THE NIGHT AND GALE

DANIEL CARRIER

SilverKnight

PUBLISHING

Night and Gale

Published in the United States by Silver Knight Publishing, LLC.
(P.O. Box 721254 Orlando, FL.)
SILVER KNIGHT PUBLISHING, knight helmet logo, and associated logos are trademarks of Silver Knight Publishing, LLC.

ISBN-13: 978-1-938083-05-1
ISBN-10: 1938083059

Library of Congress Control Number: 2012934363

This book is a work of fiction. Any references to real people, events, establishments, organizations, or locales are intended solely to provide a sense of authenticity and are used fictitiously. All other characters, incidents, and dialogue are drawn from the author's imagination and are not to be construed as real.

Cover art by: Aldren Gamalo

DEDICATION:

Dedicated to my wife, Amber, who believed in me and encouraged me to strive for new heights and accomplishments. This is for you.

TABLE OF CONTENTS

CHAPTER 1: GALE

I love watching the water. Staring at the cold waves, meshing different shades of greens and browns while wreathed and framed with a thin crown of white displaced folds as they roll alongside one another. The waves make me forget about the world around me; for once...the world makes perfect sense.

The ferry I ride every day brushes past the busy waters below, as it heads toward Port Clinton, a friendly little town located about seventy miles west from Cleveland, Ohio. I live on Kelleys Island, a fifteen-mile wide piece of land laying peacefully on the surface of Lake Erie, surrounded by beaches and trees.

I love everything about Kelleys Island. Sure, there are plenty of obvious historical landmarks to go see, like the glacial grooves and the forest canyons, as well as the beaches and winery ruins. Most people travel the entire island on bicycles, scooters, or golf-carts, taking only the given roads leading around the different sights. But to me, someone who's lived here for so many years, I get the divine experience to see a different side of things. There's a heartbeat on the island, and if you rush off to see nothing but landmarks and social gatherings, you'll miss it entirely. The lush forests, covering most of the island, not only surround the land near my home on the northeast peninsula, but tend to hide the more timid secrets of the island itself. For starters, whenever the wind picks up, I love being outside so I can take in the smell of vibrant leaves and fresh lake water. The sheer liberating aroma of nature at its purest makes me want to run as fast as I can, then spread my arms and fly off into the sky, never to land again.

The nights are equally as enchanting, especially when I'm alone, standing in the east quarry. The moon glistens softly over the water below, the light glowing on the face of the water allows for the softest shades of a faint blue and grey tone, rippling over the onyx surface. For those who cherish the island, its as if the dreams of a heart that yearned for a peaceful place actually rose up from the depths of the lake and waited to be found. I'm always reminded of something my father said when I was growing up; *All treasures come with splendor of one sort or another, but nothing compares to secrets shared with a welcoming place like Kelleys Island.*

I felt my cell phone buzz in my pocket, breaking my train of thought; the sudden cry for attention pulling me from the solace of the water's calming effect to a more insistent reality. I looked down at the screen and saw a text from one of my friends, who was waiting for me in Port Clinton.

Gale, r u almost here? The waiting is making me go CRAZY!! LOL!

I smiled behind a small snicker, while shaking my head. "It never gets old, that's for sure," I said to myself in a low voice.

I pressed the reply button, then typed, *We r pulling 2 port in 5 mins. calm urself.* I put my phone in my pocket without looking at the time, honestly, I did it on purpose. I had decided to ask the ferryman near the back of the ferry instead. He wore those ugly light brown shorts which wouldn't do even the most gorgeous man justice, along with a blue t-shirt with the ferry name in cursive on it. I loved his hair; short, light brown, with a few tussled spikes of what remained of his bangs, standing up in front. His face was stern, with well-sculpted features behind soft looking skin. He was a rather gorgeous looking creature in my book.

As I walked over, he was getting ready to start directing cars and people after the ferry docked. The ferry began to rotate completely around, moving slowly, until it steered backward toward the docking area. I tapped his shoulder and he turned to face me. At first, he looked a little annoyed, but as his eyes met mine, he froze. To my amazement, I couldn't speak either. His eyes were a beautiful, deep cobalt blue, with solid eyebrows hovering intensely above each one, as if silently attesting to a troubled mind. He stared at me with much the same captivation, which made for a more awkward silence floating between us.

Gathering the courage to talk to him was pretty much the only reason I'd ridden the ferry. I'd been watching him for over a month now, and I felt as though I was about to blow it. "Uh, hi. I was sort of wondering," I heard myself say out loud, "Could you, uh, do you happen to know what time it is?" At last, after a month of planning the perfect momentary ice-breaker, the words managed to stumble and fall out of my mouth like a crippled animal. I felt my face take on a slight shade of red while I gently bit down on my lower lip to help maintain my composure. He shook his head a bit, followed by a blink, like he was caught in a trance, then looked at his watch—twice. "It's, uh . . . it's fifteen after three," he said with a calming smile.

Barely noticing the ferry had docked, I glanced around at everyone lining up, and getting off. I looked back at him one last time, just as the wind picked up. It only added to my fascination with him, by blowing his shirt hard against his defined chest and abs while he waved once and said, "Well, um, thanks for riding us." He suddenly caught up to his words, "I, I mean the, uh, ferry! Thanks for riding it *with* us. Heh . . ."

At that point, his awful attempt to be cordial to me was nothing short of adorable. I smiled back warmly, and said, "Thanks ...for, um ...the ride." *Oh, for the love of God, Gale, just shut up and walk away before you scare him off by saying something tremendously dumb*, I thought to myself, and then pictured my palm slapping my forehead. I turned and joined the others leaving the ferry, watching out for the row of cars that carefully exited, as well. Even as I made my way out of the docking area, I could feel him still staring at me from the ferry.

I couldn't help but smile, my nerves were on edge with excitement from my brief talk with him. I pulled out my residency card, a type of yearly passport for those who live on the Islands of Put-In-Bay, and showed it to the window clerk, who nodded and smiled as I made my way through the gate-maze, leading to the parking lot.

As I entered the last stretch of the exiting line, I heard the familiar sound of bubbling laughter and the clop of open-toed, platform sandals from none other than my best friend, Shannoea, who was pulling and shaking the fence from the other side a few steps ahead of me. She had on a cute bluish-gray, spaghetti-string dress with splotches of black and white tie-dye on it, fluttering in the wind, her rich brown hair, of which I was always jealous, joining the motion of the dress before laying against the small of her back.

I smiled and stepped into the parking area, and she scampered over to me with a glittery smile about her. "Hey hey, look at you! You're looking happier than usual!" she said, giving me a warm hug, followed abruptly by a heavy gasp. "Oh, and I love that outfit, Gale! That whole one shoulder thing suits you so much! Kinda gives you that strong, sassy look."

"Thanks, Shannoea. You look stunning yourself, as usual!"

I half hoped my shirt would've helped my confidence during my fumble of words back on the ferry, but in the end, I found no courage from it. Tight, black, and extended over my left shoulder, it became a tight sleeve down my arm, leaving my right arm completely bare. I wore it thinking it would compliment what Shannoea and I had always agreed were playful curves, but at the same time, I also felt it made me look like a model without a cover-shot. I wore a pair of midnight blue pants which brought the whole look together by hugging my legs and tucking into my favorite black-heeled boots. The pants themselves had studded belt-loops along the waist, which gave me a daring sense of adventure every time I wore them.

"Where are Brenna and Sarah? Didn't they come?" I asked, looking around for the most expensive car, knowing Brenna would never settle for any common vehicle. My eyes rested on the sleek, gun-metal curvature of a Lincoln Navigator, which sat with proud majesty among the collection of average cars surrounding it.

"Well, duh! Brenna drove, and Sarah's with her, of course!"

The door on the Navigator's driver side opened, and a pair of legs, wearing four-inch gold heels each with a serpentine heel-strap wrapping around a perfectly manicured foot stepped out, one after the other. Brenna, another friend of mine I'd met as a girl growing up on Kelleys Island, originated from St. Paul De Vence, located in France, but ended up in Ohio after years of almost constant travel. Even though she'd spent so much time around us simpler folk, with our laid-back humor and bad grammar, she almost managed to keep her proper grammar, as well as her heavy accent, intact. Over the years, though, we would catch her using phrases and slang that would probably shame her in her own country.

She always had expensive taste in not only her clothes but her lifestyle, as well. And it showed in a big way. Her golden blonde hair pulled back into a tail and seven-hundred-dollar sunglasses mounted proudly over her sky blue eyes were all I could see before she closed the door, revealing her pitch-black dress which mimicked a trench-coat, with sleeves that rolled up and buttoned at the elbow, yet hung six inches above her knees.

The other door opened, and out stepped a pair of white sandals strapped along the open-toed feet of Sarah, who I'd known almost as long as Shannoea. She always dressed conservatively, khaki capris and loose hanging yellow tank-top with embroidery along the chest-line leading to thin shoulder straps.

"Wow, you cut your hair really short this time, Sarah! That's a sharp look on you!" I said in a bit of shock, as I took a good, long look. I had never known her to take such daring strides, except when Brenna influenced her. Her hair used to be long, red, and feral, hanging down to her hips, but now it stopped just below her jaw-line. I could see under the rich, red, top layer a hint of black hid, peeking out only slightly behind the breaks in the red – a shorter version of her original hairstyle, for sure.

"A rather brilliant look for her, wouldn't you agree? I had my finest stylist give her a more radiant look a few weeks back. You're looking at a powerful fifteen hundred American dollar work of art, by Armonde, himself," Brenna explained, with a warm, yet fiercely cocky smirk across her bright pink lips.

"I actually like it, Brenna's stylist really knows what he's doing," Sarah added happily as she ran her fingers through her wine red strands blowing gently in the wind. I gave a few nods of approval, then hugged her joyfully.

"I don't mean to change the subject, I mean, this is all well and good, but does anyone else care to get a bite to eat, anytime soon, or are we starving to death today?" Brenna protested.

Suddenly Shannoea put her hands on her hips. "Hang on, there's something I gotta ask . . .what's the story with *you* lately, Gale? Now you're riding ferry-boats and dressing up way more than usual, even for a visit from *us* . . ." she interrupted herself with a gasp, "*Oh my God*, it's a hot guy, isn't it? You're dating someone really attractive, aren't you? I should've known from the start!" She put her hand over her mouth while she jumped from conclusion to conclusion without losing a single breath, one of her more prominent personality traits.

"What?!" Brenna snapped her attention to Shannoea, then me. "Gale, is it true? Are you keeping a boyfriend from us?" Now Brenna tossed questions at me. She was always too nosy for her own good, but now she had backup. "And just who *is* this mystery man?" she added with a tilt of her shades, showing her eyes.

I couldn't believe this, even Sarah looked curious, a dash of 'point him out', on her face! All I could do was hold a silent smirk, while I strained hard not to blush. Despite my best efforts, I lost my composure and carefully let out a heavy quivering sigh. I draped my long, black hair over the side of my head and pretended not to notice him walk past us. It was hard enough for me to talk to him on the ferry, which I felt was a disaster on my end, but it proved even *harder* not to let my eyes devour the sight of him as he passed us in the parking lot.

Brenna stared intensely at him, as did the other two. He caught them glaring, and started to look restless.

He made his way toward a nearby white Land-Rover, glancing back repeatedly until he bumped into the door. He unlocked it, and got inside, uneasily.

Even watching him stumble to get into his vehicle was adorable, somehow. Suddenly, I heard a disgusted sigh, which broke my concentration. "Wait, wait, wait..." Brenna scoffed, "*That* is your boyfriend? Gale, you can't be serious, the poor fool isn't even all that good-looking! With all the strong, well built men floating about, you wind up choosing a social disaster like him?" said Brenna sternly, chuckling.

I shot a glare at her that could've killed, hoping she'd get the message to back off the subject.

"I don't know—he looks like the type who has a deep, gentle side, almost like his sheer simplicity is what makes him so interesting. I guess with lives like ours, dating a guy like him might be the best kind of escape," added Sarah, flicking her hair.

I looked at her with newfound respect. She'd hit the nail on the head with one comment, but it left me wondering how I was going to tell them I hadn't been dating him; that, even at my most courageous, I was somehow petrified of talking to him.

Shannoea stepped forward and broke their chain of judgment

to say, "Well, I think he looks kinda cute. So, if you're all finished stabbing at Gale's choice in men, maybe we can decide where to eat now. My poor stomach is growling like crazy over here!"

Brenna's eyes lit up, even behind her shades. "In that case, we should go to Nagoya! They have the most splendid swordfish teriyaki I've ever tasted. Not to mention, the atmosphere is much better than some of the other places around here."

"I was actually thinking more along the lines of a place called Bell Mell, honestly. It's a sports-bar, but I've been meaning to go there for a while. I hear their quesabellas are one of a kind," I explained with a shrug. I could see Brenna was unamused as always. Whenever her chance to burn through a wad of cash which could feed a third-world country was compromised, she felt her credit cards huddling in the corner of her pocketbook, crying like starved babies, or so it seemed.

"A sports-bar? You're kidding right? This is—this is some kind of sick joke, right? Your way of pay-back for insulting your boy-toy a few seconds ago?" she continued, in contempt, looking at each of us with that 'please tell me you're just kidding' look on her face. "Oh great, that's just marvelous." She turned her head away from us. "I can see this day is going to be an absolute nightmare," she said in a low voice, folding her arms in front of her and sighing.

I smiled back without saying a word. It's not often, but sometimes, I get a chance to burn down her little pompous attitude with a few well-placed comments or suggestions I know Sarah and Shannoea will agree on, leaving poor Brenna in a flaming rubble of discomfort for once.

I don't dislike her or anything, I just can't stand how judgmental she can be. She always tries to keep a high profile, even when no one is around. I came to the conclusion long ago that she's merely playing a character. She's never really done anything in her life that stands out, so she jumps at the chance to look accomplished, whenever possible.

Shannoea walked alongside Sarah and I, keeping pace while flicking her hair behind her head. "Do they have pizza? I'm in the mood for a huge slice of pepperoni heaven, myself!"

"Yeah, and they even have an outdoor area where we can sit. It's not far from here," I said, while we made our way to the car. Shannoea and Sarah followed happily beside me, while Brenna angrily walked behind us, clutching the keys in silent protest.

CHAPTER 2: LUCAS

"Seriously, Brent, can you hurry up? I really need to eat something soon!" I hated having an empty stomach. Well, to be honest I didn't mind having an empty stomach while at work. Being on a ferry, with the way it shifted and swayed, made it hard for me to keep from hurling sometimes. In either case, I tend to keep to myself anyway, so even if I *did* throw up, it's not like it would affect my immediate status with the passengers. The crappy blue shirt and tan shorts from the seventies made sure to keep my social appearance as laughable as possible.

As soon as I'd clocked out, I went to the locker room and changed into what I deemed as normal clothes, immediately. I'd gotten it down to a science, I could be in and out, in less than three minutes. My favorite gray t-shirt and black cargo pants topped off my worn, white sneakers. Afterward, I headed over to Brent's house. He was in a nice neighborhood, with a quiet setting, most days. Now all that was left was for Brent to get himself in gear, then we could grab a bite to eat.

Brent is a lot of fun to be around, most of the time. He's a bit of an easy going, gamer-jock. He's into just about every kind of music, game, sport, movie, or book. You name it, he somehow manages to know about it, or he's actually done it. The guy has a network of friends in every kind of social group in school.

That's probably due to working at a restaurant which gets a lot of attention from the locals over on Fulton street, called Bell Mell. It sits alongside the street, just barely hiding among the rows of houses. As a tourist, you'd most likely never even know it was there, but for those who live in Port Clinton, Bell Mell brings in the masses. Obviously, Brent loves to mingle with just about anyone who walks through the door. I swear, sometimes I think the owner wants to leave the whole place to him, when he dies.

"Dude, hey, I gotta stop at work to pick up my schedule, so let's just eat there to save gas, okay?" Brent insists.

"That's fine, let's just get going, I just wanna grab a burger and relax. Work was heavy today." I leaned back in one of the chairs in the kitchen, picturing a plate of food in front of me. It made me drool in the back of my mind. The idea of a plain and simple cheeseburger waiting to be devoured was more than I could handle.

Brent came out from his laundry room and had thrown on a white Cleveland Indians shirt, and a pair of khaki shorts with his gleaming white and red sneakers.

"It's about time! I was about to tear off the door to your fridge and raid it like a starved animal! I'm *that* hungry!" I joked, before hopping up from my chair.

"All right, 'ya goof, let's head out then! I don't need you ravaging my stash of turkey and ham again!"

Before I had time to react, he wrapped his arm around my neck and put me into a headlock, then tapped my head lightly

13

with his knuckles before letting me out of the hold.

I looked at him with a coy smile and said, "You know, you're just lucky I'm exhausted from work, or I'd have to annihilate you, in your own house!"

He looked at me and snickered, while I pretended to crack my knuckles, then shook them like I was in pain.

"Well, we can't have that now, can we, Mr. Big-shot? The carpet is imported ya know," he answered, holding his hands in front of himself in surrender. We both looked at each other with blank faces for only a few seconds, before smiles and chuckling snuck into the silence. This was exactly why I enjoyed hanging out with Brent. Always light hearted, he made me feel comfortable, like I could act brave if I wanted and he'd go along with it, no matter if it was false bravado or not. It was as if he was a long lost brother, one that respected me as a person and not some random nerd at school. Whenever I got the chance to hang with him, I felt like I could be at home.

I'd known him for nearly two years, my last year of high-school and my first year of college. We'd had the same science and math classes together in high-school, so I ended up helping him with his work from time to time. He started inviting me to different events and gatherings, until I was permanently threaded into just about everything he was doing, in some way or another. The only thing I hadn't been pulled into was his life on the school football team. Something I'd declared self-neutrality from forever.

We left his house and got into my SUV. I usually drove while Brent texted his friends on his cell along the way.

"You said work was heavy earlier. You seem more distant than usual, man. Heavy like how? Like bored outta your mind heavy, or like time went slower than usual?"

"More like . . ." I hesitated, and then sighed, "I'm not sure I feel like talking about it right now."

"Now, come on, dude, you know that ain't fair-play. I'm tryin' to have a simple chat with you here. The least you can do is tell me what's got you so dead silent."

"It's no big deal, really. I just . . ." I let out another slow, heavy sigh. "There's this girl that's been riding for about a month now." I watched Brent's eyes widen, like he was about to declare this a holiday of some kind. I knew I should've kept it to myself after seeing his reaction.

"She's always there during my shift. I'd never thought much of it until today."

"Wow! It sounds like she's totally stalkin' you! Is she good lookin' at least?" he shot back with a smile.

"She, uh..." He managed to catch me off guard before I'd even answered him. A flash image of her hung in front of my train of thought. I blew off his question about whether she was good looking or not, entirely. "Well she's never actually come near me...until today. She came right up to me and asked a question." I could feel my hands starting to sweat on the steering wheel. I pictured every detail of her face with ease. The same as a priceless work of art, smooth and precise, the curve of her features were guarded by a black silken flow of playful hair, and she had a soothing smile that made me ache inside with an unfamiliar sense of longing.

"What did she ask you? Did she try to get your number or somethin'?" His grin was getting bigger while he waited for me to go on.

Just as I went to answer, I helplessly recalled her hair blowing away from her face while she stared at me intently with deep, burnt sienna, almost wine-red eyes. I'd already fallen in love with her eyes—I'd never seen anything more gorgeous in my life. I felt a welling of jealousy toward the wind. Allowed to comb through her hair anytime it wanted while I was forced to watch, tortured at arms' reach. My thoughts rushed back to me; I felt overly obsessed with something so simple.

"She, she asked me what, uh," I stammered, my thoughts returning to driving. "She wanted to know what time it was." I glanced over at him, briefly. As I thought, Brent's face had gone from excited to a more bewildered look.

"Do *what*, now? Are you frikkin' kidding me, Luke?"

I shook my head, keeping my eyes on the road.

"Okay, bro, lemme get this straight; You had a hot girl come onto *your* boat," He stopped himself quickly, leaned over to me, and asked, "You did say she was *hot*, right?"

"What?" I hated when he did this, he used the term hot like it was a requirement of some kind. It bugged me a lot. "Brent, why does it always have to be hot girls with you?"

He cut off my sentence instantly. "Okay, mister conservative, so a good looking girl was on *your* boat, and from what you're sayin', she's practically been stalking you, even though, let's face it; there's not much room to stalk someone on a ferry deck. After all that, all she wanted to know was the time?" His disappointment was obvious.

I could've sworn he was waiting for me to jump up and say, *Hah! Gotcha! I sweet talked her into giving me her number! Had you goin' for a second, huh?*

"Lemme guess, you didn't even capitalize on any of it, did you? No phone number, no email, no nothin', right?" I shrugged my shoulders at him, "I really gotta say Luke ol' pal, you've got a winning posture when it comes to females," he said, unamused.

"That's just it, I don't get why she needed *me* to give her the time, she had a cell in her hand when she got on the ferry," I answered. I didn't know if I was too slow on grasping the situation, or oblivious to her true intentions, but I couldn't figure why she'd approached me at all!

"No offense, bro, but you need schooled in hot-chick-ology. Seriously, if you didn't notice, she was tryin' to get the hook up with you! She wanted *you* to give *her* the *time* to get to know you! Get it? Not literally stare down at your watch and shoot off the pole meridian, like a geek!"

I didn't really care what he thought about it, all I cared about at this point was getting some food. I saw the familiar yellow siding of our destination in the distance, followed by the wooden balcony railing that lead to the sign which stuck out from the side of the building itself. I pulled into the closest available spot and we got out, heading toward the front stoop. As I entered, the cool air was a nice welcome to the kind of atmosphere I had always enjoyed. Brent came in behind me, and I made my way around the bar counter trying not to bump into the bustle of patrons.

The familiar setup around me was friendly and welcoming, numerous signs and posters with sport teams names and beer company logos gave me a sense of barring. The low-level lighting was relaxing in its own way, but made it hard to dodge the oncoming traffic of customers and employees.

"Okay, I'm gonna go grab my schedule, you find us a good seat. Maybe we can catch some of the game on TV," he insisted, and went through the employee door.

I walked out through the doorway leading to the white fence enclosed yard, dodging a few waitresses and guests while following the paved walkway. I passed the handful of round white tables in the grass shaded by huge umbrellas, then stepped into the wooden deck area. I sat at one of the several tables that had green marble patterns, coupled with green chairs on either side of the eating area. I noticed the TV's were already tuned to the baseball game.

Bell Mell was always slammed with business whenever there was a game. especially involving Ohio teams. It was also

Saturday, so it was even more crowded than usual with game-seekers. The Indians were playing against the Tampa Bay Rays, and they were losing, from what I could see.

I was never savvy in sports, but Brent helped me along by giving me key points of interest from time to time. He said it was blasphemous for any guy to live outside of sports, but even with his crappy opinion about it, I seemed to manage life just fine.

Some of the people at the table next to me became irate at the uphill battle the Indians were apparently facing. They left in an angry huff after slamming down their tip for the waitress.

"That's a load of bull! Let's get outta here, before I throw up from disappointment!" I heard one of them say.

"No frikkin' doubt, man, Cleveland needs serious help if they can't even beat those grade-schoolers," another one said, as they left.

Dana, one of the waitresses approached me, and took out a pencil and note-pad, backed with a quaint smile. "Hey, Luke, good to see you again," she was always enthusiastic, I smiled and nodded to her, "I'll take good care of ya sweetie, what can I get you to drink?" she asked in a cheerful voice.

"Actually, I already know what I want. I'll just have my usual hamburger, well-done please, with American cheese and mushrooms this time." I'd been craving one all day. My brain even drooled while I pictured my order in my head.

"You want that with chips and pickles, honey?"

"That's fine, sour cream and onion flavored please, and put in an order of fries, too," I answered, as I leaned back in my chair.

"Awesome choice, and what did ya say ya wanted to drink with that?"

"Oh, uh, I guess I'll have a cola." An ice cold soda sounded awesome enough to me that I started to drool in my mind.

"Okay, then, I'll have that right out to ya!" She scampered back into the sea of patrons seated around me. Dana had a way of making anyone who walked through the door at Bell Mell, feel like they'd just walked into their own kitchen at home. She acted cheerful, sympathized with any and all who shared stories or news with her, and always had a down-home kind of attitude. It made the place feel warmer, and more welcoming than most other restaurants.

I sat there a few minutes, taking in the entire day and settling while I waited for Brent to find our table.

Dana returned and set down my drink with a smile.

"Yer food will be out soon, Luke, 'til then, relax and enjoy this ice-cold soda." she said, holding on to her cheerful tone. I smiled and nodded once in approval.

Finally, after about five minutes had gone by, I saw Brent walk through the doorway. He waved once and plopped down in the seat across from me. It always took him a million years to get anything done, only because everybody knew him, and he mingled like a spy at an enemy ballroom. It reminded me of the movie where the husband was secretly a government agent, but had a front as a sales rep for a computer company. Not that

I figured Brent was even capable of anything epic, but, even so, the thought made me smile amidst the irate Indians fans.

"So did you order yet, cause I had Amy put an Italian sub in for me?" he said."Yeah, I got a burger with fries on the way."

"So what about the game? Are we winning?"

"Not really. Tampa's holding onto their four points pretty well," I replied, folding my arms on the table. I let my head plop down onto them. I was already getting tired of waiting for my meal. The drink was doing its job, but my stomach demanded something solid. It gurgled from under the table, making me shift uneasily in my seat.

"Seriously? Well that just plain sucks. If Cleveland loses, my sub won't taste right at all." Brent's comment made me want to laugh. I'd never cared much for sports, so I never understood why people were passionate about them. I kept my laughter to myself, and focused my attention on my drink.

I took a sip of my soda and ascended to a state of pure carbonated bliss as the flavor from the bubbles twinged across my taste-buds and coated my throat with icy, refreshing splendor. Any hard day dealt to me could easily be rendered forgotten after such a stupendous experience from such a simple beverage.

"All right, so about this girl you've got glued to your shadow. Let's hear more about her. At least give me that much, maybe it'll make up for all this crap with the Indians." He just had to bring that up again.

Frustrated, I sipped in a few more gulps of my soda, and

stared at him, hoping he could see how annoyed I was getting.

"What did she look like?" he asked, wide eyed.

"Are you kidding me? You can't just pretend we never talked about that?"

"Uh, not really. No." His face held a sarcastic, yet serious look, a look I'd grown familiar with quickly. It meant he planned on poking and prying with witty comments until I cracked, submitting to his interest.

CHAPTER 3: LUCAS

My head came crashing back to reality from atop the cloud nine I had floated on from the first sip of my drink. I knew better than to fight his curiosity, he was relentless when it came to females as a whole. I only had one option, tell him everything.

I let out a resigned sigh, "Okay, look, if I tell you, then you have to drop it. I mean like, don't bring it up ever again. That's the deal, take it or leave it." I wondered if he would even honor that kind of deal. He wasn't the type to pass up a chance at hearing what he liked to call chewy details about girls.

"Yeah, okay, fine... whatever, just tell me already! Sheesh, you act like it's a broken leg we're dealin' with!" Contrary to his comment, I hesitated to admit it, even to myself deep down, but I actually felt excited about telling him all about her.

"She was about my height, with long black hair and brown eyes that have a hint of dark red in them, kind of like a deep shade of burnt sienna." As I described her to him, my mind ran back to that moment when I saw her face up close, and I felt myself melting inside. "She seemed kind of confident, like she had a strong and brave posture." I wasn't looking at him, still picturing her in my head. I zoned out entirely, holding her image in my mind like a desperate thought that threatened to fade away forever.

"So how old do you think she was? I mean, I don't know any women that sound like that! Usually, the chicks I see around me are party animals and run-down, gray-sky, manic teen mothers!" I saw him glowering, his comment as ice cold as his expression, I quickly got the notion he couldn't stand those kinds of girls.

"I don't know, maybe around my age, I guess. She had a few friends meet her in the parking lot after we docked." A bad move to mention since Brent was single, as well. Now he'd pry even harder, despite my take it or leave it deal earlier.

"Whoa, whoa, *whoa there*, now! She had friends with her, too? You never said anything about *that* before! What were they like?"

I let my head fall straight onto the table with regret. He'd never shut up now. He loved chatting about girls even more than sports! I gave it all some thought, then, after taking another sip of my drink, I figured I should stop fighting it. It wasn't like there were any better topics out there to go on. I gave in altogether.

I sighed heavily, once, "There were three others with her. One was pretty much a stuck-up looking snob with a French accent, and another looked sort of timid and quiet, like she was the smart, reserved one of the group." I watched Brent's eyes get wider and wider as I described each of them.

"The one she talked with the most was an energetic looking, happy-go-lucky kind of girl, the kind who'd be friends with anyone. They seemed like friends from out of town and when I passed them, they all stared at me, all except the one who's been watching me," When I thought about it, I wondered why she put her hair over the side of her face as I passed her in the parking lot. It hadn't occurred to me until I told Brent the story.

"So-o, they all gave you the stank-eye treatment? Oh man, I'm sorry I asked," Brent answered with a chuckle.

"What about you? What kind of girl would *you* wanna date?" I leaned to one side in my chair, propping myself up with an elbow on the table, my shoulder against the side of my head. "I mean, you sounded kinda frustrated earlier when you were talking about party animals and manic mothers."

He shifted a little in his seat before he shook his head. "I don't know, really. I'm just so damn sick of the same old crap when it comes to women in general." His tone changed, he started to sound like me, happy, but lonely all the same. "I wanna meet someone who takes good care of themselves, not a reckless, wild, party-animal. I get enough of that when I go out on the weekends, as it is, bro." He looked at me, sincerity in his eyes. He'd never opened up to me before, but now that he had, I was at the edge of my seat, soaking in every word.

"I want someone who's smart, funny, and has kind of a deep personality. Someone I'm nothing like, because let's face it, Luke, opposites attract. It's like... I dunno, a ninja dating a cowgirl, or somethin'!" He snickered.

I smiled back and chuckled with an approving nod. That was officially his first nerd joke ever. It was corny and subtle, but it was still pretty good. "So you see yourself as a ninja looking for a cowgirl?" I chuckled, picturing Brent doing anything martial arts related. I couldn't help but grin uncontrollably at the idea.

He rolled his eyes and shared a sarcastic smile as he said, "Oh, har-har, King-Dork's got jokes!"

I chuckled a bit, then answered, "Okay, all right, I get it. I'm not funny, I know. Go on, then."

"Anyway, I guess what I'm saying is I want a girl who can be sophisticated when she has to be, but still has a fun, wild side. Self control is the key, really. Ya know, a feisty, adventurous girl, who can let her hair down and have a good time." While he described the perfect female to me, I started to wonder if that kind of girl actually existed at all! "It's so hard to stay confidant with so many trashy, simple-minded girls, who'll take any guy they can get, even a guy that *beats* on them." He looked frustrated.

I figured he was reminding himself of past girlfriends he'd lost to a few jerks.

Just then, Dana came to our table and sat our food in front of us, followed by a bottle of ketchup, and said, "Here you are, fellas! Let me know if there's anything else you two need."

Brent nodded to her, and she walked away smiling.

I dove into my burger like a starved raccoon storming a knocked over trashcan. The first bite was heavenly. The tender flavor of the meat came forth, then the cheese followed suit. After that, the mushrooms entered the swirl of deliciousness, ending with the closing flavor of fresh hamburger bun. I thought I heard Brent saying something to me, but I didn't care. A hard day turned into a journey into burger-heaven, almost at the drop of a hat.

"Dude, are you even listening?"

I finally heard his question to me. I swallowed my food, and looked over to him. "Sorry, I zoned out... what were you saying?"

"*I said*, you spilled your drink! It's in your lap, ya lunatic!"

I hoped to God he was joking just to get my attention, but he wasn't. I looked down to see a wet lap quickly becoming a wet leg. I glanced around in terror, looking to see if anyone had noticed. Thankfully, though, no one had paid any attention. They were all glued to the game on TV.

I grabbed a nearby menu and held it near the incriminating spot climbing down my thigh while I headed toward the exit. The distance between the exit of the deck area and the bathroom seemed farther than ever, as I held onto the menu for dear life. I carefully avoided every manner of human contact, pacing myself out to the lawn area, trying desperately to look inconspicuous with my shiny menu held against me, yet still flapping in pace with my legs. I could almost swear that every eye was on me. I could see glances of humorous intrigue flash across the different faces I'd passed as I trekked across the path into the bar area. Deep down I hoped it was just my own paranoia.

"I'll get us some boxes to go. We can meet up in the lot and head over to your place, if you want, bro." I heard Brent say behind me. I turned to nod in approval.

As I turned to continue my pace to the door leading to my salvation, I was caught off guard by someone blocking my way.

"Oh, uh, I'm sorry, I didn't see you," I said quickly. I realized how bad the situation was becoming. There, standing right in my path, was the girl from the ferry! I felt my blood freeze instantly and my thoughts went completely blank as she started to speak.

"That's okay, no harm done." Suddenly, she recognized me, "Hey! It's you!" She stood dead center of the walkway, staring at me with those rich, brown and red eyes and a smile that made me feel even whiter with fear, hoping to God she didn't realize I was trying to escape . . .

Without thinking, I glanced at my watch. "Oh, it's, uh, ten after four." I blurted like a dork. *Why did I just do that? Brent is right, I'm an idiot,* I thought to myself.

Her eyebrow rose a bit, then she smiled again. "Th-thanks but I didn't need to know the time," she replied with a hint of surprise.

"Actually, I'm glad you're here. I wanted to apologize for earlier," she went on. "Some of my friends may have given you the wrong impression back at the ferry's parking lot."

Was she serious? She was actually trying to apologize for her friends glaring at me like a pack of vicious animals? My leg was getting wetter and colder by the second, and the menu I had to guard the mess would be nowhere near big enough to cover it much longer.

"They're usually pretty welcoming and good natured, although Brenna can be a bit icy at times. If you have a second, I'd be happy to introduce you to—"

I politely cut her off. "Maybe, uh, I'm sorry, but, maybe another time... Look, I'm sorry...but I really have to get going. I was uh, on my way to the restroom . . ." she looked at me with a puzzled face, glancing down at the menu, against my leg. Damnation, she just *had* to look at the one thing that kept me from dying of embarrassment!

"Uh, what's with the menu?"

"What? Oh this, uh this is just..." I had to think fast, "reading material. Yeah, I usually take something with me to read. It helps me, uh, relax." Somebody stab me in the head, before I say anything else! I felt my face start to turn red a bit.

"You're taking a menu into the bathroom, to read, while you... go?" Her eyes squinted, like she was both confused and grossed out at the same time.

Oh, shut up and move outta my way, you gorgeous raven-haired goddess, please Lord, do not let her notice the spilled soda crawling down my pant-leg! I heard myself say mentally.

"Yeah, I, I do. Now, uh, if you'll excuse me," I said behind a breath of fear. Then I made my way around her, making sure I didn't expose my leg in the least.

Just as I had made it to the doorway, I bumped face first into the worst possible person on the planet, Nathan Hughes, a guy who always had a bad attitude. We fell, knocking not only him down, but his three other cronies as well, spilling his chili all over his chest, staining his white Tampa Bay Ray's shirt.

"Oh, my frikkin' *God*!! Who's the *dead-man* who just *ruined* my *shirt*?" he growled.

I knew it was all over now. Nate was about to yank my arms off for ruining the shirt of his favorite team.

"It was that geek, right there, man, let's bust his ass!" I heard one of his buddies say, as they all scrambled up at once.

Nathan grabbed my arm, lifting me up with almost no effort. "Stand up, loser. I want you to die *before* you hit the ground!" His tone was full of fatal assurance.

Eye-level with him, I dangled from his arm, helplessly. His eyes were almost buried under his low hanging brow and his brown hair stood up like a field of spikes above his Neanderthal features. This was the face of the reaper, and he was about to send me to coma-land.

"Hey, let him go! It was an accident!" I heard a voice of reason break through the silence of my standing funeral.

The girl I just tried to get away from and she looked steamed!

I glanced around. Everyone, and I mean *everyone* was watching us. I was stuck, hanging like a piñata from a tree, helplessly waiting to either be saved or get punched in the gut until my bones spilled out of me like candy.

"*I said* let him go, you jerk! He didn't do anything wrong!"

"Aw, is that your girlfriend, ya geek?" He glanced over at her. "What are you gonna do if I don't? Bite my ankle, ya stupid little poodle? You best keep on walkin' before I add *you* to the body pile, lil' girl!" he sassed.

Then I felt it—a sharp, stabbing sensation ringing its way throughout my ribs. He had punched me with his free hand, and it felt like a car parked on my guts, then decided to spin its tires. I almost blacked out from the collision, but somehow I didn't.

Then I saw the group of girls from earlier, the ones who glared at me so devilishly. They got up and surrounded him—the tough-looking rich girl was the most intimidating creature I'd ever seen! She stepped right up into Nathan's face, like she knew she could demolish him in a fist-fight.

"You heard what she said, you knuckle-dragging caveman! Let him go, right now!" she ordered. I felt his grip start to loosen.

Just then, one of his friends spoke, "Hey, do you know who the hell you're talkin' to, Barbie?"

She glared at him, which silenced his attitude quickly. "I beg your pardon, do *you* know who *you're* talking to, *little boy*?" He backed himself into the huddle of Nathan's cronies quietly.

"I won't bother to repeat myself again, unless of course, you'd like to try pressing your luck against someone like *me*?" Her teeth gritted as she threatened him, her accent made her sound even more vicious, as if she'd been waiting for a fight all day.

I felt him let go of me almost before she finished. I couldn't believe it! She just turned him into a scared little three-year-old right in front of everybody! He backed off, only briefly before staring me in the face again.

"Yeah, whatever, lady. Me and you'll play later, geek. This ain't over by a frikkin' long shot," he said, strutting off with his crew of trouble-makers.

"What the heck just happened?"

I looked back to see Brent, standing in the entrance to the enclosed eating deck. "I take five seconds to pack up our chow and you're on the grass, surrounded by," suddenly, he realized who they were, based on my description from earlier, "Well now, this *is* a nice little surprise!" he said as he approached us.

I looked over at the black-haired girl, then over to her snobby accomplice. "Thanks for, uh, for helping me. How did you do that?" I asked.

"I didn't do it for you. I did it because he disrupted the meal I was sharing with my friends. Besides, all men fear me. Naturally, he didn't want my six-hundred-dollar shoe, up his twelve cent behind," she said with a powerfully evil grin.

I was at a loss for words! No one had *ever* run Nate off like a scared little dog before! I knew better, though. He'd be back with his boys to regain his foothold of confidence, no matter the cost. He'd been to jail more times than anyone I'd ever known. Every law had a backbone in his eyes, and every backbone gets broken by him, eventually. Even cops have had a run for their money with him.

My train of thought was broken as a gorgeous, lone hand was held out in front of me—the mystery girl, waiting for a handshake.

"My name is Gale, by the way, Gale Anning," she said to me. Even her nails were perfectly manicured, with elegant soft-looking gloss that glistened in the light.

I placed my hand into hers and she wrapped her fingers around my palm with grace. Her grip was somewhat overwhelming, but also careful, almost like she was trying to hold back from crushing my fingers like a handful of twigs. I quickly gained the notion that she hadn't shaken very many hands.

"I-I'm Lucas. Um, Lucas Carmicheal. My friends call me Luke." I said with a mental gag on words. How cliche' was I being? She wasn't stupid, she knew the variations of my name and here I was, spouting off like a moron, *again*. I closed my eyes and pressed on, hoping to regain composure, as I introduced *my* friend.

"Uh, speaking of friends, Gale, this is Brent. We graduated high school together. Over at Port Clinton High."

Brent held out his hand, "Hi, it's good to meet you, Gale! I gotta say, Luke didn't miss a single detail, when he described you to me!"

I was caught off guard, I felt my face flush, and then I shot to attention with embarrassment. I glanced over to Gale, who was beginning to blush. Seeing her flawless cheeks take on a faint shade of red kind of made me feel better, now that she knew I'd talked about her.

"And who might you be?" he said, holding his hand out to the snobbish girl, "I gotta say, I know I'd remember seeing a classy lady like you."

She looked down at his hand with a cold stare, then scoffed, turning her head from him.

Brent's face went from a warm smile to a confused gape as he lowered his hand back to his side with disappointment.

"Don't mind Brenna, like I was saying before, she can be a bit harsh sometimes," Gale said with a giggle, "This is Shannoea and Sarah. I've known them all pretty much my whole life." She pointed to the quiet, red-haired girl, and the bubbly mannered girl next to her.

"I-I don't think I've ever seen you, or your friends, before. Do you ladies go to school somewhere around here?" Brent was quick to regain structure on the conversation, like always.

"Actually, no. We, um, we're all from a digital-classroom program. You know, like an Internet schooling program? Our families travel a lot, so naturally, we can't stick to a solid location," she replied, her tone seemed odd, like she was uncertain about the answer she gave.

Shannoea walked over, and waved playfully at us both, using only her index and middle finger held together, "'S'up guys, it's nice to meetcha!" Then she leaned close to Gale's ear and whispered, "He's even *cuter* up close."

Gale started to blush as she pushed Shannoea away, who was still giggling.

Then Sarah slowly approached us, her sky blue eyes stayed transfixed on Brent, who oddly enough, seemed to be staring right back at her, their faces totally frozen. I couldn't help but wonder what they were thinking as they approached one another. I'd never seen Brent act like that—totally out of the talkative character I'd come to know.

"Uh, hi. I'm Brent Weismann." He sounded almost breathless.

I couldn't figure it out at all. I saw Shannoea and Gale look at each other with an *Aww, how cute are those two?* look on their faces. Was Brent actually attracted to her? Brent, who had a knack for captivating all sorts of girls, was actually captivated by *this* one?

She held out her hand slowly and just as his hand met hers, she gasped softly, like he'd shocked her with an arc of static buildup. "I'm Sarah Nite."

I could've sworn I saw a glisten in their eyes as they shook hands, slowly, staring at one another, neither of them noticed, or cared that everyone was looking at them. Even I was drawn unwittingly into it!

Suddenly, I saw Gale's eyes drop toward my leg. "Uh, did that guy you ran into have a drink?" she asked, drawing his attention from Sarah.

Brent nervously cleared his throat, followed by Sarah, who backed away until she was standing behind Shannoea, her eyes still glued to him.

Brent and I glanced at each other. He shot me a raise of his eyebrows, which meant he thought I should play off the rebound I'd been handed.

"Um, I, yeah. He lost his drink on me when we collided. It was, uh, cold." I heard myself say like a blathering idiot. I was no good at social skills of any kind. Most of the time, Brent took care of my talking by filling in for me when my train of thought dried up. I guess he saw a golden opportunity to see how far I could coast before stalling completely in front of this kind-hearted girl. I wanted to die before I embarrassed myself, or her, any more than I had already.

"Well, listen, it was an absolute pleasure to meet you, Gale, as well as your friends, but Luke and I really do have to get going."

"Oh, well, here, don't forget your cell phone, Lucas." She reached down, and picked it up from the grass. "I think you must've dropped it when that jerk-wad ran into you." she said to me while handing my cell to me.

I took the cell and put it back into my pocket. For whatever reason, Shannoea had a sly smile on her face, standing behind Gale. I didn't know why, but I felt like she was up to something that even her friends didn't know about.

"That reminds me, can I borrow your cell for a sec, Gale? Mine isn't getting a good signal out here," I heard Shannoea say. Gale handed off her cell without taking her eyes from us. I caught Brent glancing back at Sarah behind the crowd of friends, and noticed she was doing the same. There attentive staring made me feel awkward, his eyes were dining on every inch of her, and she was doing the same. I just wanted to go home...

"Thanks again. I guess I'll see you around, maybe on the ferry," I replied with a sense of hope.

"I certainly hope so. You never know when a woman will need to know the time." She said behind a glistening smile and narrow eyes as she handed me the menu I had dropped.

"Don't forget your reading material, Lucas." She added.

I grabbed the menu and held it against my leg while my eyes shifted in every direction. I looked at Gale who was still smiling, but also shaking her head.

"What?" I asked, hoping she wasn't onto me.

"Nothing. I just think you're a very strange, and interesting person, that's all," she chuckled gently.

I felt my nerves jump the minute I caught up with what she'd said. No one had ever said such a thing about me, least of all a female! I was always the rear-end of every joke, both in and out of school. I stood there, void of words. Void of, well, everything really! She had me on the ropes and I had no way of responding. Just then, I felt Brent tap my shoulder.

"We gotta go, bro, you're drivin', remember?"

"Oh, right. Well, see you later, Gale." I'd actually made it through a conversation with a female *outside* of the nerd-community! Despite the fact that I was nearly killed by Nathan, I felt pretty good, so much so that I felt my confidence start to build, just a tiny bit.

She waved as she and her friends walked back to their table. I saw Shannoea begin to gossip to them about us. It was obvious, after all my years of listening in during lunch at school. Sarah sat down with her friends, and tried not to look over at us while we picked up our food. I could see her from over Brent's shoulder, she was sneaking peeks at us while we finished.

CHAPTER 4: LUCAS

The drive back to Brent's house was the same. He couldn't help but gab about the handful of women I had surrounding me, after Nate nearly tore me apart.

"So that was your stalker-girl, eh? She's a frikkin' bomb-shell-fox dude! But that snob girl, Brenna, was a real freak with an ego problem!"

"Yeah..." I was barely listening to him, Gale's enchanting image still hung like a painting in the front of my brain.

"You're still thinking about her aren't you?" He smirked.

"Yeah, I mean, she seems nice and all, but it's not like I'd even know where to begin if I really had any chance to date her, anyway," I felt hopelessly lost in the sea of society around me. I barely had any experience with anyone outside of my own group of friends growing up, and they were all like me: dateless nerds with no sign of dignity, pride, or confidence.

"Well, that's what I'm here for, bro! I can teach you the art of socializing with girls! Honestly, I'm really happy to see you acting like you're alive for once. Lord knows, I've been trying to get you to be more socially active for years, and now you may have yourself a knockout of a girl at your door, It's exciting, man, you gotta admit!" He patted my shoulder.

He was right; I did feel excited about maybe getting to see

her again. Like the world around me started to take on a brighter shade of color altogether, the thought itself warmed my brain, and reminded me of his encounter, as well. "So tell me, what was all that about, I mean with Sarah? Are you gonna try talking to her anytime soon?"

He froze up, but his eyes widened. "She was really intense, wasn't she?" I could see he was at a loss for words. "I can't explain it. She took my breath away, dude," he answered nervously.

"I guess that's a good sign in her favor then, huh? Maybe if I see Gale again, I'll ask her about it, maybe see if Sarah's mentioned wanting your number, you know?" I said, with a smirk of my own.

Brent looked at me and smiled. "Now you're starting to sound like a true friend, you know that?"

It felt good to bond with him in this new territory. I was beginning to enjoy the concept of hooking Brent up for once. After his years of loyal friendship, I finally had a chance to give something back.

"Look, go ahead and drop me off at my place, if you want. Since you're gonna get a shower, we can maybe hang tomorrow, if you feel up to it."

"That's fine. We're almost there anyway."

I pulled into Brent's driveway and he grabbed his to-go box before he got out. He closed the door, and hung just inside the window. "Well, take it easy, dude. Get some rest, and we can hang tomorrow." He held his fist out. I tapped his fist with mine, and he walked to his house.

I drove home in silence. Gale stood strong in my thoughts, like a statue in the middle of an open field. It seemed as if I was obsessed with her. I'd only just met her and I already felt knots in my stomach. I tried to ignore them, but it only got worse when I pictured her smiling at me, after the incident with Nathan.

My head spun. I pulled into the driveway to my house. The familiar beige-colored structure greeted me with the warm glow of light as I parked in the garage and tried to compose myself before I went inside. I couldn't let my parents see me in such a messy, distracted state. After a few deep breathes, I was able to water down my thoughts enough to head inside.

Thankfully, just after I entered, I found a note from my parents on the counter in the kitchen. They were out shopping for groceries and wouldn't be back for hours. I made my way upstairs and closed the bathroom door.

After I showered, I changed into my lounging clothes. I always wore a pair of wind-pants and a light t-shirt when I had nowhere to go for the day. I sat down at the edge of my bed, and dug through my pants pocket so I could charge my cell for a bit. When I looked down at the screen, I noticed a number on the call history that I didn't recognize. I hit the call button, and waited to see who would pick up on the other end. The song that played in place of the ring was violin music, which was odd, but soothing. Then, I heard a voice on the other end interrupt.

"Uh, hello?" The tone was familiar, almost as if it was hers, but how?

"Hi, um, I'm sorry but, who's number is this? It was in my call history, but it doesn't look familiar." I asked, but even so, I hoped it really *was* her!

I heard her take in what sounded like a breath of shock. "Lucas? Is that you?"

"Yeah, it is. Is that you, Gale?"

"Well, yeah, but how did you get my number?" I could tell she was smiling slightly as she asked.

"I don't really know. Like I said, it was on my call history, I just figured I'd call it to find out where it came from."

I could hear her put her hand over the speaker, then I heard her whisper briefly to someone in the background, "Shannoea! I can't believe you used his phone to call mine! I know it was you; you're the only one fast enough to pull a stunt like that!"

"Well, I don't see you hangin' up on him! I did you a favor, you should be thankin' me!" I heard another voice laughing, and then I heard a door closing in the background.

I wondered, if what Gale said was true, how her friend could get my phone without me or anyone else seeing her, dial Gale's number, hang up, and then lay it near me in the grass all with ninja-like reflexes.

My train of thought was broken when I heard Gale say, "Well, I've never called your number before, either, but all the same, it's nice to hear from you after you and your friend left so quickly. I started to wonder if it was something I said," she said behind a tiny laugh.

"That's impossible for you," I stopped myself cold. Like a coward, I curbed my tongue before I could tell her how hearing her voice had become a soothing experience for me. Not only would it creep her out, but something deep down was screaming to me that saying something like that was far too fast a move for just one day.

"What's impossible?"

I had to gain control of the situation before I cornered myself yet again. "Uh, nothing. I was just looking at a picture Brent sent to my email. It's not important." I lied through my teeth, hoping she'd bought it.

"Oh, I see. So, um, why did you and Brent take off so suddenly, if you don't mind me asking?"

Oh, crap. I had forgotten he'd said that to help me escape before too many people noticed my soda spill. I pictured Brent giving me the same 'take the rebound' look he gave me earlier.

"Well uh, he'd forgotten some things he had to get done around his house." I hoped she'd buy my lame excuse. "He only wanted to stop there because he needed to grab his work schedule anyway."

"Huh, well, I wished I could have had a chance to talk more with the two of you. Shannoea just left to meet up with our other friends; they all went to shop at a few stores around here," she sounded lonely. "Hey, if you're not busy at the moment, maybe

you'd like to meet me over at Toft's, for an ice cream? I'll buy!"
Her voice was soft and sweet, like she was singing to me.

I couldn't resist,, not even a little and I couldn't hold back
my thoughts. Without hesitation, I spat out, "Sure, that sounds
great. I'll head out right now and meet you there!" What was
I thinking? I found myself frightened, all at once. I imagined
myself alone with her, blurting out all kinds of stupid things.
Brent was home, probably playing video games, and I was about
to meet this mysterious girl who had simply waltzed into my
world earlier today and insisted on hanging out with me!

"Fantastic, I can't wait! See you soon!" she replied.

"Heh, yeah, I... uh... I can't wait either." I trudged through
just before she hung up.

I went back into the bathroom and splashed some water
on my face to help get my thoughts together. The mirror over
the sink did me no justice, showing just how shaky I was. My
forehead furrowed with concern, my hands trembled, and my
mouth was quivering like crazy. It all reminded me just how
badly I needed to get my act together. After staring at my
reflection for almost thirty seconds, I decided to just grit my
teeth and do my best. This gorgeous creature invited me to spend
some time with her, and I already said I would. Just then, I heard
my phone buzz—a text from Brent.

Dude, I just beat Barbarian Rage 3!! The ending is a killer!!
lol

As soon as I read the text, I hatched an idea. I hit the reply button and typed, *Hey, somehow Gale's number ended up on my phone. When I called it, she answered! She asked me to stop over at Toft's and have an ice cream with her... I might need u 2 help me so I don't blow it...*

I waited for a few seconds for his reply. As I waited, I slid on a blue polyester button-up shirt over the white tee I wore. It had a black tribal looking pattern which climbed up the back. I liked wearing over-shirts, it made me feel like I had a fun side about me, somehow. I always left the over-shirts unbuttoned because I enjoyed the breeze crawling up my back.

I heard the phone buzz again, Brent had finally replied. *Look man, I can't hold ur hand thru everything. It's cool she wants 2 hang with u, but if I'm always there she won't stick around long. It looks bad for ur maturity. Just go scarf sum ice cream & stay calm bro. She already likes u. Just try not 2 shut her out like u do every1 else. Lemme know how it goes, and don't 4get to ask about Sarah. lol*

I couldn't believe it. But he was right, as usual. I do shut people out. Maybe it was time for me to get a grip and try talking to her. I hit the reply button one last time.

Ur right man, I'm gonna go have a good time. Thnx 4 the advice. I put the phone down with a sigh of renewal. Then I threw on a fresh pair of khaki pants, and shoes. I picked up my phone and saved Gale's number in my contact list. Then I selected text message and began to type to her for the first time, *I'm on my way. Be there soon.*

I finished getting ready, and headed downstairs, and made my way back to my SUV. I got in and drove off to meet her. Traffic was a bit insane; I seemed to catch every red-light.. All it did was make me even more anxious to get there. My nerves were tingling enough, without having to wait longer. In the back of my mind, I relived the moment when she and her friend stepped in and saved my hide from Nathan's wrath at Bell Mell. Such a spellbinding girl standing against a beast like Nate was somehow an attractive situation to me, considering it was *me* she was defending.

I'd always heard Nate had been a monster to just about everyone he encountered. His gang of thugs never made a move without his say-so. Rumor was he used every kind of drug out there, and he would do anything to get them, even assault authority figures, like cops. It was hard for cops to arrest him. He'd been in and out of several correctional facilities and even landed in rehab from a court sentencing. Nate was a cold and calculating individual. I heard he faked a complete turnover for months, then when he was released, he took his rage out on anyone who crossed his path.

His time in jail taught him ways around most laws which helped him get out of severe sentences and maintain his reign of terror. I had watched him do horrible things to some of the students at school. I remember one time when he waited for Tim Hestner, a guy who had to wear braces for almost a year and a half, to come out of the bathroom. Tim was getting a drink at the fountain and Nate grabbed him by the hair and slammed his mouth against the part where the water shoots out. Tim swallowed a lot of teeth and blood, and even parts of his braces that day. As for Nate, he was suspended for most of the year.

I cringed at the thought of Tim screaming, his hand over his blood-soaked mouth, tooth shards falling onto the floor. He couldn't even scream very loud since the attack knocked the wind out of him. It took most of the teachers from the lounge to calm him down until the school nurse showed up. Last I heard, Tim was doing fine these days. He went through about five surgeries and looks normal enough.

There were other times I dared to remember briefly, but never for too long. Nathan was a different kind of monster altogether. I knew he would hold true to his word and he would fit me into his busy little head-stomping schedule at some point. The one time he was minding his own business, I, like a buffoon, unwittingly ruined his mood. Even if I bought him a brand new shirt, he'd still kill me for sport.

I saw the plaza a few streets ahead, where Gale asked me to meet her. I made my way to the parking lot and found a spot near the ice cream shop. I could see her sitting on the bench, just out front of the shop itself. She smiled as soon as she saw me getting out and hopped from her seat to meet up with me.

"Hey, again! You finally made it!"

I couldn't help but smile slightly. "Yeah, traffic was kinda rough. It usually is whenever I drive." Well, that wasn't too nerdy a thing to say, I'm off to a good start, I hope. I let my eyes crawl all over her, trying not to become nervous at her presence. She was undeniably captivating. The sunlight lay over her smooth features and gently rolled over her neck as it glistened against her long, flowing hair. I soaked up every detail, helplessly, while she looked at me with her gemstone eyes. I collected my thoughts and tried to stay focused, before I started to weird her out.

"So, uh, you like ice cream, eh?" I heard myself say, like a dumb ox. I jerked my head slightly to one side in detest of my own words and winced briefly. I tried to compose myself before she asked if I had a nasty twitching habit or something.

"Well, yeah, actually, I love ice cream. This place serves the best flavors I've ever tasted, so I always come here when I get a chance!"

My face went a little numb, followed by my hand when she grabbed it and led me into the parlor.

"Come on, let's get inside and I'll show you."

I harbored no resistance as we approached the counter. The woman behind the counter was overly friendly and gave us a warming smile. "Hello, welcome to Toft's. What can I get you two?"

"I'm thinking I'd like the black sweet cherry, with a scoop of blueberry, on a waffle cone! I've been craving one of those for a few days now," Gale said. She bit her lip gently with anxious excitement.

I found myself fascinated by how adorable it was, seeing her so eager for ice cream. I don't think she noticed me enjoying the moment, her fixation for her frozen treat was far too deep.

"And what can I get you, sir?"

I barely heard the woman ask. "Huh? Oh, right." They were both looking at me. "I, uh, I think I'll just have a cherry amaretto fudge on a waffle cone."

"All right!" she said, scooping our orders, and placing them into the cones. "Here you go!" She handed us our ice cream with a napkin. Gale was already beginning to work on hers, as we walked to the counter.

She reached into her pocket and handed the cashier a twenty-dollar bill. The cashier handed her back some change, followed by a smile as she said, "Thanks, and enjoy!"

Gale found a table for us, and sat down carefully. I sat across from her, and she giggled to herself. She reached into her other pocket and pulled out something small, but kept it hidden in her hand on the table.

"So, Lucas, tell me, do you like games?" Her eyes were shining playfully behind her question.

"What, you mean, like video games? Well, sure." Honestly, I wasn't sure what she meant. But if she liked video games, then she was definitely the type of girl to hang onto.

"No, silly. Here, let me show you," she said and opened her hand. She held up what looked like an ancient coin; something a pirate would have in a treasure chest, buried on an uncharted island.

"This is a Corvidae ducat. My dad gives me one every year for Christmas. I love shiny things, call it a weakness, if you will. Anyway, notice that one side has a raven on it and the other has a face," she explained, while slowly flipping the coin in order to show me both sides.

"I'm going to flip this ducat, and you call whatever side you want, heads or tails. Ready?"

I nodded once, nervously, and she flipped it.

"Heads..." Sure enough, it landed on the table, heads side up. Gale was grinning.

"Well then, that means you get to go first. Ask me any question you want. It doesn't matter what it is, I have to answer, since your side was up."

What kind of game was this? I'd never played anything so nerve-wrenching in my life! The possibilities flooded over me like a heavy gust of wind. I was on the spot and she eagerly waited for my question. I had no idea what she had in mind. Was she being playful or somehow, hidden in the twisted rules of this game, was she hitting on me? Maybe she was hoping for some kind of dirty question regarding a racy secret she'd been dying to tell someone about. I kept thinking of every possibility, it wore on my thoughts to think that this would turn into a cliché game of raunchy secrets. Oddly enough, aside from the employees, we were alone enough for the game to sway in that direction, even though I was hoping it wouldn't. Mostly because I didn't have any racy secrets to toss back.

I reached for the nearest question I could think of. "What's your favorite kind of music?" I asked, with a heavy mental sigh.

"Mostly abstract sounds. I enjoy heavier dark music, as well as some lighter tunes. I don't like rap or R&B. I hardly ever enjoy pop music, either. Country can be fine at times as well. Your turn. Favorite music?" she asked with a lick of her ice cream.

"I suppose I listen to, uh, mostly video game sound-tracks, really. I like bands that recreate the old game songs into rock or metal versions. I sometimes listen to techno, and movie scores. I don't enjoy mainstream radio at all. Sometimes, I listen to German-metal-bands in my car too."

"Interesting," she replied with an upward inflection "I would never have guessed that about you." Then she went for another flip of the ducat. It landed on tails this time and I felt my blood turn cold.

What else would she ask someone like me? She was obviously having a blast, and she could probably see how shaky I was, which made her smile even more. This was her game, and she knew it, I was obviously the feverish mouse, and she was the hungry cat.

"Hmm, what's your favorite color?"

"Um, Copenhagen blue, it's a few shades richer than, royal blue," I said with relief. "What's yours?"

"Violet. Always has been,." she said with a bite of her cone.

She flipped it once more. It landed on tails again and I felt another jolt of spotlight fever.

"Hmm, well, how old are you?"

"Nineteen, you?"

"Uh, Nineteen, same as you. How about that? Heh." She said it like she was hiding something drastic, and did a horrible job of masking it. I played along with a friendly nod.

She flipped it again, and it landed on heads. My mind was still a blank, so I spat out the one question I knew was familiar to me.

"Do you play video games?" I felt like such a dork asking her that, but it was all I had.

"I do. I'll even add to the answer and say that I own an X-Box 360, and that the best games are ones I can play with friends. I play online games from time to time, and I love action adventure games the most. My father hates having a video game console in the house; he says it's a useless distraction from the importance of reality." I chuckled as I pictured her dad tearing out his hair over a game system sitting there, innocently entertaining the family. "How about you?"

My brain let out a heavy sigh of relief. She was a gamer! I could hardly believe it! I couldn't help but grin to myself in a nerdy fashion. "I actually play games every day. I love online games too, and I also play emulators for the PC when I want to play old-school games from the eighties and nineties." I hardly noticed I was spilling over, I rattled on without pause, "At one point, I even dreamed of getting a job in the game industry, but now I'm not sure if I'll go that route at all." I caught myself rambling and stopped cold before I could blurt out my life story, and bore her to death. I clenched my palms with the tips of my fingers to try and calm myself. They were clammy to the touch, which made me even more nervous.

She looked strangely pleased with my long-winded answer, though. "Sounds like you're pretty passionate about it," she said, a coy look on her face as she flipped the ducat once more. It landed on tails.

"Let me ask you this—A guy like you, with such a fascinating personality," she said playfully, "do you happen to have a girlfriend?"

My face felt like it had just slid off my skull and flopped onto the table. Did she really think a guy like me was all that fascinating, like she'd said? Or even for that matter, that I'd have a girlfriend? I'd only had one girlfriend in my whole life, and that was back in third grade! Gabby Botch was her name, but all the other kids made fun of her. They called her Gabber-box because she liked to talk a lot.

Either way, there was no way to avoid telling her the honest truth. "Um, I don't. Girls kind of avoid me, like I'm a social reject, most times." *Oh, that was smooth,* I thought to myself and lowered my head slightly.

She gave me a confused look—almost like she didn't understand what I meant. "Well, I'm single, too. My dad usually scares everyone off before the end of the first date. That is, if I manage to find anyone brave enough, and interested enough, in me. I guess most guys are intimidated by me, somehow, as well."

I was shocked to hear such a thing and I listened startled at what she said..

"I don't know, maybe to them I'm some kind of freak..." She stopped herself cold, "Oh, Jesus, listen to me going on about it like a drama queen! I'm sorry, Lucas." She rolled her eyes at her own comment, then put her hand on her forehead, rubbing it in frustration.

"Why are you sorry? You're not a freak at all! Are you kidding me?! If those losers even had a clue what they were missing out on, they'd be lining up at your door!" I was so angry about guys treating her like a freak, I hardly noticed I was ranting openly. My logic was being blocked by my mouth, and I was shooting wildly. "You, you've been nothing but nice to me, and I never would've thought a girl like you would even want to be seen in public with me! Anyone who treats you like that needs their eyes cut out. They," I sighed heavily, "don't deserve to look at you, if they don't want to see you for who you really are!"

My mind caught up with what I'd said, and I felt a shiver of fear run up my back. I could hardly believe I just spat out such a thing! She wasn't moving. Even an inch. *Great.* I probably just blew the moment, and she was probably scrambling for an excuse to leave to escape my psycho-talk.

She stared down at the table with her mouth slightly open.

She held up the ducat, and showed it to me with an awestruck look on her face, before she placed it on the table, tails side up, and held it down with her index finger. She looked up at me, holding back a smile "And what do *you* see when you look at me, Lucas?"

My eyes widened as I stared at the ducat under her perfect little fingertip with the dark purple nail-polish. I realized right then, I had just backed myself into a corner. My palms started to sweat even more, I felt my face flush. She looked at me, waiting for an answer, and I was staring back, mentally scrambling and stumbling for the most absolutely perfect thing I'd been dying to say from the day she first talked to me, all the way up to this very moment. Then, out of the haze of my anxiety, as I gazed into her eyes from across the table, the dark brown, with its hint of red somehow gave me a calming sensation. The words I'd been aching to say came to me like the sound of piano music silencing a rainstorm.

"I see an honest, beautiful person, someone who's a lot of fun. The kind of girl you'd be crazy not to like. Someone with a warm, golden heart." I let out a resigned sigh, "I didn't mean to lash out in a ramble earlier. I just can't stand how some people treat someone who's unique. I don't want you to think I'm some angry, psychotic nerd, that's all." There, I said it. Oddly enough, I felt a veil of relief brush over me, and I felt a bit vulnerable all at the same time.

She gently looked me in the eye, and replied "Angry psycho?

No. Nerdy, absolutely. But I have to admit," she put her hand on top of mine. "It's part of what attracted me to you in the first place. I see a deep and fascinating person in you, Lucas. Someone I feel like I can talk to. Someone I really hope to spend more time with. Maybe even date, if that's all right with you?"

I felt my heart jump and slam into my rib-cage, like a car crashing into a brick wall. I was speechless, but insanely happy. Gale, a girl who could have any guy she laid eyes on, was actually interested in *me*! I scrambled to compose myself before I reacted.

"I'd love to! Absolutely! That's so awesome," I managed to get out. I chuckled a bit and she laughed along with me. It felt nice to get a chance to share a light-hearted moment with someone other than the friends from school. I was now out-of-bounds in the eyes of the social classes of the established world of stereotypes. It was the first daring thing I'd ever done, and it felt dangerously good.

"I've been meaning to ask you. I've been thinking ever since we sat down," I was still reeling from the last thing she said, so I was barely prepared for whatever else she had on her mind. "Can... I try some of your ice cream? It looks so-o good!"

I didn't see that coming at all. I held out my cone to her lips. My eyes were frozen in place as I watched her gently drag her cute little tongue over the surface of my ice cream, then, she managed to scoop a small dollop onto the end of her tongue, and pull it into her mouth before looking over at me, with what sort of looked like a flirtatious gaze. The mere sight of her enjoying my ice cream, then looking at me with those innocent, doe-like eyes, nearly made me lose control entirely. My mouth hung open slightly, and I think she knew it!

"Mmm, now *that* was amazing, I'll have to get one of those next time you bring me here."

I struggled mentally to snap out of my trance from her arousing taste test, and nodded in agreement. "I would probably take you anywhere you asked me to, that is, if you gave me a napkin. My ice cream is melting like crazy, onto my hand," I helplessly told her. Not only was it true about it melting onto my hand, but I also needed time to lower my heart-rate, as well as my physical excitement from watching her elegantly tasting my ice-cream. I wasn't about to give her the chance to ask if I'd like to leave and take a walk with her, standing up at that point would've been extremely embarrassing.

"Oh, hurry and eat that while I get you a few!" she said, and got up to find the nearest dispenser. As soon as she was far enough away, I had the strangest urge to do something nerdish. I turned the cone around and checked to see if anyone was looking. Then, I quickly licked the end she had tasted. I don't know why, but just the idea of licking the spot she had tasted, not only made the frozen treat seem far more delicious, but also put me into a state of geeky bliss. I figured, maybe since this was as far as I'd ever gotten with a girl this nice, and good looking, and since no one was watching, I'd treat myself for hanging in there, just this once.

I just shared an ice cream with a beautiful goddess, even if it *was* only one tiny lick...

I looked over at the counter, and saw the woman who'd taken our order earlier. She was looking right at me, giggling to herself with her hand over her mouth. I know my face went red as a stop-sign, instantly. I wanted to die so bad. At least now, my excitement had faded, and I could stand up and leave, without being laughed at even more.

"Here, I got you a few napkins. If you can't finish it, then go ahead and throw it away. You'll just have to owe me another date if you do," she said with a wink. "Something to think about."

I took the napkins from her, and covered my face as best as I could, not realizing what she'd just said until I felt the redness fade from my cheeks. *I'm on a date?* I asked myself mentally. My first date ever, and I didn't even realize it. Brent is gonna flip when he hears about this!

As we sat at the table, sharing in countless laughs and smiles, I noticed from time to time that she glanced over at the door. I couldn't figure out why. Maybe she wanted to ask me if I'd go for a walk or something, but it was becoming more obvious as the minutes passed.

"Gale is everything all right? You, uh, kind of seem, well, anxious about something."

"It's nothing really. I'm just waiting for Brenna and the others to pop in here and put a dent in our perfectly smooth-flowing moment. They should be done shopping soon. I just wish I had more time to enjoy our day together."

"Yeah, days are sort of cruel like that," I agreed as the door opened, and Brenna stepped in. The other two stepped in after her, and they stared at me with coy smiles, except Brenna, who had her arms crossed.

"So Gale, you've decided to have your sweets early. And look, you've even got an ice cream as well! How charming," Brenna said sarcastically.

"Hi Luke! What a nice surprise!" Shannoea added, with wink toward Gale, and a wave at me.

Gale looked back at me, and signaled for me to follow her to the door. I got up, and walked closely behind her, passing Brenna's piercing attitude.

"Brenna, you're so rude sometimes. Look, now you made Gale mad!" I heard Sarah say as we exited the shop.

Gale stepped onto the curb, and I stopped in front of her. She had her hands folded in front of her, almost like she was disappointed in Brenna, but knew she would act the way she did.

She looked up at me and said, "I'm sorry, Lucas, sometimes Brenna..."

I calmly interrupted her. "I know, she's harsh at times. Look, you don't have to explain her. I don't want to ruin any of your plans with them. I mean, to be honest, even though it was kind of short, I had a really great time."

"That's so relieving, because I almost figured she'd ruined

everything. But since she put a stop to our little gathering, what are you planning to do now?"

"Uh, I'll, probably go home and sit at my computer, with my cell phone by me, waiting."

"Waiting for what?"

"A, um, a call, from you. Maybe." I shied away from looking her in the eye. I couldn't even believe I'd said something so idiotic, it made me feel like such a loser.

I watched her face turn red, then I felt mine doing the same all over again. She reached into her pocket and pulled out the ducat, and reached for my hand. She freed my fingers from my palm without effort, and placed the ducat gently into it before closing my fingers. She then pulled my closed hand up to her lips and softly kissed the spot just above the knuckles.

"There, something shiny for a golden heart like yours," she said to me in a low whisper, and slowly walked back to the doorway to Toft's. She opened the door, and looked back at me over her shoulder.

"It'll be hard *not* to call you after such a wonderful time," she said with a cute looking smile.

I nodded slowly. My senses were numbed after having her that close to me. She kissed my hand! My whole arm was completely numb with pins and needles. All except the spot she placed her lips on, which was cold from the passing breeze. This was the greatest date of my entire life, and all I could do was stand there, looking down at my hand like any nerd would do after an encounter like that!

I suddenly felt my cell phone buzzing in my pocket. I snapped out of my trance, and pulled it out. It was Brent, he'd sent me a text saying: *How's it goin'? U didn't leave her hanging did u? Please tell me u went 2 meet her Luke!*

I hit the reply button and wrote my victorious text with confidence: *It went great. We had a real awesome time, & she wants 2 spend more time with me! Does that mean we r dating? Like... boyfriend & girlfriend?* I hit send, and waited for his reply as I walked to my SUV, and got inside.

I took a few deep, cleansing breaths, before I started the engine and felt Brent's reply text buzzing in.

Brent – Right on! U got a girlfriend dude! U gotta call me & tell me the details man! R U home right now?

I smiled and wrote: *No, but I'm on my way now.*

I would remember this day for the rest of my life.

The next two weeks were filled with Gale. Each experience was better than the last, as we started to feel closer to each other with every day that passed. Every moment I spent with her seemed to make me feel stronger somehow, and more confident. It was like I knew, deep down, that as long as I was with her, nothing else mattered. Brenna became easier to tolerate, and the other two, Sarah and Shannoea, were becoming more and more fun to hang out with. Gale and I shared more ice cream, and even went for walks along the path on Kelleys Island near the water's edge. I hoped it would never end.

By the third week, Brent was nagging hard about getting a chance to wedge himself into my newfound group of friends. In all honesty, I couldn't figure out whether he was really trying to fit in, or whether he was trying to get another chance to flirt with Sarah. Either way, I was easily coerced into making plans for the six of us to get together.

My dad had bought me a sports-boat about a year ago; a speedy, night-black boat designed mostly for wakeboarding and racing. It was one of many attempts to get me out of the house, away from video games and chat-sites.

I pulled out my cellphone, and sent Gale a text...

Hey there, r u busy at the moment? That was a quick, subtle way to start 'phase one' of my diabolical plan, I hit send before I had a chance to press Erase Text Field. I waited for what felt like a million years before my phone buzzed with her reply.

I'm never 2 busy 2 text u, Lucas. Wuts on ur mind?

There was no turning back now, and somehow, amidst the pace of the moment, I wasn't afraid or panicked. I felt slightly brave and anxious all at the same time. I looked back down at my phone, then started typing to her.

CHAPTER 5: LUCAS

"Dude, this is *so* gonna rock, you have no *idea* how solid-rad this is gonna be," Brent was more enthusiastic than usual, but this time, he wasn't alone. We were waiting for Gale and her friends at Lakefront Marina, sitting near the docking area.

I looked over at him, trying not to grin too heavily. "I still can't believe I let you talk me into this, I've only driven that boat about three times,"

He laughed, "That's why I'm here, bro!" I rolled my eyes at him. "I love boating, and what better way to enjoy a day like this, than to ride the waves with a good friend and a handful of sexy chicks on-board?"

I didn't admit it out loud, but he was right. This was an opportunity I couldn't resist, I wanted to impress Gale, let her see a different side of me. The only way I could think to do that, was to take her and her friends out on a boat ride.

I saw their car pull up, then felt my eyes dry up as they went wide. Brenna was the first to exit the car; she wore a very revealing, solid black, string bikini, with gold trim. She stretched with a grin, making sure to turn all the way around, revealing a very promiscuous G-string, which dove playfully between the perfectly tanned curves of her butt.

She wore the same sunglasses as before, only this time, her

hair was free to blow in the wind. The only thing that broke up the amount of flesh she was advertising, was a very thin, black silk that she had hanging around her waist like a loose, see-through belt of sorts. I nearly fell over gawking. Most of the people on the docks were staring, which made me regret the idea of letting Gale bring her at all.

"Holy crap!" Brent said, panting, "Those are some fatal curves, on a dangerous woman," he wiped the drool from his chin, just as Sarah got out of the car.

She had on the most conservative bathing suit I'd ever seen, a calm, quaint little sleeveless red shirt, with white lilies patterned all over it, hanging just above her white bikini bottoms, but just low enough on top to show off her small, but cute bust-line.

Shannoea emerged from the car next, wearing a bright neon blue two-piece, with bright purple and yellow palm tree leaves patterned on both. For whatever reason, she had on a white baseball cap, which seemed to fit her impulsive attitude pretty well. Just the sight of her being her bubbly, warming self was enough to make me crack a smile, despite Brenna's insatiable urge to make a scene.

I was on the edge of my nerve, wanting to see what kind of outfit Gale had picked for our little adventure. I broke away momentarily, to see Brent already working his magic on Sarah, who was blushing like a schoolgirl. Brenna, on the other hand, was already surrounded by a multitude of both guys *and* girls, all flirting with her like she was a lost, but available supermodel. Shannoea was standing by the car, waiting for Gale to get out, but waved to me as soon as she'd spotted me on the deck area.

I waved back with a smile, then the driver's door opened as Gale stepped out. My heart literally jumped out of my chest as soon as I saw her; she was wearing a very dark, violet, two-piece bikini that hugged every curve of her body. I was instantly jealous of every single thread on her outfit; it was allowed to touch her all over, while I was stuck watching her from arms' length. Her hair rippled in the wind as she and Shannoea made their way down to the rest of us. I stood there like a statue, mouth hanging open, with my hands over my lap.

It was like everything was stuck in slow-motion, I watched her gracefully step down the walkway, enjoying every single second as her hair flowed over her shoulders and her chest slowly bounced down and rose up with the rhythm of her steps. My eyes sank to her perfectly sculpted stomach, defined like a powerful warrior goddess, all the way down to her hips, swaying in a hypnotic dance, secretly dedicated to me.

Everyone eventually gathered around the dock where my boat was docked. Gale stepped closer. "I wanted to thank you for inviting us, Lucas." Her lips glistened in the sunlight, "I didn't know you owned a boat, or I would've asked you for a ride myself!"

Brenna scoffed, "On the boat or him?" she said in a low voice.

Shannoea nudged Brenna's arm, and gave her a narrow glare, "You shut up—it's not like your plans were all epic-win, compared to going out on a boat-ride! Not everyone wants to fly all over Ohio, teasing guys in every town we land in,"

Brent raised an eyebrow, "You guys do that?" He glanced over at me, then back to Shannoea, "Wouldn't flying all over the place like that be kind of expensive?"

Gale slapped Shannoea's outer-thigh, then cut in, "Uh, well, Brenna's family is pretty, uh, well-to-do. They own most of the businesses that station in France, so they usually send her all over the world, looking for ways to expand."

The way she explained it almost sounded desperate. I broke away from the group, then started to untie the boat from the dock before anyone could notice the effect Gale's gorgeous body had on my lap.

"Oh, well, that makes sense, I guess," he answered back. "I'm glad you came, Brenna, everyone needs to just escape every once in a while, ya know?"

Brenna responded by shaking her head, then folding her arms in front of her.

Suddenly, I heard a voice behind me, groaning in perverted delight, "Hey, honey, how'd you like to date a *real* man?" I looked back and saw a very hairy, out-of-shape guy hitting on Brenna, who looked pissed at his cheesy one-liner.

"Look here, you fat slob," she scowled at him. "I'm a wealthy, stunning woman, who doesn't waste time. Do you

66

know why?" she asked.

He looked confused, but from the look on his face and the sound of her answer, he hoped she was about to tear his clothes off, right there on the dock.

"It's because I know the value of a dollar. Time is money, and right now, you're wasting time. *my* time. And when someone wastes *my* time, they pay out of *their* pocket! I'm willing to bet, by the look of you, that any money *you* have, belongs to the girl you're trying to cheat on, right now. *Piss off*, hairball."

He took a second to soak in her answer, then stormed off in a mad huff. I never imagined I'd actually cheer Brenna on for such a cold move, but I did. I laughed to myself as I boarded the boat, then turned the key, starting it up. The roar of the engine got everyone's attention, and they boarded, taking their seats.

"So, Lucas," I heard Gale's voice behind me, "what's the name of your boat? Don't all boats have to have names?"

I hesitated, for nearly twelve seconds, "Uh, Wave-Blaster." I tried to sound intense when I said the name, but I felt embarrassed, all the same.

"Let's blast some waves then! Punch it, Luke!" Brent exclaimed, patting my shoulder. I smiled, and then hit the throttle as soon as we'd reached the exit of the docks, slowly bounding into gear, ripping through the wind.

CHAPTER 6: GALE

We spent nearly an hour on the lake with him, Lucas' boat
was fast. I loved the feel of the wind tussling my hair. I didn't
dare admit it out loud, but seeing him behind the wheel, his gray
shirt fluttering against his toned arms, making me bounce around
as we shot over the waves; it was a serious turn-on for me!

I already felt attracted to him before, but the idea that he'd
invited all of us out for a day of thrills, as well as his company
was enough to make my heart want to sing to him. Shannoea
and Brent were watching Sarah do some wake-boarding, while
Brenna lay sprawled out, across from me, catching some sun on
her well-oiled body.

"Wow, girl, you're a natural at this," Brent hollered, followed
by a series of cheering whistles. Sarah was holding on for dear
life, hardly budging at all, she looked a little scared, which was
justified by her hatred for being wet.

"Maybe you should pull her in for now, she's been at it for
nearly ten minutes!" Shannoea laughed.

Brent tilted his head, while nodding in agreement, but just as
he reached up to signal Lucas to stop the boat, Sarah wiped out.
She fell out of stance and hurtled into the water. "Oh, crap, Sarah
took a spill, guys!" Brent announced before hopping into the
water after her. I was actually shocked to see him dive in after

her, I'd never seen a guy so insistent on such a thing.

Lucas drove the boat back around, carefully approaching the two of them, while Brent helped to keep her afloat. She looked extremely agitated.

"Here, I'll help ya back on board," he said, lifting her with his massive frame. "I'm gonna grab your waist, then you hop as high as you can, that should be enough to get'cha back on the boat, okay?" he explained.

She nodded, her insecure eyes locked on him. He did just as he'd promised, and she hoisted herself onto the side, then stumbled back to her seat, shivering from the ordeal while she unhooked the board from her feet.

As Brent hopped back aboard, he had a very intrigued look on his face, he sat down next to Sarah, then wrapped a towel around her. "That's an awesome tattoo you have on your back there."

My blood nearly froze in my veins.

"Where'd you get it done? I've never seen a tattoo artist who could detail their work like that, in my whole life!"

Sarah's face dropped, along with mine "I...uh... I..." She was nervous, when she was nervous, bad things happened. She was already starting to pant, and averting her eyes from him.

Even Lucas seemed intrigued. I had to think quick, I couldn't leave her on the spot, nor could I let her tell him anything that would put him, or the rest of us, at risk.

Shannoea and Brenna both sat up, then Brenna spoke up, "It

was a gift from me, for her eighteenth birthday."

My eyebrow arched as high as it could at her answer.

"She nagged me for two months, until I finally caved and paid for the entire two-thousand-dollar job."

"Whoa, now *that's* hard-core, girl," he cackled. "First you put us all to shame with your ninja skills on the wake-board; then, you turn out to be a steel-hard tatt-collector! I'm gonna need a few seconds to catch my breath from bein' near you, Sarah—you're a crazy awesome-saurus!" He had her smiling from ear to ear with his artful cunning, which made the rest of us smile as well. It was a special treat when she reacted with the rest of us, as she seemed unplugged, most times.

It wasn't long before Brent had her laughing, she even allowed him to brush the hair away from her face, showing him even more of her charming features. I had to admit, I hadn't seen Sarah connect with anyone so well, not even Brenna. It was refreshing to see her finally letting someone in, who seemed to care so much, after so little time with her.

She seemed to forget she was soaked from the lake, due to his valiant comedy. Even so, I couldn't tell if it was *his* efforts, or hers that drew them so close. It didn't matter, so long as she was having a good time and felt safe.

Brenna seemed angrier than usual, most likely due to Brent's overall appeal to Sarah. Shannoea on the other hand, was enjoying the moment as much as I was.

Our time on the lake drew on, we each took turns

wakeboarding. When it was Brent's turn, he showed off as much as possible for Sarah, who watched like a little girl enjoying a birthday clown. We shared laughter as he wiped out several times, but refused to admit defeat at the hands of the waves.

After about three more hours, we'd had our fill, and Lucas drove us back to the docks.

I walked over to him as the others made their way to the car, "Thank you so much for inviting us out today, Lucas." I couldn't help but run my fingers through his hair. He shivered with a smile on his face, then started to blush. I loved his bashful side, it was an irresistible trait of his that I enjoyed triggering.

"It, uh, it was nothing really, I just wanted to show you a good time." He was so cute when he was fragile with his words; it made it harder to leave.

"Well, I certainly had a fabulous time, but it's getting late. Maybe we can spend the rest of the day texting one another?"

He froze up as soon as I'd suggested it, then nodded, "Absolutely, I'd love to touch you," his face turned white, as soon as he'd caught up to himself, "I mean *text* you! All, um, all night."

I felt myself taking on my own shade of red as he cleared his throat.

I gathered myself, acting as coy and alluring as I could. "Well, then I'd be happy to oblige you. After all, you deserve it after today."

He looked both confused and excited as to whether I wanted

his touch, or a text. I approached him, running my index finger across his chest, "You look cold, Lucas. Maybe you'd like a hug, to help keep you warm?"

He nodded slowly, shaking wildly. I reached into him, wrapping one arm over his shoulder, while the other laced around his waist. He gradually followed my lead, letting one hand rest shakily on my shoulders, while the other trembled against the lowest region of my back.

I snuck in a very soft, yet quick, kiss on the side of his neck, making him turn hot to the touch. I couldn't help but grin to myself as soon as he reacted. Eventually, I broke away from him, then winked at him as I rejoined Shannoea and Brenna.

Brent was escorting Sarah to the car personally, keeping her smiling the entire time, which seemed to make Brenna angry on the inside. I almost hated to go, but it truly was enough excitement for one day. I had much to attend to, much collecting that needed to be done for the night.

Brent held open Sarah's door for her. Then suddenly, Sarah hugged him, just out of nowhere! "Thank you for saving me, Brent, you're a true gentleman." It took about ten seconds for him to catch up to the moment, but when he did he hugged her back, making sure her towel was still keeping its warm hold on her back.

"Aww, I'm glad you had a good time, Sarah. Honestly, it was nothin', I'll save you anytime you want." He tilted his head to one side and asked, "That, uh, sounded corny, didn't it?"

Sarah laughed, putting her hand over her mouth. "Yeah, just a little." She stepped into the car, and waved to him, with the reddest cheeks I'd ever seen her with.

I took one last look at Lucas, who was still standing in the same spot, his hands in his pockets smiling to himself as he waited for Brent to tear himself away from Sarah.

Brenna scoffed from the back seat, across from Sarah, "Can we seriously go already? I've got a hair appointment in an hour!"

Brent reared back, acting as though he'd been snapped at, by a vicious feline, and then waved to Sarah with another smile. The way he took Brenna so lightly was enough to get a giggle out of me. I slowly drove off, making my way back to town, the image of Lucas still hanging in my thoughts. As simple as the time we'd spent with him, it would be in my fondest memories for a long time, indeed. He'd shown me a side of himself I didn't even know he had, he seemed braver, more confident than what I'd already come to expect.

It was refreshing to finally be in *any* relationship with a guy who didn't seem so hell-bent on sex, or ego-boosts, something that seemed null and void in Lucas' mind. It was that very part which seemed so magnetic to me—the part of him I wasn't used to, and the part of him that seemed to dwell elsewhere. It made him seem mysterious, yet simplistic at the same time. I hoped deep down, that in time, he'd share those sides of himself more, to give me passage into the areas he'd kept from everyone else around him.

More-so, I hoped that someday soon, I could open up to him as well, and share with him the secrets I'd kept for so long, secrets I'd never wanted in the first place, secrets that ached and thrashed inside me, burning at the chance to be told.

But, would they draw him closer, or would the shards of my tattered, shrouded past be more than enough to drive him off? One thing I knew in my heart for absolute certain, I would need time to consider such actions; neither of us were ready at such an early stage in our relationship.

The side of me I'd kept hidden for so many years was a risky one, to say the least. The other thing which I'd come to decide in the recesses of my heart—the longer I kept it all from him, the longer I could simply enjoy being seen as normal—normal enough to finally be happy.

Normal enough perhaps to finally live a simpler life, without so much arcana threaded into every breath I took.

CHAPTER 7: GALE

Even though I'd spent the last few weeks with him, he still somehow made me feel the same way I did when we'd first met on the ferry. I couldn't explain it, but his mere presence made me feel nervous and excited at the same time. I'd decided to take what we had between us to a higher level. I called his cell and waited for him to pick up.

"Well, hey there, what's up?"

My heart jumped the moment he spoke, and my skin froze over with excitement. I even stood on my tip-toes for a split second before lowering myself into a calmer composure.

"Hey, yourself!" I shot back, smiling uncontrollably. "I just called, because I wanted to hear your voice, but then I thought, why stop there? Instead, how about something more?" I cleared my throat as best I could, "You, me, a night of the hardest metal money can buy, at none other than the Twin-Silver-Orchids concert. They're playing at the Wolstein Center in Cleveland, and I just happen to know the two of them personally, and they sent me two tickets. Maybe we should go, like tonight-ish." I said it in such a way that I made sure it didn't sound like I was asking and waited for his reaction.

I could hear him gasp slightly on the other end. It made me smile even more. "Did you say Twin-Silver-Orchids? as in *the*

Twin-Silver-Orchids . . . from Ireland?"

"None other. So, now that we've established the entertainment for tonight, all that's missing is you, agreeing to go with me! I'll get pretty lonely if I'm forced to stand all by myself, so just say you'll go!" I knew he couldn't stand the thought of me being lonely; Lucas had an adorable way of being generous to those he cared about. It was a hard trait of his to resist.

"But, uh, it's five thirty p.m.. Is that really your idea of night-ish?"

"Don't get coy with me, just go look out your front window." I could tell my answer confused him, but that was all part of what I had in store. I waited on the phone until I saw him move the curtain and peek out. His face lit up when he saw me outside in a black jean-jacket, over a black evening dress, standing next to a sleek, shiny, black limo in his driveway.

"Hurry up and get ready, we'll be cruising in style, so wear something sharp!" I winked at him, hoping he could see it. Instead, he tilted his head slightly, like he was confused.

"Holy crap, you're serious, aren't you?" He stared at me with a shocked look on his face before he started to smile. I could see his excitement building, even from the driveway. It was nice to see him so anxious for a night with me, since it was our first official night together.

I smirked back and said, "I'm going inside to greet your parents. That way, not only do I get to finally meet them, but it gives you a reason to hurry. Go, get ready!" I laughed, then hung up my cell, putting it back into my handbag as he put the curtain back. The night I had planned for us was going to be perfect. I'd taken every stride I could to see that it would.

I walked up to the front door and rang the doorbell. The door opened and an older guy, I assumed was Lucas' dad, stood in front of me.

He had a kind looking face, with the same comforting eyes as Lucas. His head was shaved which in my opinion made him look more casual. He had a peculiar looking shirt on. It was a white button-up, with dark brown and black triangles flowing in rows, straight up and down, their points facing one another. It almost made me dizzy just looking at it. His simple blue jeans were honestly the only thing that kept my eyes from spinning out of my head. I fought off my vertigo and smiled with my hands folded in front of me, trying to look as pleasant as I could.

He must've been caught completely off guard. He glanced at me with a heavy sense of confusion before saying, "Uuh, wow." His eyes grew wide as he scanned me over, then he leaned back into the house and hollered in a sarcastic tone, "Honey, I'm leaving you, and I'm running off into the sunset with this lady at our door. Okay?"

Lucas had told me his dad was extremely light-hearted, and always found humor in just about everything. I played along, staying silent and cordial, smiling at his father's comment.

In the distance, I could hear a woman's voice answer back,

"Not even the neighbor's dog would run off with you while you are wearing that horrid shirt, you nitwit!"

His reaction almost cracked a laugh out of me. He raised his eyebrows, looked down at the incriminating article of clothing, then his brow furrowed like he was hurt. When he saw me holding back my laughter, he gave me his best sincere look.

"Is it true? Does my shirt really suck that bad?" he asked with a wink. I took his wink as a gesture that I could be honest or coy, he could handle both.

I chuckled a little. "Um, yeah it kinda does. Sorry."

He slapped his forehead, and let out a defeated groan, like he'd just been shot before he suddenly went into formal mode in a split second. He held out his hand and I leaned forward a bit and shook his hand.

"Hi there, I'm Gale, I was wondering if Lucas might be home. Is he, by chance?" I asked, knowing full well he was upstairs, franticly looking for something to wear. The front door opened a bit more, and an energetic looking woman pushed her way in front of Lucas' dad. She had on a far more conservative outfit, a brown, short sleeve shirt, with Khakis. Her dark brown hair was pinned back, but it looked like she'd pinned it back in a hurry earlier. It still looked nice.

"Oh, my goodness, Drew, it's Gale!" she exclaimed, her eyes racing over every inch of my outfit, from the smooth, midnight black surface of my form fitting dress, to my black, knee-high, four inch heeled boots. "It's an absolute pleasure to finally meet you. We've heard so much about you, sweetie! I'm Suzanne, Luke's mom, and that loser with the ugly shirt is Drew, his dear ol' dad. Please, please, come on in, have a seat while I go get Luke!" She took my hand, and led me into the living-room, right on the other side of the front door. I sat down in the soft brown chair near the couch, and folded my legs to one side while she walked over to the hallway.

"Luke? You have a stunning young lady waiting for you down here, sweetie. Don't keep her waiting, or your father says he's gonna run off with her, you hear me, dear?" she hollered carefully up the stairs.

In the distance, I could hear him banging around, still getting himself ready. I heard a door crack open somewhere upstairs and then he answered, "Okay, hang on mom. I'll be down in a minute." The door closed again, and I glanced around the room. It was a warm and inviting layout, with light brown walls, met with a cozy fireplace, with several pictures of the family on the walls, each one carefully hung throughout the room.

His dad sat down on the couch and leaned back slightly. "So, aside from what Luke told us, tell me a bit about yourself, Gale. It isn't often our son has a guest of your caliber come to visit him." He smirked from across the room.

I smiled back warmly, and said, "Well, now, that depends on what he's told you."

He chuckled and ran his hand over his head. "I think he'd probably try to kill me for telling you," he said, glancing around the room, acting like he was being spied on. "You seem nice enough to take a bullet for, so I guess it's okay!"

Although he was having fun with the situation, I was actually on the edge of my seat with excitement. I felt small surges of anxiousness pulse through me as I leaned in closer.

"He had a hard time even telling me anything, he gets embarrassed easily. But when I did manage to get him to answer, he said you're..."

Suddenly, I heard Lucas from clear upstairs calling down the hallway...

"Dad, remember your promise from the other day?"

Drew made a double-take, from me to the stairway, then back to me again before he said, "Uh, yeah, don't worry, I got ya covered! I was, uh, just telling your awesome new friend about this cool show I saw on TV earlier." The second he finished shooting off his evasive fib, he leaned in quickly and whispered all in one breath, "You're the nicest girl he's ever met, and you're all he thinks about, and he hasn't even touched his video games for almost a week. I'm pretty sure he'd go so far as to crap out a dragon egg with a diamond ring in it, if you asked him to." He inhaled hard and let out a dramatic sigh that made me giggle behind my hand. His eyebrows raised while he nodded slowly, his mouth open like he was in shock. "Yeah, you heard right."

I wasn't sure if he was being coy or serious. *Just how big an impact have I had on Lucas?* I wondered, my face stuck in shock.

"Okay, your turn!" He folded one leg over the other and clasped his hands over the top knee casually, then tilted his head.

Oh, boy, where to begin. "I've lived on Kelleys Island almost my entire life, and even though there's a lot to do on the island itself, it wasn't until I'd met Lucas that I actually started to enjoy everything the island has to offer." I could see from my answer, I had managed to knock the breath right out of him. He was against the ropes with shock, which made me beam with joy inside.

"You mean, he actually socializes? With socializing people? In a social environment? Are you sure you're at the right house, lady?" he asked behind his coy smirk. "The only socializing Luke has ever done that I know of is when he's chatting on that online video game he's always playing! I swear, he's always on that thing, when he's not hanging out with Brent!"

He put his elbow on the arm of the couch, rested his head on the knuckles of his hand, and cleared his throat. "So, uh, are you taking him on a date, or did you dress all dark and dapper just to impress us? Coz if you're trying to impress us, it's totally working!" He let out a prestigious chuckle.

I couldn't help but laugh along with him. He was far too fun to be around. I felt comfortable, like I was being accepted without effort. I loved it.

"Actually," I smiled back, "I *am* taking him on, well, sort of a date tonight. I thought I'd take him to the Twin-Silver-Orchids concert for an intense kind of evening. Maybe even a limo drive around town afterward."

Drew's eyes grew wide, and his jaw nearly hit the ground. "Wow, I totally hate that band. But only because he played their CD for an entire summer once. But even so, where the heck have you been all those years ago when he *needed* a date?" He seemed to be enjoying the idea of the reverse role being played, the girl taking the guy out.

Before he could ask, I gave him a preemptive answer. "You probably think it's odd for the girl to ask the guy." He nodded, still smiling along with me. "The truth is, I'm not the normal kind of girl anyone is used to. I really like Lucas' company, and I felt the need to take the initiative, and ask him out tonight, or—"

He calmly interrupted me, "He probably never would've been brave enough to ask you." He nodded to me, I silently agreed by nodding back once. "Believe me, I know how he operates. I was like him, once upon a time." His smile was still warm, as was his reassuring tone. I was honestly shocked that he was aware of Lucas' meek attitude toward women, until he said, "Suzanne was the strong one between us. She used to drag me all over the place, showing me off to her friends like I was some great prize; but honestly, I didn't see it at the time." He looked like he was having a mental flashback, which only made him smirk a bit more. "But then along came the day when I was able to be there for her when her dad passed away. She was devastated, but because I was there, being strong beside her, she pulled through."

I suddenly felt a rush of nerve-racking chills run over me. I couldn't help but shiver at the thought of my father dying. It would be more than I could handle.

He must've seen me shiver, for in that split second, he sat up, and began to look worried. "Oh, crap, I'm sorry. I didn't mean to creep you out like that. This is supposed to be a nice, romantic evening and I'm ruining it."

"It's—it's okay. Don't worry about it." I reassured him, trying to break the mood with a smile. It seemed to work, as he was starting to look calmer as I leaned back in the chair. "I'm just sorry to hear that he'd died. It sounds like she was close to him, which isn't too different from *my* life."

I heard Suzanne enter through the door near me. "He's almost done up there, so I figured I'd get us some refreshments," she said, holding a tray with a few glasses on it. "Gale, would you care for some of my famous Berry Grove blast?" She handed me a glass of the dark bluish, purple drink. I held it up to my lips, smelling its rich aroma. The cold air from the crushed ice made it easier to smell a blend of raspberry, blueberry, and kiwi, with a hint of strawberry in the mix. I eagerly took a sip, and was sent to a level of bliss I'd never experienced before from one simple drink.

"Do you like it, dear?" she asked with a hopeful look on her face.

"This is incredible, Mrs. Carmicheal. Did you come up with

this recipe yourself?" I took another, heavier sip.

"Please, Gale, call me Suzie, or Sue. I can tell, you and I are not formal kind of women. And as for the drink, I did. It has berries of all sorts, as well as an organic fruit mince I make from scratch for added flavor boost! Bet you couldn't tell from smelling it, eh?" She smiled with content and satisfaction while I enjoyed another sip. A few minutes passed while the three of us chatted, it was nice to have a normal, undisturbed moment with such warm, loving people for once. The way these two kept the atmosphere of our conversations both humorous, as well as intriguing, it was like being welcomed home. I was nearly finished with my glass, when I heard Lucas coming down the stairs. I perked up and looked toward the staircase near the front door.

"Well, look at that! He *does* have something other than sweat-pants and gray shirts, after all!" Drew cackled, holding his glass up.

We all looked at Lucas, and when I saw what he was wearing, I nearly dropped my drink. He was dressed in a sharp pair of black cargo pants, with a white, loose hanging button-up shirt. He also had on a smooth dark-blue jacket over top of the shirt, which made him look casually enticing, in my eyes. I even caught myself drooling a bit, just looking at him! I took a napkin from the tray, and wiped my mouth before anyone had time to notice, before getting up and going over to him. I held out my hand and bit my lip to hold back my uncontrollable smiling.

He took my hand and I ran my other hand up the sleeve of his jacket.

"Wow," I whispered to myself. He must've heard me from the look on his face, which made me start to blush heavily. I scrambled to take his attention away from my embarrassment. The only thing I could think to do was make my way back over to the chair, and get one last sip of my drink. While I did, his parents surrounded him, his dad took a picture of him with his cell phone, while his mom kept brushing his sleeves with her hand, making sure he didn't have any dust or hairs on him.

"Can you believe it, dear? Our son is finally dating! And it's a date with a *HUMAN!*" Drew was pretending to cry on Suzie's shoulder, making sure Lucas heard every sarcastic whimper. Suddenly, he shot up from her shoulder, and slapped Lucas on the back. "The best part is, you know for sure that your date is actually a woman, and *not* some twenty-five-year-old fat guy playing an online game as a level seventeen, female Chaos-Mage, am I right?"

I almost cracked up laughing when he said it, but I could see that Lucas wasn't amused. Not one little bit. "Come on, you remember Marla Faustus, dont'cha?" Lucas rolled his eyes with a disgusted sigh.

"Oh, knock it off Drew Howard Carmicheal, you're such a terd!" Suzanne slapped his shoulder.

"Hey, I did it for *Luke's* own good!" He seemed rather serious, dropping his comedic tone. "I mean really, son, I know

I'd already talked about it before, but I'll say it again; The only way to live a healthy life, is knowing who you're talking to! Take Gale here, for instance," he gestured to me while he spoke, "you can see her, standing right here. She's a real, flesh and blood human being, who is *clearly* a tangibly alluring female! If it wasn't for me pulling that stunt, you probably would've *never* even met her in a trillion, kajillion years!" He had my interest peaked as to this stunt he was referring to.

"All right, that is quite enough! Don't mind him, you two, I'll handle him. You'd better get going, while the night is still young!" She smiled at us before turning to her husband, who was standing behind her, looking at the picture of Lucas he'd taken. "As for you, good sir, it's off to your room! Go and sit in the corner and think about your behavior! That should serve you justice!" She stamped her foot down and pointed toward the bedroom door.

Drew reacted without missing a beat. "You're not my real mom! I don't have to do what you . . ." She interrupted him by grabbing his ear and pulled him toward the doorway. "*Ow, ow, ow*, lady, that hurts! You know it only takes twenty-five pounds of force to tear off the human ear? That means you break it, you bought it, toots! Oh, and Luke, about the concert tonight, don't go streaking while covered in blood like they did in that one music video of theirs, okay?" Suzie pushed Drew into the bedroom doorway and shut it promptly behind him, shaking her head. "I already own your sorry little behind, now go think about how you're traumatizing the poor boy with your antics, young man!" she demanded.

Lucas and I headed outside to the limo. The chauffeur opened the door for me, and I got in. Lucas stood for a second next to the door, his expression awkward.

"What's wrong, Lucas?"

He looked at me through the open door with a hesitant stare, "Sorry. I – I've never been this close to a limo, let alone a limo driver!" Seeing him act like this was kind of adorable in a way, but we still had a schedule to keep. "So, do you ever get to ride in these things, or do you just drive them all day?" he asked the chauffeur.

The driver smiled back and said, "I get that all the time, man. Long story short, when I get that question, I usually tell em; I love drivin' these babies. In the long run, they're more expensive than just about every car we park next to. So either way, drivin' or ridin', it's high-rollin', to me." He winked and patted Lucas on the shoulder, respectfully. "Now if you'll just hop inside, Mr. Carmicheal, I can get back to making you two look beautiful in the back, while I look beautiful at the wheel."

Lucas cracked a smile, and got inside, sitting next to me. "Thanks, Will," I said with a thumbs-up. I knew he'd get Lucas back on track fast, he was always good at getting down to business. He shot one back and closed the door carefully. Lucas shuffled in his seat uneasily. I could tell he was definitely a fish out of water, and I was now his only bearing. I leaned over and nudged him with my shoulder to snap him out of his fidgety trance.

He looked over at me, almost as if he'd forgotten I was right next to him.

"So tell me, who's Marla Faustus?" I asked coyly. His face went blank, and I chuckled to myself. I knew he was unamused, but I simply *had* to know the details on what Drew talked about back at the house.

He sighed and turned his head slightly away from me, "Oh, God, you had to hear him say that, didn't you?" I was surprised when he surrendered to my curiosity. I half expected him to get a bit angry, but instead he groaned and said, "Marla Faustus was a prank my dad pulled on me. *HE* was Marla. See, he bought a copy of this online game I was playing at the time, and created a female character, then she pretended to be interested in me the whole time we were going on several quests and missions together." He wasn't even looking at me when he laid out the situation, it was clearly not one of his father's better pranks. "When Marla reached her seventh overall level of experience, she revealed herself as my dad. He laughed his butt off for hours, telling me I had all the skills I needed to talk to people from playing that stupid game, and that I should spend some time socializing with *real* people."

"I'm sorry, Lucas, that sounds pretty awful." I started to rub his hand gently out of sympathy, the only thing I could think of to comfort him. I even felt guilty for asking him about it. I felt a stem of anger flicker inside me from his father's cruelty. At the same time, though, I fell into a whole other level of understanding. Even in a family as warm and welcoming as his, he still felt like an outcast. The feeling of mutuality began to outweigh the anger, and I smiled to myself. "He was right, you know."

I snapped out of my musing and looked over at him again.

"If I still had that game, I'd never have met Brent, or...or you. Chances are I'd still be wasting my life, instead of living it." Those gorgeous eyes of his were locked with mine as he spoke. It was enough to make me want to kiss him, right then and there.

CHAPTER 8: LUCAS

"So, wait, how do you know the twins?" I needed something to distract me from remembering my dad and his hair-brained ways.

Gale shot back a clever looking smile, and shrugged her shoulders under her jacket. "Nova and Naya? Uh, well, let's just say; we go back a ways. I remember when they started that band of theirs, they had the hardest time getting off the ground, but look at them both now."

I stumbled to speak. It was absolutely fascinating that she was even remotely connected to such a legendary group that hailed from as far away as Ireland. "They had trouble starting T-S-O? That's..." I tried to ask, but I couldn't find the words, at all.

"Strange? Well, if you knew them the way I do, then you'd know they're both very demanding. Not like Brenna. They do have better manners, but when they ask for something, then the subject is closed until they get it. That's part of how they got to be so famous."

I barely heard her answer, I was still in shock that she knew them! I'd never told anyone, but I had a huge crush on both Nova and Naya a few years back. I shuddered to think what she'd do if she ever found out such a thing, which didn't take long. Without thinking, I chuckled and said, "Man, I used to have such a huge cru . . ." A brush of fear swept over me briefly. I caught myself a split second too late. She was looking at me with her head tilted slightly to one side.

"A huge what?" she asked. I felt my face turn a slight shade of red, while hers stood firm without expression for a few seconds, before she let out a playful giggle. "Let me guess, you had a huge crush on them, am I right?" She put her hands on her hips, sitting there with an unsurprised look on her face.

I knew I was getting redder by the second, with no way to hide it.

"Oh, Lucas, seriously, every guy does at some point when they see them! But for your sake, don't tell them that!" She laughed.

"What, wait, what do you mean? For my sake?" Now I was confused.

"Everything they do is part of their act. The things they say and do are all part of their stage presence. They are very good at acting promiscuous. If they get the impression that you're interested in them, they will tease you and play along nonstop. If you thought you were embarrassed when you told *me* that, then you haven't been through anything yet!" She giggled a bit more with her hand over her mouth. "Besides," she leaned in and wrapped her arms around me, and stared deep into my eyes, "I don't think I could fight off the two of them if they started groping and pawing at you."

I tensed up, instantly, her gaze was soft but hungry. I couldn't help but feel frightened inside. I knew Nova and Naya were ravenous by nature, just from seeing a few of their concerts on TV, as well as some of their interviews a few years back.

Gale and I made small talk for almost an hour. We talked about the times in high school when my friends and I used to hide comic books inside our textbooks and read them during class, and she told me how she used to love playing hide and seek during recess. She said she was so good at hiding that she accidentally fell asleep in her hiding spot. When she woke up, school was over for the day and every teacher was outside looking for her. It made me laugh when I pictured her curled up, sleeping behind a bookcase or a tree.

The limo pulled into the Wolstein Center parking lot, then made its way around the building, toward the rear entrance. The layout was enormous, with floodlights lining the outside walls, and tall trees standing in rows, complimenting the sheer warmth of the building itself. It was gorgeous, considering I'd never seen it until now. I started to feel my nerves clench up, while butterflies fluttered in my stomach from the excitement.

The chauffeur parked and opened the door for us. We got out and headed for the door leading inside the backstage area, but as we neared the door, we were stopped by a pair of large security guards.

"Gale Anning?" one of them asked. She nodded and we looked at each other. "The twins wanna see you and your guest immediately. Just hand me your tickets and I'll take you to them." Gale handed him our tickets, and he tore off the top, then handed the stubs back to her. "Right this way, please."

The guard led us down one of the hallways until we came to a singular doorway with the Twin-Silver-Orchids logo painted on it. It was two silver orchids, side by side, wreathed in thorns in the shape of a heart with blood spats all around it. The guard unlocked the door, and let us inside. "The twins will be here, momentarily. They requested that you make yourselves at home until they arrive," he informed us before he shut the door.

Their room is insane! I thought to myself, in a gasp. There were baby-dolls hanging from steel twine all over the place, and an ashtray with a huge cigar smoldering in it, surrounded by cigarette butts. Every one of them had dark ruby lipstick on the ends. I looked over at the mirror, and it was cracked from where someone had stuck a large ominous looking dagger into the top. The crack looked like a spider web, with branches reaching out in all directions. There were pictures of the twins with various people, all tacked onto the border of the mirror with black electrical tape. Each one looked like it was from a different country. I caught sight of a painting sitting against the wall next to the mirror. I looked closer and saw the twins along with what appeared to be Gale. They were wearing Victorian clothes! It was a perfect likeness of Gale, but she was just a bit younger, almost like she was fifteen years old. The painting creeped me out in a way I couldn't even begin to express, I turned away and saw Gale looking at the Gothic-looking couch at the end of the room. It had dark red cushions and a pitch-black wooden frame. I took a closer look and noticed the frame was detailed with hundreds of tiny carvings of naked humans sprawled over one another. It made Gale blush slightly, which was kind of cute to see when she looked up at me.

"Just feel lucky they didn't decorate *your* house, Gale," I joked.

Gale looked back at me with a shake of her head.

"The couch isn't as bad as this," she said, before holding up a small stack of adult magazines that had been sitting on the corner of the couch itself. Each one was dirtier than the last, with pictures of morbid and even unspeakable positions on the covers!

Gale's face was getting redder by the second, so I took the magazines from her and slid them under the couch. She glanced at me briefly while biting her lip, before feebly clearing her throat and walking over to the other side of the room. I could have sworn the look she gave me, was one that showed a keen interest in keeping those raunchy magazines.

The door opened, and my blood shot cold. Nova stepped into the room, followed by her sister, Naya. I grabbed Gale's hand and held on for dear life. Nova had on a black ruffled ribbon-top which tied to a single red orchid below her collar-bone. The corset she had on hugged her savage curves with several belt-straps climbing down the front of her body, and pushed out her chest, which she flaunted with a proud sense of joy. A black frilled, thigh-high dress bloomed out from the bottom of the corset, teasing the eyes of any who dared to look. I watched her enter the room, with widened eyes. Each step she took tugged at my nerves furiously. The mid-leg, orchid lace leggings, and belt-strap boots didn't help matters, at all, The loose ends of the belts on her boots swung and whipped around with her movements as I gripped Gale's hand tighter.

Nova's dark emerald eyes locked with mine and her ruby lips cracked a playful smile. She brushed her shoulder length nightmare black hair, layered with blood red tips, from her face, revealing a cluster of orchids painted over her right eye and down her cheek.

"Oy! Look, Naya, Gale's here! And she's brought a friend! *Céad míle fáilte! Cad is ainm duit?*" Nova said with the heaviest, most beautiful Irish accent I'd ever heard.

I had no idea what she'd just said, but it made my skin tingle to hear her foreign language! Her sister, Naya, approached us with a smile, as well. Her outfit was a gleaming white version of Nova's outfit, but it had soft silks instead of shiny black vinyl, and white fur boots. Her hair was ghost white with black layered ends, and the orchids painted on her face were white, making her an exact opposite to her sister.

Naya held out her hand, and tilted her head to one side quaintly. "He's lookin' a bit 'onna tasty side, eh, Gale? I can see why ye keep him at arms' length! Name's Naya, what's yours, *milseáin?*"

I couldn't speak at all. I'd never heard such a hypnotic, entrancing accent before, ever. I felt my insides fluttering all over the place, like a bird trying to escape a cage. It was absolutely crazy! I felt Gale put her hand on my shoulder and whisper into my ear. "Remember, stay focused, don't give them the chance to start hitting on you. Oh, and don't keep her waiting, she'll just force you to shake her hand, if you do." She gripped my shoulder a bit tighter.

"I donnea understand it, is he broken or sommin?" Nova asked, with her hands on her hips.

I scrambled for something to say. I took in a deep breath and exhaled slowly, as I spoke. "I'm Lucas Carmicheal. It's so awesome to, uh, meet my favorite singers from one of my favorite bands! Strom-Garden was the first album I ever bought. I even played it non-stop for the entire summer, like six years ago!" I felt my brain take a sigh of relief, before I lifted my hand to hers.

She gripped my hand and said "a whole summer, eh? Did it drive everyone insane?"

"Only my parents. They, uh, hate anything heavy, especially Irish metal, thanks to me!" I laughed nervously.

"Well, Lucas Carmicheal, me sis and I are glad to finally get to meet Gale's boyfriend; ye're top o' the list in our book! To show ye how much we appreciate your love for the finer sounds of music and metal, Nova and me wanna present to ye, our most rockin' Maglairin's Pog, a seal of approval!" Naya stated. Her skin was so soft and her grip was gentle, too, but only for a second. She wrapped her fingers around my palm and pulled me right up against her, nearly knocking the wind out of me. My forearm was planted against her chest, with the top of my hand in front of her face.

"This here's how we like greeting our V.I.P's!" she said with a wink, before she licked the top of my hand once slowly, then kissed it lightly, all the while looking into my eyes. It happened so fast. At first, I was just shocked at her sheer strength. She was able to yank me over to her with no effort whatsoever, after which I was powerless from her grip. But after she licked my hand, then kissed it... I was in serious need of another Bell Mell menu. This time, it wasn't going to be covering a pop spill. I was suddenly thankful for having wore a large, loose-fitted button-up shirt.

"There we are now, have a look-see! Now ye're holding me official V.I.P seal of approval, what we call; The Orchid's Kiss. Better than any day to day autograph, and it's way more fun to give," she said with a sinister chuckle. "Now the security back here won't mugger up your time backstage," she went on with a smirk as her sister Nova began to walk up to me.

I looked down at my hand and saw a glistening red stamp of lipstick staring back at me. It was the strangest thing I'd ever had done to me! These two were known for being unorthodox, and I had just been a victim of their testament! I glanced over at Gale, Nova was giving her the same seal of approval. Gale's face looked awkward as she allowed her hand to be licked, then kissed.

"Is this really how you greet V.I.P's these days? I mean, it just seems a bit excessive," Gale asked, as Nova let go of her hand.

Nova sighed and put her hands on her hips. "Look, *milseáin*, Twin-Silver-Orchids is a strong, hard-hittin' name-brand that people respect. We have an obligation to everyone we come across to uphold a constant, shall we say, flow of stage presence and simple bloomin' continuity! We cannae be breaking away from who we are, even for ye two."

"It's all in a bit of fun, Gale. We used to have lots of fun when we were growing up." Naya added with a flick of her pearl hair.

"Yeah, I suppose you're right," Gale replied, looking down at her kissed hand.

As they passed by each other, Naya put her hand on Nova's arm and spoke in a low voice "Oy, his hand tasted like a bit of heaven," I heard her say softly as she glanced at me from over her shoulder with hungry eyes, before she whispered into Nova's ear a little more. All I heard were the words "I really wish I could taste..." before it became inaudible for my ears.

Gale however, heard every word, or at least I figured as much, considering her jaw had dropped and her eyes got to be as wide as planets.

"You two are so perverted. Lucas would *never*..." she stopped herself before she let too much out too soon, "...do *that*." She giggled lightly, with a hint of uncertainty.

Nova and Naya looked at each other and then looked back at Gale. "That donnea mean *ye'd* never do it," Nova said in a sadistic tone. "I know ye're a naughty lil' lass deep down, Gale. I've seen the books ye grew up readin'! We even brought ye some tasty looking magazines from over in Germany! They're over here, on the couch." She gestured toward the couch, but saw they were gone. "Oy! Where'd they go?"

Gale's face turned pink, then red, with embarrassment.

"I bet he'd do anything ye asked, the quiet ones always be tasty perverts underneath." Naya chuckled.

I felt awkward standing there. Everyone was talking about what I would or wouldn't do and, oddly enough, I actually started to wonder just what kind of perverted act it was they were arguing about. Deep within my mind, I pictured Gale asking me if I would, and with every syllable she spoke, my heart tingled with a familiar twinge, a twinge that attested to the adventurous side of me. I would, I honestly would do anything for her, no matter how obscure it was.

The thought of Gale having a bad side actually made me see her in a new light; like she was waiting to show me that side of herself when the time was right. As I looked over at her, trying hard to keep from becoming more red in the face, I enjoyed the thought of her having a bad girl side. I felt a smile crawl across my face, which made her turn pinker yet, when she saw it.

"You two suck so bad right now," Gale told them both while she tried not to make eye contact with me.

"Oh, hon, ye donnea know how wrong ye really are—we're actually quite *good* at suckin'," Nova replied without missing a beat.

"Oh, for the love of... *Will you please just quit?*"

They giggled at each other before Nova approached me, and held out her hand. "'Ello *milseáin*, name's Nova, obviously, let's have a shake, eh?"

I looked back at Gale in hopes of getting some kind of support from her. They were intimidating as hell and I was actually being man-handled by them in front of her, which felt kind of odd. Gale wasn't paying attention though, as Naya was busy chatting and playing catch up.

Suddenly, I felt my body slam against Nova's. She was very impatient and had decided *for* me that I was greeting her, whether I liked it or not. I was a knife-tip distance from her lips, and her eyes pierced me with an emerald glare of intense starvation.

"Donnae be shy Luke, dear, I wonnae hurt ye, nae without Gale's say-so, eh?" she said, leaning over to my neck.

I felt myself become hot with worry. I was overcome with a rush of excitement while she hovered over me; I hoped to God she didn't notice just how excited it made me. She was holding me against her like a tiger preying on a helpless goat.

"What, what does *milseáin* mean? You keep, uh, calling us that," I asked, as my voice shivered and tensed up.

She loomed over my neck, and inhaled slowly through her nose, like she was letting her senses take over the situation. I could've sworn she was thinking of me as some kind of human cheeseburger. She let out a slow, steady sigh of satisfaction before she leaned back in front of me. Her hot breath rolled onto my face with intensity, which only made me even more uncomfortable, as I stood fixated against her. She slowly loosened her grip, and I stepped back. Her expression was frightening as she stared at me, mouth open, panting heavily behind quivering lips, almost like she was fighting the urge to maul me right then. All I could do was try to keep my shirt from advertising my present dilemma, as I pulled it down as far as it would go.

"Och, it means 'sweets' in Irish, and *that's* nae far from the truth!" She winked. "Naya's right, ye really *are* a tasty piece, indeed. I dinnae think I've had a scent that enticing in years," she said with her intense stare.

"I think she likes ye, Luke! Gale, what do *ye* think? Let me sis get in a bit of *sproai-am* with him?" Naya laughed.

I seriously hoped she was kidding. Nova looked like a violent, starved animal who had just found a tiny morsel to feed on.

"Uh, did you just ask me if your sister could eat my boyfriend? That is so not happening ladies, sorry." I was relieved to hear Gale say that.

I looked back at Nova, and she was still staring at me with silent, heavy breaths. She was also gently chewing on the end of her index finger, licking a tiny trickle of blood from the tip behind her teeth. To a sadistic sex maniac, she would look irresistible right now.

"Nae, I asked *ye* if she could get in a bit o' fun-time, nae a nibble. Ye need your ears checked *milseáin!* Besides that, I was only joking, anyway. Ye always take everythin' so heavy-like."

Gale put her hand on my shoulder and brushed her hair over her ear, almost like she was marking her territory. It made me feel safer, honestly. "Sorry, ladies, Lucas belongs to me. If anyone's ever going to eat him, it would be me."

I stiffened up with what she'd just said, and turned to face her. "Can we not talk about eating me, please? It's disturbing as hell." even if it *is* a handful of gorgeous girls bickering over what flavor they think I am.

"See what I mean? Ye both freak out over everything! Cannea even have a laugh these days eh? What's this world comin' to, sis?" Naya said, looking over at her sister, who struggled to snap out of her trance and reply.

"Huh? I mean, yeah, it's going to the birds. Donnae worry, Gale, I wonnae be nibbling on your boyfriend. He does look tasty, but I have to watch me figure! Anyway, we gettin' sommin' to eat after the show? Maybe a couple o' pizza's. I'm starving like mad over here!"

"Pizza it is, then. Where did you wanna meet up after the show?" Gale asked, holding out her hand, waiting for one of them to give her an approving high-five.

"What about the roof, we can just grab a few lawn chairs and relax up there! It's nice and quiet up there at night. Should be good for a sit and grub, eh?" replied Nova, who gave Gale the high-five approval she'd waited for.

"The show gets rollin' around nine-thirty. We put ye both in the front row with our best guards to make sure nobody will mugger up our V.I.P. friends! Ye two go have a good time, and we'll see ye out there."

CHAPTER 9: LUCAS

The opening bands were incredible, first was Fire-Shy, then came Zombie-Ninja-Mayhem, and after that, was my favorite German group, Shackle. I didn't even know they were part of the show, but when they came out, they did two of my absolute favorite songs *Kolben-herz (piston-heart)* and *Feuer Fleisch (Fire flesh)!* Gale and I were having the time of our lives, we threw our fists in the air with each rhythm and riff, then swung our heads to the beats that poured from every amp in the room. After the smoke cleared, the room slowly became quiet. The only sound was a low rasping buzz, followed by an occasional scraping noise. It sounded like a metal pipe being dragged across a sidewalk panel.

"It sounds like the twins are about to get started; are you having a good time, Lucas?" Gale asked, nudging my shoulder.

"I've never been to a concert in my life, this is really awesome! Thanks for bringing me with you!" I was grinning uncontrollably. I couldn't help it, she'd given me a night to remember for the rest of my life. I reached over and put my hand over hers. I was having such a great time I hardly realized I was being brave for once! She smiled and looked deep into my eyes.

"Well, I had other reasons for bringing you..." she said. I jerked my head back in slight confusion. "I have a special surprise that I've put together, just for you." She had a very sneaky look on her face, one that was anxious, as well as nervous. "I hope you enjoy it."

Just then, the lights faded out completely and the crowd started to cheer louder and louder. The lights turned a deep shade of ice-cold blue and the metallic scraping noise became more prominent. I was getting more and more anxious when I heard a woman's voice speaking in Irish. It was an old prayer of some kind, and some of it sounded like it was being spoken backwards.

"Is this a new song or something?" I asked Gale, but as I turned to her, she was gone. I looked everywhere, my skin went cold while my nerves went frantic. *Did she ditch me, or is she just going to the restroom?* I asked myself as I glanced at the millions of unfamiliar faces around me. I was getting more and more worried, barely noticing the show in front of me. Then, as if out of thin air, I heard a voice in my head; it asked me to look up at the stage.

There was so much fog crawling over the surface, like a graveyard with laser-lights flashing all over. A huge spotlight faded onto the center of the stage, and a single shape emerged from the darkness. A raven sailed gracefully out of the fog and, just as it landed, it transformed into the shape of a woman. The crowd erupted with heavier cheering as the spotlight revealed the woman's features, my face nearly froze over.

There was Gale. She was on stage! She was holding a violin

under her chin, her eyes were locked with mine from clear at the edge of the stage. I nearly fell over from shock! She started gently playing the violin, her notes matching the mood-set of the song which played ominously from the shadows. It was cold and gradual. The Irish prayer faded off, and two ghost white wolves emerged from the fog on either side of Gale as she played on!

As the drums kicked in with a medium-paced beat, followed through with a gradual hiss from the cymbals, the wolves jumped into the air, toward each other. Crossing in front of Gale, they took the shape of Nova and Naya, then landed on either side of her and started to head-bang with the beat, just as the sound of a heavy percussion started to match the drums.

I felt my chest pulse with every strike of the drums rhythm, from clear on stage, while both of them bent over almost completely. Their heads bobbed with the drums and violin. The bass guitar swooped in with a low hum, followed by a very sinister lead guitar, wailing an almost grunge-metal sound, with a dark, gothic baseline. As the songs beginning reached its climax, the crowd was getting louder and louder, and then they both pulled out their microphones and started to sing...

"*My heart beats fast, I sense ye near,*" Nova strutted over to Naya, and placed her hand on her sisters shoulder, then slid it daringly across her neckline to the other shoulder.

"*My love for ye is feral, dear.*" Naya grabbed Nova's hair, and yanked her head back hard.

"*I ache inside to be this close.*" Nova then wrapped her arms around Naya's waist.

"That's what I really need the most." Then Naya did the same.

"Unleash the wolf, deep down inside," Nova chimed in as they stared at each other.

"And run with me, forever mine!" She finished singing and they both spun around and changed into white wolves again, and to everyone's surprise, they howled in perfect tune with Gale's violin! They even kept a perfect matching vibrato to each note from the strings! It was the most surreal thing I'd ever seen, and from what it looked like, the same thing could be said for everyone else, too! Some cheered wildly, while a lot of others had tears in their eyes while they shot their fists into the air to the beat. One girl even fainted!

I stood there, mouth hung open, wondering how all this was possible. How did they pull off these illusions? And how did they get wolves to howl in perfect tune with a violin? *A show this elaborate must cost them a serious fortune,* I thought, still gawking.

The rest of the song was intense. Nova and Naya moved gracefully throughout the entire thing. They did everything they were famous for doing, from cryptic, breathtaking shows and lyrics, to dark, provocative poses that would give every fan they had a permanent truck-load of hot-dreams every time they tried to sleep.

The whole time, Gale stood perfectly still, playing her violin like she was in a heavy trance. Seeing her up there, along with the twins, it was hard to fight off tears of my own. As the song came to a gradual close, Gale's violin was eventually the only remaining instrument playing. The twins shifted into the two ghost-white wolves and Gale put down her violin. The three of them ran, full speed, toward the crowd and dove off the stage!

Everyone gasped as the wolves vanished into a veil of smoke, while Gale disappeared, as well, and the raven emerged again, flying off over the crowd and into the darkness. A single caw from the raven echoed slowly throughout the room, as everyone fell dead silent. As the raven's caw faded, the entire place erupted with wild cheering and screaming all over again. It went on for several minutes. I was starting to get a ringing in my ears when I suddenly felt my phone buzz in my pocket.

I pulled it out and saw a text from Gale: *Have the security guy next 2 u take u back 2 the dressing room. time for intermission.*

I put my phone away and tapped the nearest security guy on the shoulder. He turned to me and looked down at my hand with the lipstick on it, then nodded once. "You ready to head back?" he asked. I nodded and he led me through the crowd, toward the back exit.

I saw Gale in the hallway near the door to the dressing room. She leaned against the wall, her arms folded in front of her. She smiled as soon as she saw me, and ran up to meet me. "So? What did you think? Did you like my surprise?" she asked, as she locked her hands with mine.

I let out a huge, enthusiastic sigh, "Gale, that was absolutely amazing!" I stammered for just the right words, but the urge to spill over was far too overpowering. "I've never heard anything so incredible! You were awesome up there! How come you didn't tell me you played violin?"

She bit her lip gently, but smiled even so. "I'm not an open book, you know, I do like having a few surprises here and there. But I'm seriously glad you enjoyed the show. I nearly had a nervous breakdown from stage-fright!" she said with a laugh.

"*You* were *nervous*?" I scratched my head. "That's hard to believe. You made playing a violin in front of thousands look like second nature!"

She started to blush slightly, her eyes shifted away from me and she flicked her head to one side, causing her hair to cover her face.

"Hey, I've been wondering—how did they do all that awesome looking animal morphing? I mean, that was completely unexpected when that raven landed and turned into you! It looked so *real*!" My question looked like it bothered her. An uncomfortable expression crossed her face.

"It's, uh, it's just smoke and mirrors, nothing fancy." I could tell by the way she said it, she was upset. I felt extremely guilty for asking. "Look, um, we should probably go talk to the twins. It's time for intermission, and they wanted to hear your thoughts on the new song." She wasn't even looking at me when she spoke, which made me feel even worse. She opened the door to the dressing room, and we went inside.

As Gale closed the door behind us, my jaw nearly hit the floor with embarrassment. Nova was changing right in front of me! She was wearing a black-lace bra, with her back to us, she struggled, trying to pull up a pair of extremely tight black leather pants, the whole time her entire rear-end was exposed to us! She tugged them gently, letting the smooth, flawless cheeks of her supple rear-end melt slowly down into the tight grip of the seat of the pants. My eyes were bulging, and I'd completely forgotten where I was until Gale nudged me.

Naya got up from the couch, and slapped the left side of Nova's butt as hard as she could, making her jerk straight up, Naya chuckled and walked over to the ashtray. Nova's pale left cheek had a glowing red hand-print on it as she pulled the leather pants over it, then strapped the belts up. "What the bloomin' Hell, Naya? Me poor butt is gonna be sore all damn day after that!" she said as she turned around.

I almost had a heart attack —the bra was extremely exotic looking, with black and red roses lining its edges. It was skillfully crafted to hold up her large C-size charms like two soft, pale globes, nestled gently within a bouquet of gothic roses.

Gale and I looked at each other, our shocked faces matched perfectly.

Nova saw us standing at the door and nearly died of embarrassment. "OCH!" She quickly covered herself with her arms, which did little good. "How come ye dinnae tell me they were back? Ye're being a real biter today, Naya!"

"I told ye they'd be back before ye could get changed! Ye donnae listen, and now they got to see your pretty lil' naked butt!" She laughed. "Poor Lucas, he'll probably have hot-dreams about ye for the rest of his life, eh?"

We turned away from Nova, letting her change the rest of her clothes.

I heard Gale whisper, very softly, *"Caithfidh me' a admhail . . ."* I had no idea what she'd said, but she was hiding a jealous smile. *"Afach, ta Ni Nova butt deas . . ."* The way she'd said it, I could have sworn she was commenting on Nova's beyond gorgeous backside. Either way, I was too embarrassed to ask.

Naya had a huge cigar in her mouth, she pulled it out and let the smoke roll out of her ruby glossed lips. The thick gray coils of smoke crawled up every curve of her face, then passed over her hair, then it faded as it silently collided with the ceiling. Even though she was smoking, which I hated seeing a beautiful woman do, she still had a daring, irresistibly sexy sense about her. I didn't dare say anything out loud, but something inside was pulling at me. It happened the moment I was being man-handled by them when we'd first met. Something lit up inside me, I thought it was just the cowardly part of me, like just me getting nervous, but it wasn't. This was something darker pulling at me the longer I stood near them.

I was absolutely petrified, but at the same time, I felt deeply compelled to give in to the subtle urges mixing in me. It felt like an angry, lustful creature was burning, screaming to gravitate toward Naya as she gazed at me. Her provocative looking smile teased the deranged, ravenous half of me, the starving mix of thoughts and emotions stirred angrily, forcing dark, dirty, and unspeakable images and words into my head. I suddenly didn't feel like myself anymore, I was letting this new, undiscovered side of me have too much time to breathe. I turned and walked right passed Gale, leaving the room completely.

I stood in the cool, dark comfort of the hallway with a sigh of relief. I heard the door open behind me.

Gale stepped out. "Well, that was a bit much, to say the least. Are you okay, Lucas?" She put her hand under my chin and gently lifted my head until she could look me in the eyes.

"I don't know. I don't feel right. It's just that those two are so ridiculous!" I shook my head, not because of disappointment from them, but because of disappointment in myself. I didn't have what it took to fight off the urges I'd been feeling whenever they were within arms' length. I wasn't star-struck or anything. This was a darker, more malevolent force. "I mean, did you smell that room? It smelled like, like . . ."

"Sex and liquor. That was what you were smelling," she said without surprise. "Lucas, those two are into some dark things, they party almost all the time, so you can just imagine what all goes on." She explained, the way she was talking, she almost sounded amused by me leaving the room. "I can't honestly tell

112

you how many times a year they throw one of their infamous dark gatherings, I got used to it after a while. What I'm trying to say is I'm here, Lucas. I'm not going to leave you alone with them, not even for a second."

I felt a little better after she said that. As I looked into her eyes, I started to feel calmer.

"How old are they, anyway?" I asked, not knowing what to expect.

"They're, uh, in their mid-twenties, even though they act like ten-year-old girls." She was giggling, I hoped she was being sarcastic, but something told me she wasn't. "Long story short, they're known for their nature, and their nature is intensely reckless. They scare most men because of the things they do to the ones that show up and convince them both to a bit of *spraoi-am!*" She did a perfect impression of them when she said the last part.

I chuckled and rolled my eyes.

"Okay, look, let's compose ourselves. You go back out and wait for me at our seats, and I'll let them know that we'll watch the rest of their show. Then we can just meet them at the roof access afterwards, and you'll have the open air to breathe instead of the smell of liquor and sweat in your lungs. How does that sound?" I nodded after she explained her brilliant plan. She turned around and went back inside the dressing room, while I slowly made my way back to the seating area.

The rest of the show was hard to enjoy. Gale did her best to keep me smiling. I did my best not to let my experience with the twins totally ruin Gale's night with me. We head-banged to a lot of the songs I'd loved over the years. Songs like *Shadow Princess, Sweet Snowy Swift, My Forever-man,* and even *Pages of a Gilded Heart,* brought back a nostalgic feeling that slowly erased my earlier concerns. I was here with Gale, she brought me here to have a good time, and I wasn't going to blow it.

When the show was over, Gale and I followed the security escort to the maintenance section. We took a metal staircase leading up to a single metal door with a sign that read: *Not an Exit* . Gale opened the door and we walked out onto the roof. It was cool and crisp outside. I could hear the multitude of fans crowding out of the building, some were still screaming franticly, while others were laughing between comments. A few minutes later, the security escort brought up four folding-chairs and sat them down near the doorway. We helped him unfold the chairs, placing them in a widened circle. "Have the twins let me know if you need anything else. I'll be downstairs," he said, closing the door behind him.

"It's a beautiful night out, wouldn't you say?" Gale asked. I turned to her and saw her already sitting in her chair. She had her hand on the arm of the chair next to her; I assumed she was trying to invite me to sit next to her before the twins showed up.

I walked over and sat down in the chair she'd reserved for me. "It is, It's not too cold and the wind is down. Kind of a perfect night for a rooftop pizza party." I shot her a reassuring smile. I didn't want her thinking I was still brooding from earlier. I really wasn't, but I needed her to know it, at least. I was just glad to be sitting next to her where I felt safe.

"Oy, there they are!" We looked over and saw both twins coming through the door. Nova had on a black vinyl trench-coat with white orchid silhouettes littering the bottom, some bigger than others. Naya had on the mirrored version, a white one with black orchids printed in the same fashion.

"So did ye order the pizza yet? I'm getting a wee-bit ravenous after a show *that* big!" Naya sat down in one of the chairs while her sister Nova slipped out of her trench-coat, and hung it over the back of her chair. This time, she wore a wine red silk top that looked like a nighty. It hung down to her upper thighs, which made it hard not to stare. She also had on black thigh-high leather boots with belt straps lining the sides all the way up to the top. As she sat down, she noticed me staring and shot me a coy looking smile as she slowly brought one leg over the other, and sat cross-legged, then ran one of her fingers over her leg, acknowledging the attention I was unwittingly giving her.

"I ordered a few before intermission was over, should be here any second now," Gale replied, checking the time on her phone.

"Well, I'll text Barny and have him bring them up when they get here." Naya whipped out her phone and sent him the text, while Nova stared at me with deep, hungry eyes. I felt the tug of that dark tension all over again, this time even more intense, like my blood was boiling while my skin went cold as ice.

Gale must've noticed it this time. She grabbed my hand and cleared her throat. "So, Nova, did the show go as well as you'd planned tonight?" She stared at Nova with defensive eyes. I could tell she was setting territorial boundaries. It made me feel so much better knowing Gale was there to be brave in my spot. Lord knows, I wasn't nearly brave enough to fend off Nova's advances.

"Well, me lass, it was pretty smooth, but I really gotta say, me favorite part of the show was our first song, Chase the Night. That one's going on the new album for definite sure!" She was looking at Gale, but I could tell she was keeping me in her peripheral vision. I knew she was, only because of her next, most obvious question. She kept her eyes on Gale while she asked me, "What did *ye* think of the new song, Luke? I thought Gale was smokin' hot on her violin." Then she turned her eyes to me with that same coy grin.

I was in the spotlight again. I felt the pressure hitting me from all sides. I gripped Gale's hand tighter and held my composure. "I loved the new song. Gale's skill on the violin was...breathtaking, for lack of a better word. I didn't even know she could play one, but now I've heard what she can do, I hope to hear more someday."

Nova's face was priceless. I figured she was hoping to get me to stumble through my words, somehow showing Gale that she could wrap me around her finger the way Gale could, but I held on to Gale's hand. It helped me maintain my composure, as well as my self-respect.

Gale smiled at me, with her cherry-red cheeks. It felt good to be able to finally defend myself, even if I did have help. Naya pulled out another one of her cigars and lit it with a match she pulled from her bra. After taking a few huge puffs from it, she leaned back a bit in her chair and said, "I thought the new song was crazy hot, I cannea wait 'til we record it in the studio! Gale, ye *do* plan on comin' out to the studio to play your violin, right?"

"I'd love to. It's the least I can do for all you've done for me over the years." She gave Naya a friendly wink, then shot Nova a quick glance before she started to gently run her fingertips slowly up and down my arm. "This was your best show yet, ladies. Which reminds me, are you planning on going to the O2 this year?"

"Wait, what's the O2?" I asked, in between warm shudders from Gale's fingers.

Nova leaned forward a bit, "Ye donna know what the Oxygen Convention is?" I shook my head. "It's only *the* biggest convention ever! Bands come from all over to play. Think of it as a non-American Woodstock, like an outdoor version of the Rock Am Ring." She seemed a little more than disappointed, but I didn't care. She was psychotic in my book, even if she was drop-dead gorgeous in every sense of the term.

"We stole the show for the last two years, if I remember

it right," Naya chimed in. "This year, we plan on shooting a live segment there, then we'll have the last bit of footage for our upcoming DVD. I think we'll probably call it *Blood of Shadows*," she said with another puff of her cigar.

Just then the door opened and Barney, their security escort, walked out with three pizza boxes stacked in his hand, and a plastic shopping bag hanging over his arm. "Soups on, ladies and gent!" He walked out to us and handed the pizzas over to Nova. He walked back over to the door and reached inside, pulling out a large wooden crate, then sat it in the center of our circle of chairs. "There you go. Now you have a table to stack those on. Let me know if you need anything else."

"Hey, Barns, ye wanna join us for a few slices, handsome?" Naya giggled playfully.

"Well, honestly, Miss Marco, Gale ordered one for me earlier. She mentioned it as being a gift for being good at my job tonight," he replied with a respectable tone.

"What job did ye have him do, Gale?" Nova asked.

"I had him secretly protect Lucas from the two of *you*," she grinned,

Naya laughed so hard she nearly fell out of her seat, Nova had a look on her face that said *Touche'* all over it.

I had no idea how to react, so I just sat there quietly, munching on my pizza slice.

Barney turned to leave, but then approached us again before handing Gale the plastic shopping bag. "Oh, uh, Miss Anning?

You nearly left these behind, in the dressing room. The Twins wanted me to be sure you didn't lose them." He handed her the bag and when she looked down inside, her face turned rosy red. I leaned over and peaked, curious. I got a quick glance. The familiar cover of one of the porn magazines sat playfully in the bag against the stack of others, waiting to be read. I quickly joined Gale in embarrassment as the twins shot us a sly grin.

CHAPTER 10: LUCAS

The next few days at work were hard to concentrate on.
The echo of Gale playing her violin with Twin-Silver-Orchids
still swept through my thoughts like a never-ending CD track.
She's so amazing and talented, I thought to myself. *I just can't
shake the feeling that she's trying to tell me something.* I glanced
around the deck of the ferry, hoping to see her pop out of
nowhere and surprise me, but all I saw were a handful of tourists
and two cars. It was the only depressing reminder that all good
things have an end, and that no matter how long that end is,
it's grueling to endure until the next good thing comes along. I
leaned against the railing and let out a long, resigned sigh and
looked to my right. Almost instantly, my eyes grew as big as
planets. Right there, staring me in the face, was a huge, lone
raven. It was as big as a full-grown crow... Its head was the only
thing moving as it tilted and angled in all directions, scanning
me over silently.

"I hope you're not the same sign as a crow, I hear they're a
sign of death when you look at em." I said as I pulled out my
phone. I opened my text messages from Gale and re-read the one
from earlier that morning.

*Lucas, our time 2gether has been nothing short of a dream.
I feel like u & I have already been thru so much . . . which is y I*

think the time has come 4 me 2 make a few decisions. As I read through the text message again, my throat was clenching and choking up.

It looked like a break-up was inevitable. She had asked me to meet her on the island. She had some things she wanted to talk about and it was important. I didn't know what it was, but it felt urgent. I had just gotten off the ferry and made my way onto the island near where Gale asked me to meet her, when my entire day went swiftly into a painful shift for the worst.

Nathan stepped out from the shadows of the trees, followed by his other three friends. They blocked me from going farther, and a couple of them were armed with wooden baseball bats. I knew what this was about, and I knew what it meant. He was gonna try to put me in the hospital for what happened to him at Bell Mell. In a drastic panic, I darted off into the trees and bushes, doing everything I could to stay calm and alive.

They chased me through the trees, yelling and laughing like maniacs on a blood-path. I tried to lose them, but they stayed right on my trail with no effort. Nathan slammed into me with all his might and I collided with a tree. It almost knocked the breath out of me, and I fell onto the ground.

"Get up, loser! You ain't done yet!" he barked, as he picked me up by the throat and held me against the tree..

"What? Did you actually think we'd let you slide after that little stunt at the restaurant?

"You're gonna pay, runt! You're gonna pay for the rest of

your life," one of his friends exclaimed.

"Yeah, all five seconds of it!" another one laughed.

I couldn't breathe at all.

Nathan was way too good at torture. He had several victims on his extensive list of past conflicts. Ranging from helpless people like me, all the way up to teachers and police officers. Every one of them beaten, every one of them humiliated forever. Tonight it was my turn to unwillingly become another notch on his figurative gun. I started to sweat feverishly at the thought. Rumor had it that Nate had even killed a few people during one of his infamous beat-downs. He'd never been charged since no one ever found the body, or other evidence, but he was certainly capable, even when he wasn't on drugs.

One of his friends handed him a wooden baseball bat, and he rammed it into my stomach. My ribs went numb for a few seconds, and then they started to ache, badly. I slumped down and held my hands over them to aid against further damage, but he grabbed my head and shoved it back against the tree.

"You're dead, nerd! Ain't nobody comin' for you! I'm gonna leave you to die, and no one will *even care*!" he scoffed.

I started to feel a twinge of anger rising up inside me. He had no right to treat me like this! If Brent were here— *No, I won't cower while he walks all over me.* Brent would help me if he could, but he can't. He doesn't even know I'm still on the island. He's safe at home, playing his video games, while I confront this jerk and his half-baked posse.

I balled up my fist and let my anger tighten the muscles in my arm before I cocked it back. This was my chance to stand against him and finally show him he couldn't push me around like some helpless kid. I screamed as loud as I could, and swung with absolutely every ounce of strength I could find. My fist raged toward his face, trembling and burning from my tight clench. It collided into his cheek, and skidded into his left eye pushing him back a few inches. At the point of impact, I felt a flash of pain surge through my arm and cause my vision to blur a bit. I saw colors of green and blue, and even red, replace my vision for a second, as the pain raced up my arm. I had no idea it would hurt so much. The whole thing went limp at my side, and I felt ridiculous for trying to defend myself. He didn't even fall down, like I had seen in so many movies. Instead, he barely moved at all. Panic soaked my body again, only this time it was harder to keep my composure, now that I'd made him angrier.

Nathan was stunned, but hardly stopped. He wiped his face with his hand to check for damages, and found a small trace of blood from his nose. His eyes widened and his anger flared even more.

I knew I was dead after such a pathetic defense.

His friends started to croon a sinister, "Ooh man, you're gonna get it now, geek!" amongst themselves as Nathan started to pummel me against the tree.

He swung the bat into my left arm, and I felt it break on impact. The pain spiked through my entire left side, burning and freezing contending furiously at the same time. I screamed in terror at the top of my lungs, while they all laughed. The bat collided against my right knee, and I felt it pop out of place. My screams went unheard, aside from the group of lunatics deep in the trees around me. I began to feel light-headed from the continuous blows of Nate's bat. I slumped down onto my remaining knee, blood pouring from my mouth and nose. He kicked me square in the collar-bone and I puked up even more blood. The sheer amount of agony was far beyond anything I'd ever felt before. The throbbing wounds and breaks were too much to handle. Tears flooded my eyes, I didn't want him to kill me, but I didn't have any way of escaping. All I could do was bleed and panic...

"Nobody ever hits me! E-e-ev-er!!!" he screamed, followed by a heavy swing of his bat. I felt the cold wooden surface slam against the side of my head before I fell limply onto the ground.

"Man, did ya see all that blood hit the tree? That was awesome, hit him again, Nate!" I managed to hear one of them say in between chuckles.

The pain was unforgiving and never-ending. My head was throbbing, my eyes swollen and aching, and my jaw was hanging open. I tried desperately to stay awake, hoping they would leave me, but they decided to kick my loose body around, laughing and hollering cuss-words as I absorbed every attack. Just as I started to feel myself pass out, I heard one of my attackers scream in pain. I saw him land in a heap a few yards from me, bleeding from his head. Someone had slammed his head against the tree he was leaning against. There was even a splintered crater where he'd hit. It almost made me smile.

"What the hell?! What happened to Travis?" I heard one of them ask, I watched one of them go to investigate their injured friend.

"I think there's someone else out here, Nate! This geek must've brought backup." The one checking Travis' body said with panic in his voice. Just then, another guy hollered before he was yanked from the group into the darkness. Everyone was on edge, looking for the source.

"Dillon? Hey, where are you, man? What happened?" one of them asked, still glancing around.

Suddenly, their friend Dillon fell out of the darkness of the trees above, landing near the remaining two in a limp heap. Nathan and his last man scattered away from his body as it hit the ground. Then they started to get worried, looking up into the trees in confusion. "He fell outta the tree, man, and I never even saw anyone grab him! He got ninja'ed! what the *crap* is goin' on here?"

"Shut up, right now!" Nathan hollered, then grabbed me by the collar and shoved me against the tree again before looking me in my bloodshot eyes. "Who's with you, geek? Who'd you bring with you?" He ground his teeth as I hung silently from his arm, unable to move my jaw. "You better answer me, stain, or I'll break your stinkin' neck, *Right the hell now!*" Just as he finished threatening me, the last of his friends cried out in pain. He turned his attention away from me, letting me fall back to the cold earth.

My eyes closed for a few seconds, but it felt like a year had passed. When I opened them, I saw a dark figure with long dark hair standing over the last guy. He had managed to catch the fist of his attacker, and was holding onto it from a kneeling position, keeping it from colliding with his face.

"*Grruuh!!* Nate! Dude, I got him! Hurry and bust him up, man! Use the bat on him, quick!" He was so busy holding the fist away from his head, he didn't have time to defend against the next attack. The figure rammed a heavy right knee, kick-boxer style, square into his face, which sent him flying into the air toward Nathan. He landed next to me, holding his face, screaming intensely behind his cupped hands and rolling around in agony. I could see the blood spilling from between his fingers, his entire face had been shattered like a coffee cup against a brick wall. All at once, I felt terrified all over again.

A random thought managed to slip past the overwhelming agony and terror. *Was it Gale?* If not, then who was this, and how did they manage to beat two full-grown, weapon-wielding, drug-abusers bare handed? I looked around, watching as each of Nathan's thugs were picked off by an unseen force, each one taken out with precision beyond human ability.

"Ya know, Matt, when it comes to fighting, you really are a moron. You need to learn to defend yourself." Nate scoffed while

Matt wretched and choked behind his hands, still whimpering in pain. Then he turned his attention back to the mysterious intruder who dared to disturb his sadistic game. "Who are you, punk? Come out and *fight like a ma-a-an!*" I heard Nathan barking as he glanced into the darkness at the intruder.

The intruder stepped into the moonlight slowly. Right then, if my fractured jaw could've dropped open any further, it would have. I could hardly believe it—*Gale*. She'd come from out of nowhere to help me! Just seeing her, made my already aching heart soar even higher than the pain could reach.

"What in the hell is this? Are you tellin' me, some random schoolgirl just beat the *holy, livin' crap* outta my crew?" He was nearly laughing. He looked around for any sign of male assistance in her favor. I guess he figured in his self-proclaimed godhood, that only a male could stand against him in battle. Not that he'd plan on losing, but he never imagined a *female* would be brave enough, *ever*. He turned back to Gale, looking closer at her as she stepped further into the moonlight.

"Hey! You're that piece of trash that tried savin' this little turd at Bell Mell! Oh, I must've done somethin' right for the reaper, coz tonight, I'm addin' *your* scrawny butt to the body pile, after all!" Nathan taunted, gripping his bat even tighter than before. He was having the time of his life, it was beyond obvious. Only a monster like him could ever enjoy the idea of hurting such a beautiful girl.

She stood with a kind of solid vigor. An unusual silence

radiated from her. She stared at Nathan with absolute certainty in her eyes. "I swear, you won't touch him ever again, not after I'm done with you."

"Aww, you're gonna get it now! *Nobody talks back to me!*"

My eyes twitched behind a curtain of blood as I watched Gale take a stance, while Nathan rushed at her with his bat positioned to swing hard. I fought against the intense agony, the urge to pass out was heavy, while I stared at them both. I blinked a terribly painful blink and when I opened my eyes again, I saw something which frightened me to the core.

Nathan swung with every bit of his girth, and Gale threw a straight-punch, shattering the bat into a cloud of splinters! Her attack against the weapon was graceful, almost as if she knew it would shatter! The sound it made was deadly, like a truck crashing through a large wooden door, followed by the sound of wood chips raining delicately onto the grass. Nate was knocked back onto his backside and he held what remained of the bat in front of his face.

The look in his eyes was worth a million dollars, but the sight chilled me to the bone. I began to feel my heart clench, trying to pump the last of my blood through my veins. The pain worsened, and my body started to grow cold and jelly-like. Blackness took me, and then even the pain couldn't follow. Even as my body trembled and stiffened up, I felt a small ounce of ease pass over me at a single thought, *At least I got to see her one, last time, before I . . .*

CHAPTER 11: GALE

"Come on, Lucas. Breathe! *Breathe*!!" I could barely see through the tears in my eyes. I wiped them away and continued my attempts to revive him. He was hurt badly and he had lost a lot of blood from the attack, but I knew deep down I had to keep trying. The light from the moon passed through the branches and leaves of the trees around me, gently highlighting his battered features with a soft pale glow. Even seeing him like this, I noticed a glint of beauty underneath his surface—one that expressed a sense of loyalty and care. My heart ached at the thought of him dying, but more so, what I would have to do once he did.

I cringed intensely at the thought, and my eyes swelled with tears all over again.

"Lucas, please, you have to come back. If you leave now, I'll have to be the one to take you. Please, don't do that to me, Lucas." My words passed vainly over his helpless body, and I sobbed into my shaking hands, holding back my urge to scream. I knew I only had a few more moments with him, and each second that passed hurt like a day of cold, relentless agony.

I placed my hand gently on his chest and took in a deep breath. It was time. I had to do it. I was left with little choice. Even so, I still felt the urge to resist. I bit my lip and cleared my mind, holding onto a mental image of him. Only then, did I feel strong, only then did I have courage. The tears I cried for him dripped from my chin onto my legs as I knelt beside him. All at once, I felt my blood getting colder, the image of him getting clearer and finally, I felt as though he was kneeling right next to me. My heart jumped at the sight of him so intensely in my mind, and I was overjoyed, briefly.

Suddenly, I saw a strange image flash across his shape in my head. A white raven, majestic and powerful, flew straight toward me, passing right through the image of Lucas like a ghost through a veil of smoke. I gasped as I opened my eyes and took my hand from his chest. Fear and confusion lanced through me. I knew what the sign of the white raven meant. It was a sign of promise, an omen of hope, strength, and a love that would never diminish. It only appears to a Corvidae who's found their empyrean destiny. Dear *God*, is Lucas my . . .even in my thoughts, I couldn't speak. I was in utter shock from such a devastating revelation, the thought of Lucas being my soul-mate tingled the hairs on the back of my neck.

I gathered myself, then I closed my eyes and saw the faint image of the white raven, once again. It flapped its pearl-white wings in slow motion, hovering over Lucas as he lay in the grass. Its eyes were a radiant gold, shimmering in the darkness. Then, just as I began to feel myself ache with sadness, I felt it speak. *Help him. Share with him the breath of life.* The voice was far more than soothing, every syllable echoed in the corners of my mind, as if calming rainfall cradled me from inside. *Protect his fragile heart, dear child. For a stray cloud always leads to a lonely storm, or a solemn gray sky.*

I looked down at Lucas' body, and it was then, at that moment, as I stayed knelt with my hand over my mouth under the moonlit trees by the calming waves of the nearby lake, that I knew. Deep inside my very being, I knew I couldn't be without him. I wept behind a trembling hand and an aching heart.

"I can't do it. Lucas, I'm sorry, but I'm just not ready to see you go. So I've decided not to let you. I know I haven't really known you for very long, but after just one day, I knew I didn't want to live in this world if I didn't get to wrap my arms around you and keep you safe with me. You mean far too much to me already," I said to his limp body, as I took in a deep breath, and closed my eyes. I lowered my head until our foreheads touched, my nose brushed against his, and I exhaled softly, watching his mental image dissipate altogether. My breath started out as cold as ice, but soon became warm, and then hot. I waited, my forehead still resting against his, and my tears trailing into his eyelashes, until at last I felt him take in a very thin amount of air.

"Lucas? Oh, Lord above." I checked for another shallow breath. "Lucas, can you hear me?" I asked him while I wiped some of the blood from his face.

"Ga—Gale? What?" his voice was a hushed whisper, a dying flame at the end of a candle, kept alive by a single hand, my hand, to cover it from the soft winds of the unforgiving night.

"Ssh. I'm here, Lucas. I need you to stay calm and quiet, okay?" I looked down at him, tears welling up in my eyes, again. I felt my cell phone buzzing in my pocket, and pulled it out. It was Shannoea, she was on her way with the others.

Gale hang on! We r almost there! Keep him calm k?

I had nearly forgotten I had called her when I finished with Nathan and his gang. Just then, Brenna pulled up and everybody got out, and assessed the situation.

"What happened, Gale? Is he dead? Brenna asked while she glanced around at my combative mess.

Nathan and his friends were starting to come to their senses, coughing and hacking from all I had done to them.

"I... I was going to meet him. I thought it was time I told him the truth, but then these brutes showed up and attacked him," I answered, my voice shaking.

"Oh, for the love of God, Gale! Why would you do something like that, huh? Have you gone crazy? What would your parents say if they could hear you right now? Maybe *now* you know how dangerous all of this has gotten." She started to scold me, but I cut her off immediately.

"Don't start that crap with me, Brenna. I'm not in the mood at all. Besides, I'm not the first of us to break the rules. There's a life on the line here and all you want to do is complain because it isn't *you* that has the spotlight."

"Yeah? Well, what do you think your father would say about all this, huh? You and this boy of yours? He'd be absolutely furious and you know it! He got himself hurt, Gale, you were planning to step out of bounds and because of *that*—"

I cut her off again, but this time I let my temper slip out. "Brenna, shut up! Just shut your over-priced mouth! That jerk would have bullied Lucas no matter who was there when it happened! I'm doing him a favor by letting him live, because I probably would've killed him, if I wasn't trying to keep Lucas alive right now!"

"Gale, I'm going to pretend you didn't just raise your tone with me. I need you to listen! You seriously *cannot* do this! You have to fulfill your duty here! If you don't, everyone *will* know! And then, not only will *you* be in danger, but so will everyone you're connected to!" She put her hand on my shoulder. "Let him go, Gale. He's as good as dead, if you don't." She tried to stare at me with concern, but I could see that behind her expression she was only concerned for her own well-being. "I'm not against you, Gale, but you're out of line here! What do you think will happen when your family asks why you've neglected your duties? What do you want me to tell them?"

I looked back at her with contempt, before shoving her hand off me, "I honestly don't care what you tell them. I've never cared about my duties, the rules, or the decree. I've told you all a thousand times. I want a normal life. I never asked for any of this. All I want right now is for Lucas to recover, and I'll make sure that happens, even if it means turning my back on everything else." My concern for Lucas was far deeper than my concern for the world, or my role in life. Nothing else even came close in comparison to what I was feeling for the fragile soul I was holding in my arms.

Lucas moaned in discomfort as the pain welled and receded from the swelling and blood-loss. Each time he screamed, I cried a little harder, silently. I held him close to me and tried to talk him down, which seemed to work well enough, until the pain returned. I looked up at Brenna, and saw her fighting back tears as she observed my deep concern for his life.

She stared back at me with a slightly shocked, defeated look on her face behind the glossy, tear-soaked eyes. She'd never heard me outright deny my duties to my family, but all the same, it didn't matter to me. I'd said my peace, and anyone who disagreed among the group would simply have to live with it.

After mentally deciding to back off, she flipped her hair, and walked toward the car, speaking in French under her breath.

Shannoea knelt beside me, followed by Sarah. They both looked at me with worried expressions on their faces. "Gale, we've got your back on this. We really do and we'll always support your decision, but all I ask is that you to consider the costs for doing this. He'll be in danger almost all the time," Shannoea insisted.

"The others might try to step in when word gets out. They'd love to dip their hands into something as big as this," Sarah warned. "Gale, I honestly hope you're ready to carry this kind of weight, because this decision isn't the kind of thing you can enshroud from either side. They *will* all be able to see what you've done, and it'll attract constant attention of an immeasurable magnitude. So much so, it may disrupt those higher than your parents. Are you certain you're ready for this?" Sarah's fatalistic tone certainly did make the situation heavier.

But, even so, I nodded in reply.

"Well then, let's get him to your house, Gale. We can finish all of this where it's safe." Sarah insisted.,

Brenna stepped out of the car, and approached us. She stared down at the three of us surrounding Lucas' body and sighed once. "All right look, if you wanna get yourselves into trouble by saving one guy's life, then that's fine by me. Just do me a favor and pretend I'm apologizing. Maybe then, I can get back to being right all the time." She was never good with humility. She stumbled for words, the same way Lucas and I had when we'd first met on that ferry. That's how I knew she was being honest. That's how I knew she'd back me up. It was one of the only ways to see through her attitude and find the good friend I knew so well.

I couldn't help but smile when I said, "Thanks, Brenna. I knew I could count on you." We each got on either side of him, carefully picked him up, and put him into the back seat of the car.

Sarah and Shannoea got in, while Brenna walked back out to where the beaten thugs were still laying.

"What about you? Aren't you coming?" I asked, as I opened

the back door of the car.

"No. I'll deal with our new friends. It's high time they learned some manners and I'm in a bad enough mood to give lessons tonight," she answered, without even looking over at me. Instead she stared coldly at Nathan, who was stirring from my confrontation with him. He moaned in pain next to the tree where I left him.

"Just don't overdo it, okay, Brenna?"

"Sure. Fine. Whatever."

I knew she'd say that. She was mad as hell, and I was in no position to argue the point. The three of us drove off toward my house near the edge of the woods. I sat in the back with Lucas' head in my lap while Sarah drove.

"Just hold on, Lucas, we're gonna get you to my house. Then you'll feel better, okay?"

I felt his cold hand searching for mine. I placed my hand into his, and he gripped it faintly and pulled it closer to his head. I watched him slowly press his battered lips against my hand, and he kissed it once. His mouth trembled against my skin. My emotions raced and my face grew warm with another overflow of tears. I closed my eyes and tried not to lose composure in front of him again. I didn't want him to feel anything outside of sheer comfort.

Such a tiny, unselfish kiss on the hand, from a dying soul amidst his own agony. It was like a silent miracle among so many tragedies that blotted out the warmth of hope I had felt for the two of us and the future I hoped we might share. Almost as though he were trying desperately to thank me for saving him, even though I blamed myself for his pains.

We reached my driveway in no time, considering Sarah was the one driving. The familiar welcome of the dark, faded blue house stood just outside the car, Shannoea opened my door for me, while Sarah and I lifted him from the back seat. We carried him up the porch steps, and onto the deck until Shannoea unlocked the front door. She joined us in carrying him through the living room, and up the steps leading to the guest room. Honestly, I wished I could've invited him in and given him the proper tour under less intense circumstances, but his attackers managed to ruin that pretty well. I hoped Brenna was showing them a night they'd never forget, no matter how much mental therapy they sought afterwards.

"Here we are. Lay him on the bed. Careful now," I informed them both. After I placed his head on the pillow, both Sarah and Shannoea stepped back from me, watching from across the room.

"It's your move now, Gale." Sarah said. "You have to make a difficult choice. I don't understand how you've managed to keep him alive, but even so, if you proceed in saving him, he'll always be a part of you, and likewise for him." I glanced at her as she spoke, feeling every deep, fatalistic word that fell from her lips. It was as heavy as rainfall from the strongest of thunderstorms. "Now is the time to choose," she went on, leaning against the dresser with her hands folded over one another.

I looked down at his face. His eyes were trying to stay open, but he was in far too much pain. I leaned down and kissed his forehead. It was hot to the touch from the fever he was beginning to run. I felt another flood of tears roll down my face, trickling onto his. I gathered myself, and put my hand on his chest. I closed my eyes and pictured him the day I had met him on the ferry, praying mentally.

It made me smile, just slightly, before I let his mental image in my mind be taken and I replaced it with a mental image of him standing next to me, the two of us standing against the entire world, and everything beyond. I marveled at how radiant he looked. It made my heart feel like it was glowing and singing at the same time. I took in a deep breath, and the image became more prominent, and then I started to hear whispers from inside my thoughts. The whispers were in a language I'd never heard, as if there were several thousand shadows watching over the moment. Then, just as before, I felt my breath become as solid as ice, but then it became as warm as the face of the sun. I exhaled slowly, just as I had done back in the woods; and the air that fell from my lips almost seemed alive as it crawled across his chest and into his mouth.

I kept praying in the back of my thoughts, harder and harder. I asked that he live, that he be given back the breath of life, itself. I started to ache inside as my eyes began to water.

The image of the two of us swirled into a mesh of fog

and light before it reshaped into a single form. A white raven appeared and emerged from the fog, its feathers gleaming with pearled majesty, its eyes shining like golden stars. Then, beyond the echo of my thoughts, a voice came from the furthest reaches of infinity, resounding in all directions, *So be it.* It was smooth, like running water, but also thundered with a calming rasp.

I felt Lucas jolt back to life and take in a frightening gasp of air. It was done.

He would live.

CHAPTER 12: LUCAS

Here I was, standing on an open plain of soft grass, with no signs of life anywhere. The grass was greener than I'd ever seen, and the sky was vibrant and blue. The only thing that didn't make sense were the clouds. They were black. Like, midnight black. I smelled no water in the air and I didn't hear thunder anywhere, so a storm couldn't be coming. I looked around again and saw Gale standing a few yards away from me. She was wearing a very thin, white silk gown that barely hid any of her features underneath. Her long, black hair began to blow, as the wind picked up, causing the gown to hug her body even more, which made my eyes want to stay open forever.

She started to walk slowly toward me, but with every step she took, I thought I could hear glass breaking. When I looked down at her feet, they were bloody, and when she stepped forward again, I noticed the grass around the two of us were shards of glass! Fear swept over me. *Where was I?*

"Gale, stop! Don't move. I'll come to you!" I hollered to her. She stopped and smiled.

I took the first step and it was far more painful than I'd thought it would be. My bare feet were shredded badly and I hadn't even moved more than two inches. *What in the world was happening?* I thought to myself. I glanced over at Gale, who was still waiting for me to come to her. Suddenly, like a flash from a camera, Gale appeared an arm's length from me, almost like someone had pressed the fast-forward button on a DVD player, whereas I was somehow unaffected. All it did was frighten me even more.

"I can't live without you, Lucas, you are all that matters to me. A field of pain can't keep me from you, and neither can death." Her words were kind, but cold. It was like she was empty and lost. I looked closely at her, but from what I could gather, she looked real enough.

The air grew cold and thick at the same time and the clouds seemed to come to life above us. I looked up and saw them dissipating and descending to the area where we stood! The uncertainty of this entire situation chilled me even further, as the clouds spiraled around us. Then I got a good look at everything. Ravens! There were thousands of them circling us. They weren't clouds at all! They all landed one after another, hundreds of thousands of ravens all landing around us. I started to fear for my life...

After they all landed, there was an eerie calm in the air. No sounds at all, not even the smallest caw from any of them. Their eyes were piercing me with stares of outrage and hunger. I looked over at Gale again and, somehow, her gown was covered with tears and rips, but she was unscratched.

"I need you, Lucas, you're everything I've been missing. *Run, they're coming for you!*" She screamed at me like I couldn't hear her at all, even though I was standing right next to her! I reached out to touch her, to let her know I heard her, and the instant my fingers connected to her face, she shattered like a window and turned to dust, blowing away in the wind. I pulled my hand back out of reflex and started to shake wildly with an intense amount of worry. This was Hell, it *had* to be Hell. There was no other explanation. The ravens around me started cawing like mad, and the sky turned black and red at the same time. Suddenly, the figure of a wild looking animal emerged from the ravens, its fur was mussed from a hundred battles, and its face was feral and sinister. I couldn't help myself. I stared into its eyes as it made its way through the mass of birds littering the ground. It looked angry and vengeful, like it knew who I was. I looked at its body. It was the strangest animal I'd ever seen. It had features from every animal I could think of and somehow it didn't seem like an animal at all.

"*Child!!* There is no place for you here! *Be gone!*" The creature howled.

I spiked with sheer terror, screaming as loud as I could. I opened my eyes and sprang up from where I lay. I felt a cold sweat on my forehead, as I glanced around to see where I was. It was a bedroom, but not one I recognized. It was actually kind of nice and inviting. The walls were painted a dark blue, which was complimented by black wooden bookcases and an expensive looking reading desk. Even the bed looked pricy, draped with dark blue silken sheets that matched the walls and a nicely decorated blanket bordered with golden thread, winding and racing along its edges. The question of where I was hung in my thoughts while I took in the detail of the room around me. I saw a picture on the desk, lying next to a stack of books.

I stepped from the bed onto the hardwood floor. With a trembling hand, I reached for its shiny black and gold frame. I took in a few deep breaths and collected myself. It was a picture of Gale. She was standing next to an older man with silvery gray hair, and a rough outer demeanor. He looked wise and full of authority with his massive build and powerful smile. Standing next to him was a woman. Her long, black hair closely resembled Gale's, but was pinned up in an almost native fashion. Her warm face and smile in the picture gave me a welcoming sensation all over. I even caught myself smiling, as I looked at the three of them. They looked like a completely innocent family, happy and safe. I felt envious.

My thoughts raced back to reality and I was filled with uncertainty all over again. *Who's room was this? Gale's, maybe? What about that dream? What did it mean?* It was so horrifyingly real, every one of my senses were tingling, causing me to feel light-headed. I sat and propped against the wooden headboard, and paced myself. As I did, I was flooded with flashbacks of being attacked by Nathan and his crew back in the woods. I felt the pain all over again. It was so fresh in my head that it made me sweat heavily. I checked myself for injuries, but I couldn't find any. I was absolutely fine, aside from being dizzy. *What was happening?* I mentally asked myself. I knew the injuries couldn't have healed this fast, but then again, I had no idea where I was, or how much time had passed.

Glancing around the room, taking in a little more detail, I noticed a TV mounted on the wall, across the room, at the foot of the bed. It was a nice, thirty-six inch, LCD flat-screen. Below that, sitting like a crown jewel, was a quaint, familiar shape; an X-Box 360. I grinned to myself helplessly. I could only guess that this was, in fact, Gale's bedroom. It was beyond ironic that I had only fragments of memory leading up to now, with the only soothing sound of her answer from our date at Toft's ice cream parlor, 'I do. I'll even add to the answer and say that the best games are ones I can play with friends. I play online games from time to time, and I love action, adventure games the most'. I looked down at her stack of games, neatly standing in a single row: *Left 4 dead, Fable - the lost chapters, Fable II, Oblivion - the Elder Scrolls IV, Banjo Kazooie - nuts & bolts, Fallout 3, Dead Space, X-Men Origins: Wolverine,* and even *Bioshock,* the kind of games a guy like me, would marry a girl, for playing.

Just then, I noticed something that caused my eyes to pop out of my head. Right there, laying on top of the X-Box, was the case for a game that made my heart melt inside; Sonic's ultimate Genesis collection. She was actually playing old-school Sega Genesis games! I felt weak in the knees, she'd not only heard what I'd said that day, but even went through the trouble of finding a way to experience it for herself! I couldn't decide whether she'd actually liked me, or if what I'd told her was enough to spark her curiosity. It made my head spin just thinking about it. Maybe she wanted to make sure we had something in common, something we could ramble on about, for hours on end? The fact that she went so far to relate to me was making my face hot to the touch, my chest was even turning a bright shade of pink. I was far beyond flattered, either way.

I sat back down on the edge of the bed, and almost out of nowhere, I remembered the rest of her answer from that day, 'My father hates having a video game console in the house, he says it's a useless distraction from the importance of reality'.

I snickered, most parents would agree, that is, until they found a game to get addicted to themselves. I shook my head in silence.

Then I heard arguing through the wall behind me. It sounded like Gale and some older guy were having it out. I decided to carefully investigate, hoping I wasn't dreaming again.

CHAPTER 13: GALE

"Father, please, you aren't even listening to me," I protested, trying to get him to see my side of things. As usual though, he stood firm in his opinion, as he always does.

"This is not open for discussion. You went out against my approval to see this boy of yours and because of this, you have neglected your duties not only in this household, but also within the roles of the Corvidae law," he replied in his usual gruff tone, not caring whether I was listening or not. His word was like stone-clad decree at my house. He was always the kind of father who seemed like an Indian chief, as if everything he stood for was life or death. It made me furious sometimes.

"I like him, father, he's the only person I've ever known that doesn't have—" I stopped myself, only because I realized he would never truly understand. He never does.

"You were about to say dark secrets again, weren't you? This kind of talk from you is nothing short of an outrage, Gale. I will not allow you to continue to use contempt toward your own race! What we do is important to everything and every creature! If we do not fulfill our function, who will? The Rostair? They are filth on this plain, and nothing more!" He ran his fingers through his silvery hair. It always made him look a little distinguished, and even though it was short, it tended to do its own thing most times. On days like this, however, it made him look like a power hungry government official.

"Are you done with these boring monologues? We aren't Colonials or Victorians, anymore. Times have changed and so has everybody else. This lifeless attitude of yours is exactly why I ran off in the first place! Now you're spouting off, *yet again*, like it's going to keep me from being my own person! I've had more than enough of this." I threw my hands up. "You never used to be like this. I just wish you'd take the time to hear yourself these days." I hardly ever stood up to my father. I loved him, I really did, but he was frightening sometimes. At this point, I didn't even care, anymore. I was not going to slave around and miss the chance to live my own life any longer.

His face was unchanged, just like I figured it would be. It stayed firm, a flat pair of lips slowly melting into a frown from years of unhappiness, and a solid, lifeless stare from countless years lost. The wrinkles on his face were each like a road to nowhere, with only the law of servitude as their map.

"Times *have* changed. In this, you are correct. It seems that children have become even more defiant than they were in the earlier days. Parents outside of an orderly home have become nothing short of a danger, not only to themselves, but those around them, as well. With hate and fury running wildly in the streets and yards of all who dwell here, it is of little wonder as to why the Corvidae have been much busier than usual, which is why we must be firm in our role."

I almost thought for a fraction of a second that he was actually going to listen to himself. Instead, he calmly snuck in another monologue of fatalistic importance.

I couldn't take it anymore. I got up and walked over to the hallway leading to where I'd left Lucas. "I saved his life."

My father's eyes got wider and his face turned white with anger and fear at the same time.

"He was attacked, nearly killed, and I stepped in to save him and there's nothing you can say that will make me regret it." That was that. I managed to anger him beyond all reason, and I loved every minute of it. He stood up from his chair, his face wild with emotion.

"How could you do this? You have betrayed everything. Betrayed the Corvidae... for this, this foolish human boy!" He was shaking all over. Whether it was from anger or worry, I couldn't tell. But I felt it was time for a change. Mine. It was time for me to make my own decisions, starting with Lucas and I.

"Actually, I don't honestly know *how* I did it. I simply wanted him alive badly enough and I did it. He's recovering in the guest room. I plan to take him home, and explain everything. Who I am, what we are, and what we do. *Everything.* Where he and I go from there, I'll leave up to him." My words were like swords to him. I thought I saw a tear in his eye, but I could've been wrong. I knew I only had a few minutes before my father tried to stop me. He might even try to *kill* Lucas before anyone got wind of what had happened. I rushed down the hall and opened the door to find him at the edge of the bed.

He was rubbing his head, and trying to stand on his own.

"Lucas, we have to leave, right now."

"What's going on? I could hear you two fighting through the wall. Your dad sounds like he's angry at me..."

I grabbed his arms and lifted him until he was standing. "You're still dizzy from the recovery, but that's okay. I'll help you." I led him into the hallway and toward the side door. His steps were careful and he was shivering. At least he was alive. We made it to the door and I led him down the stoop.

As I turned to close the door, my father stepped out and moved me aside, then threw Lucas hard enough to send him flying into a nearby tree. I was out of time. He was going try to end it before we even had a chance. I had to think fast. Only one phrase came to mind and it was in a language I hadn't spoken in a very long time.

Just as he darted over to Lucas, I took in a deep breath and closed my eyes. *"Gimhera ikkna, nir bevorhn, niluhr."*

My father's head perked up.

"Shulna tef Cihs Ravi itarrah!" I yelled the words and my father halted in mid-strike. His hand was only inches away from landing on Lucas' neck, but he froze all the same, like a statue in the wind. Lucas was staring him right in the eyes with ice-cold fear, the same way a wounded animal stares at its captor. I waited for him to speak.

I could hear him. His breath was shaking from the tears in his eyes. I hadn't seen him like this since his wedding day. "How, how, after all this time?" he asked, his voice quivering.

"I told you before, father, I don't know, but it was there and so was Lucas. You can't kill him now. I've vowed myself to him."

"I heard you." He gritted his teeth.

"If you kill him now, the blood on your hands will never wash off. You'll be shamed and resented in every tribe and clan. Then everyone will know, the way that I know, what kind of person you've become."

"I said I heard you." He was grinding them now.

"Then get away from him!" I'd never ordered my father before, but I couldn't let him slaughter Lucas like some trespasser. I needed to get him out of here, before my father could think of some other means of stopping us. I walked over to Lucas, who was still trying to stand, and picked him up. My father had his back turned. I could feel the outrage of the situation permeating from him, while I slung Lucas' arm over my back, and began to walk him down the path to my car.

"Fyett! Rhune, er unde' silont, tef Cihs Ravi myara't??" he asked me through a shaking breath. I didn't figure he'd ask me the same question twice, let alone, use my birth-name. But he did. If he wanted to know if I was sure about what I saw, then a sure answer is what I would give him.

I turned around, with Lucas still holding onto me, and

answered him. *"Tiatne'. Nil omeh ecna simpara, Xander."* I was done talking, even in the old languages. Lucas and I turned back around, and continued to head toward my car. The sleek, black form of my Audi was a welcome sight amidst the arguing. I love luxury sports cars. My last argument with my dad caused me to buy this latest 2010 model. A gift to myself for enduring his never-ending babble over the years.

"What language were you two speaking back there, Gale? It was kind of awesome." Lucas' breath was knocked out of him. It was cute. His obliviousness to the fatal situation managed to get me to smile, slightly.

"I'll tell you more later. For now, let's just get you out of here so you can rest a little better."

"Where do you think you are going, Gale? You cannot do this. He is a mere boy!" I heard father say, his back still turned.

"What does it matter to you? I won't stay here and listen to you blather on about laws and secrecy, anymore. I've told you hundreds of times, I won't be a part of this stupid fighting. And just so you know, Lucas is more than just some boy to me. He's been the greatest thing that has happened to me so far! He doesn't treat me like I'm different at all, and he's not afraid to be himself... Maybe you ought to take a few notes from him." That was all it took, he turned and faced us as

"I am your father, Gale, you will do as I say! I will not allow you to defy me." I cut him off hard before he could rabble on.

"It's obvious my *real* father's gone. When he gets back, tell

151

him Lucas offered to let me stay at his place until I can sort out my life, and decide what I want to do with it." Deep down, I'd hoped my snappy comeback hurt him enough to make him see a bit of sense.

Lucas looked at me with a confused look on his face and whispered, "I, uh, I don't remember telling you that, not that I'm complaining."

"Don't worry, I've got a plan. Just leave it to me," I whispered back.

"And what of your mother? Do you not even care what she will think of your actions?" I stopped dead in my tracks. He actually played a tricky hand, for once. He used his trump card and I had nothing to defend against it. I felt a tear crawling down my face and decided to keep walking. When he told her the situation, she would most likely side with him. Then again, she was always an old fashioned kind of woman, so if she had seen how happy Lucas made me, she might side with *me*. Either way, it didn't matter. She was far from here, taking care of some business out of state.

We reached the car and I opened the passenger door. Lucas got in and I walked to the driver side door and opened it. I looked back one last time and saw my father. He was still standing there, helplessly watching me take my stand against him. He was trying not to show emotion, and was doing a horrible job of it. I could see I had finally put a crack in his solid stone heart. A crack that proclaimed my yearning for a life the outcome of which I could decide. Still, even with my tiny victory over him, I felt awful about it.

I sat down and closed the door. I smiled at Lucas before turning the key and we drove off to the port together.

CHAPTER 14: LUCAS

Gale was driving toward the port where the ferry docked. She had angry tears in her eyes from her fight with her dad. I was seriously confused by the whole ordeal. All I could do was try to comfort her by holding her hand. Her grip was strong, really strong, in fact. She must have noticed she was cutting off the circulation, because she loosened her fingers a bit.

"Look, I'm sorry I've put you in the middle of all this madness, Lucas. I wish I could make it up to you, but there's nothing I can do to make up for him attacking you like that—"

I couldn't help but interrupt her. "Gale, please, just calm down; take a minute and breathe. All I want are some answers. Like, for instance, how did you punch a baseball bat into a million pieces with your bare hands? Or, for that matter, how am I not in a hospital?" I hoped she would have some logical explanation that would solve all this madness. It felt like I was in some kind of crazy dream.

"I can't give you answers, not right now, I'm sorry," she said in a low voice.

I couldn't believe she shut me down like that! She pulled her hand from mine and put it on the steering wheel, staring forward. An offended sensation boiled up inside me.

"Oh, so what do you want me to do, forget it ever happened?

That's gonna be a little hard. You realize that right?" The whole mess of things made me angry. I couldn't help but lash out.

"Lucas, please. I'm not asking you to forget anything! I just need a little time to soak all of this in, that's all."

"Your dad's insane. I can see why everyone who meets him ends up running away from you." Somehow, it just slipped out. I didn't even mean to say it out loud at all, but the fact that he threw me against a tree seemed to make me even angrier.

Gale looked shocked, even offended I'd even think of such a hurtful thing. The second I said it, I felt horrible. She pulled to the side of the road and stopped.

"You don't know anything, Lucas. You have no idea what's going on around you or your perfect little world!" She was agitated, her grip on the wheel tightened as she turned to look straight at me. "For you to say something so ugly, after all the beautiful things you've said to me." Her face was full of hurt and anger at the same time, but when I looked into her eyes, I could see a glimpse of understanding. Like, she almost expected this to happen.

She sighed. "I realize you've been through a lot, but so have I. In case you didn't notice, I just broke my father's house-rules and stopped him from attacking you! This whole mess goes deeper than you think!" She stopped herself cold. "Let's just get back to Port Clinton. I need to drop you off at your house for now, then we can meet up later. I need some time to sort out this mess, so I'm gonna meet with Shannoea and the others. Would you at least give me that?"

After staring at her for a few seconds, I nodded my head in defeat and looked back out the window. "I'm sorry, Gale, I didn't mean to." I barely got to finish apologizing before she put her hand on my chest.

"Look," she shook her head while she spoke, "just forget about it, all right? You have every right to be angry. Just like you have every right to have your questions answered, but I need some questions answered, too. Just give me a little time to get my answers. Then, when I see you next, and I've explained everything, maybe you'll be able to answer one of *my* questions."

I wondered what question she had in mind. I hadn't realized she'd been saving any inquiries for me, or us, at all. I couldn't imagine what they were, even though I tried.

"This is gonna sound kinda crazy," I tried to smile, but I was too busy replaying it all in my head. "I just can't get out of my head, the way you two were arguing. It sounded like you two are hit men for a government assassins group, like he wants you to join the ranks and be some death-bringer for hire," I said in a calmer, lower voice. She glanced at me, periodically, a bewildered and almost amused look stayed on her face as I rambled on.

"Then there's this Corvidae law. I keep thinking that's the name of the group he's working for or something. That's the only sane explanation for your dad throwing me into a tree and trying to snap my neck. You know, like some spy covering his tracks."

She looked at me with an even more amused look on her face than before. All it did was confirm how wrong I was, which was comforting in all honesty.

"I know, now I sound like some nerd with a wild imagination." I felt like such an idiot trying to figure this all out, like it was some crazy video game plot-line. The explanations I guessed seemed to make her smile more with each passing second. She even giggled to herself a little before covering her mouth with her hand to hide what she obviously thought was an insulting reaction, while shaking her head.

"That does sound a bit extreme," she laughed softly, "but if it means anything to you, I'm glad you're taking it so well. It really means a lot to me that you haven't run away from me after all you've been through." Her voice was gentle and sincere.

I could tell she wanted me to assure her that I wasn't going anywhere, that I'd stay with her despite all the madness and mystery.

"If you can promise me that you'll answer me, that you'll tell me what's going on— "

She jumped in again, before I could finish. "I promise you, Lucas, I'll tell you everything. Just give me some time and I'll give you every answer you want, and more."

"That's really all I wanted to hear. Now, where will we be meeting up?"

"Perry's Monument, on South-Bass Island. It's somewhere I like to go when I need time alone. I have a friend who will let us go up to the observation deck after hours."

We finally reached the port on the island and Gale pulled into the loading area. One of the ferry-men approached the vehicle. I recognized him instantly, with his trademark baldhead and biker mustache. It was Tom. He was always a hard worker and he was always fun to work with. I rolled my window down so he could see me.

"Hey, Luke, how's it going?" he asked with a friendly smile.

"Not bad. Did you have a good vacation?" My efforts to change the mood in the car were fleeting at best, but I pressed on, in order to help Gale and I both cool off.

"Oh, you know, the wife and I had a blast. I took her to a Gunhammer concert. You know how she loves that Gothic industrial metal," he said with a laugh, "then we went to see her parents in Texas. It was fun! So what about you? I see you've met a new friend!" He held out his hand to Gale, who was still holding on to the steering wheel. She gave him a careful shake, and a warm smile.

"Hi, I'm Gale. Nice to meet you, Tom." She pretended to be in a good mood and she was only half-way good at it.

"Likewise, it's not every day Luke here brings anyone with him on the ferry. I'm just glad it was me who had the pleasure of meeting you first. The other crewmen are a bit immature at times, makes for a bad impression. Uh, again, it was good to meet you, Gale. Oh, and Luke, give me a call whenever you get some free time. Maybe we can go for a cruise in that Jag of mine you like so much," he said with a wink.

"Uh, yeah, I'd like that. Sounds fun." It was all I could do to answer the guy. I really enjoyed Tom's company, but all this secrecy from Gale was making it hard to enjoy the moment at all. What was she hiding? I couldn't help but let my mind wander.

She parked the car on the ferry and for the entire trip, she stayed silent. We both sat like statues in our seats. She stared down at her legs, her hands clasped together, while I looked at the clouds passing us outside.

When the ferry reached the docking area of Port Clinton, she finally looked over at me. "Are you going to be all right, Lucas?" she asked.

There was a sensitive look in her eyes. We both needed time to soak all this in. I needed to unwind, but I didn't want to go home.

"Yeah, I'll be fine. Just drop me off at Brent's house. It's on East Karlite Drive. I really don't wanna deal with my parents right now."

"If that's where you wanna go, then, sure."

She drove the car like an expert, turning and braking with expert precision. I was so busy watching her driving skills I hadn't noticed she was already turning onto the street where Brent lived.

She slowed as we drove down the street. "Here we are. Which one is his?" she asked with a glance.

"4766, Right over there." I pointed to the white, vinyl-sided house. She pulled up to the driveway and I opened my door.

"A tree," she said out of nowhere as I was getting out of the car.

"What?"

"He hit a tree with his bat. I was lucky. I barely managed to get out of the way. You must've been starting to hallucinate from the pain." Her explanation was almost insulting, but what else could it be? Her hand wasn't broken or bruised, and we *were* in the woods. I caught myself looking back on the whole ordeal before she snapped me back to reality.

"Don't worry too much about it, Lucas. Everyone sees unbelievable things in their life. Even me."

Her expression was uncertain, as if she wanted me to keep thinking about it. If that was her plan, it worked. I closed the car door and leaned into the window. She glanced at me a few times, but wouldn't look me in the eye.

"As for meeting up, I'll text you, when I'm ready."

"Well, that's one answer at least. Be safe." I turned away and headed for Brent's front door while Gale drove off. I admitted to myself, I was angry at her attempt to avoid answering my questions, but I felt bad about treating her the way I did. In the back of my head, I knew there was more going on, but it was only fair to give each other the time we needed to take in everything that had happened.

I knocked on Brent's front door. After a few seconds, he opened it. "Hey, Luke, my man! What brings you to Casa De Brent's-house?" He had a football in his hands. That meant he had company—the sports jock kind of company—the kind of company that eats a heaping bowl of helpless nerds before every game they play. If I stayed, I'd be leaving with a monumental wedgie I'd never forget.

"Sorry, man, I, uh, I hope I'm not interrupting anything. I just needed some down time from, well, home and everything else."

"Well, that's fine by me, I was gonna head to the backyard and toss the football with a few friends. You can join in if you want!"

I hesitated, suddenly, I didn't wanna drag him anywhere near the situation. After thinking about it for a few seconds, I decided to leave. "Look, uh, I'll talk to you later man. I forgot I have some stuff I gotta go do." I turned and started to walk off, but he caught up to me.

"Luke? Bro, what's wrong? Come on now, talk to me, man. What's goin' on?"

"It's nothing, really, just . . .don't worry about it." I started to back up, hoping he'd let the situation play out to the point of my escape, but he stepped in front of me and raised aneyebrow.

"If I didn't know better, I'd say you needed to get your mind off somethin'." He put his hand on my chest and shook his

161

head slowly. "I'm not lettin' you leave, 'til you've passed some pigskin with me and my buds. I know you'll feel better after you burn some energy, trust me, Luke."

Always so insistent, I couldn't think of one time when he was otherwise. I was quick to humor him. Brent was the only friend who'd ever actually pushed me to do things that would benefit my life. He would drag me to parties, cookouts and anything else to expand my life skills. Today, though, he was more aggressive than ever. He'd never had to physically stop me before, so I knew he was serious. I nodded in defeat and followed him back inside his house.

"Whoa, Brent, who's the new guy?" One of the guys standing at the counter broke from the other two and walked up to us.

"Oh, this is Luke, he's cool. He's a good friend of mine," Brent said, gesturing toward me to greet his friends. "Luke, this is Chad. I've known this guy for like a trillion years. Those other two Bozo's are Mark and Aaron. Don't mind them, they're just here to eat all my food," he went on before slugging Chad in the shoulder.

Chad pushed Brent back and smiled. "Yeah, Brent's a total punk, so don't let him tell you different. He sucks at sports and women, so he follows me everywhere I go. Maybe someday, he'll be as cool as me, the Chadness hath spoken." Chad laughed. The nickname he gave himself sounded so egotistical, I almost cracked a laugh, but I didn't want to draw attention.

I was caught off guard as normally *I'm* the one being made fun of, but, Chad had all his friends joining in. They laughed along with him as Brent stood there next to me, a sly grin on his face, shaking his head slowly.

I smiled slightly and held my ground with the only friend I had in the room.

Brent crossed his arms and said, "Whatever, dude. You're full of crap. I guess you forgot it was *me* that got you a date for the prom last year. With the girl from the pizza shop, the one who had a thing for putting mayo on everything she ate. You were drooling over her for like a week!"

Chad's mouth nearly hit the floor and his eyes almost fell out of his skull.

The other two at the counter began chuckling. I could tell Chad hadn't seen Brent's comment coming at all.

Mark spoke up, "Oh, man ,Chad, I remember her! She was so gross, dude! I watched her eat two whole cheeseburgers smothered in that crap one time! I almost threw up, man!" Even while he was talking, he nearly gagged. Aaron had his hands over his face and ears. I figured it was too gross a subject for him to handle.

"Yeah, you're a real funny guy, but now you're gonna get it." Chad said, behind a fading smirk. He tried to put on his best poker face, but it was pretty shoddy. Even Brent saw through it. "Grab your boy here and get your butt out back for some football! You're both goin' down, with a busted frown!"

I looked at Brent and he shot the same look back at me. Chad's crippled wordplay skills were laughable only neither of us could push out a chuckle. He struck me as the type that should've been associated with *my* stereotype; the nerds and antisocial sorts. Usually, those with bad or cheesy slogans and tag-lines are noted as hopeless geeks. I guess he deserved major points for being brave enough to be what I couldn't. He was socially acceptable. I started to feel a little jealous as I thought about it, but, then, looking at Chad's demeanor, it was easy to see a glimpse of familiarity between the two of us.

Brent's work was easy to spot; clearly he'd done for Chad what he was trying to do for me. He pulled him from God only knows whatever failed social group and showed him a healthier way to live. Chad was a well-built guy, with broad enough shoulders and a toned enough stature to be a football-playing maniac, but underneath he had the personality of a true-blue geek. Almost like looking into a mirror from a parallel universe!

Brent nudged me back to reality and motioned for me to follow him to the back yard. I did, even though I didn't want to. "Don't worry, Luke. Just give me the ball and I'll run it. That way, you won't have to worry about gettin' pummeled," he said, with a reassuring slap on my back. Normally his back-slaps hurt like hell for hours, but somehow, it didn't even tingle today. It caught me by surprise.

We all made our way to the backyard, and Brent sat the football on the ground next to him. "Well, ladies, here's how we're gonna do this." He looked over at me and shot me a friendly wink before looking at the other three, standing across from us. "We're gonna do some warm-up passes, then we're gonna need to decide who's gonna coach. Three against two ain't good odds for pansies, like you guys, so we're gonna even everything out and play fair." His smirk was getting bigger the more he spoke.

"Hey, now wait, just a damn minute!" Mark jumped in with an insulted look in his eyes. "First off, I ain't no pansy. In case you don't remember, it was *me* who won the game for us, last summer! I ran that last twelve yards, *without* a single one of you clowns backin' me!" He began to look a bit angry and started to approach us with an evil glare. "Second, who the hell says you make the rules, huh?" Brent stiffened.

I felt a strange jolt inside, telling me his dominant side was about to emerge. I backed off slowly as the feeling grew stronger, I didn't know what else to do.. I'd never felt anything like this before. It was like I could actually see the pheromones and testosterone building and rolling off them both, like dark blue steam. It made me gasp to myself.

"Ooh, wow, you're right, Mark, I did forget about that! A whole twelve yards—and all by yourself, too! That really *is* amazing, little man!" Brent continued to taunt and Mark grew even more defensive. I half expected him to slug Mark in the head, but the other half of me knew he'd toss a quick joke into the mix and end Mark's pride with subtlety. Just then, I caught a glimpse of something strange. The color of Brent's attitude changed. It went from dark blue, to a confident looking orange! Seeing these colors rolling off the two of them made me white with fear. My breathing became sporadic, and I started to panic a bit.

I rubbed my eyes, hoping I wasn't hallucinating or stressed beyond reasoning. When I looked again, the colored steam remained, barely visible, coiling from them both. I was petrified—and I wanted to throw up, right there, in Brent's grass.

Brent leaned in and put his hands behind his back, neatly folded, one inside the other. "I guess I could see how that's all you'd remember, considering how short-sighted you are, Mark," The humorous glare Brent flooded Mark with, was frightening to say the least; he knew this guy well enough to know he had him against the ropes, so to speak. He was toying with Mark's insecurity, and Mark knew it.

"But if you'd bothered to look behind you, during your so called 'epic-win', you'd have seen how Darren kept Roy and Kyle from tackling your ass in the first three yards of your 'oh-so glorious' twelve yard scramble. So, next time you call someone a clown, make sure *you are not* the one juggling with your damn foot in your mouth, bro. Then, maybe you won't fall on your ass in shame."

"Yeah, dude, Brent's right." Chad walked into the fray and stood between them. "Mark, you really gotta stop putting yourself above everyone else, guy. Brent and Darren were

backing you, and you just tried to shoot 'em both in the face!
Not to mention all the other players who safety-net your ass!"
The translucent steam radiating from Chad was a neutral shade
of gray, he was trying to keep the peace and have a good time.
I didn't need hallucinations to know that much. All the same, it
was relieving to see maturity unfolding inside their little group.
The fact that they weren't fighting almost made me forget about
the colors I was seeing.

Honestly, I was used to seeing fists flying by now, but
these guys had a strong sense of loyalty to each other. One that
reached into the depths of a truer sense of the word 'friend'. I
began to feel safer with them, even accepted in a way...

"You're a good running-back, Mark, but way too egotistical
about that one game, dude. You'll never make the big leagues
with that kind of attitude, trust me," Brent did a great job of
thinning out Mark's anger with soothing wisdom. A trait he
didn't even seem to realize he had. "You gotta learn not to take
every joking gesture I make so seriously, man! Just lighten
up and have a good time! Like Luke over there, he's ready to
play some friggin' football, am I right, bro?" He pointed to me,
standing almost seven feet away from their group, hoping they'd
forgotten all about playing 'kill the nerd with the ball'.

"All right Brent, fine. Let's do this. I've been mad as hell
ever since Katey left last week. Gotta get my mind off it," Mark
said. His attitude faded to a dark brown, with traces of gray.

It was strange to actually *see* the color of someone hurting.

It made me wonder what color I was. Either way, I needed to focus. I needed to ignore these mirages and keep myself from getting clobbered, or I'd be seeing plenty of black and blue on my body. I took a deep breath and pretended the colors weren't even there—for the time being.

"We'll, get your mind off her, bro. It's her loss anyway. Just take it out on the ball, that's what I'd do," Aaron said, with a brotherly grin.

Brent handed the ball over to Mark, who wore a defeated look on his face. "Here, Mark, why don't you start us off? Throw the ball to me, and I'll throw it over to Luke. We'll warm up, then we can get things rollin'."

Mark nodded and took his position, while the others did the same. He threw the ball as hard as he could and Brent caught it without effort. It was like watching two well-oiled machines with a cannon arm, firing a single shell at each other with precision.

"You ready, Luke? It's your turn, buddy!" Brent launched the ball at me, like a ballista hurling a stone.

The minute the ball left his arm, I felt my senses heighten. My focus clicked on like a laser beam and every muscle in my body tensed all at once. My hands had a life of their own. They stood ready, even before the ball made it half-way to me! As it came in range, my hands latched onto it with ease.

"Whoa, Luke, good catch! Now, throw it back to me!" Brent hollered from across the yard, already in a readied position.

I looked down at the ball. My hands were holding onto it for dear life. I'd *never* caught a single pass in my life, not when I was a kid and certainly not over the years, up to now. Usually, I dropped whatever was hurled at me, followed by bruised ribs as I landed on the ground in a broken heap. I looked at Brent then something welled up inside me. The urge to throw this thing took over. For the first time ever, I actually wanted to throw a football. And I wanted to do it right. I lined my fingers up to the laces, cocked my arm back, and closed my eyes, before I launched it as hard and straight as I could, right at Brent's chest where I knew he'd catch it easily.

When I opened my eyes again, Brent was on the ground, looking at me with a seriously frightened look on his face. His friends stared at me with the same expression—which made me extremely uneasy.

"Dude, what the heck was *that*?!" Brent asked between coughs. The ball rolled off his chest, into the grass.

"Did you see that? He almost killed Brent with that throw!" Chad exclaimed, running over to Brent's aid.

Aaron stared at me like I was some kind of lunatic, his face nearly sliding from his skull, while Mark started toward Brent. Mark and Chad finally managed to help Brent stand on his own, then dusted him off, glancing at me the whole time. Brent signaled them both off him, then grabbed the ball, and gripped it against his chest.

"Luke? . . .Do that again," he said, his tone more serious than

I'd ever heard before. The color of his attitude was a dark shade of grayish-red, a color that seemed to mean he was intrigued and determined—maybe even a little angry. He tossed the ball again, harder this time.

I caught it with ease, again. This was the second time I'd caught anything thrown at me, but it felt almost like it was coated with the gray-red attitude he was showing me. I was scared out of my mind. Not because I caught, or even threw, a football for the first time. I was scared because for the first time ever, I may have unwittingly made Brent angry with me. I'd never seen him mad, except one other time when one of his ex-girlfriends tried to have him beaten up, in which case he walked away unharmed. I hesitated in cocking my arm back again, I really didn't like where this was going. The farther back my arm got, the darker the color of Brent's attitude as it fumed off his shoulders, like a barely visible wall of flames. I threw it as hard as last time, only this time, I managed to keep my eyes open the whole way. It sailed over to him, like a missile tracking a jet, then, as it shot into Brent's chest again, he managed to catch it. But as he did, he was knocked back a few steps. I watched in shock as he tried to regain his footing, walking backward for at least five strides before stopping completely.

The others were gawking at me, then at Brent, then back at me, all over again, their faces white as ghosts.

"Ho . . .ly crap!" Aaron exclaimed, breaking the silence. "Luke's totally got gun-arm!"

I looked down at my hand, wondering what 'gun-arm' meant. I hoped it was somehow a good thing.

"Man, Luke, I've never seen anyone put Brent down like that! How come you never tried out for the team, bro?" Chad looked scared and excited, all at the same time. He walked over to me and held up his hand, trying to get me to high-five him. I held mine up and he slapped it lightly, with a brotherly grin.

"Yeah, seriously, we could've won by default after Luke put the other team in the hospital from passes like that!" Mark cackled.

Brent stood silent, his hands still wrapped around the ball, staring at me with a look of uneasy concern on his face. Eventually, he walked over and pushed the other three out of the way, carefully, before handing me the football again. His eyes stayed fixed with mine, his face still showing concern. "Hey, guys, can, uh, can you gimme a minute with Luke? There's some stuff I gotta ask him about, real quick." He turned and looked at the three of them, and they slowly dispersed toward the back patio area, muttering to each other the whole time.

He leaned toward me and said in a low voice, "Luke, I'm gonna be perfectly honest man, I've never seen a throw like that. And I'll even admit, I never figured you'd have it in you. In fact, I think maybe I should be a little worried, bro. I can usually read people pretty well and when I caught that ball, both times, I felt a vibe from you I'd never felt before," he went on. "It felt like you were angry—maybe more than angry. I need you to talk to me, right now, Luke. What the hell is goin' on with you?"

I tried to look away from him, but every time I did, he leaned back into my line of sight. "Brent, please, don't do this. Not right now. I... I just can't. Okay?"

"Luke, you know you can trust me. If you want me to get rid of the other guys, so we can hang a bit, then I'm game. You just gotta say the word."

The way he was so willing to accommodate me just to get answers was enough to make me want to break down. But, I held back every painful second, hoping he'd forget about it long enough for me to get through the day since he insisted on having me join him and his friends. "I think I just need what Mark needs. I need to get my mind off of things for a while."

His eyes were reassuring and even his silence told me the offer stood. He nodded a few times and asked, "Then, what would you say, if I asked you to run the ball? That'll get your mind off just about everything! Running and dodging, there's nothing more exhilarating—or distracting."

I admit, at first, I was reluctant, but the offer seemed irresistible. I looked down at the football in my hands and smiled. Brent smiled in return. He knew me well enough to know what I was thinking.

He signaled for his friends to come back, then said, "Do your best, Luke. I wanna see what other hidden skills you've been keepin' secret. And don't worry about gettin' hurt; these guys know they'll answer to me, if they rough you up."

"I don't know, Brent. How far am I running with it, exactly?"

"Just get past all three of them. I'll be watching from over by the house to see how you do," he said with a wink, then turned to the other three. "Okay, you guys. Try to tackle Luke. Let's give him the initiation he deserves for showin' us his mad throwing skills."

"That's cool. I could use the run," Mark scoffed.

"Sounds good, man. Let's see what the new guy's got when he's on the move," said Aaron, his arms folded over his chest.

"Mmm, fresh newbie meat. That's why I love this game, fellas." Chad's comment made everyone turn to him, their faces winced and un-amused.

I almost laughed at that one.

"Okay, you guys ready?" he asked all three of them. They nodded and he turned to me, "You ready, Luke? Just get by all three of these goons and you win."

I nodded once as I stood ready, hoping I would walk away from this alive. My palms were sweaty and my legs clenched up. The colors I'd been seeing faded away and my focus was on survival. I felt time suddenly slow down, as if my entire body was getting ready for an intense battle of some kind. Almost as if it thought I was in genuine danger.

Brent lifted his arm. Then, just as he lowered it, he yelled, "All right, guys . . .*GO!*"

Instantly, I bent down, gripping the grass under me with the edges of my sneakers, before shooting toward the three obstacles in my way. Adrenaline flooded my veins the closer I got to them. They came at me like three monster trucks closing in on a tiny go-cart; Mark and Aaron came in from the sides, while Chad shot at me head on. Mark reached me first and tried to slam into me with his shoulder from the right, but just before he connected, I went into a running crouch and slammed into his legs. He fell over the side of me, rolling into the grass. I glanced for a split second, watching him tumble, before turning my attention back to the others.

Aaron immediately came at ramming speed on my left side, diving directly toward me, hoping to grab me and drag me to the ground. I stopped briefly and then leaped as high as I could. He closed his arms around thin air as I sailed right over him. I was shocked to find I'd had enough time to look down at him as he slid empty-handed into the grass before I landed next to him.

I turned my attention to Chad, who was still charging at me. He looked really aggravated and worried at the same time. I was too energized at how well I was doing to sympathize. I had to finish what I'd started.

I ran straight at him, trying to think of a way to get past him. Suddenly, I stopped and tried leaping into the air one last time. He must've read me pretty quick. He grabbed me with every ounce of strength he had as I lifted off. I watched as we both sailed for nearly thirty feet before he lost his grip and fell like a brick to the ground below.

I landed, kneeling quickly to absorb the fall, and looked back carefully at the three of them, hoping I hadn't seriously hurt anyone. They were all staring at me. Only this time, they weren't moving from where I'd left them. Everyone, including Brent, was speechless. As the situation caught up to me, I felt a large swell of fear rise up within me.

CHAPTER 15: LUCAS

My eyes crept open. I was in the corner of my bedroom, huddled in the shadow of my half-opened bathroom door. The lights were off. I was still shivering, my legs like jelly, and my hands colder than I'd ever felt them. I could almost see my breath, as if I were outside in the cold, even though the whole house was a cozy seventy-two degrees. I'd barely moved from my spot in the corner for three and a half days. Nothing made sense anymore.

My gaze shifted to my cell phone. I slowly reached over and pawed at it, until I managed to get a grip on it. I carefully held it to my face, hoping I wouldn't drop it like I did five times already, as I lay against the wall.

0 new messages - 0 new text messages - 0 missed calls

It hurt to see those three little zeros. I actually felt my heart ache every time my eyes counted them. *Why won't she call me? Or text me for that matter?* How hard could it possibly be to take five whole seconds to type something quick. I'd never do this to *her*! I yelled to myself. The pain of not knowing where she was, if she was all right, or even *alive*, started to set in. I held onto the phone for dear life, wanting desperately to feel it buzz, ring, or even light up.

Several minutes passed as the phone remained silent and

still. I carefully laid it on the side of my head, near my temple then let my arm fall lifelessly to the carpet. The emptiness of my room matched my thoughts. I went mentally numb as the minutes melted into hours. I wanted that damned phone to come alive, to feel it buzz against my skull, to break not only the silence, but take away the numbness that clung to me, deep inside.

My parents were worried; I could hear them through the wall. My mom was convinced she should call a therapist, but dad stood firm against the idea, pleading with her to let him try to talk to me. I cared, I really did. I was as worried as they were, but some sick, sadistic part of me actually *wanted* them to worry. Deep down, I wanted someone to feel like I did right then. Abandoned, aching with a cold, worried feeling in their chest. Maybe it would justify everything I felt. Maybe it wouldn't hurt as bad if someone else shared it with me. Maybe I didn't care either way, so long as I had company.

A twinge of anger stirred my thoughts. It started as a single, solitary cloud, but soon became a furious rainstorm in my head. I gritted my teeth and clenched my fists. Still huddled, laying on the floor, angrier than I'd ever been in my whole life. How could she do this to me? How could she just *leave* and not even care? I saw her as a threat to my sanity, the sheer notion that she'd left me, torn up and bleeding inside like some disposable plaything, made me want to *kill* something.

None of this insanity happened before I met her—just since

that day in the woods. I stopped dead in thought. My eyes widened and my breath became heavier. Somehow, she was connected to all this madness. She *must* have some idea what's going on with me. *She* shows up and everything turns crazy! And now, when I need her the most, when I'm scared and alone in the dark, she's ignoring me!

The mental picture I had of her was starting to be painful to look at. Her eyes felt poisonous, cutting further into my heart. Her smile stabbed against my chest; it made me furious to know she was smiling while I felt like I was dying. Even her stance was sickening to look at—she was so damn confident, so fearless, so heartless. I punched the carpet in front of me with my weakened arms. It hardly made a sound, which angered me even more. I felt so helpless, like even my fury taunted me.

The guilt of putting my parents through this kind of hell didn't comfort me, in the end. The guilt outweighed the sadistic purpose and I felt terrible for it. My eyes burned with hot tears. I put my hands over my face and cried as hard as I could.

My mom could hear my broken sobs through the door. She sat on the other side and joined in my pain with tears of her own.

"Luke, son, please, if you can hear me I just want you to know, I promise, I won't leave this spot. I won't let you be alone." Mom cried harder than I, every tiny gasp stabbed into me like a sword covered in barbed wire. "I love you, Luke. Whatever is hurting you inside, I'll be right here. I'll always be right here."

As her gasps grew heavier and she could hardly breathe at all, it made me curl up even tighter. Everything I felt—guilt, shame, apathy, it all numbed me and I slowly fell asleep, still crying to myself.

CHAPTER 16: LUCAS

I suddenly opened my eyes, somehow alone, in a cold room. No sound—no light—nothing. I knew it was a dream, almost instantly—it had to be . . . Right? The sadness I'd been going through was dulled here, but the loneliness was thriving. It was everywhere, like the grim reaper himself was ready to reach out and grab my shoulder. I didn't care. I wasn't afraid at all. I'd already died once and yeah, it scared me the first time, but that's when I had something to lose. This time, things were completely different.

Still huddled on the floor, unable to move, I looked more closely and saw a thick layer of ice coating my skin and most of the ground around me. I was somehow frozen to the ground! I glanced around the room, seeking any sense of bearing, but nothing looked familiar. The only thing that stood out was a single raven, lying on the ground next to me. It looked dead, but I could see it breathing. Its chest was moving at the same pace as mine.

I started to panic. Thoughts of where I'd been and how I got here rushed through my head. Even as I strained to remember, nothing came to mind. I lifted my head and saw the raven near me do the same.

"So, you're alive after all." Just as I started to speak, I froze in shock. I could've sworn it spoke at the same time I did! I quickly thought of something else to say and watched more carefully before I spoke. "So, how'd you get here?" I asked. The raven's beak matched every syllable! This is surreal! I slowly lifted my head and the raven matched me perfectly, like a perfect reflection in bird form. I managed to wrestle off some of the ice on my arms and struggled to free myself. The raven mimicked every movement I made, which scared me a little.

Then, I stopped as I had a startling revelation. I looked back at the raven and it looked back at me. Every blink, every breath, and every twitch was mine. This *had* to be a dream. The raven wasn't just a mimicking reflection, it was me!

"Is this real?" I asked.

The raven stared back at me. The beak hung open the same way as my own mouth. Then, it leaned forward and looked me square in the eyes.

"I'm as real as you. If you die, I die."

The look in its eyes was painfully sincere. It chilled me to the bone with fright, but even so, I was oddly drawn to the company.

"Who are you?" My question seemed ridiculous, asking a bird such a thing. But it was all I had to go on. The situation didn't make sense anyway, so I just gave in to it.

The raven tilted its head to one side, then whispered, "My name is Lucas Carmicheal." As soon as he finished speaking, I felt my heart stop! The ice caked over me shattered, and the entire room fell silent. The raven vanished in a cloud of thick, black, smoke. I gasped for air like a drowning animal. Something shook on the side of my head, breaking through my panic, like a rock smashing a window. It shook again, this time a little harder, then harder again.

I snapped my eyes open and saw the familiar layout of my room. The bed sat across from me and the dresser stood next to my feet. I was relieved, but frightened at the same time. Suddenly, I felt the buzz against my head again. I reached up and felt around until I realized my phone was sitting on the side of my face. I got excited and struggled to sit up for the first time in days. I fumbled to keep my balance and checked the phone for messages.

31 new messages - 6 new text messages - 25 missed calls

I held my breath as I clicked on the text messages icon, frantically hoping at least one of them was from her, hoping whatever her text would say, that it would comfort me, and chase away everything I'd been put through. I scrolled down and saw Brent's name next to all six text messages. Even though he was my closest friend, I was actually disappointed to see his name instead of Gale's. I clicked on each one and read them quietly.

Message 1: Brent - *Hey, bro, where have u been? Ur mom & dad are freakin' out like crazy! They said u locked urself in ur room. Is that true, Luke? Call me.*

Message 2: Brent - *Dude, wut is wrong? R u ok, or do I need 2 come out & bust ur door in? Ur mom says she's gonna call the hospital! Wut the hell? U need 2 call me ...like now.*

Message 3: Brent - *Luke, u seriously need 2 text me back, bro. Ur work just called my cell. They said u haven't been in over 4 days. I told em u were sick. I don't mind backin' u up, man, but, u gotta give a little back, every now & then. I'm ur friend, bro, this aint bein' fair 2 me. just call, or text me.*

Message 4: Brent - *I just tried callin' u. Y won't u answer? Ur startin' to freak me out! Ur parents told me u haven't eaten since u got home. Y don't u meet me for a burger? We can just hang. u don't hafta talk, if u don't wanna. Just get ur butt outta that room. Everyone is worried about u.*

Message 5: Brent - *I'm coming over. This is stupid, Luke. I won't let u do this 2 urself, not while I'm breathin'.*

Message 6: Brent - *Last chance buddy. Ur dad says I can bust ur door in, if u don't answer me. I'll do it, if u don't. U know damn well I will, Luke. Don't play it like this man. Text me, or it's comin' down.*

I exited the text screen and entered the missed calls menu—Brent had called twenty four times and my employer called once. I let out a long sigh and dropped the phone against the wall in defeat. As soon as it hit the floor, the door to my room flew open and slammed into the wall beside it, violently.

Brent charged into the room, followed by my parents. Each of them had the same strange, bluish colored glow radiating from them.

"Luke! Come on, get up! It's time to stop this, right now!"

Brent insisted, grabbing my arms and slowly helping me stand.

I leaned on him for support, my legs lost in a sea of pins and needles from so much lying around. I didn't really want to stand, but was far too weak to put up much resistance. The second I was on my feet, those annoying sparks of light appeared everywhere, floating around and then disappearing like tiny fireflies. After that, the room spun a bit and my chest started to get warm.

My dad stood next to me, pressing gently on my back, assisting Brent in holding me up. "Let's get you downstairs, Luke. You need some fresh air." My dad sounded so calm, despite what I'd put him through; it was almost enough to make me tear up all over again.

"Thank you for coming and helping us, Brent. God bless you. God bless you so much, for this!" mom said, her voice quivering.

"Don't worry about it, Sue. I'm always ready to help, whenever I can, you know that. But seriously, what I think Luke needs right now, is a little dude-time. I'm gonna take him with me, maybe get him somethin' to eat, go for a cruise, you know, stretch his legs," Brent insisted as we made our way down the steps.

"I think maybe Brent's right," my dad agreed, heading for the door to let us out. "Let's give 'em some room to breathe, honey." He put his hands on her shoulders, trying to comfort her while she sobbed.

"But we just got him out of his room! Now, you want me to just sit back and let him leave, again?" My mom was losing it badly.

Even as Brent held me up, I felt weak in the legs. I wanted to run over and hug her, to tell her I'd be all right and was so sorry for doing this to her and dad. It wasn't fair at all. It was selfish and immature.

I stopped Brent. "Hang on." I strained for words; it was extremely hard to say anything, but I needed to try. I owed them that much. I shambled to my parents, before leaning against my dad. "Mom..." I shook my head slowly, desperately hanging onto my composure, "I'm sor...sorry. And I love...both of..." I couldn't say another word. It hurt to speak. My eyes flooded with tears of shame and sorrow.

My mom wrapped her arms around me. Her grip felt tight and warming at the same time. My dad rubbed my back carefully, while my mom continued to hug me. She whispered to cover her choked response. "It's all right, Luke. At least we knew where you were. At least you were home, safe and sound, where we could be close by, if you needed to talk." Her words trembling, she barely breathed out the syllables. It made the situation heavier.

I leaned my head on her shoulder, looking down the curve of her arm. The thin, colored mist was still rolling from her. I put my hand in its path as it climbed over her. The coils traced through my fingers and around my palm, just like smoke from a cigarette, then faded away. I still didn't understand what it was—but I gathered it had something to do with the mood of that particular person. The blue tint on her began to turn a lightly tinted orange. I figured it must mean she was feeling a little better.

"Luke, you know we're here for you, if you need anything. Just please, don't scare us like that, ever again. Your mother and I couldn't take another round of that." Dad patted my back a few times. "Go on, now. Brent wants some dude time. He went to the trouble of kicking your door in, so you probably shouldn't keep him waiting." My dad was trying to be clever; he always had a way of keeping things smooth, even during a crisis or tragedy. I slowly broke away from my mom and headed back over to Brent, who helped me out the door.

The drive proved calming. Seeing the outside world after so much time was like being born all over again. Every color was more vibrant than I remembered and I could hear everything going on outside of the car, even though the windows were rolled up and the stereo was on. I heard people talking as we passed by, music playing in other cars, and sounds from the bustle of people on the sidewalks and streets! It was amazing in a way words couldn't describe—I became worried all over again.

Brent broke my train of thought by handing me a few bags from the back seat. "I picked up some grub from work, before I left, man. Go ahead and dig in. I'm gonna find us a good place to park, so we can relax," he said.

I ravaged the bags of warm food, looking for anything familiar and tasty. I found a juicy looking cheeseburger and a container of French fries in their own bag. My eyes lit up and my throat clenched at the thought of devouring both.

"Wow, dude, you must've been starving! Look at you go!" Brent laughed.

I tore into the burger like a ravenous animal, swallowing big bites whole. I couldn't help it. I hadn't seen food at all the entire time I was on the floor of my room. The thought of eating never occurred to me.

Brent pulled into the parking lot of an old, rundown apartment complex and parked in one of the spots. We sat there, listening to the stereo, while I kept up a constant attack on the bags of food in my lap. The music played on, killing the noise of me eating and Brent breathing as he lowered his window, to rest his elbow on the doorframe.

"So, how's the burgers treatin' ya? Good, eh?" he asked with a grin.

I nodded with approval, glancing at him once.

"That's cool. I made a few of them, before I left today." He looked out the window for almost a minute before he glanced back at me. I devoured every drop of food in every bag in less than five minutes before I realized he left an unopened soda in the drink-holder. He handed it to me and I gripped it carefully. I wasn't about to get another lap full. Not this time.

The first sip was incredible, the ice-cold chills crawling down my throat were enough to make me sigh, heavily. I cleared my throat and noticed my voice wasn't cracking like it had back at the house. After a few more cleansing grunts, I took another sip of the soda and looked at Brent, who was casually looking back at me.

"Thanks." My voice was still shaky, but I managed to get that out, at least. I cleared it again and tried to keep talking. "Seriously Brent, thanks for every...everything." It was getting easier to speak, it was still a slight chore, but it felt good to be making progress.

Brent smiled and nodded, then turned the stereo down a notch. "You're always welcome, bro, you know that." His tone was reassuring enough, but the color surrounding him was gradually turning gray. "I'll always be there for ya, Luke, I think of you like a brother. I just wanna know, what would make you lock yourself in your room for three or four days?" His tone changed on the drop of a dime, he was trying to tread softly, but being seriously worried made it hard for him to stay calm and controlled.

I swallowed hard. This was it—time to face those I'd put through hell and back. He wanted some answers and so did my parents. I knew he'd tell them anything he learned about my actions. It was only right that he be the one to give them the kind of reassurance they'd been after, on my behalf. I felt sick. The attention was on me and this time, I didn't want it. I let out a familiar, defeated sigh.

"Something is seriously wrong." My voice wasn't cracking anymore, but it was still shaky, "Things are different, Brent. I don't know how to deal with them."

"What kinda things? I mean, you're gonna have to be more specific."

"Like, everything—everything is different. Days, nights, *you*, me...everything! I don't know how to explain it. It's been real hard to deal with." I was getting a little upset, which also didn't make a whole lot of sense, considering the amount of respect I'd always had for Brent. Mood swings were something I'd never experienced much, but when I did, I was usually alone. I'd always made sure of it.

He looked at me, surprise on his face. I didn't know what he was thinking, but the color radiating from him was almost green.

"What do you mean, I'm different? I'm no different than I was a day ago! Luke, I didn't throw a football harder than a tank, like *you* did! It also wasn't me who put my best three guys on the football team in the dirt, like they were third-graders chained and dragged to a speeding school bus!"

His defensive tone staggered my thoughts, and I was getting angrier, but sadder, with every word he said. A spiral of emotions swirled within me. I wanted to tell him everything, badly.

"Luke, you're the one that's different, no one else is acting different—*just you.* And now, you're—"

I cut him off, as carefully as I could. "Brent, that's not

what I meant! I didn't say everyone is *acting* different, I said every *thing* is *just*...different. Nothing seems right anymore. A lot has happened to me in the past four days that I really don't understand." I was doing everything I could not to break down in front of him. For once, I wanted to be in control of myself. Just once, I wanted to be brave enough to stand on my own. I looked him in the face and shook my head slowly, "I don't even feel like myself anymore, Brent. Ever since that day on Kelleys Island, things started changing."

He raised an eyebrow. "What happened, Luke? What day are you talking about?"

"I went to see Gale—she had something to tell me. Something important..."

He stopped me before I could go on. "Luke, you better not tell me you locked yourself in your room over some damn girl! I'll slap you here and now, if you tell me you did!"

I winced. The thought of him slapping me made me cringe. "Are you planning to let me finish?" I asked with a disgusted tone.

He nodded a few times and rolled his eyes, half expecting me to confirm his theory.

"But, when I got there, Nathan and his goons," I choked up a bit, but pressed on, "They were there. I tried to get away, but they caught up to me in the woods."

Brent's eyes narrowed, the color on him was turning reddish, black. He didn't like where this was going.

"What happened when they caught you, Luke? They didn't hurt you, did they?"

"I, uh... I think it was worse." My eyes started to gloss up with tears. His face went white with concern. I looked to the front of the car. I couldn't look at him while his face was so full of dread and fury. "They beat me with, uh, a baseball bat." Brent gripped the steering wheel with all his might, I could hear the plastic and leather stretching and cracking under his palms. That kind of noise always sent chills up my back.

"They what?!" Instantly enraged, the color on him emanated the darkest red I'd ever seen in my life. "He's so dead. Man, if I *ever* see that chump again—"

I put my hands up, signaling him to stop and calm down. Then, I looked him in the eyes and said, "Brent, please, settle down. It's hard enough to tell you any of this, but it's even harder when you're this angry."

He started to inhale deep breaths, his eyes still narrow, but he was calming down at least. We sat there for almost two minutes before he settled.

"All right, man, I'm okay. Go on. What happened, after that?" He was straining himself, trying not to explode.

I took a careful deep breath, and went on, "What I'm about to tell you isn't gonna make much sense. But, I really don't know any other way to explain it."

His eyes closed in on my face, he was preparing to hear whatever I had to say, no matter how obscure.

191

"They broke a lot of bones—my arm, my ribs, and my collarbone, even my leg. And then, while I lay there, something happened."

Brent looked confused despite my warning. He looked over every inch of me, searching for signs of fractures and bruises, something to make this story add up, but it didn't. "Luke, are you sure you're feeling all right? I mean, I don't wanna sound like I'm calling you a liar, bro, but you've never looked healthier! You said it's been five days since that happened, right?"

I nodded, staring at the dashboard. "That's the part I don't get either, Brent. I told you, it wouldn't make much sense. When I was lying there, someone came out of nowhere and took down every single one of Nathan's friends, then beat the crap out of Nate himself! It was insane, how quick it all happened!" As soon as I'd said the part about Nathan being beaten up, Brent's face lit up with joy. I couldn't help but smile along with him.

He leaned in a bit closer and jumped in, "Wait, wait. Step back a sec. First, you're saying you were beat up by Nate and his gang, then, you tell me they broke your arm, ribs and collar. *Now* you're sayin', someone just randomly showed up and kicked their butts? Who *was* it, dude? And how are you *not* in a hospital?"

I paused. This part of the story was the part that made no sense. Telling him would make so many loose ends even looser. But, what else could I say? Who else would ever believe me, let

alone listen to me? Even more, he'd never laughed at me when I
confided in him before, he was always supportive, even when I
made no sense. I looked at him as he waited for my answer and I
stumbled for the right way to give that answer. "It was...Gale."

Silence was his reaction. He looked shocked, but also
overjoyed, somehow. It was hard to get any kind of reading the
way his face was frozen. Even the color radiating from him was
stuck between red and gray and brown.

"It was your *girlfriend?!*" He sounded stunned. "What
the heck, man!? Is she a girlfriend by day, ninja by night, or
somethin'?"

I had to agree with him on that one. Seriously. That was a
pretty outrageous, yet intriguing guess. "I told you, it didn't
make much sense," I said, turning my eyes to the window.

"You're right, Luke, that doesn't make sense at all. In fact, I
don't know if I can believe it, really."

Somehow, deep down, I knew he'd say that. Even so, it was
still a shock to hear it.

"You should be dead, if you took that much punishment. But,
you're not—no marks, no bruises, no nothin'." He was getting
agitated, that was obvious.

It was enough to make me rethink telling him anything, ever
again.

"I... I did," I barely managed to say that much as my throat
stiffened, but I had his attention again.

"Did what, Luke?"

"I died, that night..." My palms were sweating; I gripped my knees as hard as I could. The feeling of life trickling from me, the dread of getting colder and heavier, all of it came racing back. I struggled to hold my composure, I wanted more than for him to listen; I needed him to believe me. I was more confused than Brent, and I didn't know where else to turn. I knew it was real, I knew it happened. I also knew Gale was hiding something about the entire ordeal, the way she spoke before she'd left made me feel more curious— like she was dropping a trail of clues, hoping I would find out on my own.

Brent looked more serious;his face went white and his hands trembled slightly. "Don't even joke about that. If you're tryin' to be funny, it's not workin'."

"I'm not. I don't understand any of this, but, I know I died that night! I bled to death against a tree while Gale took down Nate and his friends!" I felt angry at his disbelief as I struggled to confide in him. "Look, I know it doesn't add up, but I'm out on a limb here, telling you all this!"

His face narrowed, he looked defensive, before shooting back, "Yeah? You're tellin' me! 'Cause right now, *I'm* on a bit of a limb myself! I mean, *come on, Luke!* This is all a bit thick! You can't expect me to be able to just drive to your house, kick your door in, drag you out to a quiet spot so you can get some of your sanity back, *then* swallow a story like that, without questioning any of it!"

This was getting heated, to say the least. I could hardly

stomach the idea that he didn't believe me.. I lost my grip, anger swelled up in me, and then gushed out before I had time to think. "I never expected anything from you, Brent! You talk like I did this to get your attention! Never once, Brent, never one damn time, have I ever tried to get anyone's attention! So, don't throw that crap at me, like I'm some kind of monster!" Even after I'd blown up at him, I still felt the pain of his disbelief aching inside. I got out of the car and leaned in the doorway, staring him in the face. "You know, Brent, I actually needed you to hear me out and help me find a bit of reasoning to something. I guess it figures that the one time I needed you the most, you act exactly like everyone else." I slammed the door enough to get my anger across, then walked away, fists clenched. I heard him behind me, repeating my name, hoping to get me to stop and turn around.

I didn't. Instead, I walked over to the nearest lamppost, closed my eyes and pushed it as hard as I could while I screamed with everything I had. It didn't make me feel any better. I opened my eyes and saw the post laying a few feet ahead of me, bent and smashed, uprooted from its base. The concrete was cracked and crumbled from the force. Terror shook through me as I looked back at Brent, gawking from his car.

"Oh, my God!" I heard him whisper.

"I, uh, I didn't mean to. I mean, uh, I didn't want to, but you said you needed proof!" I was so scared from destroying property that wasn't even mine, my anger was completely melted by the fright of being arrested like some vandal stealing a car, or breaking a window. I didn't think. He'd made me so angry, I had to do something. *Why did it have to be that?* I asked myself.

"How, Luke, how did you *do that*?" He pointed with a trembling finger.

"I told you, things are different. I wish I could explain it better, but I can't." I walked slowly toward him, trying not to frighten him, or myself, by doing or saying something outlandish. He paced his way toward me, until we were finally standing two feet away from each other. "My only clue to what's happening to me is that after Gale saved my life that night, I woke up at her house, and everything started getting weird." I watched his face the entire time. It was frozen with fascination. I couldn't even see the color he was radiating anymore, it was like he was so awe-struck the mist around him didn't know what color to turn.

He shook his head a few times, trying to reassure himself that he'd seen a thirty- five foot lamp post get pushed and uprooted from a cement base, by a simple nineteen year old nerd. "Whoa, dude, it's pretty obvious she must've done something weird to you, coz I've never seen anybody do *that*, let alone, *you* do that!" he said with a sarcastic tone. He was trying to lighten the mood, which made me feel a little better. "What about a car? Do you think you could keep a car from moving?"

I hadn't considered actually testing my newfound strength, so the idea intrigued me. I shook my head, "I'm not exactly sure,

196

Brent! I've been locked in my room for days; the only thing I've moved was a dresser, and that was with one hand."

He looked excited. I knew he was dying to try the idea of me stopping his car like a superhero. There'd be no shutting him up now, until we did it.

"Let's try it, Luke! Come on, it'll be crazy fun!" He was getting bouncier as he spoke.

I couldn't help but laugh, which also made it hard to resist his offer. I chuckled a little and nodded twice. "All right, fine, let's try it. But, don't run me over, Brent!" I could hardly believe I was about to try to hold an entire car, while he slammed on the gas! The idea was thrilling and terrifying at the same time. I wanted to do something to take my mind off of everything, maybe this would help.

"Will you just relax? Man, you're like a jittery mom, always worrying about the possibilities, instead of *loving* 'em!" He laughed, settling behind the wheel.

I signaled for Brent to hit the gas, while I put my hands down on the hood and pressed gently. He eased into it at first, signaling that the needle on the gauge was at five miles per hour. Then he hung out the window and kept me posted as he accelerated.

"Fifteen, bro! Seventeen! Twenty-two! *Holy cow, Luke,* it's already pushing thirty!" he yelled over the tires squealing.

I was barely pushing down as the car shook and revved, trying desperately to topple me and speed off.

"Forty-seven miles an hour, dude! This is *intense*! Fifty-four!

Sixty!"

I slowly pressed down a little harder around the sixty mark, but the car had yet to budge an inch! I was exhilarated, but scared. No human was supposed to be able to do such a thing, but, here I was—holding a speeding car in place, with very little effort.

"*Severnty-five, seventy-freakin'-five!*" I heard him yell, as he let his foot off the gas.

The car slowly wound down, until he was able to turn it off. The smoke from the back tires cleared and the odor of burning rubber lingered everywhere. I hated that smell—like burning hair and rancid garbage. I took my hands off the hood and rubbed them against my pant-legs.

Brent got out of the car and leaned against the door, shaking his head with a smile, "I really don't know what to say, I mean, I didn't even believe you, at first! But, now, I'm not sure what to think!" He was stuck in a state of awe, but then again, so was I. Neither of us knew how to handle anything like this! We stood there, in silence, for nearly twenty seconds, before he spoke again.

"What the hell did she do to you, Luke?" His voice was calm, yet serious. His concern outweighed his fascination.

"I seriously don't know. I wish I did, none of this makes any sense." I shook my head slowly.

He scratched his head before his eyes shot open wider. "Maybe she's like that chick, Noria, in that video game we played, a couple months back, ya know? What was that, Crystal something?"

"Crystal Moon: Solace. And I really doubt it, Brent," I answered, staring at the ground with my hands in my pockets. The game was a deep story about a woman who lost her true love and to get him back she asked the spirit of the moon to bring him back. Long story short, the moon agreed, but only if she chased down and captured every shooting star, then brought them back to the moon spirit. I guess the shooting stars were spirits trying to escape the moon's kingdom in the sky or something. Simple, but romantic, in its own right. Even so, this was far from some fantasy world in a video game, this was frighteningly real.

I was doing everything I could to hold back the worry in the back of my mind. "When I died that night, I was in total darkness; it was cold and I was falling, really slow." The memory of it came back, like a rock breaking a window. As I re-lived the incident, describing it to Brent, I could mentally hear the sound of my bravery being shattered by fear all over again. "I fell through all this dark smoke around me. Then, right as I'd started to see a light around me, I saw a raven swoop out and grab me." I leaned against the side of the car, one hand resting on my leg, the other gripping my wrist, holding onto my composure for dear life. Brent was staring off into the distance, but I knew he heard every word. I knew that now, after all the proof I'd given him, he believed me.

"After the raven grabbed me, I woke up and saw Gale kneeling over me. She was keeping me alive somehow, even with all those wounds and all the pain and fatigue. She was holding me together. I even heard her talking to me, saying things about my soul and how she didn't want to be forced to take it, and how she refused to let me pass away." It was getting harder to talk, the full gravity of the fear of that night had begun to shake me from the inside. I took a deep breath and looked back at Brent. He was looking back at me, his face expressionless.

"Why didn't you ask her about all this? I mean, this isn't something that'll be easy to hide, bro," he said, folding his arms against his chest.

"I *did* ask her, but she didn't give me any kind of straight answer. Instead, she bottled up and said she needed time to give me answers. I'm starting to think *she* doesn't even know how she did it."

His posture stiffened. "Hold up. *What?* Luke, how could she *not* know how she saved your life? That doesn't make any sense! Did you try calling her? Maybe get some answers that way?"

"I did. I sent texts during the time I spent in my room. I got scared, Brent. I didn't know how to handle any of this. But even after all the phone calls and the text messages, she never called or wrote back." My heart ached as I laid it all out for him. The thought of her disappearing so suddenly was painful, but Brent's presence made things a little more manageable.

"So, you *did* lock yourself in your room because of her! Luke, I oughtta smack you, like I said I would, but knowing how much of a hulk you are now, I don't want you punchin' my head off!" He was being both serious and sarcastic. "So she ditched you and stayed gone for *four days*, without so much as one answer? And you didn't bother gettin' ahold of *me*? What's wrong with you, man?"

"What do you mean, what's wrong with me, Brent? Isn't that what we're out here trying to figure out? She saved my *life*—if it wasn't for her, I wouldn't even *be* here! So, don't make her out to be some horrible monster!" In the heat of the moment, I'd totally lost my cool. Sure, I was angry about Gale leaving me with nothing to go on, but Brent had no right to be angry with her. I was the one this was happening to, not him. He'd always been socially accepted, whereas I've always struggled to keep any social status.

He leaned in closer this time, a stern look on his face. "She treated you like dirt, Luke. She's gotta have some idea about what this is doing to you. Not to mention, the sick fact that she left you high and dry for four days, like some blind date gone bad."

I looked away. He was seriously agitating me.

"Don't talk to me about heroics, I appreciate her saving you, buddy. Believe me, if I were there, I'd have done the same. But, if she cared for real, she'd have at least checked on you, or contacted you, at some point."

"Just stop talking, Brent. Please, you just need to stop. I really don't wanna argue the point, I don't. Im so sick of arguing with everyone any time there's a change in my life, so I'm through doing it, right now." Just as I'd finished, I heard my phone beep in my pocket. I pulled it out and pressed the button to open my inbox. My eyes widened and my blood froze instantly.

0 new messages - 1 new text messages - 0 missed calls

Message 1: Gale - *Lucas, I'm ready 2 speak with u. I'm sorry it's taken this long 2 contact u. plz, giv me the chance 2 fulfill my promise 2 u. Giv me the chance 2 giv u all the answers u asked 4. Plz, Meet me at Perry's Peace Monument, on South-Bass Island @ 11pm. -Gale-*

I felt my lips quivering as I silently read the text over and over to myself. My heart sighed with intense relief at each word.

"It's her, isn't it?" His question broke my train of thought.

I looked up and saw him staring at me with disgust.

"Lemme guess, you're gonna go running back to her, after all she's put you through. Am I right?"

"She asked me to meet her at Perry's Monument, over on Put-In-Bay. She said she wants to give me some answers, Brent. You know I have to go. I *need* to figure all this out and I also need you to put away this anger and help me!"

Brent's eyes slanted in anger. "Help you? Dude, that's exactly what I've been *trying* to do! And now, you're gonna go chasing after her, like she's some angel in the dark? If she wants to give you answers on anything, you need to tell her to just call you, or come to *you*, Luke! Instead, she snaps her damn fingers and you go runnin', like a hungry dog."

"So, is that what you think of me, then? Just some stupid, hungry dog? Really?" I looked him square in the eye. I could hardly believe him shooting at me with an insult like that! I needed to get out of there before I said or did something I'd seriously regret. *"Fine."* I snapped and stormed off, fists clenched hard, teeth gritted and aching. I heard the car door slam behind me as I made it half-way across the parking lot. A few moments later, Brent pulled up beside me, keeping a slow enough pace to keep up with me while I tried to ignore him.

"You know that's not what I meant, Luke. I just got angry. I don't like the fact that she left you hangin' like that! It ain't cool, bro." He was doing all he could to sound sincere.

I could tell he was still angry, but at least he wasn't raising his voice anymore.

"Look, at least let me drive you to Port. Since I know I can't stop you, the least I can do is support you. All I'm askin' is that you don't let her walk all over you, the way she did when she left the first time."

I stopped and looked at him through the window of the car door. Slowly, I relaxed and allowed him to see how relieved I was that he at least tried to see things my way. I nodded and he opened the passenger door. I got in and he drove off, stereo blaring.

CHAPTER 17: GALE

Send to: Lucas - *Lucas, I'm ready 2 speak with u. I'm sorry it's taken this long 2 contact u. Plz, giv me the chance 2 fulfill my promise 2 u. Giv me the chance 2 giv u all the answers u asked 4. Plz, Meet me at Perry's Peace Monument, on South-Bass Island @ 11pm. -Gale-*

I hit the send button and prayed he didn't hate me. It had been five days since I'd seen him, and my eyes burned to see his face again. Every ounce of me clung to the hope that the face he showed to me wouldn't be one of anger. That is, if he planned to show at all. That thought shook me.

I stood waiting for him at the doorway to the Peace Monument, the place I told him his answers awaited. Tonight, I would give him everything he asked for. I checked the time on my phone. 7:16 p.m. The monument didn't close until around 10:00, and since Lucas worked on the ferry, he should have a ride to the island all worked out.

I began to type another text message, this time to Shannoea.

Send to: Shannoea - *I've arranged to meet him at Perry's Peace Monument, 2night. It's time he knew the truth. I'm asking u 2 promise me, right now, that u will forego telling any1. Not Sarah, or Brenna, or even my mother & father. As my dearest, closest friend, I need u 2 promise 2 support my decision. The*

White-Raven decrees that we must obey its holy message, & truth be told, it told me 2 save him the night he died. I cannot ignore what the White-Raven, or even my heart, are telling me. Plz, promise me this. -Gale-

I hit send, waiting mere moments before receiving her reply.

1 new Text message;

Shannoea - *Gale, u know I can't stop u. Sure, it's dangerous, but this is LUV ur talkin' about! The White-Raven told u 2 keep him around, then that's kool with me. I think Luke is fun, anywayz. Besides, I don't have the authority 2 butt in. This isn't my territory, remember? If any1 asks, I'm gonna pretend I don't know a thing about any of it. But, if any1 tries 2 step in, u know I got ur back! Just send our usual signal, if u need me. Peace, girl!*

Deep inside me, anxious fear stirred and ached. Even knowing Shannoea supported any of this seemed to mean nothing against the weight of the situation. Never once, in my entire life before I'd met Lucas, had I felt this kind of uneasiness, this kind of worry and terror from what was to come. It made me feel slightly human.

I thought back to how I'd left him standing there, in the street near his friend's house, that day. He'd looked so lost. I could feel every single emotion in him that day, his mixed feelings had rattled inside, like a caged animal pawing to reach a morsel of food through the bars. I wanted to comfort him, to give him whatever he wanted or needed, but I just couldn't. I *had* to leave.

I *needed* to find the answers myself. It was hard enough to keep from telling him too much too soon, but, it was shattering to my heart to drive off, leaving him with little more than another lie. A lie I knew he saw right through.

Nathan struck a nearby tree with his bat, Lucas. I barely managed to get out of the way, when he swung. I could tell by the certainty in his eyes, he didn't buy into that. Part of me was glad he didn't, but the other part trembled at the thought of putting him through all of that, in the first place. He was the first normal person who had ever been in my life and tonight, I was about to complicate everything. I felt disgusted with myself as I thought about it. I didn't deserve him in my life, at all. I looked at my phone to see the time again: 8:32 p.m. The longer I stood there, the more it seemed as if time itself was angry with me— silently glaring down wishing I would vanish forever.

Tears welled up in my eyes as I leaned against the outer wall of the monument. It felt good to let things out, for a change. I barely ever had such chances. I was about to step further over the line than I ever had before and in doing so leave the fate of our relationship up to him. As I stood there, reflecting on everything in my life, anxiety weighed heavily on me—a cast iron shadow pressing on my shoulders, trying to break my will, trying to crush my bravery.

Am I really doing the right thing? I've already gotten him hurt, what if I can't protect him? What if he doesn't understand? He's going to leave me, I just know it, I thought to myself. The question hung, mimicking icicles at the edge of my thoughts. The idea of not having him, of losing him for good, made the pains of worry even stronger. I wiped my eyes, but covered my mouth, trying desperately to keep my lips from quivering, hanging on tightly to my composure. I let my back slowly inch down, sliding against the wall of the monument, until I was sitting on the cold, hard pavement. I could barely breathe.

I ran my fingers through my hair and gently draped it over most of my face. My chest ached terribly. I knew this was going to end badly. Ever since I started talking to him, I'd caused nothing but trouble for him. And here I was, waiting on him to show, so I could finally tell him what I am and what I do every single night. I took another look at my phone, after an eternity of tears—9:00 p.m.

The longest evening of my life was beginning.

CHAPTER 18: LUCAS

The Elevator was slow, building suspense for what Gale was going to say. It made me nervous and I caught myself fidgeting with the buttons on my jacket. I pulled out my phone as soon as I felt it buzz.

A text message from Brent: *I called ur mom & told her you'd be hangin with me 4 most of the night. Either way, it'll buy u sum time. If things end early, or u want 2 come over when ur done, just call. I got ur back.*

I smiled, knowing Brent had me covered, I felt brave. I only wished I could repay him for everything he'd ever done for me.

When I finally got to the top of the monument, I saw Gale leaning against the brick railing, which traced around the entire balcony. She was staring out into the night, arms folded, hair flowing gently in the breeze. She had on a black jean-jacket with black quills sticking out from under the collar, one of the oddest things I'd ever seen. I walked up beside her, and leaned against the railing, as well.

She turned her attention to me.

I felt as if I was in a trance when her eyes locked with mine. They were a deep shade of purple tonight, like two gemstones reaching out to me.

"I'm glad you came. I wasn't sure you would, to be honest,"

she said, sliding her hand over the top of mine. "Before I start explaining, can I ask you something?" Her expression was soft, like she was being careful not to upset me.

I leaned against the railing, looking at her with a calm, careful stare in return. I wanted to be angry about all the secrecy, but just looking at her made me feel detached from everything.

"I don't see why not." My answer was slow and steady as I stared at her. Chills started gathering like ice crystals over my skin. The cold breeze at this altitude added to the situation. I raced through hundreds of thoughts, trying to guess the question before she asked.

As she moved closer, I felt overwhelmingly frightened. I was ready to hear what she had to say, but I was distracted by her eyes. I'd never seen anything like them in my entire life. They were so deep, they almost glowed... They looked hungry, somehow.

"Do you enjoy being with me?" she asked, slowly running her finger down the side of my face.

"Well, yeah, absolutely." The sensation of her finger tracing down my face made me shiver with delight. I had trouble finding the right words, let alone saying them without stuttering. "I don't...wanna sound like an obsessed psycho, but you're all I've thought about, pretty much since the day you first spoke to me," I answered, behind several more shivers from her touch.

"That doesn't sound psychotic to me, Lucas." She chuckled softly and smiled. "That's actually good to hear because I like being with you, as well. That's why I asked you to come here." She sighed heavily as she looked down at the ground. "I love the quiet air on nights like this. It helps me clear my head when I've got too much on my mind."

Her eyes climbed back up to mine as I stood there, wanting desperately to lean in and kiss her. I'd never kissed a girl before– in my entire life, but the urge was there, pulsing deep inside me like a time-bomb. A big part of me wanted to toss away that feeling of angst and wrap my arms around her. Somehow though, I couldn't move. The depth of her eyes were captivating in a way that no word ever spoken, or written could describe. She was trying to give me answers and I could tell it was taking everything she had to do it.

"I, uh, I haven't been very straight with you," she said carefully, "so I chose tonight to clear everything up. I want to explain everything and then allow you to choose where we'll go from here."

"I need to say, you left me hanging—worried sick about you for four days!" I felt the hurt welling up. "What you did was wrong. It wasn't fair in the least bit! I mean, seriously, all I want are answers, Gale. I just wanna know what's going on," I said in a huff.

"I... I'm truly sorry. I didn't mean to put you through so much." She sounded shaky, like I'd managed to hit a nerve. "But, there are things I feel you should know about me, about who I am, Lucas. Who I am and, more importantly, what I do.

You see, uh, there's more to me than what I've shown you—a lot more." she stammered as she tried to explain herself.

"I'm a Cor—" She stopped herself. "Good God above, this is so hard and even if I manage to explain it, you'll probably think I'm crazy, anyway." She looked down at her trembling hands. She covered her face with them, and then ran them through her hair.

"Listen, Gale," I sighed and leaned in to look her in the eye, "if it's *this* hard for you, then maybe I should just go. I... I don't need the guilt of knowing I'm getting you into trouble with your family. I appreciate you helping me with Nathan and your dad, I really do. But I can't let you put yourself through this because of me anymore. If you wanna tell me anything, maybe you can text it to me instead." I started to walk toward the door to the elevator, but she grabbed my arm. Her grip was intense and so sudden it sent another frightening chill through my body. I couldn't take another step.

"Please, Lucas, don't leave, not yet. Telling you the truth isn't just something I have to do, it's also something I want to do."

I looked back at her. She glanced toward the spot where I was before I walked off. I took it as a sign that she wanted me to go back to leaning on the brick railing. I slowly took my spot against it again, and waited for her to speak.

"I need you to be patient with me right now. But even more than that, I need you to stop jumping to conclusions and listen," she insisted. She began to pace her breathing, obviously looking for the right words. Whatever she was trying to say, it was, without a doubt, a heavy burden. I recognized that feeling immediately. I'd been there plenty of times. She needed comforting words from someone who'd walked the road of loneliness and I was glad it was my turn to help her.

"I know what it's like to want to talk to somebody. You've been there for me through so much already, I guess, maybe now, it's my turn to be there for you. You need to trust me, Gale, the way I trust you, without hesitation, or fear." My heart swelled from her awkward attempt to confide in me. I could almost feel her crying out to me, wanting nothing more than to give me her secret so we could finally be that much closer than we had already become. It pained me to see her fighting so hard to speak, but I could see relief in her eyes after my heart-felt confession.

I held up both of my hands. "I came up here, nervous, but ready to either hear what you had to say or leave here single. But the longer I stay, the more I see how we're really not so different." She looked shocked and confused. "I don't want to lose you, Gale, I really don't... But I can't let you dump me off for long stretches every time you can't cope with something! I trust and care about you with my life, don't you see that?"

"You, you trust me that much?" Her face became soft and innocent, and her eyes glimmered from the starlit sky.

"Well, yeah! I mean, when I was dying in those woods, it

was cold and deep and even darker than I ever expected! I was falling through a thick black fog and even though I wanted to, I couldn't move at all! I was alone, falling forever..." I looked deep into her eyes, every moment of that day rushed back into me. But this time, I wasn't afraid at all. I only felt the rush of my heartbeat as I started to realize. She really *had* come to me! The weight of the moment took its toll and my eyes widened. "And then you came out of the blackness. You told me you'd decided not to let me go, and then somehow you changed into some kind of dark black bird, and flew into me like a ghost. I felt calm, like I was finally safe. The fog around me thinned out, and I was back in the woods, lying on the ground, like I'd never left. Then I woke up with you next to me." I shook my head with absolute certainty "I'll never forget that night, not in a million years."

"A raven," she said, looking at me with grinning eyes.

"Yeah, it *was* a raven, I think! Only this one had purple, glowing—" suddenly, I knew, I was staring at the very answer she had been trying to show me the whole time! Sparkling like twin moons on the surface of a lake, the silently attested answer to Gale's secret—the same eyes of the raven that had pulled me from the yawning depths of oblivion stared me right in the face! The moment suddenly became extremely frightening, but at the same time, I couldn't help but feel even more curious. I felt an urge to try and escape, to run for my life, but another part of me, a strangely deeper part of me, told me to stay. My legs didn't budge. I was trembling, trapped on this balcony, over three hundred feet in the air with a woman who was both terrifying and undeniably attractive.

Now it seemed she was far more than that. She knew about everything I'd experienced that night, even the mysterious raven that came out of the blackness and carried me back to the world of the living. I was cold with fear; I could see my breath coiling from my mouth.

"Please, Lucas, don't be scared. I've been trying so hard to... to find a way to tell you," she said in a gentle, shaking voice, as she wiped her eyes with her sleeve. "But I... I didn't want to lose you!" She sniffled and gently put her hands on my arms.

"You mean, the raven was really *you*? But I don't understand!"

She sniffled and said, "You'd lost a lot of blood, you were dying. I was left with two choices..." Tears raced down her cheeks while she tried to explain, "I could help you survive and push you back into your body, or let you die and carry your soul to the afterlife. I know it was selfish, but I didn't want to give you up. Now you know why this is so hard to talk about!" Her hand rested on my chest and I could feel it shaking.

"I knew I saw you break Nathan's bat! Why did you lie to me?" I asked and put my hand over hers to help calm her.

"What did you want me to say, Lucas? I... I had to stop him from hurting you, and to do it I had to destroy his weapon! I'm sorry, I just... I lose control when people I care about get hurt! Besides, if I had told you the truth when you asked, would

214

you really have believed me? You had to see certain things for yourself! So I made sure you got to *see* those certain things. Like me at the concert, or the bat being destroyed. Lucas, you need to understand. Just you having a *slight* clue as to what I am puts you in serious danger! Both sides would come for you if they had any idea." She shook her head as she looked me in the eyes.

I was confused. She sounded uneasy with every word. "I'm sorry. Both sides? What does *that* mean? And are you saying that you're a raven that eats souls?" It was all so frustrating. I did everything in my power to understand, to take it all in, so that the situation wouldn't feel so heavy. But it was heavier than what my mind could carry in so many ways.

"Lucas, there are more than just my kind out there, much more. And we don't really eat souls, more like, we drink from them. We call ourselves Corvidae, a race of creatures that can—"

I interrupted her with astonishment, "Change from humans, into average sized birds!" I was glad I was leaning against something at that point. I felt my heart racing as I lost the feeling in my legs! I was rescued from death, by a...a *girl* who can change into a *raven* whenever she wanted to, or so she claimed.

"Look, I understand this all sounds crazy. I can't really blame you." she said, while she cupped my hand with both of hers. "I... I just wanted you to know the truth, even if it means I risk losing you in the process." Her lower lip quivered, small tears slid down the curve of her face, and fell from her jaw-line.

"Well, I, uh, I have to say, that *is* a bit hard for me to take in." I rubbed my forehead with my free hand. "That's nowhere *near* the kind of answers I thought I'd be getting! But, oddly enough, I believe you. I'm not sure how to explain it, but I can sort of feel your sincerity inside me." Her words felt like pulses of warmth against the strain of a cold, dark truth. It made my heart ache for her even more.

She let go of my hand, then began backing up and ran her fingers through her hair, brushing both sides behind her ears. "I need to show you, Lucas. You need to see what I truly am. Then you'll understand the full weight of everything I've told you." She stopped about six yards away from me. Then, without warning, she darted toward me and jumped into the air. She spread her arms, arched her back, and held her legs together like a diver from the Olympics. Then she was engulfed by what looked like traces of black smoke with billows of gray that mimicked a plume of feathers falling and coiling in all directions.

As quickly as the smoke had appeared, a pair of familiar purple glowing eyes pierced through the darkness, followed swiftly by the even more familiar form of a raven. It was flying straight toward me, and I fell down at the sight. It was absolutely chilling to see a dark bird with such a determined look in its eyes flying right at me! Like the reaper itself was calling me to my death all over again! In a panic, I shielded my face with one arm, and held the other straight out.

It was an instinct I had no control over, I felt dread in every bone of my body while I shivered on the floor of the rooftop. Suddenly, I felt my arm become slightly heavier, the feeling of sharp prongs gently gripped my forearm, and a brush of feathers against my fingers. I put my arm down from my face very slowly and saw the raven perched on my arm. At first, the sense of dread engulfed me, but gradually, I realized I was not in any immediate danger. I began to feel a sense of security as I marveled at the moment. This raven, this beautiful creature with onyx black feathers, and enchanting amethystine eyes, was Gale.

At a loss for words, I took in the majestic sight of her standing proudly on my arm. She opened her beak slightly and let out a single gentle caw, then looked at me with her head angled down, almost like she was smiling behind her round eyes.

I cleared my throat, and stumbled to speak, "Ga-Gale? Oh, man, is that really *you*?" My voice shook between each syllable, my eyes stood wide open. The raven slowly nodded once, holding its gaze firmly on me. Nothing in my entire life could've prepared me for this... I was completely stunned!

"Wow, you're *amazing!* You're even gorgeous when you're like *this*!" I managed to gasp. I lifted my free arm, and gently approached her head, wanting badly to stroke the back of her neck. She must have sensed my intentions. She stood straighter, with her head down, waiting for me to touch her. I placed two of my fingers on her smooth little head and slowly traced down her back. I could tell she enjoyed every moment of it. I knew because she closed her eyes and let out a soft sigh. I continued to run my fingers through her feathers on her back and then I ran them down one of her wings. She carefully extended her wing as I did and her breathing became heavier with bliss. I was caught deep in the moment, so much so that I didn't ever want this fantastic moment to end. I was literally at arms' length with the most dangerous creature I'd ever encountered, a raven that could drink the life force of other living creatures.

I slowly realized what she meant about the weight of her dilemma. She'd risked everything—her darkest secret revealed. She wanted me to know, to choose carefully what would happen between us. The thought of not having her in my life made me ache, I couldn't imagine how anyone who knew such a fantastic creature could live with turning her down! She said I was in danger for even knowing *this* much about her, which made the situation more staggering.

I finished stroking her wing, and she leaned forward gently and pressed her tiny forehead against mine. It was warm and smooth to the touch, I sat quietly her head nestled against mine, and began to *feel* her voice in my thoughts.

"Lucas, this is what I really am. I don't want to keep secrets from you. I have to confess, I've fallen in love with you, and for the first time in my life, I've never been so scared of anything! Being alone is something I can't contend with anymore. There's nothing in my life that matters more to me than you. I proved that when I dove into the trenches of death to keep you. But if you decide otherwise, if you don't feel the same or this is all too much, I'll honor your decision and I'll leave." Her words were as clear as moonlight in the darkness of my thoughts. She spread her wings and took flight from my arm. I got up from where I sat and she landed in human form next to me, her arms behind her back and her head down just a little. She looked as if she was preparing to be shot in the chest.

"Gale." I grabbed her waist and pulled her close, putting my arms around her. I couldn't hold back anymore, she was just as scared and vulnerable as I felt. Everything she'd told me seemed unimportant. All that mattered was the moment we were sharing. I understood her better than she realized. She was trapped in a world of secrecy, a world I knew far too well. No one else could've taken a fair look at her the way I had. For once, I began to feel absolutely liberated. I put my forehead against hers while I stroked the back of her head, running my fingers through her hair. I'd been dying to touch her hair for so long, and after the chance to feel her raven form against my fingertips, now they were gliding through a million miles of midnight splendor. Each strand flowed like water past my hand and I felt her breath against my neck, as she sighed again blissfully.

"Please, Lucas, I don't want to lose you," she whispered against me.

She held onto me, desperately, one hand around my waist, the other holding a fistful of my coat from the back. Almost as if she hoped the moment was real and not some elaborate dream. I worked up the courage and kissed her forehead. Her skin felt warm, radiating a heat that made me feel weak at the knees, but I held onto her nonetheless.

"It's okay, Gale. I'm not gonna go anywhere. You stayed with me through death and trusted me with your secret that puts you in a risky situation. Even so, I plan on staying here...with you." I reassured her by brushing her hair from her face and looking her in the eyes.

She smiled, uncontrollably relieved. My eyes fell deep into hers. I pressed my index finger softly against her lips, and she kissed it gently.

"This is all so intense. I wish this night would never end." I knew it sounded corny to say, but I didn't really care. I was lost in the moment.

She looked back at me with a glistening smile, and said, "Even if it does, I'll just fly around and follow you throughout the day. I've done it before."

I jerked my head back a few inches, shocked. "Seriously? You-you do that often?" I asked with a sense of flattered embarrassment. The thought of her stalking me, a gorgeous woman showing interest in me, gave me goosebumps of the best kind.

Her face turned a pale shade of red and she turned her head to hide it, but it was far too late. "I, uh," she cleared her throat a bit, "actually, I've been doing it since, um, since the first day I saw you on the ferry." Now her face became redder than before. She tried desperately to fight it off, but all she managed to do was bite her lower lip and avoid eye contact. I couldn't help but find her embarrassment attractive.

"Wow, my very own stalker! I'm... I'm flattered! I dunno, I kinda like knowing you're obsessed with me. Usually it's the guy that stalks the girl," I said with a chuckle.

"Well, I'm not the usual girl, now am I? When I decide I want something bad enough, I don't give up until I get it," she answered, a sexy glare in her eyes.

"I don't know why you'd want to be with a nerd like me that badly. I'm still not sure why you're so attracted to me. I've never even kissed a girl before." Just as I'd said it, she let go of me and took my hands into hers.

"What about a woman?" she asked me.

"What?"

"I'm no girl, Lucas. I'm a woman. Girls are young, most usually like being called girls until they're in their early thirties, but me—I'm two hundred and fifteen years old. I'm well past the whole girl stage in my life."

I felt my heart stop. I couldn't believe what she was saying! Beyond the fact that she could turn into a raven and had incredible superhuman strength, she was also over two hundred years old! I felt a bit anxious after what she'd said caught up with me. Such a beautiful, not to mention powerful, woman, wanting to be close to me? I wanted to take her up on her offer right then, but something burned inside me, telling me that out of all the imperfect aspects of my disastrous life, I needed at least one perfect moment, and that moment had to be both flawless and unforgettably unique.

My thoughts were running in circles. Not even the elaborate video games I've played over the years, with immortals and Gods and mythic creatures, could've prepared me for this! Still, there was that nerdy, geeky part of me deep down, that sprang into an excited frenzy at the thought of being kissed by a two-hundred-fifteen year old raven-lady.

Gale ran her fingers across the back of my neck, sending prickly chills through me. "If it helps, I've, uh, I've only been kissed by one person," she said with a nervous tone, "way back during the Victorian era."

She was right. It did help to know that. It meant that, at least *she* knew what she was doing, because I sure didn't. I couldn't decide which was going to be harder–turning her down, or telling her why. In the end, I decided to go with both.

"You're the most amazing and unique woman I've ever met, Gale. Quite frankly, I don't know how to say this, so I'm just going to say it." I took a deep breath. "My life has always been a disaster. No matter how hard I've tried, it always goes badly for me. Just once, I'd like something to be perfect." She looked puzzled, so I tried explaining it in simpler terms. "If I did get a chance to kiss you for the first time, I'd want it to be something just as amazing and unique as you." I watched as her eyes lit up and I could swear she was glowing on the inside at what I'd said.

"That's the absolute sweetest thing anyone's ever said to me,

Lucas," she answered as she bit her lip behind a bashful stare.

I was relieved she took being turned down so well, but my decision to wait until the moment was right was something I'd longed and planned on, for years. It was one of the most important things in my life and I would see it through to the end. Even with her reaction though, I still felt kinda bad.

"I'm glad you see it that way. But still, I'm really sorry, Gale, it's just that this means a lot to me, and—"

She gently put her fingertips over my mouth, and looked at me with warmth in her eyes.

"Lucas, it's all right, I completely understand." She shook her head slowly as she spoke, "You don't have to explain anything to me. I want you to have your perfect moment! I'd wait ten thousand years if that's what it took, for just ten seconds of bliss with you."

I slid my fingers in between hers, and slowly pulled her hand from over my mouth and rested it on the collar of my jacket. "You'd do that, just for me?"

She gripped my fingers with her own and guided my hand over to her, until she stopped and rested it just below her neck. She was unbelievably warm, and I could feel her soft heartbeats at the ends of each of my fingers while she held my hand in place. "I would." She looked me square in the eyes with deep determination. "I decided a while ago that every beat my heart takes, is devoted to you. A rhythm that promises to keep going, a rhythm that will protect you and stay with you forever."

As she'd spoke her mind, I wanted to break down and start bawling my eyes out right there. *Finally, I found someone who wants to understand me.* I thought to myself.

I don't really know what came over me at that point. Maybe it was a spark of bravery or maybe it was an urge to be playful. I stepped away from her, still holding onto one of her hands, and she looked at me with a puzzled expression on her face as I hopped onto the edge of the balcony.

"Lucas, what on earth are you doing?"

"So, by protect me, you mean if I fall you'll be able to change into your raven form and catch me?" I asked in a sly tone, still gripping her hand while standing on the ledge. She looked a bit scared, but she had a smile creeping across her face. That was a sure sign for me that she was confident in her abilities.

"You're ruining our moment, you know, I ought to let you fall just for *that*." She giggled with a playful glare.

"Wait, hold on now, that's not what you just said. What was all that about not wanting to lose me and not letting me go earlier then, hmm?" I asked behind a coy smile, as I stepped down from the ledge.

She put her hands on my chest, and put the tip of her nose to mine. I could feel the warmth of her breath across my face as she sighed. She leaned forward and closed her eyes, but stopped suddenly. I thought she was going to try to kiss me, but she opened her eyes just as her lips were a razor's edge from mine.

"So you like a hint of danger in a relationship, eh?" Her smile looked kind of sinister.

"Only if the woman I'm dating has magic bird powers," I replied, flippantly, "then I'd never have to worry about danger ever again." I smiled back.

Gale's mouth dropped and her eyes widened with playful unamusement, followed by a heavy gasp. "Lucas Carmicheal! Are you making fun of me?" she asked with a cute laugh.

"Me? Never," I said with a straight face, "Well, maybe just a little."

"Well, just so you know, I like being dangerous!" she said. Her eyebrow quirked, then settled, as she cracked an evil smirk. Then, suddenly, she shoved me over the edge of the balcony!

I gasped as I sailed over the side of the deck. I didn't actually think she'd push me over! I stiffened up and terror wrapped every inch of me with solid hands, the same terror that engulfed me back in the woods on Kelleys Island had returned instantly. I flailed helplessly, the edge of the balcony climbing further away from me with every second.

"Oh, my, God! Gale. . .Gale! Help me!" I screamed at the top of my lungs, desperately clawing at the air rushing by me, hoping she'd save me with the powers she possessed.

Just as the terror in me reached its peak, I saw Gale dive over the side, trailing after me. She was moving faster than I was falling. She shot like a bullet down to me and I saw a huge smile on her face, as if amused by my fear! She put her arms around me and locked her eyes with mine. She quickly pulled my lips to hers. The fear melted away as fast as it had come and I desperately wrapped my arms around her and closed my eyes. Time stood still as we plummeted toward the ground below with only the cold air of the night and the race of emotions we shared surrounding us.

Our first kiss, ever—terrifying and altogether magical beyond measure. My words came rushing back to me like a flash of lightning–*If I did get a chance to kiss you for the first time, I'd want it to be something, just as amazing and unique as you.* My heart pounded a thousand times faster than normal, and my entire body grew warmer as her lips embraced mine. They were smoother than silk, like a soft pink ribbon sliding gracefully across the surface of my mouth.

Slowly, I felt myself become light as air. When I opened my eyes, I wasn't falling at all! Somehow, I was looking through the eyes of the same raven that had saved me before, only this time it was covered with a very thin, glowing mist of some kind. Gale was sailing across the night sky like a shooting star. I looked around to find my body, but it was somehow missing...as if I was part of the raven itself! I felt her speak to me with a calming voice in my mind, just like before.

"Lucas, you don't ever have to be afraid. I'll always be there for you. I'll always catch you, no matter where you fall, and then we'll fly away together."

It was incredible! She'd actually changed into a raven and

we were actually flying! My heart raced with excitement as buildings passed below us. I could see the water glistening below and Gale somehow felt my thoughts.

"Get ready, I'm gonna show you how a Corvidae rules the skies!" she said, and made a heavy right turn. She swooped down hard, then passed under the branches of a few nearby trees before shooting back up into the sky, followed by a well-timed barrel-roll.

"This is amazing, Gale! It's so great to see the world like this! But how are we, I mean, *you* doing this?"

"My Corvidae bloodline carries with it unique gifts, aside from changing into ravens. I can carry a person along with me as fast or as far as I like. Right now, you're little more than a thin layer of smoke around me. I've tethered your soul to me. That way, I can carry you with me in this form."

What she'd explained made sense, even if it *was* out of the ordinary. I watched the world through the eyes of Gale's raven form, soaring into the night like a whisper echoing through a silent, empty valley. "That must be why I feel light as air. We've really gotta do this more often!"

"You haven't seen anything yet!" she said with a heavy flap of her captivating wingspan.

We were traveling so fast, everything else paled in comparison. Gale reached the water's edge and she swooped down. The surface of the lake raced passed us, but the sparkling reflection of the moon stayed with us without any effort. She lowered closer to the face of the water and dipped her dark gray talons into the water as she shot across the winds with breathtaking grace.

I could smell the fresh cascading lake as Gale lifted her talons and dipped the tip of her right wing into the water and let it drag across the feathers at the end. Suddenly, she shot up into a fast moving, upward barrel-roll. Her wing splashed water all around us like playful drops of rain. She leveled out, and glided like a kite across winds. She headed toward another island in the distance.

CHAPTER 19: LUCAS

"What island is that?" I asked, watching it get closer by the second.

"That's Marble-Head, it's where we're going to land. There's a really quiet spot I want to show you," she replied as the form of a lighthouse took shape in the distance. She swooped down, heading straight for the red guardrail wrapped all the way around the white tower. As she came within reach of the railing, she thrust her wings flat and upright against the wind, stopping in mid-air before she gripped the rail with her talons. She hopped down onto the terrace of the lighthouse, and in a flash of black and gray mist followed by the familiar purple light, we both emerged, her arms still wrapped around me, and mine around her.

The entire moment took my breath away, completely. She freed my arms from around her and pointed with a gesture of her nose toward the rail's edge, followed by a quaint smile. "Check this out, Lucas. It's one of my favorite places to be. I love the view from way up here," she explained.

I looked out and saw the water. It was swaying all around, chasing the wind, and crawling up the rocks below. The trees that surrounded the lighthouse were swaying along with the waves, some swaying more than the rest causing them to make the sound of wood bending, almost as if the waves and trees were actually talking to each other under the silent eye of the moon. I marveled at it.

"This is fantastic! I've never taken the time to listen to the world like this!" I confessed while listening on.

"That's not all you're going to notice from now on." Gale's stern and chilling tone broke me from my trance.

"What do you mean?"

"Lucas, when I saved your life, I had to take it first. I sipped from your soul, and then I somehow poured it back into you. I've never done it before, but I know some who have. The people they did it to started having a side effect from it. I guess it has something to do with their Corvidae energies mixing with human ones."

The cold breeze that passed over me felt even colder after hearing her say such a thing. I stared at her with newfound clarity. The speed, endurance, hearing, and strength I'd been experiencing, it was all due to her saving my life. My soul was touched by hers! I felt excited and confused all at once. It made perfect sense the more I thought about it!

She cleared her throat and put her hands on the sides of my arms.

"Your senses will heighten at first, the usual hearing, sight, taste, and smell; even your brain will function more clearly. Then the bigger effects will set in. It's different for everyone, so there's no way to know for sure what you'll experience."

"I already know, Gale. I've been trying to figure what happened since the day I woke up in your bedroom." Without thinking, I turned to her and said, "You didn't warn me before, so I didn't know where to turn. After you dropped me off at Brent's house, he managed to get me to play a game of football with him and his friends. I guess I figured I needed to get my mind off of things, just for a little while."

Her face began to change from a gentle demeanor to a more concerned one.

"Lucas, tell me you didn't..."

"Didn't what?"

"Tell me you didn't do anything to draw their attention!" She looked more concerned than before, like she was afraid for my mortal being. "Good God, Lucas, what did you do?" She stared me square in the eyes with fright.

I wasn't sure how to respond after the look she gave me. The fact that she was so worried made me wonder what telling her might do. "I... I didn't make a big spectacle, if that's what you're getting at! If anything, I was more shocked than they were! I had perfect aim when I threw the ball, I out-ran all three of them when they tried to tackle me, but then, later, I was worried that something was seriously wrong with me." Her reaction was confusing. She looked thrilled that I was experiencing the side effects, but something didn't seem right in her eyes. She almost looked hurt, and she looked ashamed of something. "And since you didn't reply to my text messages for over four days, I kind

231

of turned to Brent, for help."

She began to shiver and then reached over to me, putting one hand on my chest and the other on my shoulder. "Lucas, that was not a very smart thing to do! What did you tell him, exactly?"

"I told him about Nate and how I was sure he'd killed me. And I told him how I woke up at your house and then I showed him how I had changed. I held his car in place with one hand, while I had him slam on the gas. It didn't move, not even an inch, Gale! He said he was going at least seventy-five miles an hour!"

She slowly shook her head while she stared at me with disappointment on her face.

"I told him not to say a word to anyone, not until I'd had a chance to get some answers about it, from you. But now that I have those answers, I'm not sure I want to put him through something like this."

She was still shaking her head, "You don't understand do you? You've already involved him enough to put him in danger, as well as yourself! You absolutely *cannot* do such things anymore. Do you understand me, Lucas?"

"Well, what was I supposed to do, Gale? Like I said, you left me high and dry, with no answers for days! I got scared! You didn't even try to contact me, even after I'd sent hundreds of text messages! I started to think," I couldn't finish saying it, I was shaking too much. The one thing I'd always been afraid of, when it came to anyone I cared about.

"What? What were you starting to think?"

I swallowed hard. It felt like I had a boulder stuck in my throat—one lodged deep enough to suffocate me. My shaking intensified when she slid her fingers across my cheeks, wiping away a steady flow of hot tears. It took everything I had to open my mouth, to give her the answer she asked for, the answer that almost drove me insane with heartache for one night. "I started to think you'd somehow forgotten about me." The words slowly came out, each one shook worse than the last. I didn't want her to see me like this, not in such a broken, frail heap against a guardrail. I knew those five nights were over and she was with me now, but the agony was still extremely fresh in my veins. It hung inside me like a burnt painting, covered in soot.

"Oh, Lucas," she said softly, with a tender inflection. "Don't you ever think like that. How could I ever forget you? You're the absolute greatest thing that's ever happened to me! I *need* you in my life, Lucas, you have to believe that!" She pulled me close and held onto me while I tried to calm myself.

"But where were you, Gale?" My voice cracked badly, my throat tensed up; it sounded like I was choking on the words.

"I was looking for answers. I've never given anyone their soul back, Lucas. I had to find out how I did it. To do that, I had to go to a place where contact with the outside world is forbidden." She held on to me with a careful, nurturing hug, which soothed my nerves and calmed me down. I'd never felt anything so welcoming in my life. "I'll make you a promise here and now, Lucas. If I ever need to leave again, for any reason, I promise to tell you beforehand, if you promise not to ever think I'd forget you."

I nodded in agreement, against the collar of her jacket, the black raven feathers which lined the collar, brushed against my face.

"I promise, Gale."

Gradually, I started to think about Brent after that.

I was already used to being made fun of by other people because they thought I was different, but this was a different ball game entirely. Gale made it seem like Brent could be attacked by a horde of ninja's for knowing too much. It was obvious that by showing Brent my newfound strength, I managed to add more pain to the pavement, as Nathan once said before pummeling a helpless victim.

"So what will happen now? I don't want Brent getting into any kind of trouble or danger, because of me! Is there anything you can do, Gale?" I was actually shaking when I'd said it.

She sighed once and looked out toward the water. "I wasn't aware of how deep a friendship you had with him, until now, that is. But if you're that concerned about his safety, I'll arrange to have him watched. If he stays quiet and keeps this to himself, no one will be the wiser. Just tell him the attack from Nathan was all a bad dream and the adrenaline rush must've still been in your system. That should calm his curiosity."

The way she came up with an answer so quickly made me

wonder how many times she'd had to cover up the truth from prying eyes. It made me feel nervous about what might happen to Brent, even if he *did* have someone watching him.

"Please, Lucas, you need to be more careful from now on. It's important that you know why I'm taking such strides to be part of your life." She looked back at me again. Her eyes were glossy from the tears she held back.

"Wha-what do you mean?" I asked.

"Do you remember how I stopped my dad from attacking you back at my house?" She asked me, as she stared softly at me. I nodded in silence.

"I yelled the words, *Gimhera ikkna, nir bivorhn, niluhr! Shulna tef Cihs-Ravi Itarrah.* It's old Avish, which means; 'Forever bound, I vow, my love. The White-Raven has shown my fate'," she explained.

I felt myself become weak at the knees once again. I thought she was yelling at her dad at the time, but after she'd explained it, the situation intensified. She was actually yelling to *me!* She'd vowed herself to me. I felt humbled and a feeling of unworthiness came over me. I had nothing to offer her in return for all she'd done, nothing except what we were sharing right now, this moment, itself. There was no way I could compare myself to her, she was perfect in every way. I couldn't help but wonder what her vow meant for the two of us.

"So if you've vowed yourself to me, what does that mean? I mean, is there anything I have to do in return?" I wondered if it meant she pretty much screamed to her dad that we were engaged by Corvidae ritual or something. It was all too new to me.

She giggled a bit before putting her hand on mine. "It means only you can claim the right of having me by your side. Everything I have, I will share with you. Every word I speak, affectionate or not, is only yours to hear. Every breath I take is yours to have. And every kiss I offer, is yours to claim. You're my white-feather-knight. You saved me from a lonely, dark world. For that, I gladly give you all I have. Lucas, I would do anything you asked of me."

Her words were so beautiful, so heartfelt, that I felt my heart swelling up, and my chest started getting extremely warm. After hearing her talk about such a deep devotion toward me, she'd managed to make this night even more unforgettable than before! I was speechless...

"As for you doing anything in return, you've already done more than you realize. By staying with me, when you could've walked away, by sharing with me the most amazing kiss ever, and flying with me to this romantic spot, you've done more than I could ever have hoped for. I've never been happier, Lucas," she reassured, her fingers locking between mine. She leaned in with her other hand behind my head, and pulled me closer.

Her kiss was much deeper than before, and I felt a few of her tears crawl from her face onto mine. The night seemed timeless, as we embraced each other. My second kiss ever turned into an eternity of bliss, one I would never forget.

My thoughts cleared as our lips embraced one another. She slowed her movements, showing me just how she liked it done. I copied everything, the gradual slide of her lips, the way she brushed the tip of my tongue with hers. Cold flames welled up inside me. I felt her running her fingers through my hair, sending a tingling sensation shooting into every nerve I had. I wrapped one arm around her waist, slid the other up her back, and pulled her closer to me.

Gale let out a tiny, soft whimper, followed by soft shivers, as if she'd waited for me to do that all night. She slowly pulled away, but kept the flow of affection going with smaller kisses on my jaw-line and chin. Each one was like a soft little star against the night sky. I started to smile uncontrollably.

"Lucas." She was looking me deep in the eyes, while stroking the back of my head "I... I don't ever want this to end." With a serious tone, behind a soft stare, she continued, "I just need to know how you feel about me?" Her sincerity was a song that waited on the face of a single sheet of paper, waiting for its ending to be written.

In return, I looked her in the eyes and sighed with a smile, "Gale, this isn't fair."

Her face went blank with confusion

"I... I just can't tell you what you want to hear. It sucks because I have had the most incredible time with you. You're the first misunderstood person I've ever fully understood."

She loosened her grip slowly, as if everything I said was beginning to hurt.

"What you wanna know is if I love you, right?"

Her eyebrows furrowed with concern as she nodded with a bite of her lip.

"The truth, Gale, is that I don't."

Her eyes filled with pain, and she started to pull away completely, but I pulled her chin back to face me.

"It's deeper than love, Gale. It's not fair, since I can't find a better, deeper word than just *love,*" I said with sincere intensity. My heart burned for her, and I almost couldn't breathe.

Her reaction quickly changed from painful confusion to a flattered loss of words. She put her hand on her chest and gasped at my answer. She blushed in embarrassment, and I knew she felt the same as I was inside.

She wrapped her arms around me, tighter than before, hugging me as close as possible. "I love you, Lucas!" she said with a few sniffles, digging her fingers into the back of my shirt.

I stroked her hair, gently caressing each inch, and whispered into her ear, "I love you too, Gale." As the night drew on, we held each other, trading breaths, and trading stares of intrigue. Then, as the sun started to rise, we brought our romantic night to a close.

"I don't mean to ruin the world's most perfect moment, but I, uh, I think it's time for us to get home. I'm starting to feel tired." I was hardly able to finish my sentence before I started to flag from lack of sleep. I leaned against the railing, so I wouldn't fall on my face.

Gale noticed then how much I struggled to stay awake and aware. She kissed me on the forehead and smiled. "All right, lover-boy, let's get you home to bed before you pass out on me," she said, then she ran her fingers through my hair. The sensation from her fingertips was enough to help me stay awake while she held my chin up and looked at me with another warming smile. "I'm gonna take you home the fast way. I call it whisking. We'll be there in about three seconds." She placed her hands on my shoulders.

I closed my eyes. I felt a jolt of energy pulse through me and when I opened my eyes, I was standing right at the end of the driveway leading to my house!

"See there, just like that! Now give me a second to change and I'll meet you on the porch." She winked.

Because of how tired I was, my mind hadn't actually caught up to what she said. Without hesitation, my yawning brain pictured Gale actually taking her clothes off and changing in the street. While the thought was a wild one that made my hair stand on end, I was far too tired to appreciate the concept. It wasn't until I'd made it to the front door that I realized what Gale was talking about.

My mom was awake and making her way out the door. She was usually up at this hour to water her flowers and weed the garden. Her hair was pinned up, leaving a few wild strands to hang freely, and she had tossed on her gardening clothes–a simple white short-sleeved shirt, and a pair of jean-capris. As soon as she turned around and saw me, she stopped.

"Luke, where on earth have you been all night, young man?" her face froze with terror, "*Oh dear, sweet Jesus above! What is that thing on your shoulder?*" she wailed, flapping her arms all around her.

I inched my eyes to my left shoulder, and there, perched proud and majestic, was Gale. I didn't even realize she'd landed on me—I was too out of it to notice anything.

"Sorry, mom. I was at Brent's. I was just hanging out over there. I must've lost track of time. Mom, this is, uh," I said the most obvious thing I could muster, "I bought a pet raven. Her name is..." I was shuffling in my mind to come up with a cool name for her, but nothing hit me. Then suddenly, I felt Gale's voice in my thoughts.

"Tell her my name is Rhune."

"Her name is Rhune, you know, like rune-stone? I was having fun spending time with her pretty much all night." I smiled to make the situation more convincing, which seemed to work. Mom was calming down, but she still hid in the frame of the front door. I shot Gale a quick smile, and she responded with a wink, which caught me off guard. I had no idea birds could wink, unless it was just another of Gale's talents.

I reached up gently, and stroked her head. Gale responded by closing her eyes, and shivering with contentment. "See? She loves attention. Do you wanna try petting her?" I wondered if she'd go for it. Mom was always a big fan of nature. Her garden was equipped with everything it needed to attract just about every animal on the planet earth. But her face told me she'd rather run off screaming until she found a broom to swat this bird.

Oddly enough, mom slowly reached out, being careful not to startle the raven's calm demeanor.

"Are-are you sure it's safe? I mean, I love wildlife and all, but-but this is a bit steep!"

"Don't worry, mom, she may look a bit scary, but Rhune is very loving and gentle. I know it sounds strange, but she's more than just a raven to me." Gale tilted her little black head and looked at me with those vibrant amethystine eyes of hers. I almost swore I saw her smile inside them.

My mom's hand finally made careful contact with Gale's head, her fingers climbing along Gale's feathers, coursing down the back of her neck. Gale reacted much the same way she did for me, it put a huge smile on Mom's face to see a creature like this enjoying human affection.

"See? She likes you!"

Mom giggled while she brushed along Gale's neck. "This is so neat, I've always wanted to know what this feels like!" She continued to stroke Gale's head while Gale took in every bit of attention she could get.

"It's like she's covered in black silk. I could pet her all day!"

she puckered her lips and started talking to Gale, as if she were talking to a baby, "Yes, I could, you're such a gorgeous little lady." She was cooing with each soft stroke. My fatigued body reminded me I needed to rest—my eyes ached and my breathing felt heavy.

I looked at Gale and she looked at me. With a yawn, I told my mom, "Sorry, I'm getting kinda tired. I really should get some sleep. I'll bring her with me after I wake up. That way, she can meet dad, too." I was rubbing my eyes with the back of my hand.

Mom pulled herself from Gale's charm and opened the door for me. "Are you thinking of keeping her in your room, sweetie? I mean, is she trained for indoor life?"

"Yeah, mom, she's trained better than most humans I know. Trust me, she wants nothing more than to be a part of the family."

"Well, all right. I guess I'll approve of her staying with us, as long as you take good care of her, as well as yourself. I don't want to have to send Brent after you, again."

I felt my nerves sink. "Mom, about that . . ."

She cut me off with a careful hug. "Don't apologize. I was right there with you, on the other side of the door. Just go back to being my beautiful son, the boy I'm always proud of—that's all I want." Her voice was calm, as if pretending nothing had happened. "See you later, Rhune. Make sure Luke makes a proper place for you to sleep in that room of his!"

I couldn't help but smile. I made my way inside and headed for the stairway leading to my room upstairs. I could see from the corner of my eye that Gale was scanning every detail of the house, enjoying her short tour to my bedroom. I took my time up the stairs, trying not to wear myself out or, for that matter, bounce Gale off my shoulder. With each step I took, I watched as her head stayed unmoved, while the rest of her body was bobbing to match my upward movement. I finally got up to the hallway at the top and headed for the door on the end.

"Here we are, your new home," I said to her and opened the door to my room. The morning sun was just beginning to crawl from behind the horizon in the distance. Its glow had already started to light its way through my balcony window and illuminated the whole room. Gale took a good look around before she hopped from my shoulder and glided over to the window. Before she landed, she changed back into her human form.

"Here, let me get the curtains. You get changed for bed," she insisted. I leaned against the dresser across from my bed and took my shoes off, slowly. It took everything I had to do it, but I managed. When I reached down to pull my shirt off, my arms felt strained, as if I'd been lifting weights at the gym. I tried again, but I just couldn't get past my chest.

Suddenly, I felt Gale's hands against my abs, her touch soft and soothing, and I let a sigh of relaxation sneak out of me. "Let me help you, Lucas." She lifted my shirt up to my neck, then she lifted my arms one by one before sliding it over my head, letting it hit the floor beside me. I could feel her breath on the back of my neck and shoulders. I leaned against the dresser while she slid her fingers slowly up my lower back. I felt her breath get warmer and I could swear she trembled with each breath she took. I was getting lost in the sensations her hands sent through me. The fatigue grew steadily behind her soothing touch. I'd never felt such a warm, pulsing flicker inside before—a deepening ache of some kind, I wondered if she was causing it.

"Something is wrong, I-I don't feel right."

She stopped me from talking by turning me around, and then she pushed me onto the bed with one hand! I was shocked at the sheer strength behind it. I barely noticed her wrapping her arms around her waist gasping as she backed against the wall and huddled next to the dresser. I took it as a sign that she was trying to restrain herself from something.

"I'm sorry, Lucas. I tried to fight it. I didn't mean to. . ." She was breathing heavily now, and shaking all over, as if she was fighting off some kind of insane urge. Then it hit me. I knew what it was she needed. She obviously hadn't fed her Corvidae side in a while and it was starting to take its toll.

"Good Lord, Gale, when was the last time you, uh, you know, fed on someone?"

She looked at me from behind a curtain of black, silken bangs with shame on her face, "I haven't drank since the first day—when I talked to you on the ferry. When I saved you on the island, I poured every drop of your soul back into you... I wanted to be sure you'd live, so I didn't bother to keep any for myself."

My thoughts froze. She hadn't fed on a soul for nearly a month! It must've been tearing at her to endure such a deep thirst.

"I-I'm sorry Lucas. I've completely ruined our perfect night together. I'm probably freaking you out pretty bad right now, so, I'm just going to go sleep outside." She started toward the window.

I got up from the bed and grabbed her arm. Slowly, I led her to the edge of the bed and pulled her closer to me. I held onto her waist as tight as I could while I sat back down. As I looked her deep in the eyes, the fear welled up in me that she might hurt me, but I couldn't let her starve. At that moment, I'd decided to be there for her, the way she'd been there for me.

"It's all right, Gale, you don't have to be sorry. And no, you didn't ruin anything. I know you're hungry. It doesn't freak me out that much, really." I placed her hand on my shoulder, attempting to show my willingness. "Here, I want you to take some of mine." The dim lighting in the room brought out the deep shade of purple in her eyes more fiercely than the night had. They sent terror shooting through every inch of me, scaring away the urge to sleep, entirely. Even so, I knew she wouldn't intentionally harm me. Her reaction to my offer told me it wasn't something she had expected. She glanced down at my hands clasped around her waist, then looked back to my face.

"I'm not letting go of you until you do it. Look, Gale, I don't have anything to offer you in return for all you've done. You've even vowed yourself to me, so the very least I could do right now," my throat stiffened, "is offer you a chance to feed on me." I spoke with as much determination as I could muster, although I knew she could tell how afraid I was.

"But, Lucas, you're way too exhausted. I can't let you do this." Her breath grew hotter and her eyes stared at me with insatiable hunger. She was more than tempted to accept my offer, to drink from my life-force, so she wouldn't starve.

I tightened my grip around her, hoping she would get the message and get it over with before I could chicken out.

She finally gave in, putting her hands against my bare chest and leaned in closer, causing me to lie on my back with my legs hung over the side of the bed. She crawled over me, letting her hair brush over my skin. The tingling sensations from each strand gliding across me was relaxing. It took away the tension. She loomed over me on all fours. Her breathing was wild and trembling as she began to lose herself.

The same sensation from before re-emerged and the second I felt her quivering lips against my chest, I closed my eyes and said, "Just promise me it won't hurt. I'm no good with pain."

"I-I'll try," she said as her hand, followed by her forehead, pressed against my chest. The pulsing sensation grew as I literally felt her drink part of my soul. It was painful at first— her hand burned like hot embers as it pressed against my body.

I clawed at the sheets in agony and grunted uncontrollably between breaths from the hot, stabbing sensation. My legs stiffened and I tried not to kick while she stayed knelt over the top of me.

I struggled more and more as it went on. Minutes seemed to melt into hours. Gale finally put her hand over my mouth to muffle my stifled cries. Then she sat down on my legs to keep me from struggling. The moment her body pressed against mine, the intense pain raced neck and neck alongside a feeling of sheer ecstasy as I screamed in the back of my mind.

The mental picture of her draped over me, holding me down while she fed on my soul, was shockingly arousing. I seriously hoped she didn't notice how arousing it was. I put both my hands over the top of hers covering my mouth. I couldn't help but bite down on her fingers as she drank harder from me. My teeth dug deep, but thankfully, no matter how hard I bit down, I wasn't able to penetrate her skin.

I heard her let out a moaning sigh of approval, while her white-hot lips barely touched my chest, inhaling wildly. I could hear her as she drank. She was whimpering with every sip she took. I had no idea how long she'd planned on drinking, but it was painfully obvious that she appreciated every drop she was getting from me. The stabbing burn was fluctuating, Gale tried so hard not to let one outweigh the other.

Suddenly, I felt her raise her head, and she gasped slowly and heavily. I opened my eyes to see hers closed tightly. Her mouth was open, and what I saw scared me. An ominous purple light kindled from the back of her throat, lighting the inside of her mouth, and a trickling arc of dark blue smoke which glowed with ribbons of yellow and white flares trailed from me as if fireflies coiled from my body and slowly passed through the fingers of her free hand, entering her mouth as she inhaled.

I began to shiver, and then I heard her whispering inside my head, *Close your eyes, Lucas. Don't be afraid... please... let me have just a little more... I've never been so thirsty...*

Under the thick blanket of agony and bliss, I managed to free one of my hands. I grabbed the back of her head and pulled her head against my chest, causing the pain to increase. I bit down on her hand as hard as I could, deciding to bear the agony to let her finish. She was taking so much out of me and it was so mind-numbingly painful, I felt woozy—everything felt heavy around me. As Gale continued to drink, I felt myself giving in to the fatigue from before, and I helplessly passed out.

"Do not worry, I'll chase away all of your pains." Her voice sounded different, almost like she was back in the Victorian era. It was both fascinating and relaxing. "When next you wake, I'll be at your bedside and you will find I have given you newfound strength. Rest yourself for now, my White-Feather-Knight. I'll ease your mind, even as you dream the night. This I promise you my dear, sweet, Lucas." I could hear her speaking to me, even through my dreams. Her voice was soft, like a cool, gentle breeze against my skin. It echoed in my thoughts as I slept through most of the day.

The experiences I had shared with her up to that point left no room for doubt on two accounts. One: she was undeniably devoted to being with me. She planned to be with me until the end of time, if possible. And two: my life had changed beyond all recognition. All I had to do was be myself. That's all she asked for. That would be easy enough, considering I was never good at being anyone else. If this kind of treatment was what I had to look forward to in my future with her, then the pleasure of her companionship and affections outweighed the pain of her need to drink from my soul. No contest.

CHAPTER 20: LUCAS

I woke up to the sound of paper sliding across the face of a desk, followed by pages being flipped and laid flat. I opened my eyes and yawned harder than ever before. I saw Gale at my art desk. She sat there, looking through a stack of pages in a spill of sunlight peeking through the edge of the curtain nearby. I stretched carefully, remembering the pain I'd experienced the night before, and hoping there was no permanent damages done to me.

"Gale? What are you doing over there?" I got up from the bed and walked over to her. Suddenly, my eyes shot open, and I nearly lost my balance with shock. "Oh, crap, uh, oh, boy." She'd found my secret stack of drawings. She must've rooted through my entire art desk and found the secret compartment where I kept the more personal ones. These weren't ordinary drawings. They were multiple drawings of her, ranging from simple sketches to exotic ones with racier pinup girl themes. I stumbled around searching for something to say, but I was stuck between a sudden urge to have a heart attack and a mental gray area.

"These are amazing," she said in a low voice, still staring at one of the exotic charcoal styled ones.

Her reaction threw me completely off guard. I half expected

her to be furious, for not only drawing her like I was an obsessed madman, but drawing her in what could easily be mistaken for a fantasizing deviant. I didn't say a word. I stood there, mouth half open, wondering how she even found the darn things.

She looked over at me as I fidgeted with my hands from the awkward situation. Gale grabbed my hands and pulled me closer, which made me even more nervous. She gazed up at me with those two irresistibly gorgeous eyes of hers and I felt my heart melting inside.

"I really love these, each one drawn in a different style. I've been up all night, looking at them ever since you passed out." Her smile was cute and warming to look at.

I could tell she was sincere, somehow fascinated by my artistic obsession of her, despite my embarrassment.

"You weren't supposed to know about those, like, ever." I felt myself blush. My cumbersome attempt to fight off the awkwardness was failing badly.

"How long have you been doing this? A few of these look like me riding the ferry!" she asked, picking up one of the scribble drawings. I loved that one. Her hair was caught in a breeze and it flowed softly over the rail of the ferry. It was a dramatic picture, which is just the kind I love to draw.

I sucked in a deep breath, defeated. Since I'd been caught red-handed, I had no choice but to confess to everything. "I've, uh, kind of been drawing you since even before you talked to me that day," I said, letting out a defeated sigh. "I didn't want you to freak out, so I kept it a secret. Not even my parents know about these drawings or the secret compartment where I hid them."

As soon as I answered her, she reacted with a worried look on her face. I was so embarrassed about the whole situation I hardly looked at her. "Oh no, I'm sorry, Lucas. I shouldn't have gone through your stuff like that." I watched her run her fingers through her hair, "I-I guess I forgot, when I drink from a soul, I also take in some of their thoughts and memories," she explained, her voice low and delicate. She seemed as embarrassed as me now. The silence in the room grew more prominent, making my hands begin to sweat badly.

"Well, my snooping around aside, I really do like your art. I wasn't kidding when I said that."

I looked at her, smiling at me with an apologetic grin on her face, which made me forget about her rooting through my desk to begin with. I couldn't help but give in to her girlish charms, I smiled back and shook my head in defeat, once again.

"You're so different from anyone I've ever known," I told her, shaking my head with a warm stare. "You're such a breath of fresh air to me. Honestly, I almost don't know how to handle it." I chuckled as I leaned against the wall next to the desk. I was so caught up with her approval of the drawings, and her reaction to them, I barely noticed how moved she was by what I'd said. She had a glisten in her eyes, the kind that was unmistakable.

Gale stood and gently pushed my back against the wall. She kept her hands pressed against my chest. I tensed and my breath thinned; I could feel my nerves freezing at how close she came to me.

Then she leaned in and kissed the side of my neck before she looked me deep in the eyes and said, "Honestly, I could say the same thing about you." Her eyes lowered to my lips, and then she pressed her index finger gently against my lower lip.

I felt she was seriously teasing me and I was on pins and needles. She made me feel so defenseless and, oddly, I enjoyed every sadistic minute of it.

"Last night was absolutely fantastic. You've opened up a whole new world for me, I know you may not realize it, but," she leaned in next to my ear, and let out a single warm breath, sending shivers down my neck while she whispered, "I feel like a whole new woman because of you."

Her white-hot breath brushing across my skin sent warm tingling waves of excitement throughout my entire body. I took in a very shaky deep breath and closed my eyes before I slowly placed my hands on her hips. Even my fingers were shaking wildly! I leaned closer and whispered to her, "If you need more, you can."

She stopped me by putting her fingers over my mouth, followed by an assuring stare, the tip of her nose brushing against mine. "Ssh, it's okay now, there's no need, Lucas. You gave me more than enough to last me for quite a while." She sighed while she nodded gently with satisfaction, "And just so you know," she looked deep into my eyes as she playfully licked her upper lip slowly, "you're the most delicious thing I've ever tasted." The way she said it almost sounded like she couldn't wait for the next time.

I was flattered, and frightened at the same time.

"It didn't hurt you too much, did it?" she asked.

"Actually, I don't know how you did it. But the pain was kind of nice. I'm more worried about you, though. How's your hand?" I remembered biting as hard as I could into it, to muffle my agony last night. I wasn't sure if I'd drawn any blood or left a scar of tooth-marks.

She held it up for me and smiled. "It's fine. Don't worry, you're only human, Lucas. I do feel pain the same as you, but the difference is you could never break through my skin." She guided my hand up to her neck and placed each of her fingers over each of mine before she pressed down, making my nails dig deep into her skin, but still not able to penetrate. I watched, helplessly as she dragged my hand under hers, down the surface of her neck, leaving the faintest claw-marks down to her collar-bone. She gasped slowly and closed her eyes while she gently exhaled through her slightly puckered lips, her eyebrows slanted and furrowed, which told me she enjoyed the burning ebb from my nails. "Pain can sometimes be intimate, if it's done right. I just happen to enjoy a lot of both." She had a sinister type of smile on her face, the red marks from my finger-nails faded and her neck returned to normal in seconds.

"Whoa, your injuries heal fast too?" I asked as I stared at her neck with amazement.

"It's just another of many perks within the Corvidea bloodlines." She winked. "And that's the least of my abilities."

I was completely amazed. She became more fascinating by the second! I honestly didn't know what to think, at first. I felt a tug of jealousy at the thought of having a fast healing rate. That would've come in handy during my school years in gym class.

"By the way, Lucas, speaking of perks, I wanted to ask you something." Her voice turned a bit more serious. She backed away from me and leaned against my art desk. "Last night, Shannoea pulled a few strings with some of her friends here in town and she was able to get us a special reservation at Mon Ami," she explained as my jaw hit the floor.

"Well? What do you think? Tonight—a romantic, candlelight dinner for just the two of us, and the finest food in Port Clinton."

I'd never actually eaten there before, mostly because it was beyond ritzy, and I'd never actually had anyone to go with. I was completely awestruck.

Gale leaned against the edge of the desk, waiting for my answer.

"I've...always wanted to go there! But-but why are you—"

She interrupted me, pressing her fingers against my mouth like she had earlier. "Why not? If you need any reason at all, let's just go with the fact that I feel like repaying you for your intense generosity last night."

I barely heard what she said, but when her words caught up

with me, my heart skipped a few beats.

"What you did for me, Lucas, was beyond the worth of money. My strength was waning and you gave me yours. That's the most thoughtful thing anyone has ever done for me in my entire life."

"I would've given you every drop, if you wanted it." My words were shaking, but I meant it. I could see by her reaction, she knew I was serious.

"I know you would. Your energy seemed pretty eager to be tasted last night. I had to pull back so you wouldn't die on me, again."

At first, I thought she was joking, but just looking at her standing there with that look on her face, that look that said, *I nearly lost you all over again.* It was more than enough proof that she was serious. I felt a heightened rush of dread spill over me after she said it. It only lasted a few seconds, but it was still strong.

"Don't worry about it. I was more than capable of keeping you alive. It's my vow to you, remember?" She pulled my hand to her lips and kissed the top gently.

"So, wait, you also eat real food? I mean, I'm not going to be the only one ordering anything tonight, right? I'd feel kinda weird." I hoped I hadn't made her mad by asking, but I seriously wasn't sure. Beyond ice cream and soda, I'd never actually seen her consume anything else, other than drinking from my soul on a recent occasion.

"Of course, I do, silly. I eat all *kinds* of normal food! I ate ice cream, didn't I?" She shot me a brief, coy smirk and gently nudged my chest with a playful slow-motion punch. "Did you think I was going to have you sit at the table eating all that lavish food while I sat next to you and drained you to death?"

"Well, no, but, I didn't know if you *could* eat other things. I've got this whole new side of you to get to know now. You're a deeper woman than I realized."

She winked at me and said, "Mmm, you shouldn't flatter a woman like me, when you're trapped in a room with her." She ran her index finger up the middle of my chest and then traced up my neck, stopping under my chin. "It's bad for your soul." She grinned, then she grabbed my neck with her hand and pulled me into a deep, romantically aggressive kiss.

It was enough to send me over the edge. My thoughts blurred while my hands seemed magnetically drawn to her. The moment my fingertips pressed against the small amount of skin peeking out from under the back of her shirt, I felt a surge of excitement shoot through me. I wrapped one arm around her waist, and the other traced its way up her back and rested under her cascading hair, against the warmth of her neck.

The only reassuring thing in having her so close, knowing she was intensely dangerous but she'd never willingly harm me, was the passionate way she kissed me. I could almost feel her heartbeat matching mine with every pulsing second we shared.

Her lips were extremely hot to the touch. I felt her tongue

brush across the tip of mine. It was more than enough to sweep the breath out of me. We must've stood there, embracing for almost twenty minutes. She eventually pulled away and stared deep into my eyes. "Don't go to work today, stay home." She had a hungry gaze in her eyes, the kind that didn't look hungry for just my soul. "Let's stay up here all day. We can still go to dinner later. I just want you all to myself right now." Her hands slid over my chest and neck. It was hard to think of anything else. She was breathing hard and pawing all over me. It took everything I had, but I managed to break away.

It was one of *the* most difficult choices I'd ever encountered. Her eyes melted me on the inside and her touch was driving my heart insane. Even so, I couldn't risk it. Losing my job would draw a lot of unwanted attention to me. "I want to. I really do wanna stay here, with you." I ran my hand over her cheek, then traced her chin-line to the back of her ear. "But I *have* to go today. It's one of the busiest days of the week—if I don't show, I could lose my job." She looked disappointed, but I had no choice. I walked over to the dresser and rooted through the drawer containing my work uniform.

She wrapped her arms around my waist and pressed one of her hands against my chest. Then she tightened her grip on me. "Lucas, my family has been around since even before the Colonial era. I've made plenty of money over the centuries. If you want, you could quit your job. I'll pay your bills forever, if you just stay here today."

I stopped cold, her hair draped over the side of my face as she loomed over my neck, clamped to me like a vice-grip.

The decision she laid in front of me turned from thick, metaphorical syrup, to quick-drying cement! She was so sure of herself, so calm and collected about me walking off my job and waltzing into the sunset with her. I fought the urge with every ounce of will I could muster. Real-life syndrome had its hooks way too far within me for me to toss everything aside, like papers in the wind. I looked at her with a careful stare. "I-I can't Gale, what would my parents say? I mean, I still have college to deal with. They would never get over it. They'd see it as irresponsible and reckless. Since they're the ones paying for most of it, I don't have much choice." I put my hand over the one she had on my chest. My fingers slid between hers and she gripped them gently between hers.

"So there's nothing I can do to tempt you into staying then, eh?"

"You've already done more than tempt me; I'd stay if I could."

She suddenly slid out from around me and walked over to the bathroom door near my bed before letting out a slightly defeated sigh. "Then I'm getting a shower at least. I've got to look my best when I stalk you at work."

I had a sudden nervous spark. "But that means I'll have to—."

She cut me off with a clever smile, "Stay in the bathroom

and wait until I'm done, I know. We can't have your parents wandering into your room with you sitting on the bed. They'll suspect something for sure." Her grin grew sinister as she stepped into the bathroom and held the door open for me.

I could hardly breathe. Defeated, I got up and walked in behind her while she turned on the water. I was a prisoner in my own damn bathroom. I sat on the toilet with the lid down while she stood a few feet away from me, slipping out of her clothes. My nerves were rattled. I stared like a helpless, cowering animal as she slowly lifted her shirt over her head and tossed it next to me. She wore a black bra with white roses edging the top. My eyes nearly fell out of my skull.

She smiled the whole time, watching me quiver in the corner. She slid her boots off and unzipped her pants, then slowly eased them over her thighs and down her legs. Then she kicked them over to join the shirt.

I began to feel hot all over. I was ready to die of a heart attack!

"Hey, are you okay, over there?" she asked, turning her back to me. She reached in and let the water cascade over her hand.

As she checked the warmth of the water, I helplessly let my eyes creep over her. I took in her perfectly shaped figure, from the soft and gentle looking curvatures of her back down her sleek, narrow waist. I caught my breath at the sight of her underwear. A very thin, black lace thong matched her bra and traced along the slope of her waistline, before diving down teasingly into the crevice of her sleek behind. The whole time I stared insanely at her dazzling, goddess-like figure, I hoped to God she wouldn't notice. I saw her peek over her shoulder and I shifted my eyes away from her and grabbed the nearest thing I could find to avert my attention and avoid embarrassment. "I-I'm fine—just, uh, checking out this, uh..." I looked at my hands to see what I'd grabbed. It was an old video game magazine I'd left here a few months back. I yanked it open and held it over my face. "...this, um, article on old-school video games from the eighties. It's a really good magazine," I stammered, noticing the magazine was upside down. My face turned white with worry that she'd seen me ogling her body like some depraved perv.

"I can see that. You must be extremely versatile; I've never seen anyone read the words upside down."

I could tell she was smiling by the way she spoke. I swallowed hard. It felt like I had a boulder stuck in my throat.

I tried my best to look intrigued by the magazine, trying not to glance at her fantastic body, while she taunted and teased from three feet away. I cleared my throat and squeezed out a small sigh. "I read things upside down all the time. I read an article that, uh, that reading upside down can, um...be healthy for your eyes." I couldn't believe what I was saying! I groaned uneasily at my lame excuse and continued to pretend I was giving my eyeballs a healthy workout.

"Mm-hmm, you know, that's rather fascinating, but it's missing one thing," she said coyly.

"What's that?" I barely managed to ask as I started to shake.

As I finished asking, an empty thin, black lace thong flopped over the top of the magazine and hung over the center.

"A sexy bookmark," she answered.

I gripped the corners of the magazine for dear life. My eyes gravitated to the thong like a magnet. My body went numb and I felt dizzy. I heard the shower door close even while I struggled to keep from hyperventilating. I glanced briefly at the shower door. I could nearly see her gorgeous figure behind the dense, cobble-patterned opaque glass—her back arched like she was posing for a photo. She had one leg straight, while the other was slightly bent and her arms were above her head as she ran her fingers through her hair.

I looked down at the lone black strip of fabric greeting me with its delicate, lacey cuteness. My hands shook feverishly as I reach up and pulled, holding the thong carefully in the palm of my hand. I was in nerd-heaven. No one would ever believe I'd held a woman's underwear in my hand, let alone a *thong!* I let out a careful, long, quivering sigh. I let my eyes savor every detail as I thought to myself, *Was she being serious? Did she really want me to use them as a bookmark, or was she just teasing me in some sick, sadistic way? Did she even realize how much of a bodacious prize it was for a guy to have a pair of recently worn underwear from a woman in Gale's sort of league?* It was enough to make my head spin off my shoulders and bounce around the room like a pinball!

She was in the shower for nearly ten minutes while I sat in the corner, holding her underwear in my hand with careful reverence. I heard the water stop before she cracked open the door and grabbed a towel from the rack nearby. She stepped out with it wrapped around her. I'd completely lost my train of thought, as I stared at her in awe. Her hair was even sexier when soaked, draped over her shoulders, as it hugged her skin. She looked like she'd just stepped from a rainstorm—nothing short of poetic.

I stood up, and put the magazine down where I'd found it.

She reached down and scooped up her pants, then her bra and shirt.

I held out the hand containing her underwear, not realizing how ridiculous and perverted it may have looked from her angle.

She smiled and pushed my hand back to me. "That's very considerate of you, Lucas, but when a woman gives you a gift, you should treasure it. Especially, if it's something intimately personal."

I looked down at my hand, awestruck. "Wow, thanks." I said in an almost inaudible voice. Next to the Corvidae ducat she'd given me at our first date, this was the second most precious gift I'd ever gotten from anyone. Immediately, I plotted to keep them hidden and protected. No one would ever lay eyes on them aside from me. By the time I finished thinking of a decent place to stash them, I noticed Gale was dressed. She sat on my former seat, on the lid of the toilet, pulling her boots back on. I carefully stuffed my new gift into my pocket until I could come up with a suitable hiding place for them. I turned to her and asked, "So, um, am I picking you up after I get off work, then?"

"Nope, you just worry about getting through the day. When you clock out, I'll bring you some nice clothes so you can get changed into something more presentable, then you're all mine!" She got up from her seat and walked past me, shooting me a quick wink as she exited the room. I followed her back into the bedroom. She had one of my dresser drawers open and started rooting through it. She pulled out my white button-up, then a pair of black dress pants. "Here, I'll keep these clothes with me. When you get off, you can change into them. We can't go out to dinner with you wearing your work uniform."

I couldn't help but feel out of place. She pampered my every step, almost like she was protecting her perfect evening plans. It was kind of cute and slightly frightening at the same time.

I finished changing into my uniform. The ugly shorts and blue shirt usually dragged me into a humiliated state of mind, but oddly enough, today was different. I didn't care today. Maybe it was due to Gale being in my life, or maybe it was due to the dinner plans she'd put together for the two of us. Either way, my life was beginning to feel a bit brighter.

The day went by quickly. Everything that normally bothered

me was easily ignorable. I spotted Gale, in raven form, a few times. She hung out on the top of the ferry's control room for most of the day, watching me with a glint in her eyes. I couldn't hold back smiling at her when she cawed softly.

At one point, Terry, another of my co-workers handed me a hot dog for my lunch break. I was leaning against the rail of the dock, ready to eat, when suddenly I heard one of the tourists exclaim in a quivering whisper, "Oh, my God, look at that raven!" I turned my head and saw Gale walking gracefully toward me along the rail, looking a bit angry.

"I think it wants your hot-dog, buddy! You might wanna give it a piece before it pecks your eyes out!" I heard one of them say while everyone stared. I heard several digital cameras going off at the same time. I stood there, head turned, fixated on Gale, who was staring me in the face from the railing.

"And just what are you doing with that hot-dog, Lucas?" I heard her say in my thoughts.

"But...I still have two hours before I get off! I was just gonna . . ." I replied mentally.

She jumped from the rail, grabbed the hot dog from my hands, and flew off with what sounded like a mix between a caw and a coy laugh. Everyone around me laughed and clapped hysterically, while I stood dumbfounded, my hand held out where the hot dog used to be.

"You can wait. I'm not going to let you spoil our plans," she said in a stern mental tone.

I was astounded to say the least. Not because she stole my only food of the day, but because she could mentally speak to me from far away. I went hungry for the rest of my shift. It wasn't so bad. As I clocked out and headed to the parking area, I saw Gale's car pulling up.

She stepped out, slipped out of her black jacket and put it on the seat, closed the door, and then walked casually toward me. She wore a dark blue dress that hugged every curve of her body, with a shiny, black belt around her waist. Her hair playfully flickered in the breeze, showing off tiny, gold, raven-shaped earrings.

I let my eyes roam over her, from her gorgeous cascading hair to her black strapped, open-toed heels. The only thing that didn't add up was the white paper shopping bag she carried.

"Whoa, who's that?" I heard a few of my co-workers ask behind me.

"That's, uh, my girlfriend," I barely managed to spit it out. I was too busy trying to breathe steadily.

"*Your* girlfriend? A fine little fox like that? Yeah, whatever you say, dude. Girls like her, they're in a league all their own and let's face facts, you're not even playin' on the same *field!*" They were laughing with each other, followed by the sounds of a few high-fives being dealt.

Their snide attitude caused a lot of anger inside, followed by an unexpected urge to lash out. "Oh, you're funny—*I'm not even playing on the same field*—like I've never heard that before! The least you could do is come up with some new material. That's why *you are* still single." I wished I could backhand all of them, but I ignored the urge and finished off their egos with an angry, sinister grin. "Why don't you guys get lost? There's a gorgeous woman who wants my attention, and I'll be damned if I'm gonna deny her because of you jerks." After I'd said it, I caught up with myself. I was shocked at my sudden spark of confidence. I felt accomplished and slightly victorious deep inside.

Gale stopped in front of me and smiled. "I've been waiting all day for you. Just like I promised I would," she said, putting her hand on my chest. "I can't wait any longer. Now you're all mine for the night."

I glanced at the group behind me –their mouths gaped open, stunned that she was talking to me and pulling on my arm.

I heard one of them saying in a low voice, "What the hell, dude! She's hangin' all over Luke, like he's got game!"

"That's messed up. It's always the damn geeks, man." I heard another one say.

I felt Gale tug on my arm again. "C'mon, Lucas, I'm going crazy the more you make me wait."

As soon as she said that, one of the guys from the group behind me quickly pulled his shirt down over his shorts and turned away.

Gale smiled at them and said in a coy tone, "Sorry boys, he's with me."

She dragged me off toward the restrooms, leaving the rest of the group stuck in awe. Then she handed me the bag she carried before shoving me inside. "The quicker you change, the sooner we can get out of here. Don't keep a woman waiting. I don't need your pig-headed friends over there trying to put the move on me."

I changed as quickly as I could, making sure to look as presentable as possible. I took a look in the mirror before I tossed my uniform into the bag and left the restroom.

CHAPTER 21: GALE

We made good time getting to Mon Ami. Lucas had changed rather quickly and the drive seemed to rush by, then we were pulling into the parking area. We got out and followed the walkway toward the front door, passing under the white wooden sign with its dark green border. I have always adored this restaurant, its beauty and elegance leave a lasting impression, not only on the lips of those who taste the divine cuisine, but deep in the hearts of those who experience the welcoming and nurturing atmosphere that Mon Ami is famous for. I get excited every time I trek down the walkway, passing between the various lush plant-life expertly placed on either side. Lucas seemed a little nervous and I could tell he'd never been to such a lavish place. His reaction added more magic to the moment, in my eyes.

I opened one of the wooden doors and Lucas stopped. "Wait, shouldn't I be the one holding the door for you?"

"You're *my* date, remember? Tonight is about you before me. That's the basis of all romantic gestures, Lucas." I winked, then reached over and adjusted his collar. "Now hurry inside, I want you to see this place!"

He walked in, smiling to himself. His smile turned into a gawk as soon as his eyes took in the layout of the interior. The soft glow from the lamps mounted in rows between each of the giant picture windows brought life to the stained-wooden paneling on the wall, which surrounded the stone fireplace. Even the floor had a crisp, warm feel to it, with each brown tile facing every which way in neat little rows.

"This is incredible!" I heard him say in a whisper.

"I'm glad you like it. I wanted to make sure our first dinner was more than special, just like you." His face turned a deep shade of red, then I felt mine doing the same. Even after all the time we'd shared, I still felt that same sensation I had back on the ferry when I first spoke to him—the kind of feeling I would always welcome when it came to spending time with him.

The hostess approached us and gave us a gleaming smile. "Hello, and welcome to Mon Ami this evening! My name is Ann. Will it be just the two of you with us?" Her shoulder-length blonde hair and blue eyes were as vibrant as her attitude. It made for a quaint opening to an already wonderful evening.

"Yes, we have a table reservation for the wine cellar," I said, smiling back at her.

"Ah, the Anning reservation, right?" she asked.

I nodded once.

She led us through the dining area until we came to a door leading back outside, to the side of the dining area. We followed her until we came to another door, leading into a different part of the building altogether. She opened the door and led us through the hall of wine barrels, each with dark brown, woodland red, painted trim. We came to a gorgeous table with a romantic setup.

A wine bottle sat in the middle as a centerpiece, a candelabra mounted through the neck of the bottle. Each candle flame danced slowly, giving a soothing sensation to the atmosphere of the room.

Ann pulled out our chairs and placed a couple of menus on the table. "Here you are, Miss Anning. I'll have your server out to you, momentarily."

"Thank you, Ann. This is absolutely lovely," I said, looking over at Lucas, who was absorbing every detail around him.

She walked off with a satisfied look on her face, while I glanced at Lucas again, "So, what do you think?"

"What? I don't know what to say, honestly! It's really gorgeous in here!" His face was lighting up, a priceless scene indeed. I loved his reaction. It gave me a sense of joy. But even then, I could tell he had something on his mind.

"What's wrong, Lucas?"

"Huh? Oh, it's nothing. I mean, aside from feeling like a fish out of water, in a ritzy place like this, I guess I was just wondering," he fidgeted with his hands, "uh, well," he stammered, looking for the right way to ask whatever was on his mind, "we're the *only* ones down here. I mean, I'm not complaining, don't get me wrong. I just had the impression that, you know, there'd be—"

I stopped him with a big smile as I put my hand over his on the table. "You thought there would be others dining down here, also. Well, that would most likely have been the case, had I not reserved this entire portion of the restaurant, just for us." He was stunned to say the least. He sat there, staring at me, mouth open slightly. I laughed to myself, still holding his hand under mine.

"You really did that?" he barely managed to ask.

"Absolutely. I don't feel like sharing you with anyone else. I asked you to be all mine, just as I am all yours. I see no reason to hold back and I dare not allow anything to distract us from having a good time tonight." He was blushing again, and I felt myself turning red, also. "I would spend every last dollar and coin I have, to have just one special night alone with you, Lucas."

His eyes started to glisten, his fingers, fidgeting between mine. He wiped his eyes with his free hand as I lifted the other and gently kissed it. The candlelight danced and flickered, bringing out his soft features. I gazed at him, grinning to myself, marveling over everything about him. He grinned back longingly, the reflection of the candle flames shining in his eyes, making my heart beat faster. A perfect moment, with my perfect Lucas.

"I know this may sound weird, but I-I can't seem to get enough of you," he said behind a shy smile. "No one's ever done anything like this for me."

I kissed his hand again and smiled, letting my eyes lock gently with his. "I can't imagine why you'd ever *want* enough of me." I shot him a playful wink and he started to become shy all over again, turning his head to one side, trying to hide his embarrassment. "The day I first saw you, I was actually leaving Ohio altogether. But when I caught sight of you, I don't know how to explain it. As I was flying past that ferry, I felt an overwhelming urge to land. When I looked down to find a suitable spot to perch on, I saw you. Then I couldn't keep my eyes off you; I landed on top of the ferry and stared. You still fascinate me, Lucas, every single day! Just when I think I've figured you out, you show me some new, unique way of thinking about things!"

"I, um, I don't know what to say. I mean, I don't see what's so unique about me, to be honest. You're this fantastic, raven-woman, with amazing super-powers and I'm just—"

I jumped in and stopped him, before he could go on. "You're just, simple. There's nothing dramatic, or dark, or secretive about you." He looked shocked, as if he was caught between flattered and offended. "Lucas, I've lived my entire life in the shadows. I've had to lie about who I am to people for so long, never allowed to be who, or what I really am , until I met you." His expression took a lean to the flattered look after I said that, which made me feel more at ease. "The truth is I wish I could give up my Corvidae life. I'd much rather live simpler, maybe learn to draw the way you do, or plant a nice, yet exotic garden, something normal and relaxing, that takes time and patience. When there's nothing but danger, nothing but diplomacy and razor-thin lines between law and war, the hardest thing for anyone living a life surrounded by strife is to reach out to something as simple as a ray of hope. The kind that only shines when you look for it after an eternity of battling and hunting in the darkness; spending time with a newfound love or planting a garden is far greater a joy in the eyes of any blighted life."

His eyebrow rose. "I guess I understand you better than I realized. I enjoy excitement like anybody else, but I don't like being in large crowds. I can even say I don't like *too much* excitement, I've spent most of my life playing video games, mostly because I can control how much excitement I'm getting."

In a very simplistic way, I understood exactly what he meant. Whenever I'd had enough of my life, I would simply escape whatever situation I was in and go somewhere quiet, whereas Lucas only had to press the power-off button on his gaming console and he was out of the reach of danger and drama altogether.

"Did I hear you right? I could've *sworn* you said you wanna learn to draw like me."

"I *did* say that. I said it because your art is beautiful! The way your lines sway and curve, it's mesmerizing to me! Not to mention, how many different styles you use each time you start a new picture! It's like you see the world through a completely different spectrum!"

He looked down at the table, then back to me. "Wow. I guess I've never thought much about that. No one's ever really said much about my art, to be honest. Well, no one except Brent."

"The point is you give me exactly what I'm missing. You're

everything I've dreamed about, Lucas." I couldn't help but run my fingers over his hand, then up his forearm as I spoke to him. "I know you don't think much of yourself, even though I wish you would. And I know what it's like to feel like you don't belong. But in my eyes, you're absolutely perfect. Now that I know you, now that I know there truly *is* a ray of hope to reach out for, I don't think I could ever truly live without you."

I continued to watch his eyes with every word I said to him. They were stuck in a state of widened, flattered awe. It made the moment feel alive with the romance I'd waited all day to feel.

His lips quivered and he started to smile uncontrollably. "You really *do* think the world of me, don't you?" Even his eyes seemed to gleam with a bright smile.

"More so." I knew he could see my sincerity. I kept my eyes fixed on him and said, "What good would this world be, if I had to be all alone in it? I've tasted not only the bitter flavor of loneliness of centuries passed, but the flavors of countless souls over endless years. And, rest assured, during those dark times, none of their essences satisfied me the way your love and compassion have." I stared deeper into his eyes, before adding, "The reason you're so full of such radiant flavor, is simple. It's because you have a kind, warm heart. The best treasures of life are the ones we work hard to indulge in. I honestly hope that in *your* eyes I've worked hard enough to finally say I've found the treasure that has always belonged to me."

Just as he started to speak, I sensed the waitress approaching us.

"Hi, my name is Julie, and I'll be taking care of you this evening! Can I start the two of you off with a drink?" She was as cheerful as Ann and just as eager. I signaled to Lucas to go ahead and order anything he liked, followed with a reassuring smile.

He smiled back softly, trying to hide his red face from what I'd said. "I'll just have a sweet tea, please."

"All right, and what can I get for you, Miss Anning?" she asked.

"I think I'll have the same, a sweet tea."

"Okay, I'll have those right out!" she said, handing us a couple of menus before walking off.

I didn't need to look at the menu. I always ordered the same thing when I came here. I'd tried nearly everything they served once or twice, but I ended up going back to a classic dish I enjoy on special occasions. Lucas stared at his menu, his eyes panned hungrily over every item on the list. I'd nearly forgotten I stole his lunch earlier, which made me feel a little guilty for thinking it was cute to watch him scan his menu like a starved lunatic.

"So, tell me, Lucas, did you learn to draw on your own, or did you take lessons?" I asked, leaning forward, one elbow on the table. The question eventually broke his concentration from the mouthwatering list of delights on the menu and his eyes climbed over the top of the page and met with mine.

"I, uh, I've never taken lessons. Unless you count when my uncle showed me how to draw a cartoon character when I was little. I took what I learned from that and explored other directions."

"What character did he have you draw?"

"Ziggy, a short little guy with a bald head and a big nose," he described him, gesturing with his hands. "I remember him handing me a newspaper comic page and then he drew Ziggy, showing me step by step how to draw him. After that, he asked me to practice drawing him. I must've drawn that same picture dozens of times and when I felt I'd mastered the character, I moved on to super-heroes."

I pictured him scribbling all over several blank pages of paper, trying to master a simple cartoon. The thoughts of a young Lucas with a crayon or pencil, drawing while he lay on the floor, made me smile both inside and out.

I chuckled a bit and said, "Well, you've made an amazing little name for yourself in my book, Lucas. I've seen a lot of artists over the years, but they lack the inner-life you capture in your drawings. And that's the honest truth."

He suddenly had a smug look on his face. "If I didn't know any better, I'd say the creepy, stalker, raven-lady is my first, official, biggest fan," he said, shooting his coy, narrow eyes at me with a curved smirk.

I shot back a smirk of my own, narrowing my eyes just as he had. "I think you're right! Do you think she knows where you live?" I winked.

"Man, I hope so. I keep the terrace windows unlocked, just

for her!" he said, winking back. I started to turn red in the face all over again, "I wonder if her name is as gorgeous as she is?"

I gasped, my face going numb and hot the second he said that. I dropped my eyes, biting back a smile, wishing my hair would swing around and cover my rosy cheeks. I absolutely adored him when he let his brave side peek out. It didn't have to be out for very long, it was a special treat for me, after experiencing so much of his meek personality. Lucas is different tonight, I thought to myself. It's as if he was being constantly observant, always watching my reactions, always looking for a way to match each one and enhance the moment tenfold. *In fact, he's been acting a little differently, since the day I'd told him the truth about me,* I went on mentally.

Every single nerve in my body spiked, the way he made me feel was hard to control. His sweet, tender words, the way he looked at me with those gorgeous eyes of his, and the way he read my every word and emotion, I felt whole. My missing half sat across the table from me, enjoying the night I'd brought him while savoring everything I offered. My heart fluttered, making me giggle slightly. I put my hand over my mouth, making Lucas smile even more.

He laid his menu on the table and tilted his head slightly to one side. "Speaking of names, uh why did you tell me to call you Rhune, when my mom asked what your name was, yesterday morning?"

"That's my birth-name. My father is German, hailing from

Schwarzwald. My mother hails from France. Since she studied ancient Germanic runes and culture as a hobby, she ended up traveling to Bad-Sacklingen, where she met my father, Alexander. His birth-name was simply Xander, at the time." I watched his fascination grow as he saw an elaborate answer to a simple question unfolding before him. For once, I actually felt proud when I spoke of my past. "They spent a great deal of time together, eventually married, and when I was born she held on firmly to the one thing that brought her to the arms of my father in the first place—Runes." I leaned forward a little, my arms folded on the table. "We sometimes change our names in order to blend in longer. That's why my name is different."

"That's so amazing! I wish I had an incredible story like that! My parents dated through high school and college, then my mom found out she was pregnant with me during a vacation in Texas. Pretty lame back-story, if you ask me."

My curiosity struck and I asked, "So did they marry because of her pregnancy?"

"Well, they were planning on getting married anyway, but when they found out I was on the way, it just gave them another reason. They've always been pretty adamant about having a strong sense of moral foundation, when it comes to family," he said with a smile.

Just then, I sensed our waitress approaching again. She walked over, carefully placing our drinks onto the table, before pulling out her order-sheet and pen.

She glanced at the two of us and asked, "Have you decided what you'd like to order, or would you like a few more minutes?"

I looked over at Lucas, "Do you know what you'd like to try?" I asked with a grin. *"You can have anything you like, Lucas. As I said, this is our night and I want you to have the very best of everything."* I spoke to him in his thoughts, sensing his heart jump at my every word.

He glanced at his menu, then looked up at Julie, "I uh, I think I'll have the Mon Ami works burger, without the beet slaw, well done, please."

She wrote in his order, then turned to me. "All right, and what can I get for you, Miss Anning?"

"I'll have my usual, the filet mignon, medium rare, please."

She wrote in my order and smiled as we handed her our menus. "I'll put that in and have it out to you as soon as possible. Until then, is there anything else I can get the two of you? An appetizer perhaps?"

I looked over to Lucas, who shrugged and shook his head. "No, thank you, but we appreciate the offer, Julie." I shot her a casual grin and a reassuring nod.

She smiled back and nodded in approval before leaving us to continue our evening.

"Not that I'm complaining, but why did you order a cheeseburger? There are plenty of more lavish items to choose from here, you know."

"I don't know. I guess if I had to explain it, it's sort of a nerd-test thing."

I was completely thrown back by his answer, I'd never heard of such a thing before, nor did I know how to respond to it in the least! "It's nothing against you, or this place, but whenever I go somewhere new, the first thing I'm compelled to try, is any burger they might have. It's kind of off the wall, I know, but I've always been that way. Almost like testing the water, really. A rite of passage, to someone like me."

I grinned helplessly, I couldn't help it. It was so cute to hear such a goofy answer from such a beautiful person. I chuckled a little, followed by a nod. "Actually, that makes perfect sense. You want to stick to what is familiar, I understand," I said as I took a sip of my tea.

He had a look in his eyes just then, one that felt curious. It didn't take long for the feeling to escape his mind and find his lips. He leaned forward a bit and said, "I don't mean to change the subject, Gale, but I have so many questions running through my head right now "

"Hmm... Well, what would you like to know?"

He looked pleased at my agreement to satisfy his curiosity. He adjusted himself in his seat and looked at me with a careful stare. "Remember when I asked where you'd gone, during that five days and you told me you went to a place where outside contact isn't allowed?" He tilted his head, "What kind of place has rules like that?"

281

Icy chills crawled across my chest and back. The mood of the moment changed to a slightly paler flow around the candlelight. Even though I knew he was bound to find out eventually, or that I'd have to explain it all someday, I didn't know if I was truly ready to defile his innocence to it all. Tension mounted as the guilt of knowing he was already in danger for knowing anything about my race or lineage started to set in hard. I looked at him with the same careful stare he was giving me and answered slowly with a resigned sigh, "I needed answers—the kind of answers that only another Corvidae could give me. There's an embassy stationed in Nevada, near Las Vegas. It has a Ravenic-Loftruhm, which is a type of tabernacle. Inside that is a library containing numerous books with a detailed stemma, which is just a large book gearing toward every Corvidae's lineage and powers." I answered him as simplistically as I could.

He suddenly winced and shook his head, breaking out of an almost motionless trance. "Wait, did you say Ravenic-Tabernacle? Like, a church?"

"Yeah. It's a Corvidae church, a place we can go if we need solace and privacy from the outside world."

He looked even more stunned, "What religion do Corvidae practice, exactly?"

"Christianity."

"You mean, you believe the same thing that human-Christians do?" He nearly fell out of his seat with shock.

I grinned, not surprised that he didn't see this coming; all the same, it was amusing. "Lucas, we Corvidae were *there* when Jesus walked the earth. We are partly human. His promises to mankind also translate to us, just like any other child of God. We make the same mistakes as you do and we go to the same person, when we ask for forgiveness. Just because we have supernatural gifts, doesn't mean we have the right of Godhood."

He blinked twice before saying a word. "Wow, I have to admit, I never would have guessed that! I suppose I have all those video games to thank for a wild imagination. I would have thought you had your *own* God of sorts."

I chuckled with my hand over my mouth. He was right, video games did make his imagination rather wild with that one. "I can see why you'd think that, Lucas, but no—we serve the same God as all Christians. Although I don't know *exactly* where we originated, or how we came to have the powers we do, I've tried studying it. But many of those tomes are missing from their shelves. I only know a minimal amount, really."

"Well, what about the name of your race? Where does *that* come from?" He became more comfortable with his inquiries, his elbows on the table, arms crossed and resting on each other.

I felt a bit puzzled. "You mean the name, Corvidae?"

He nodded and grinned.

I'd never had the opportunity to share where our name and I actually felt a twinge of excitement at the chance to explain. "There are only a handful of us who remember our history. My father is one of those few; he used to tell me all sorts of stories of our heritage as I was growing up. One story he often told me was that our race stems from angelic guardians, assigned not only to help lost souls find the after-life, but also to battle other supernatural beings."

His intrigue grew with every word I spoke, the candle-flame captured his eyes perfectly, as he soaked it all in. "When I asked him that same question, regarding the name of our race, he told me it was the name of the first kingdom ever established by our kind; Corvine Dae Anhar, the citizens of the clouds. And the citizens of that kingdom came to be known as Corvidae by the lands and people around us."

"That is seriously awesome!" he said as his face lit up completely.

I took another sip of my drink and sat back in my chair.

"Gale, everything about you is so incredible! But seriously, it must be so hard." His gaze changed from fascination, to sympathetic. "Having all that proud heritage, all those histories, every memory you hold onto for dear life—It's gotta be so hard to keep all that fantastic stuff bottled up inside!"

Right then, I wanted to kiss him. I wanted to stand up, toss the table across the room, knock his chair back, and drape myself over him on the floor, kissing him until he passed out. I knew then, the full gravity of his understanding of my troubled lifestyle. The life I'd struggled to keep a secret, the years of fond memories and pains I'd held onto with no one to share them was finally being appreciated. My heart let out a sigh, one that gave me a warm, cozy feeling, deep down. This night had just gone from perfect to divine, with his one, heartfelt statement.

I felt my throat clench before I spoke, "You're such a gem, Lucas." I almost choked up saying it.

He had a slightly puzzled look on his face, so I tried again, "What you just said was something I've waited centuries to hear." I quickly wiped my eyes and dried my hands on my napkin.

"Well, I don't think *anyone* should have to go through life in silence. It's not healthy. Besides, everything you've told me so far has been epically amazing, Gale! I'd never be able to keep those kinds of things to myself; it would be way too hard for me, I guarantee it!" he said with a half-smile.

I could tell my eyes were watering and knew my face had to show my sincerity as I looked at him. I leaned forward again, taking his hands into mine. "It *has* been hard, Lucas. Every day holds another secret I'm forced to keep to myself! Night after night, chasing after souls lost in the shadows, sticking close to strict codes and laws, and always trying to fend off other clans and creatures!" I shook my head with tightly closed eyes. "It's not the life I want. I don't know what I'll do if I have to put up with another night of..." I lost my composure; I felt so ashamed, ruining our moment with my problems. His grip on my hands grew tighter; I could tell instantly, his strength was still being affected by my Corvidae energies from the night I'd saved him. It was by far, more firm than during our first two weeks of dating.

"Please, Gale, you're such a strong woman. Don't cry or you know I'll start crying, too. I'm way too soft to handle seeing you upset. Besides, you know I'm here for you." His tone was soothing, making it harder to fight off the tears.

I took in a slow breath, then eased myself back to being calm again.

"Listen, you don't have to explain anything to me. I get what you're going through, all pent up inside; but you know you have someone you can talk to, when things get too heavy! I mean, you did vow yourself to me—so if nothing else, try and remind yourself we're in this together, Gale." He may as well have been singing to me. My chest was fluttering out of control as I clutched his hands, carefully, but firmly.

"Lucas, that's just it, I'm not as strong as you think. I just wish..." The sigh I let out stopped me from finishing—a sigh heavy enough to pull the words right our of me.

"Wish what?" He asked, as I wiped my eyes gently, so as not to smear my eyeshadow.

Just as I was about to speak, our waitress arrived with platters holding our food.

Lucas started to put ketchup on his burger once the waitress left. He tilted his head slightly and said, "What did you mean by saying you're not strong?"

I'd nearly forgotten since the waitress showed up and

interrupted the moment. Actually, it was a blessing in disguise. Her approach unwittingly gave me a chance to regain my composure and calm down a little from my earlier gushing. I didn't want to ruin anything about this night, so deep inside I was extremely grateful. I smiled at the thought of repaying her with a hefty tip for saving my evening, even if she had no idea.

I snapped back to reality, hoping I hadn't been sitting there for too long in silence. I back-tracked my words as quickly as I could, "After being alone for countless centuries, being forced to take part in a blood feud I've refused to fight in, then finally finding someone who understands even a *fraction* of my sorrows I've realized, I'm not strong. My past is cold and heavy; I can't carry it much longer." The weight of the moment rushed back, but I was able to keep myself better contained. "I wish I hadn't put you in all this danger. It's not fair; you deserve someone who can offer you a life without fear and worry." I was able to handle my emotions better this time. "You deserve to be safe and happy, but now, because of my selfishness, you and I will both be in danger forever. I've broken sacred codes by giving you back your soul, Lucas. Not only that, but I also soaked it within mine! That's why you're experiencing all these supernatural abilities."

He didn't look concerned at all. In fact, he looked more at ease than I'd ever seen before. "Gale, I've already told you this," he took a sip of his drink, "you're a serious breath of fresh air to me. Sure, I get it, I'm in danger. But I was in danger in other ways, long before I'd even *met* you." His tone was slightly different, as if he felt more confident. "Nathan was the school bully throughout most of my life. He'd have found a reason to pound me sooner or later. And let's not forget my life in general. I was on a boring road to nowhere, before you showed up! There's always a danger of never finding a suitable girlfriend to take home and show off to mom and dad! I mean, I've always been afraid of spending the rest of my life alone. I've never been proud of anything in my life, Gale, not until I had you in it."

I objected with half a grin, "Well, that's actually very romantic of you to say, Lucas," I cleared my throat carefully, "but I'm not talking about bullies or boring futures, Lucas. I'm talking about something much more dangerous!"

He started to pick pieces off his burger, listening to me as he ate slowly.

"Remember when I told you, on the night of our first kiss, about there being much more aside from Corvidae?"

He nodded, placing another piece of his burger in his mouth.

"Well, there are. For instance, the Shen Di, a race of owls and falcons from Asia, that work as assassins. Then, there are the Feranarr—a mysterious and *silent* tribe of hunters who have powers that the Corvidae haven't begun to fathom!"

He was paying far more attention as I piled on the opposition of his argument. "Then there's the absolute worst ones of all,"

Lucas froze as I spoke.

"The *Rostair*. Their powers aren't natural at all—and no Corvidae of my generation has any idea who founded them or where their power originates." Just the thought of them made my blood come to a boil, yet made my skin grow cold as ice. I hated and dreaded them. "They are extremely hard to defeat and even harder to predict. They've always lived by a singular code of ferocity that has kept them on constant watch by our most elite watchmen, for generations."

He swallowed hard. "Well, *that's* starting to sound kind of frightening." His face went a little pale. "What makes *them* so, uh, deadly?"

I almost didn't want to divulge any more, but I knew it would come up again and continued, "The Rostair are the ones involved in the blood feud I'd mentioned earlier. They use magic in order to take on the shapes of any creature they've killed and drank the blood from."

Lucas started to tremble.

I cupped his hands, hoping to calm him. "That's what I worry about most when I say I've put you in danger, Lucas! They would be the first to try and harm you, but, God willing, I won't let that happen."

He began to get nervous, realizing the kinds of things he was up against. It did nothing to sate the guilt I'd brought on by saving his life. I was more fearful now than I'd been when my father attacked him. "The worst part is, their power doesn't limit their form at all. That's why I hate fighting against *any* Rostair. They can change a given part of their body to one kind of creature and a separate part of their body to a different kind of creature altogether."

He looked at me, eyes squinting as he absorbed what I'd said. "What? You mean, like, a chimera? They can change their head to a lion-head and their body to an alligator type of body, or something like that?

"Yes, but they usually keep their human body intact, changing only their appendages to match a given enemy or obstacle, unless they feel outclassed, or cornered. Then they change into one sort of creature and try to frenzy. But even *that* depends on the type of Rostair encountered. Some use other types of powers, like sorcery."

His head reared back, still staring at me. "Okay, *now* this really *is* starting to sound like the type of thing from one of my video games!"

I could see how badly he wished he could laugh, but my look of concern caused him to chortle instead.

"I guess the next best question, is whether or not you know any good Rostair "

"I know of a few. You do as well, Lucas. You know two of them."

He stiffened up instantly, "Wait, you mean, I have two friends, who are Rostair?!" I could see him mentally listing everyone he knew, hoping to find some sort of signs that should have given them away.

"Yes. You went to their concert with me, not long ago." I watched his eyes grow wider with the revelation.

"Nova and Naya?!"

I nodded in silence while he let his jaw hang open. He was absolutely floored; he put his hands over his mouth and started breathing through the tiny gaps between his fingers. I couldn't tell if he was trying to be funny, or if he was having a seizure. I couldn't help but smile, just a bit. I could hear him speaking in mumbles behind his hands, almost as if he were repeating the news to himself, soaking in every detail, hoping he wasn't stuck in some sort of intense dream.

I chuckled and smiled, "That's why their shows are so cryptic and extravagant—they don't have a stage crew. There's no risk of exposing their secrets."

After he calmed a little, he pulled his hands from his face, but kept them cupped about eight inches from his mouth, then asked, "What about the others? Brenna, Shannoea, and Sarah? Are they Rostair too?"

"No, Brenna is Corvidae, as well as Sh-Shannoea," I stammered before I could finish. He was taking in so many things in one sitting, his fascination with it all was amazing and flattering "Sarah on the other hand is, uh," Just then, I sensed our waitress coming back to check on us.

Lucas glanced over at the entrance and saw her come through the door, before signaling me to hold onto my answer.

Her cheerful nature was the perfect intensity breaker as we responded that we currently needed nothing else.

We waited until she left again to continue our conversation. I looked at Lucas after I heard the door close. "As I was saying, we're all part of what mankind would call supernatural creatures—Sarah, Shannoea, Brenna, Nova, and Naya. We're all around, hiding in plain sight, doing our best to blend in."

He leaned back in his chair, a slightly shocked look on his face, staring into space. I knew at that point, he'd had enough for one night. I took a sip of my tea and cut into my filet, smiling, hoping to lift some of the weight from the moment. "Lucas, I just want to say, I'm sorry I worry so much. I'm also sorry that every single woman you know is something dangerous and deadly," I said, after swallowing a beautifully prepared fork-full of my filet. "I know I told you I broke sacred codes by saving your life, but I never said I'd broken any laws."

His expression changed, he snapped out of his trance and looked at me again. "Not that I'm complaining about being surrounded by deadly women, that part is unbelievably invigorating, but what do you mean by you haven't broken any laws?"

I shook my head, holding onto my reassuring smile. "The law of our people states that the White Raven is the purest of our kind. Any decree of the White Raven is a decree that *must* be followed."

He looked frightened, as if he had seen a ghost. *"I saw a white raven!"* He exclaimed in a quivering whisper. "When you brought me back to life, I saw one behind you! It glowed, looking down at us from a tree branch behind you!" He almost sounded hysterical and had it been anyone else he'd said such a thing to, they would have put him in a mental ward.

For me, however, all it did was comfort me. It was confirmation that my actions were in fact pure, not only for me, but for my race. I reached out and opened my hand as it rested on the table, inviting him to lay his hand in mine. I wanted to show him how comforted I was by what he saw that night. He slowly put his fingers into my palm and I gripped them with careful nurture.

"The fact that a human, like you, was able to see a *White Raven* at all, means only one thing," I hoped he could see the sincerity in my eyes as I spoke, the same way he'd been reading me all night. "You have a pure enough heart that you were able to see past the veils of this world. It proves how right I was, when I said you're worth far more than gold." I watched his face slowly change from fright, to one of confused excitement. "No human has seen a *true* White Raven in quite a few centuries, Lucas. For one to show itself to you is a sign of prosperity and life! – one that reaches beyond the fingers of death itself. That's why I was allowed to dive into the ethereal winds of the afterlife and carry your soul back to its body."

He looked attuned, like he understood it all. But there was still a hint of curiosity in him. "That explains why you said you needed answers about how and why you were able to bring me back to life! But what about the Rostair, or for that matter, these other races? I take it they don't care about any White Raven decree?"

"No, they don't. In fact, they want to overthrow the Corvidae. The Rostair have been the most prominent about their goal to see us driven off. They claim we're unfit to oversee human existence, saying that Corvidae have no right to drink from the souls of mortals and that it's an act of arrogance that the Corvine guide the souls of those passing into the afterlife."

He looked puzzled after I'd explained.

"The way you're saying it, almost sounds like you're agreeing, Gale?"

I was at a loss for words. I let my eyes slowly shift in all directions, stammering mentally for the right words. Deep down, Lucas *was* right. "In some aspects, Lucas, I do agree with the Rostair. I just don't think our abilities are as simplistic as everyone is making them out to be. I mean, there *must* be more to it, as well as, well, us—Corvidae, I mean." I knew he could tell I was a little aggravated by the whole ordeal, I hated everything about the entire subject, but I refused to deny him answers ever again. "Not to mention, everything that's been happening in the Corvine clans and families is starting to point in obscure directions."

He clutched my hand a bit tighter and asked, "What do you mean by obscure directions?"

"Well, for one thing, the books and schematics removed from the Loftruhm—those were seriously important tomes! Only a

Corvidae serving in the Pillar-of-Wings, a type of presidency for our kind, can remove those kinds of books from such a sacred place!"

"Unless, they were stolen," Lucas added, catching me off guard briefly.

"Highly unlikely, Lucas."

He squinted. "Well, why is it unlikely?"

"The books that are missing are wider and bigger than a fifty-seven inch television. They're thick and bound in an oakwood cover, and locked with a steel hasp." He shot an interesting look back at me and I could almost see him trying to picture a huge tome being dragged out of a heavily guarded fortress, with nobody hearing or seeing anything. I almost chuckled at his expression, his mouth half open, eyes squinted slightly. But I'd had enough marring thoughts for one evening. "Lucas, do you mind if we find something else to talk about? I don't mind answering questions, but we're going too far into what I call dark territory."

"Sure thing! I really don't wanna spoil our time together with all this mystery and secrecy. I sometimes tend to get caught up in that sort of thing." He cleared his throat. "What would you like to talk about?"

I was overjoyed he was willing to move on. It was the sort of thing I admired about him—able to leave troubles behind, able to make room for better things.

CHAPTER 22: GALE

The rest of our evening went well. Lucas and I shared stories of our lives. Even with the life he'd un-affectionately called a shut-in lifestyle, he still had plenty of things to share that managed to make me laugh.

He told me of a time when his mother had asked him to help her with dinner—once. I noted the word once, mentally, as he'd said it. She asked him to prepare mashed potatoes, so he grabbed a bag of potatoes from the pantry and a hammer. I saw exactly where the story was going and even before he had time to finish, I had my hand over my mouth, laughing hysterically. He smiled, shaking his head, letting out chortles of mutual amusement.

When it was my turn, he asked me to tell him some of the funny things that happened to me while in raven form. Instantly, I told him about a time when I'd had a snow fight with Shannoea. She was searching everywhere for me in *her* raven form and I swooped in with a clod of snow wrapped in a cloth and dropped it on her head!

He began to laugh, picturing it as I described it. I loved the innocence of it all. Every story we told was priceless, yet equal and shared fairly. I didn't want it to end. Laughing and loving the way we were at that very moment, I felt as though I'd finally found a home, a safe-haven, where I would always feel joy and comfort.

Eventually, we finished our meal and decided to take a walk under the stars. I stopped by my car and grabbed my jacket, in case Lucas got chilly, but ended up wearing it myself. For her unwitting save earlier, I left Julie a hefty one-hundred-fifty dollar tip. It was only right in my eyes that she be rewarded for saving the evening I'd been planning for days from my rush of tears and whimpers. That being said, Lucas was still having a very good time, which made it all worth so much more. We walked slowly, clutching each others' hands, still sharing stories as we made our way into the night.

I loved the warm feeling of Lucas' fingers between mine. I could almost feel his pulse through the tips of each of his fingers. It was calming. The soft glow of the moon across the details of his face complimented the shimmer in his eyes perfectly. Inside, my heart melted. He looked right at me with those gorgeous, icy-gray eyes, a warm shiver crawled over my neck and chest, and then he asked, "Can I ask you something about your past? It's nothing serious really, it's just something I started wondering when you told me your real name."

"Sure, what would you like to know?"

"What were your past names? I mean, you said you changed your name each time you moved around, so I was just wondering what some of your names were, before I'd met you."

I smiled, chuckling as I clutched his hand closer against my arm, "Do I honestly fascinate you *that* much, that you would want to know *all* my past identities, Lucas?" I felt the same familiar twinge of pride and confidence I'd experienced when he began to ask more about my past, earlier at the restaurant. It was all too surreal somehow, my complications only made him dig deeper, yet somehow, I found myself submitting. Every question he asked was a chance to step further away from my former life, a chance I burned inside to have. He nudged me gently as we made our way further into the night.

I locked eyes with him and he nodded slowly, smiling at me carefully. "You don't have to answer that if you don't want to. I'm not gonna pressure you."

That was all it took for me to fold. I smiled back and took in a gentle breath. "It's all right, I don't mind honestly. It's just, well, I've had nearly two-hundred names, so it would take quite a long time to list them all. But if you *must* know, I'll give you a few of my favorite ones." I winked. "I used to go by: Amber, Annette, Rose, Heather, Talona, Kurstie, Jeannette, Sheena, Dawn, Whitney, Trista, and Nayomi, just to name a few of the more modern-day names."

He looked dumbfounded, almost as if I'd mentally knocked him off his feet. He was silent several seconds before he reacted, "Those are names from all over the world, aren't they?"

I nodded, grinning. "The name Dawn, for instance, comes from a tribal name, Dawn-Chaser. It served as *my* label, after I'd helped a tribe of Northern Indians defend against a rival clan of ours, the Rassah-Dek, who have Corvidae blood, but use it for malevolent ends."

He got that same gleam in his eyes again—that fascinated, anxious stare that made me want to pour myself out to him, just to keep that expression on him forever. "Wait, wait, there are *evil* Corvidae, too? Good God, that must drive your people crazy!"

I closed my eyes, shaking my head, "You honestly have no idea. It's just more dark territory in my already tattered past." I knew he'd catch my drift. He was doing an exquisite job of reading my emotions, as well as my words. I knew I didn't have to try very hard to steer him away from the more shrouded areas of my life, or my culture.

He cracked a smile, then asked, "So, what about some of your earlier names? I mean, Rhune is probably *the* most exotic name I've ever heard."

Just then, I had a jewel of an idea. Something that would make this night even better. I stopped walking and looked to make sure no one was around. When I was sure the coast was clear, I turned to him. "I'll tell you what, let's forget about my past names. Instead, let's go somewhere more private and familiar, than here. Does that sound better?" I gave him my best alluring gaze, hoping he'd be pulled in by my attempt to charm him. He looked stunned, almost excited, but still unsure of what I had planned.

"Sure. That sounds fine. Are we taking the fast way or the slow way?" The coy look he shot at me was more than enough to show me his adventurous side.

I leaned in, close to his ear, and whispered, "Let's fly—I feel like stretching my wings." Before he could react, I wrapped my arms around him and jumped straight up as hard and high as I could, then, after twenty or thirty feet, I took on my raven form, wreathed in Lucas' veiled essence around me. Even within the mist against my feathers, I could feel his heart racing out of control, invigorated by the rush as I swooped toward the ground below, dodging trees and branches. I flew faster than I'd ever dared, surging through the air, gliding across the night sky.

"Gale, is it possible for me to throw up when I don't have a body? If so, you may wanna slow down, I'm feeling kinda queasy."

It wasn't long before we reached the water. "Hang on Lucas, I'll help you relieve your swimmy feeling," I told him as I plunged into the water, shooting straight in like a bullet, then recoiled, breaching the surface before sailing gently across the cool night breeze.

I felt Lucas calming down.

"Oddly enough, that actually *did* kind of help, a little." Just then, as I'd hoped, he noticed the familiar setting around him. "Is that where you are taking me to?"

"Yes, it is. We're going back to where it all *truly* started, the place where the darkness of our lives was lifted by the glow of our hearts, the place where limits were broken and the love we declared for each other made us both whole." I glided softly toward Perry's Peace Monument. Its welcoming stance held proudly against the blanket of stars above. I circled it once, then drifted down closer, until I was close enough to safely re-form without dropping Lucas from too far up. We both landed safely next to the door to the elevator, and then I released my arms from around him.

"I don't think I'll ever get used to that; it's always a thrill." he said, wiping his brow. "But why are we all soaked? I didn't think we could even *get* wet if you were in raven form and I was in, well, whatever form that is!"

I let my sopping wet hair drape over one side of my face, trying my best to give him an alluring look. "You mean, you don't like a refreshing dip in the cool night lake, every once in a while?"

"I, uh," he stumbled for words as I gazed at him, smiling with all the allure I could muster. "I'd do it again, if you asked me to," he replied bashfully, averting his eyes with a sheepish grin.

I smiled with a sigh of contentment. "Thank you, Lucas. I really needed that flight-session. My wings were getting restless."

He interjected with a raised eyebrow, "I should be the one thanking *you*! I mean, I honestly enjoy it every time! Thanks for taking me with you!"

My heart skipped a beat. I loved his quaint reactions, the way he felt as though I were gracing his life with all these experiences made me feel more at peace. I kissed his cheek then ran my finger down the length of his nose. "My pleasure, I assure you." I felt him shiver with delight. It was the cutest thing ever. It gave me a sense of importance, as well as a sense of confidence. It assured me he didn't mind, even for a split second, that he was victim to my affections, and I claimed him. He was *all mine*. I backed against the wall next to the elevator door, leading him by the arm to keep him near me.

He reached up, slowly, almost as if unsure I'd let him move without penalty, then brushed a few random strands of my soaked hair behind my ear. His fingertips gently grazed my cheek.

My breath exhaled with a soft quiver. I realized I was as much under *his* spell, as he under mine. He knew it, judging by the look on his face—a satisfied grin and a shimmer in his eyes revealed by the moon above, I was captivated all over again. I felt drawn to the very pulse of his heart as we stood in silence atop the most romantic location in our relationship, under the humbling stars of a soothing night. I leaned in closer, my eyes locked deeply with his.

"Luc," I barely managed to whisper his name before he leaned into me, locking his arms around my waist, kissing me deeply. I couldn't hold back, either, and closed my eyes, drowning in a flare of passion, hungrily aching for every part of him, giving in to his demand for my deepening affection.

I kissed him harder, driving him over the edge. His hands crawled underneath my jacket, then he dragged his nails across my lower back, all the while pulling me closer. I gasped, biting his lower-lip, allowing myself to exhale ragged and slow as his nails came to a gradual stop. The pain and pleasure matched perfectly with the taste of his lip against my tongue, sending me over a cliff of absolute bliss, reading my every urge like an open tome in the throes of the wind. I wanted him, *needed* him, and I knew he could tell. For the first time ever, I was completely helpless as I felt my heart submitting to him, and I could barely even breathe.

Every move he made was almost more than I could handle. His hands glided across the open-back of my dress, then one of them raced downward, sliding over my back-side, all the while still kissing me with sweet passion. I raised my leg slowly, wrapping it over his waist, using it to pull him as close as possible. He gently bit my lip, then tightened his grip on me before diving into another heavy kiss.

"I love you so much, Lucas," I whispered into his thoughts, *"I want to hear your voice. I want to hear you promise forever. Please, Lucas, promise that you'll give me forever."*

He moaned gently against my neck, letting our white-hot breath roll over each other. Lucas put his hand under my chin, then locked his eyes with mine and whispered, "Forever isn't long enough, Gale," he whispered back. Then he kissed me again, spiking my taut nerves. "Just like the sky wasn't black enough, during all those nights alone," he whispered then kissed me deeper "My life had no meaning before I met you." He did it a third time, nearly stealing my breath entirely, "I'll give you forever, Gale, but I promise to try and give you so much more." He kissed me yet again, then gently, he slid his hand from my chin, to the side of my neck, before breaking from my lips completely.

"What is it? What's wrong, Lucas?"

He stared into my eyes, his face soft in the moonlight, as was his expression.

"There's nothing wrong, Gale." His soft smile warmed me. I loved seeing him this way, innocently soaking in the moment we were sharing. It made him beautiful to me. "You know, I never used to notice this place before." He glanced around, then turned his attention back to me. "The water, all the trees, this monument, none of it really mattered to me, until the night I came up here. The day you shared everything with me."

I bit my lip, trying to hide my smile, but it was a useless attempt. I lowered my head, but let my eyes reach up to meet his.

"You wanna know what I've thought about, ever since that night?"

I nodded eagerly, silently holding onto my smile. My arms wrapped around his waist.

"The plain and simple truth?"

His answer confused me. My smile dropped as I felt my expression change to accommodate my confusion.

He put his hand under my chin and raised my eyes to meet his. "The truth is none of it matters without the two of us, up here, sharing everything we have."

My heart skipped a few more beats as he said it. I felt myself pull at him from the inside, as if my entire being was trying to engulf him desperately before he could find a reason to allow any space to exist between us.

"Without you, Gale, this is just a lifeless brick tower and without the life you've given me, everything around us is a dead, gray, faded painting. I think about all my decisions up to this point, all the things I scared myself out of doing and every single time I think about that night, I feel way more than relieved that I didn't turn back."

I put two fingers over his lips, hushing him. "Sshh, you're putting too much effort into reflection and not enough on who you are *now*, Lucas. You're here, with me, and you're happy and safe. I've watched you grow as a person," our eyes remained locked deeply "in a short span of time. I've watched you become stronger and braver and far more confident than the first day we met. I realize it must've been difficult for you when I asked you to come alone, but when you did, I showed you how even a woman like me, who fought countless battles, killed numerous foes, and spent ageless years alone in the dark, has scars of loneliness." I watched his eyes tear up softly as I spoke. "I was just as frightened as you were, that night. In fact, I spent the entire day crying, thinking I was about to scare you off." My eyes joined his with tears of remembrance. "I showed you the craven side of me, Lucas."

He wiped his eyes, then wiped mine with his thumb.

I shook a little, remembering the worry I'd felt, but the feel of him wiping my tear-soaked face was comforting beyond all measure.

"That's exactly what I'm talking about."

I didn't understand what he was trying to say, or where he was leading the topic; all I knew was whenever he stood up and spoke his mind, it meant he'd given the subject serious, careful thought.

"You've spent a lot of your life trying to escape from the dangerous side, the secrets, the shadows, the endless nights of hunting and fighting and now you've found me. Someone you trust; someone you find blissfully simple!"

I shook my head softly, still confused as to what he was saying, "Yes, as I've said before, but why are you bringing this up again?"

"Because, I want you to know—" he shook his head quickly, correcting himself. "No, I *need* you to know that you don't have to do any of it alone, ever again, Gale."

I could hardly believe my ears! He almost sounded like a completely different person! This fragile human being, a mortal bearing no other gift, aside from a kind and pure heart, was claiming protective rights over *me*! The stern look in his eyes was more than enough to give me assurance that he was willing to die, in order to back his statement. I felt a cold chill quickly rush over me. I could hardly find a breath in me or words to express myself. All I could do was stand there stunned, silent, and humbled.

He put his palm on my cheek and smiled. "Don't run away from it anymore, Gale. Instead, let's face it, together! I don't want to spend my entire life doing nothing but directing traffic on a ferry, playing video games, and watching videos! I'd rather toss myself over the side of this monument all over again, just to feel the thrill of you catching me, like the first time we kissed!" He gestured the motions of himself falling, making me chuckle. I put my hand over my mouth to stop myself, but he took it and placed it over his heart. "I'm only a human being, Gale. I might live to see eighty-five, maybe ninety at best. I'd hate to think I'd wasted my life in my parents' house, when I have an amazing woman in my life, who can fly anywhere in the world in the blink of an eye."

I blushed more than ever before. I tried to turn my head, but my eyes kept sneaking back to his darling face. I couldn't help but smile; he was far too smooth a talker and I was hardly in the mood to fend off his charm. "Lucas, you're making me blush."

"All I'm saying is that you don't have to give up *every* aspect of who you are. Everything about you fascinates me. I know, I've said it hundreds of times, but it's true!"

The redness in my cheeks grew hotter with every word he spoke.

"I want to experience your world! See it, feel it and hear it! I know I sound like I'm out of character, right now, and I also realize I may be asking a lot, but there are times when I feel like going *crazy* from boredom!"

At that moment, I finally figured out what he'd been trying to tell me. He wanted to be assured I would help him get away from the tedium of everyday life in Ohio and whisk the two of us to wherever the winds rested.

I gathered myself, fighting off the redness in my cheeks and neck, trying to find the right words. After a few seconds, I was able to speak my mind, "I would gladly take you anywhere you desired, from the tip of every mountain, to the furthest reach of every ocean. The ends of the earth will forever be ours."

He smiled at my reply, but then, I became serious in return. "But I refuse to willingly allow you to see the darker side of my life, Lucas. All the malice and secrecy, being at the razor edge of diplomacy and total war—those are things I cannot and *will not* allow you to experience." I hoped that if he was still able to read me, as well as he had been the entire night, he would see how serious I was about keeping him far out of reach of the shadows in my life. "I don't want that for either of us," I went on to say.

"I don't want that part either! I'm saying, forget about *that* part, but be proud of who you are, Gale! You seem so ashamed of what you are, but you shouldn't be!"

"Why should I be proud to drink from anyone's soul, I don't see how that is anything short of barbaric."

He leaned in, holding his forehead to mine and out of nowhere I heard the faintest whisper in my thoughts, "Because

I'm proud of you; because I'm proud to *know* you; proud to have you, and very proud to be the *one* you come to, whenever you think you're alone."

I stiffened and my eyes shot open wide as I gasped. He was speaking to me mentally! I listened with bated breath.

"I don't know how I'm able to do this right now and, to me, it doesn't matter. What matters is that our relationship is strong enough to allow it! Details are sometimes overrated, but loving someone isn't and neither is the distance a person is willing to go for another person to prove it! I've started to feel more and more proud of myself, every single day I wake up with you in my life, Gale. I'm starting to see I needed a purpose, and that purpose is *you*."

I started to cry.

He backed away from me carefully, then ran his fingers through his hair.

I stared at him, tears streaming down my face, struggling to speak, "Oh, my God, Lucas! How did you do that?!" I choked up. The weight of it all was more than I could handle. I put both of my hands over my mouth, trying desperately to hold back every mixed emotion threatening to flood over me.

"I honestly don't know. I just figured it had something to do with what you mentioned about having side-effects from when you fed on me."

I took several deep breaths. The situation demanded explanation, to be sorted out and it rested on my shoulders to do so, before it could go any further.

"I remember saying that, but there's never been a recorded case where a human can speak mentally! It requires you creating a mental bridge, from one mind, to another! That part alone takes several years for a Corvidae to master! It was different when I was speaking to you, because you were simply crossing the bridge I'd already created!"

He shrugged his shoulders. "I guess I'm a quick learner, then. It's like I said, though, none of it matters. What matters is us!" He put his hands on my shoulders, shaking his head. "I just don't care about the details, Gale. Even if all these changes are permanent! My life changed for the better the second you walked into it and now I'm saying to hell with the rules, to hell with secrets and misery! Something is changing between us, it's changing our world, the one you and I share, and for once..." he moved in, then put his hand through my hair slowly, "...I'm not afraid. I know you'll be there with me, standing right at my side, and I promise to do the same for you."

He was right. Something was changing our world. Everything we saw in each other was becoming more vibrant, more alive; even the tone in his voice, when he spoke of enduring it all beside me, sounded sturdier and committed.

"Are you truly so sure this is what you want, Lucas? I mean, once you see the horizons of my world, there's no turning back." I tilted my head to rest it lovingly in his hand. "The other Corvidae, not to mention all other creatures and races, will be able to sense my energies within you. They'll know what I've done, and they'll try to destroy us both! I want to do as you ask, I honestly do, but the selfish part of me wants to keep you hidden away, far from danger!"

"But you're not safe, Gale! Your dad knows you saved my life; he also knows you haven't been bringing the souls of the recently deceased to him—since you left him that day! How long will it take until your dad has to answer to someone about that?" He broke away from me, then leaned against the railing of the balcony. "Corvidae obviously take their jobs seriously and if they find out he delayed telling whoever it is he answers to, they may hold him accountable! I don't want him being punished for something *we* decided to do!"

In all honesty, I hadn't even considered the fact. I looked at myself inwardly, but with great shame. I inadvertently placed my own father in grave danger by rebelling against him. He may have been able to help me find a suitable way to avert disaster. Would he have favored my decision to save Lucas' life? In my heart, I was still sure he would never see things from my perspective—that there is far more to life than duty. Even so, I still felt guilty. I could only imagine how hard it was for Lucas to find a way to say it. Such a thing would have sounded harsh to an ignorant heart. I wasn't sure where to go with my thoughts. What started as a simple choice had turned into a web of complexity. I contended with the notion that Alexander was more than capable in handling the situation on his end, but what would I be facing, should Lucas suffer for my actions?

"I told you, I've broken no law among my people. My father has more sway than you realize, Lucas. He will not answer for a thing, but they *will* hunt for you and I." I wasn't trying to sway him from his choice to see my world for himself. If nothing else, I needed him to know the full gravity of this newfound choice he was making. "I'm not saying you don't have a valid point, he does face danger because of my saving your life, but the true danger comes when the Rostair hear about it. They've tried for ages to find a way to harness our powers, using dark sciences. If they find an exiled Corvidae, they always try to capture them alive to experiment on them looking for ways to add our energy to theirs, making it possible to overthrow us with our own blood in their veins!"

"So we're in more danger than your dad, is that what you're saying?"

I nodded slowly. "Luckily, however, I have Shannoea and the others to back me up, should things turn for the worst."

"What about Nova and Naya, can they back you up too?"

"No, they're mostly neutral to any cause, even for their own kind. They've been known to get involved if they feel bored enough, or if their career somehow hangs in the balance, but otherwise, I've only seen them active in the ranks of Rostair affairs during the earlier ages." I pictured many times I'd heard others of my kind speak of battles and such, during which Nova and Naya disguised themselves as servant-girls in a bath-house in Greece, slaying many in secret, who apparently discovered the existence of both the Rostair and the Corvidae. Those slain were later eaten, leaving only the bones to dispose of. An entire army vanished in a week because of their efforts, leaving their leader no choice but to throw himself at the mercy of the emperor, who had him thrown in prison for madness. I grinned at the morbidly fond memories I had of those two and their mischief.

"Then, if your dad has things well in hand on his end and your friends are willing to defend us," he hopped onto the ledge, holding his arms straight out to his sides. "There's nothing stopping us! Show me the world through your eyes again, Gale. Show me everything!"

He'd broken the dreariness of the mood perfectly. I didn't even notice I'd blithely walked right into his attempt to goad me into fulfilling his desire to see what kind of world I'd lived in before the blissful pleasure of having him in my life. I was cornered, but it gave me an idea. "How about another flight, but this time, let's make things more interesting, just for you?" I winked.

"What did you have in mind?" he asked, puzzled.

I walked toward him slowly. As I did, I gathered a pulse of Corvine energy, inhaling deeply before allowing it to glow around me. The dark swirls of purple danced playfully across my entire body.

Lucas squatted down on the railing, mouth agape. "Wow, what is—" he attempted to ask.

I broke into his question, releasing the gathered energy into an arc of bright purple lightning, which spiked into the clouds, rumbling beyond our sight above.

"I used some of my energy to send out a signal; one that will call someone familiar to join us."

Just as I'd explained, Shannoea swooped in, her human form still intact, but her large, onyx raven wings spanned from her back. She landed next to me, flapping her wings a few times before folding them neatly behind her. "You rang?" She smiled, winking at me.

I smiled back at Lucas, who was gawking at us both, "You see, I can disperse a beacon of my energy, to call on any one of my friends. The signal was specially attuned to Shannoea and she was able to find me, in seconds!"

Lucas nearly fainted. *"You can keep your human form and have your wings out? That's totally amazing!"* He exclaimed, almost oblivious to my explanation. *"Gale, can you do that too?"* His eyes nearly fell from his head as he shot his attention to me.

I put my hands on my hips. "Sadly, no. While I'd love to have such a trait, each Corvidae inherits a different array of gifts. Shannoea *can* transform into raven form, but has the ability you've just witnessed as well."

She stepped closer to us, grinning from the flattery, as well as having a coy shine in her eyes. "That's not all. I can even hypnotize my targets in both forms and I can make each feather on my wings as sharp as a razorblade! Sharp enough to cut through tempered steel, baby!" She was showing off by such bragging, but neither I nor Lucas minded. She never had many occasions where she was able to feel appreciated, so to her and I this was a special treat.

He marveled at her as he hopped from the ledge. His face lit up as she approached him, slowly wrapping her wings around him from nearly seven feet away. He hesitated, but eventually, his curiosity overcame him and he ran his fingers over a few of the longest quills at the tip of her wing.

"It's like black silk!" he said in almost a whisper. "Can I see them, when they're sharp?"

She crossed her arms in front of her then nodded. "As long as you're careful, honey. I don't need Gale harping on me for cutting your hand off or anything!"

He took his hand from her wing and she clenched up, causing her quills to sheath over with shimmering black, crystalline edges. Each one glistened with deadly majesty. He was more careful this time, as he ran his fingertips over the side of a few of her quills.

"This is blowing my mind! It's just so incredible—I don't know how to tell you how awesomely cool this is! Seriously, this is beyond amazing, Shannoea!" I watched as he chuckled in amazement, shaking his head slowly as he stared into her wingspan, still gliding his fingers over each quill.

"Why don't we go for a ride, Gale? Looks like your man needs some air after being so close to us Goddesses of the night sky!" She gave me a glimpse of a smile and I nodded in return.

"Why not? It isn't everyday a mortal has the honored company of two Corvidae!" I replied in the same playfully arrogant tone Shannoea used. I knew Lucas well enough to know, he saw us as glorified celebrities. Shannoea always made it difficult to fight the urge to be dashing and daring when she was instigating it. "Well, Lucas, you did say you wanted to see my world. Now is your chance!"

"It's a chance I've wanted for a long time. Even before I knew you were out there, I've wanted a chance like this, Gale. I don't wanna waste another second, let's do this!" His words were full of enthusiasm. Before I could react, he dove over the railing, disappearing over the side.

Shannoea quickly looked at me and then back to the rail. "Did he? What the *hell?! Gale! Luke just—are you kidding me?!*"

Her shock was enough to make me laugh a bit. I gingerly rolled my eyes above a guilty grin. "It's a long story. Come on; let's go catch him, before he hits the bottom!" I dove after him, shooting toward him as he plummeted toward the unforgiving pavement below. I sensed Shannoea close behind me as I met him halfway down. Our eyes locked, he shot a strong smile directly at me, one of trust and assurance.

I grabbed him, pulling him close to me as I began to take on raven form. Just before I did, he leaned in and spoke into my ear, "I knew you'd catch me. Just like you said you always would. That's how I know you really do love me and that's why I promised you forever. I'll always love you, Gale."

"I love you as well, Lucas. I'll never allow you to fall from me. The winds of the night will always carry me to you, never letting distance, nor trial stand between us." I almost felt his heart glowing as I finished transforming, causing me to feel the same twinge within my being. "Now, let's enjoy the anxious call of the night. Shannoea and I want to show you a flight to remember!" With that, I swooped back up, spinning like a top until I was able to level out at a higher altitude.

Shannoea joined me, flying just above us.

"All right, you two, enough of the mushy stuff! Let's do some serious air-time!" she exclaimed, banking to the right, then swooping into a dive roll.

I followed behind her as we sailed and chased into the drifting winds, dodging around people and trees, vehicles, and buildings of all sorts. This night belonged to the three of us and we would claim every single moment, nothing was going to stand in our way.

CHAPTER 23: LUCAS

My eyes crept open, the soreness was short lived, but the light from the window was unbearable. Suddenly, I felt Gale lean onto the bed. She climbed on top of me and draped her hair over the ray of light that tried to blind me.

"Thank God for that gorgeous hair of yours. I thought I was gonna be stuck seeing that bright green splotch in my vision all day," I chuckled with a painful yawn.

She smiled, "I'm glad you're awake. Did you have fun last night?" I barely even heard her question. I stared into her eyes as I stretched my legs. They fluctuated between their normal burnt sienna and a faint swirl of lavender.

"Gale, your eyes—is something wrong? They're acting strange, like you may have to feed, again."

She cleared her throat, "Uh, yeah, I hadn't realized how much energy I used to send out that signal to Shannoea, last night." She almost seemed sheepish about it, like she felt guilty, "I don't want you to worry about it, Lucas." Her answer did not amuse me at all. When she acted like it was some sort of inconvenience for her to have to feed on me, it was annoying. If she needed to be reminded of how willing I was to satisfy her, then I'd gladly do it.

I put my hand on the back of her neck, pulling her down to

me, until her lips touched my collarbone. "Lucas..." She tried to act resistive, but I knew her instincts were telling her to take whatever I was willing to give.

"I've already told you, Gale, you don't have to feel guilty or ashamed. Drink from me, take all you need." I held onto the back of her neck, tightening my grip until she understood my sincerity. I felt her lips grow hot, the pain lanced over me, I held my breath, clutching the blankets with my other hand. Several minutes passed and she lifted herself from me. I felt a cold breath crawl over me as she poured some of my essence back into me. It was enough to calm my nerves, as well as wake me up completely.

"Thank you," she whispered, kissing me gently.

"Anytime, you know that." I ran my palm over her ear and neckline, "Don't take this the wrong way, Gale, but honestly, I can't help wondering why you're using up so much of your energy." She sat up at the edge of the bed, while I uncovered myself, then stood up next to her. "I did have fun last night, by the way." My mind swirled with pain from Gale's feeding, but was still conscious enough to recall the details.

She gave me a quick glance, but averted her eyes to the mirror I had standing in the corner, next to my dresser. "I think it's because it actually takes energy to pour energy back into a living body. Since I've never done it until I met you, I can only assume that as the explanation."

The guilt of questioning her about it fell on me almost

instantly. She was already reluctant enough when it came to feeding on me. I half expected her to vow against feeding on me forever, just for asking about it!

To my surprise she leaned in and kissed my cheek. Then she whispered into my ear, "Don't act as if I don't drive you crazy, when I'm drinking deep into you," her extremely hot breath sent violent chills over me, "I can tell you love the pleasure and the pain as much as I enjoy the flavor of ever single drop you willingly pour into me." She had me on that one, and she was right. I had fallen in love with the experience. My face turned red as she lightly bit down on my earlobe, then slowly pulled at it, until it recoiled from her teeth.

"When you do things like that, you make me wanna give you more every time," I said, even before I'd thought about it.

Her eyes lit up, followed by her smile. "Don't tempt me, I'm still thirsty enough, I assure you." Her hand slowly crossed my chest then rested on my stomach. "But I want you to be conscious enough to enjoy your day, as well as the night."

I tried to sneak the blanket over my lap, but it was too late, her eyes narrowed above her sly grin. She'd caught me, just as I attempted to hide my fully excited lower region. She was eating up her victorious moment, the same way she drank from my soul like a ravening goddess. It hurt worse than the day I'd gotten beat to death, but the fact that such a gorgeous creature was so close to me, tasting every drop of my inner-being made everything about it simply beautiful.

She pulled the blanket, putting it back where it was before I'd grabbed it, giggling warmly, "I don't mind, Lucas." her eyes glided down to my out-stretched, fully pitched black boxers, then back to my apple-red face. "I think it's rather flattering that I have this effect on you." The way she spoke took the feeling out of both my legs, my chest went cold, and I got redder in the face, as my boxers tented even more in reaction. If she came anywhere near me at that point, or dared to touch me at all, I was gonna lose control and be in dire need of another pair of boxers.

She started to lean in closer, but I grabbed the blanket and jumped out of bed, holding onto it for dear life while letting it drape down over my lower half. "Uh, I, uh, I think I need a quick shower!" I shook the words out like sand from a beach towel.

Her eyes stared at me hungrily, playing with my nerves from clear across the room.

"A, um, shower, cold, nice." I'd lost so much circulation in my head from her seductive toying, I scrambled my escape phrase like an idiot!

She giggled at my stumbling attempts to gather myself, making it even harder to compose myself.

"Why a shower, do you have plans for the day? I mean, it is your day off, you know." She shot me a shy wink as she stood up from the bed.

I stumbled in mid-thought, hoping she hadn't planned on finishing what she started, or maybe hoping she would. "I, uh, I don't have any plans, not for the day, that is." I could hardly inhale a single breath, I was against the wall, still clutching the blanket.

She stood with her finger on my chest, slowly tracing small figure-eights all over. "What about tonight, then? Do you happen to have any plans?" Her voice was a bit querulous and gave me the sensation that she was curious about me in some way. She backed away and leaned against my art desk. "I mean, you know a lot about me, but aside from your art and a few finer details, I don't really know much about you!"

Honestly, I had no idea on where to start. I'd never thought much of myself which was more than enough to stifle any answer I could come up with. The only thing that came to mind was something I was used to doing every third week of the month. I hesitated as it seemed extremely nerdy. I felt a heavy straining clench in my gut. If I told the truth, I knew she'd burst out laughing and leave forever. I stared into those gorgeous eyes of hers and began to melt. The purple had gone away and was replaced by the warming swirl of faint red, cascading in a sea of forest brown. The innocent look she gave me numbed my worry. "Well, I usually meet with my friends online and play video games. I have a game room in the basement. We play at least once a month, give or take. Nothing fancy." I watched her eyes light up, like I'd just given her an idea.

Deep down, I hoped she was interested in joining us, I remembered her video game collection in her room from the night she'd saved me. I badly wanted to see her skills. Not only that, but a very mischievous part of me wanted to show her off to my friends—the greatest thing to ever happen to a guy like me. I wanted everyone to see her with me, to make them all jealous, maybe even envious. My friends were the type to talk big, but never back it up with dedication of any sort. They wanted to be game designers, movie directors, and writers, but whenever the opportunity presented itself, they gave themselves reasons and excuses to back out. I'd always hated that part of them and being surrounded by their kind of influence made it hard to be ambitious, but whenever Gale was around, I felt like a champion. I knew she'd already changed my life, but somehow, somewhere in the back of my heart and mind, I knew she would change me even more.

She stood silent for nearly two seconds before she smiled and said, "Oh wow! You have a *game room*?! That sounds like an absolute blast!"

I couldn't help but grin at her. It seemed so out of the ordinary for a woman to be enthusiastic over anything related to video games, aside from Super Mario Brothers.

"I wish I had a place like that to go to. I loved going to the arcades during the eighties and nineties, but now, whenever I get a chance, I play online games."

It was like she was singing to me and I nearly melted into the floor when she'd mentioned going to arcades. I held back the urge to faint.

"Nowadays, I've only been able to play online or locally

with Shannoea. She's really good at first-person-shooters, like *Call of Duty* and *Unreal*."

I tried to keep my composure. Then I cleared my throat and said, "Well, tonight I've only got three friends coming over; Dwayne, Jimmy, and Melissa. They're pretty nice, once you get to know them." I said.

She tilted her head to one side, "What games will you be playing tonight?"

A coy smile on my face, she saw it I could tell, but I still pretended to think about it, like I was going through a huge library of games, picking the perfect ones for our night of adventure. "I was thinking, maybe, *Left 4 Dead* and *Grand-Theft-Auto IV*. Then maybe we'll finish up with some *Mortal Kombat*, or even *Street Fighter*. What do you think?" I grinned, hoping that having one familiar title in there would be enough to rope her in.

"I think that sounds like a fantastic list, for a fantastic night of fun! All those games sound really good, despite the fact that I only have two of the four you mentioned."

I stiffened up, "Two? Which two do you have?" I remembered every title stacked next to her console, but out of the list I'd given her, I only remembered *Left 4 Dead*.

"*Left 4 Dead* and *Ultimate Mortal Kombat 3*, I used to play them a lot, until I started dating you, that is." She winked at me.

I could hardly believe my ears, she actually played *Mortal Kombat*, one of my all time favorite games! I could hardly contain myself; everything about her was beyond perfect! A gorgeous woman, incredible intelligence, topped off with an interest in video games! The kind of woman any guy like me would die for!

I'd completely forgotten that she could have downloaded games onto her hard-drive! Even so, I didn't expect her reaction! No laughter, no scoffing, or eyes rolled at me; just a playful grin coupled with a shine in her eyes. Overcome with relief and joy I wiped the cold sweat from my forehead and let out a comforted sigh.

She walked over and placed her hand on my collar, tilted her head to one side, and stared at me with a gentle, yet piercing look. "Lucas, you don't suppose I could join you, tonight, do you?" The hopeful stare she gave me, nearly made me fall over from sheer bliss alone, but the feel of her gentle, warm breath on my face and neck made me blush. I held my breath and slowly nodded as I fought off yet another embarrassing growth from below deck. All my devious dreams were about to come true, tonight.

Her face lit with joy

Seeing her so happy about being involved in my life gave me a sense of elevated delight I'd never felt before. It proved almost as surreal as our night together, sharing our first kiss in mid free-fall, and then flying as a raven over the waves of the lake.

She rooted through my dresser, picking out the clothes she liked and handed them to me. "I think you'd look stunning in this outfit, Lucas. Go get your cold shower, then try this on." She winked before opening the door to my bathroom.

I didn't feel awkward over her rummaging through my dresser. My mom did it all the time as I grew up, so to me, it was just another part of any relationship around me, be it family or girlfriend. I had forgotten that I'd confessed to needing a cold shower, in order to hide my arousal from her seduction earlier. I groaned on the inside; I hated cold showers.

"Maybe I should take one a little later, I'm awake enough, now." I fought off the urge to blush, I knew she'd caught me trying to calm myself down; my shy physical nature seemed to give her a new sense of power over me that brought her immense joy.

I walked past her just as her cell phone chimed, signaling a text message. She pulled it out and read the screen. "Brenna and the others want to meet with me today, they say it's urgent. I guess they want to meet in Cleveland." She didn't sound enthusiastic, this was something she obviously felt forced to do. I slid on the new pair of black cargo pants she'd handed me and put on the fresh pair of socks.

"Well, if it's urgent, Gale, then you should go! I mean, it's not as if I had any real plans to begin with." I said, pulling the new shirt on. As I left the bathroom, I saw her staring out the window. She turned and leaned against the sill with a dissatisfied frown.

Her phone went off again, signaling another text message. She pulled it out and read the screen, then let the phone fall onto her chest with a heavy sigh. "That was Brenna, yet again. She wants to know if I'm ready to meet with her and the others. I'm sorry, Lucas, I really wish I could stay, but I can't. I swear, it's as if she knows I'm having a good time and wants to stifle it, just to go shopping."

"I know how that is. I've had friends like that before. Tell you what, just go get it over with and I'll be here most of the day, playing a few games with Brent online. If anything changes, I'll text you."

She carefully rolled onto me, letting her phone slide onto the bed as she pinned my arms down by the wrists. I tensed as her hair draped over both sides of my face; it felt like I was trapped inside a silk tunnel with a playful goddess staring at me, a hungry grin on her lips. She closed her eyes and lowered her lips to mine, kissing me until my legs went numb, which didn't take long at all. She pulled away gently, letting her mouth barely touch mine, her nose brushing the side of my own.

I lay there, pinned down, letting her steal my breath with hers. I loved the feel of her heartbeat against me. Through small, bated breaths, I managed to faintly pick up the aroma of her hair. It swirled my senses, lilacs and cherry blossoms permeated every cascading inch around me. I was in absolute ecstasy.

She opened her eyes slowly, locking with mine. "I wish I could kiss you forever, Lucas, but since cruel reality plays its hand on another flawless moment, I'll try and hurry back as soon as I can." Her low whispers poured over my neck, making my hair stand on end with excitement, thrilling me all over.

"God, I love when you do that, Gale." I said, closing my eyes.

She tilted her head to one side and whispered, "Do what?"

I couldn't believe I'd said anything, the thrill must've overpowered my shyness. I lifted my head, doing the same as she'd done, I held myself just out of the reach of her lips and whispered, "I love when you talk the way you do and when you take my breath away. The way your heartbeat feels against me; I feel like I'm drowning in you. I love everything about it."

She blushed deeply, which made me follow suit. "Don't tease. I'll never be able to leave if you talk like that."

Slowly, she gathered herself, making sure her hands slid teasingly down my arms, over my chest and across my stomach as she stood. Tingles spiked across every path her hands had taken, even through my shirt, it was enough to cause goose-bumps across most of my upper body. She was clearly milking every second, trying not to rush off. It made me smile inside and out.

She ran her hands through her hair then walked to the window.

I got up and went to her. "Have a good time, Gale," I said with a smile. I unlocked the window and opened it.

She winked and said, "You'll be the only important thing on

my mind. And, I'll miss you."

I felt the slight shade of red stain my cheeks before she morphed into her raven form and hopped onto my arm.

Gale leaned forward, nestling her head against mine. *I love you, Lucas. I'll return to you, as soon as I can, my knight.* I heard her say, deep in my thoughts.

"I love you too, Gale. Be careful, I don't want you getting hurt or anything."

She gave me a soft, reassuring caw, then spread her wings, and flew off. I watched her climb into the clouds, vanishing behind them. It didn't matter how many times I saw it, watching her change into a raven, was a marvel. Watching her fly was beyond what words could express. I stared at the clouds she'd flown through; the feeling of separation wasn't as painful this time. I knew she'd be back, that she felt a need to be with me. It still hurt not to have her near me, but it was a pain worth enduring.

I walked over to my TV and turned on the video game console. Just as I sat on the edge of the bed, I felt an ache course through my hands. Almost as if they mourned at the thought of not resting between her fingers, the way I'd grown accustomed during our relationship. I pulled out my phone and sat it next to me, then pressed the button on the controller to start the game. I saw Brent's avatar and profile picture right away. He was already online, waiting for me to join in the action. I pressed the start button again and was thrown into the heat of battle, without warning. Even between the explosions, the bullets, and the hordes of enemy soldiers, I found myself glancing from the screen to the silent cell phone lying silent next to me.

I sighed and smiled to myself. This time, I felt stronger. This time, I knew she was out there thinking of me, loving me, wanting nothing more than to be at my side, forever. I made my character lock and load his gun, then had him kick open the nearest door and mow down everything that moved. Even though it was a game, it was a symbol in my eyes. A symbol that signified a cornerstone in the way I once lived and how I planned to start living from here, on. This was my time and I planned to make every moment in my life count. Every shell spent in this game, symbolized a chance I'd taken. Every bullet landed, a surge of bravery, courage, and maturity. In my own secret world, I wasn't just playing a video game; in my bedroom, I was also secretly becoming so much more on the inside.

CHAPTER 24: GALE

From: Brenna - *We need 2 talk. Urgent. Meet @ Lonz. Tell ur bf we r shopping in Cleveland.*

I read the text shortly after landing on Middle-Bass-Island, where Brenna and the others waited at the old Lonz Winery. I hated lying, most of all to Lucas. I didn't know what made them want to come to such a secluded place, but it must've been as urgent as Brenna had claimed, if Sarah and Shannoea let her send the text. I put my phone back into my pocket and walked along the little road that lead to Lonz itself. The familiar salmon-colored sign with red lettering welcomed me high above the faded brick of the building. The bushes and shrubs still hugged this place as warmly as they had long before the fires of the nineteen hundreds repeatedly claimed it. I smiled, walking slowly up the staircase to the loft-deck, thinking of each vintage memory of this place, as though it were mere hours ago.

This humble building had seen much over the years; dignitaries of all kinds, social gatherings, prohibition, and even battle. Many rival clans and races attempted assassinations here, staging fires and attacks in order to topple their opposition, anyway they could. I heard the others inside already, just as I'd stepped onto the deck surrounded by a thick wooden guardrail.

The door opened and Shannoea walked out followed by

Brenna and Sarah. None of them were smiling. I leaned back against the railing, watching them glance at one another.

Then Brenna stepped forward and spoke first, "We have a bit of a dilemma. The Rostair, have been rather busy, Gale. There's been a multitude of killings in the area and even a few sightings." Her tone was cold as always, but had a tinge of concern. "We need to go to your father, ask him for assistance, and bring them down before things get out of hand."

I raised an eyebrow. "Killings? What do you mean—? " I didn't get a chance to ask, before Sarah answered.

"Humans, Gale. They aren't only killing animals, anymore. There's been fifteen human deaths and several animals have turned up dead at the city zoo in Cleveland." She looked me deep in the eyes, and said in a serious tone, "All of them were mangled and drained of most of their blood."

That was all it took for my breath to freeze in my throat. I pictured a pile of animal carcasses, shadowy figures standing over them, blood dripping from their hands and teeth, eyes insane with death-lust. I felt a draft of cold air rush over my arms and the back of my neck. Combined with the thought of them, it caused me to shudder.

Shannoea looked distressed. I wasn't used to seeing her so concerned. It made me feel more uneasy. She was usually my only bearing when it came to sanity, during a time of urgency or crisis, but this time she looked soaked with dread over the situation. I turned to Brenna once more, who looked ready for action, as always. I could tell she was worried, but I imagined it was a deep welling concern over getting her new outfit dirty. "Do you know how many there are? Or for that matter, what they're after?" I asked the three of them, hoping for once that the answer would be simple.

Shannoea spoke softly, "If they're killing humans, then I'm betting they're a Mongrel-Class—at best, sloppy newborns of some sort. It's hard to get a head-count until you're actually near them in the field."

Sarah nodded her agreement as Brenna folded her arms leaning to one side in stern protest.

"This is absolutely ridiculous, a waste of time!" Brenna growled. "Here we are, rambling about a handful of brutish mongrels, when they're out there, spilling blood and gore all about the land!"

I agreed with a nod. She was right. If they were here in Ohio, or even in town, something needed to be done. Normally, their presence would have gone unchallenged, but when their behavior becomes erratic, we're forced to step in and take action, to reestablish balance and justice. I hated doing it, putting myself in danger for a cause I barely wanted any involvement in. On the other hand, I didn't want Lucas getting hurt, should they pick up my scent on him. Secretly, during the kiss I gave him before leaving, I placed a redolent scent-mark on him—a fragrant trail from my hands and lips—to make it easy to track him should anything go wrong. I had a bad feeling when Brenna sent me the text, asking me to lie to him.

In the back of my mind, I knew my actions were justified. The scent-mark would last mere hours and I hoped he wouldn't figure out what I had done. Even if he washed his face, or his arms, the scent would stay on him. Yet, even behind the self-justified notions I gave myself, I still felt guilty for marking him without telling him.

"Gale! Are you paying any attention?" Brenna exclaimed, breaking through my thoughts.

I snapped back to the situation, hoping I hadn't missed anything dire. I glanced at each of them, "Um, sorry. I...uh, I just have a lot on my mind."

"By a lot, you mean you have a lotta Luke on your mind, don't you?" Shannoea chimed in with a witty smile.

Brenna scoffed, "I still cannot believe you're seeing him! You do realize, he's going to leave you, the moment you tell him what you are, don't you? A human dating a Corvidae is just plain wrong! It's not natural!"

"Brenna! Will you please stop badgering her about that, please?" Out of nowhere, Sarah interjected catching us all off guard. "It isn't your place to tell her how to live. You're being far more uncouth and your attitude is more addled than usual, and if nothing else, it's getting a old!"

Brenna's mouth hung open slightly, her eyes dilated with anger and vulnerability. Only on a select few occasions did Sarah speak out against Brenna, but when she did, not only did Brenna pay attention and heed her words, but so did the rest of us. Her anger was something the three of us had witnessed one time and it quickly became something the three of us never discussed, or provoked.

The silence between the group lasted several seconds before I broke it by clearing my throat. "Thank you, Sarah. Lucas isn't going to leave me. I've already told him everything about us— what we are, what we do, *everything*."

They looked stunned; even Brenna looked far beyond shocked! They stared at me, eyes widened, faces frozen.

"You what?" Brenna gasped, "Gale, the Ravenic Order is going to *kill* him and perhaps even *you*, when they find out! The Corvus Avian family will be tossed out and exiled from their territory, for this! It's *treason*, Gale! *What the hell were you thinking?"*

I glanced at Shannoea, who remained quiet and reserved. I knew she wasn't ashamed of keeping secrets. She was doing a good job of fulfilling her promise, by acting as if I hadn't told her a thing.

"I wasn't *thinking* anything, Brenna!" I shot back.

She whispered something snide in French under her breath, which made me even more furious.

"I did what I had to do; it wasn't an easy choice! The choice was made *for* me; just before I was about to pull his soul from him, *I saw it!*" I had everyone's attention now. Their eyes all raised to stare at me at the exact same time.

Sarah tilted her head. "Wait, you don't mean...?"

Shannoea looked at her then glanced back at me, still pretending to be caught off guard, whereas Brenna raised only one eyebrow as she maintained her stone cold expression.

"I do. The White-Raven came to me; it told me to save his life! The White-Raven's word is law, in the Corvidae lineage. And so is the vow of fidelity I gave to Lucas, just before I left my father and my home behind me."

"Tef Cihs Ravi, The White-Raven," Shannoea whispered the words in old Avish to herself.

It wasn't often that my friends were stunned or confused by anything we'd been through. But the way they reacted now gave the impression that Brenna and Sarah were having a hard time believing me.

Sarah cut in, *"Er unde' silont, Gale? Ver luhrnsikarra, nir hurut unde' adeemt ym?"*

I didn't know what compelled Sarah to speak our old language; whether it was the sheer weight of such a heavy revelation, or the surrounding area—a place which held as much history as we had shared in Ohio. Either way, it didn't matter. I, for one, was enjoying the sound of our ancient, native tongue from my dearest friends.

I wasn't the least bit surprised that Sarah wanted to know, just as my father did, about whether I was sure I'd seen the White-Raven. I looked at her and smiled as I assured her, *"Nir adeemt ym. "*

I knew she wanted to know the reasons, so when she asked if I saved Lucas' life for loves sake, or by command of the White-Raven's decree, I gladly answered, *"Ohn vos iknuntes."*

She smiled warmly. "You did it on *both* accounts? Gale, you're so lavishly romantic, I just love it!" she chimed, breaking away from our Avish tongue while giggling at me.

I couldn't help but join in her playful reaction, I giggled as much as she did. It lightened the mood greatly.

"Unde' bivorhnen yhunsima si meha?" Sarah asked, glancing back at Brenna and Shannoea, then to me.

I nodded once, slowly.

Sarah was completely stunned. I'd forgotten I hadn't told any of them, except Shannoea, about vowing myself to him until now, so the way she'd asked if I had almost came off as objective. Then, her face lit up with a glimmer of joy. *"Gale, domi'es yimcydekk! Tef Cihs-Ravi jes uttemn unde'! Qoh unde' ealdi vohu noll thi'hes venn deshu a'Corvidae tiat felav cyne's?*

I was relieved to see her smiling, a sparkle in her eyes. I was also glad she thought it was incredible that I was given a chance to follow the decree of our most sacred messenger. She was right to ask if I realized; how *long* it had been, since a Corvidae had seen such signs. The staggering absence of our beloved White-Raven among our race made my situation more savory.

Brenna sighed, breaking the moment, yet again. *"Hello-o-o?* Rostair mongrels, on the loose? Big, dangerous fight ahead?" She glared at me, then snapped her fingers a few times. "Or are we planning to invite them over to Luke's house for pizza and a movie?"

Sarah rolled her eyes and leaned against the rail beside me.

Shannoea spoke up, "Well, does anyone even know *why* they're here in the first place?"

We looked at one another, but nothing came to mind. Whatever they were after, it gave them confidence enough to become brash killers, despite the consequences from nearby races and clans, as well as from their own leaders. No matter the case, by Corvidae law, we had to confront them—and if they didn't cooperate, we would be forced to kill them.

I looked at Brenna and said, "You're right. What we need to do is plan our attack. They're sure to come here looking for any Corvidae in the area. By the sound of things, they're actually trying to draw us out. We can't allow this to go on another night."

Brenna was beyond pleased, grinning and clenching her fists.

I hated admitting she was right. It made me feel unclean, somehow.

Sarah cut in with an eager glance, "Why don't we simply go out there and capture one? Just lure one out, somehow, then question them?"

I froze.

Sarah had a good point; they couldn't help but leave a trail to follow, making it easy enough to track them down and stop them from ravaging the area. It seemed a simple enough plan.

Shannoea gasped, "You're right, Sarah. I say we bust some heads!" She put her hand on Sarah's shoulder and looked at me. "Gale, after we snag one of them and get the answers we need, you go stay with Luke and guard his folks tonight. The three of us will warn your dad. We're gonna need some answers, as well as some numbers, if we wanna win this!"

I nodded as Brenna stepped closer. *"La mort apprivoiser les mechents."*

We all looked at one another, Shannoea and I were more than a little confused, having no idea how to speak a word of French.

Sarah laughed and explained, "It's a French saying from her clan back home, meaning; *Death tames the wicked.*"

After a few seconds of silence, I started to laugh. Somewhere in that diabolical saying was a tinge of dark humor. It felt as if Lucas were standing next to me right then. I knew in my heart, he'd have found Brenna's words humorous. He was always allured by anything obscure. The others must have found the same humor from its context, as my laughter became infectious.

I felt my cell phone buzz in my pocket. I took it out and saw it was a text from Lucas.

Text message: *Lucas - I'm going for a quick walk outside, I need a break from Brent slaughtering me on every online game we play. lol brb*

I pressed the reply, *Be quick & careful plz I'll be home in time for our night of gaming, I promise.* Then hit send.

It didn't take long before his reply reached my phone. The

others were still chatting about a plan against the Rostair, while I seized the chance to speak with Lucas through text.

Text message: *Lucas - Sounds good. I have a surprise 4 u when u get here. ;)*

My nerves spiked. I loved surprises. It made me want to abandon my friends and rush home to him, just to see what it was! I'd never gotten a single gift from any relationship I'd been in, so this was obviously something I yearned for. Lucas would soon be the first to 'break the cycle' as humans so cleverly phrased. In the back of my mind, I knew better than to leave. I had to prepare whatever defensive tactic it took to make Lucas, as well as his family, safe. I pressed the reply button and sent him a smiley-face in return, then focused my attention back to the group.

Sarah looked at us. "When we have our forces ready and the head-count made, why don't we try and lure them into the industrial zone? It's shut down and secluded at night, so we'll have plenty of room with no human casualties, should they decide to attack us."

"I like that idea. All we need now is the head-count! If we know how many and what breed we're dealing with, our plan might actually work!" Brenna answered in an eager tone. "This is it ladies, it's *us* against *them!* Gale, text Luke and keep him off the streets. They won't pick up his parents' scent if they're indoors most of the time, so guarding them won't matter. We'll go to your father after we question the one we capture while you

340

guard Luke. We'll need your father's help since he's the keeper of this territory. Sarah and I will go find the rest of these vile bastards, get a head-count, and then come find you. If anything goes wrong, or if something changes the plan call or text us."

Even with all this madness gnawing at us, I refused to let it ruin the plans Lucas and I had for the night. The Rostair threat was heavy, true enough, but I eagerly awaited a chance to join Lucas and his friends in an epic night of video game mania. This game night he held each month sounded extremely fun and I wished nightfall would get here so we could play. To me, it didn't really matter what we planned, as long as I had the chance to experience Lucas in his natural state and surroundings. I'd nearly dried up his entire social life and it made me feel rather guilty.

I snapped back to reality, thinking about the urgent duties ahead of us. "Lucas is planning an online gathering with some friends at his house tonight. I think you should have some idea where I'll be, should you need me." *They need to know,* I told myself.

Sarah looked at me, a strangely confused expression on her face. "What are you two planning to do there, if I may ask?" She was daring when she somehow sensed my excitement.

I felt almost bashful, hiding my face behind my hair, fruitlessly trying to conceal my embarrassment. I pretended to clear my throat. "I'm, uh," They gazed right at me, "he invited me to play video games with him."

Silence blew past like a dying wind.

Suddenly, Brenna shattered the silence with her hand over her mouth, laughing to herself hysterically.

I rolled my eyes at her, shaking my head.

Shannoea's eyebrow lifted on one side, more confused than before, while Sarah looked somewhat eager to hear more.

"He did? Which games?" Sarah asked.

"He mentioned *Mortal Kombat, Left 4 Dead, Street Fighter,* and *Grand-Theft-Auto IV.*"

"Oh, wow, Gale! I *love Mortal Kombat* and *Street Fighter*! I'm seriously jealous of you guys, now!" Shannoea's reaction nearly knocked me right off my feet.

Sarah held up her index finger. "Uh, hang on. What exactly is *Mortal Kombat*, or for that matter, what's a *Street Fighter*?" She asked over Brenna's incurable laughter in the background.

Shannoea's ears perked up and she turned to Sarah in the blink of an eye. "You mean, you seriously don't *know?!*" Shannoea's voice almost cracked. "They're video games! She explained it to Sarah with extreme enthusiasm. "It's awesome, Sarah. There's a ton of characters to choose from and each one has special attacks they can use to help them win! "

Sarah blinked once, "So, I'm guessing *MK* is an acronym for *Mortal Kombat*, right?" she asked.

We both nodded with grins on our faces, it was obvious that Shannoea and I had years of gaming experience, when it came to those two particular titles.

"I've never played anything even remotely like that. It sounds like a lot of fun! The only game I've ever played is Dungeons and Dragons, a board game from 1985!"

I heard Brenna scoff in the background then she approached us in a huff, "I'm going inside for a moment. Sarah, when you've finished whatever it is you're doing, come meet up with me. I can't stand here and listen to this dribble about video games and dragons." She complained then opened the door and went in. Once again, Brenna had effectively slain the moment, hoping to focus our attention on anything she deemed worthy.

The three of us looked at each other. Snickering broke out before Shannoea covered her mouth to hide her giggling.

She spoke softly to Sarah and I, "She's just mad because she sucks at *MK*. I owned her, last time we played!"

That was all it took before I began giggling as well, at which Sarah looked confused all over again.

She put her hand on the back of her neck and tilted her head, "Wait! What does 'I owned her' mean? I've never heard that terminology, before."

Shannoea stopped laughing long enough to explain. "It's a modern-day term; it means I won with hardly any problems! I think Americans call it 'gamer-talk', or 'chat-room-talk'." Even though she'd explained it, I'd never heard the actual category for modern speech used among gamers, but it made sense. Shannoea looked back at me and said, "I, uh, heh, I spent a lot of time in chat-rooms and forums a few years back. Some of the stuff they said on those sites kinda got stuck in my head."

The way she tried to explain herself only made us chuckle even more, Shannoea's free-spirited attitude had a way of leading her directly toward trouble. Usually, what started out as an urge to go to a party, or club, resulted in her needing to be rescued by Sarah, Brenna, or me. I dared to imagine what kind of trouble had been wrought during her time surfing the web.

I felt my phone buzz in my pocket.Lucas sent a text asking if everything was okay. I looked at Shannoea, then to Sarah, "I'm sorry, I really should be getting back to Lucas. He's probably starting to set up for his game-night, as we speak."

Sarah cleared her throat carefully then shyly glanced at me. "So, um, this game-night, I was wondering..." Sarah's tone was fragile, as if she were treading carefully and trying not to say too much, too soon. "Are all his friends, uh, 'gamers', as well? Even this friend, Brent, he seems so close to?"

I couldn't tell if she was being coy or if she was honestly oblivious to the truth.

Shannoea rolled her eyes, above a smile that practically screamed, 'Oh, brother'. Then she slapped her own forehead, giggling through her entire reaction.

"Um, yes. I do believe they're all gamers, I've heard Lucas talk about he and Brent playing a few games, online, on many occasions. Why do you ask?"

"Oh, uh, no reason." She was a terrible liar, at least when it came to anything she found interesting. There was definitely something going on behind those sky blue eyes of hers. "I was simply inquiring based on a conceptive interest for video games. I may consider buying one and playing it as recreation, that's all."

Shannoea shook her head, then put her hand on Sarah's shoulder, "Whatever you say, girl, whatever you say." She laughed softly. "Maybe you should let Brenna know we're ready to go. Gale has to get back to her man, so we should get this plan rolling soon."

Sarah nodded and then went inside Lonz to get Brenna, who was probably droning on in French somewhere.

"It's all right, I hope you have an awesome time tonight, Gale, and don't let anything ruin it, not even these Rostair meatheads."

I loved when she had that quaint grin on her face, the grin that says; 'I'm always happy to help. I've got your back whenever you need it.'

"Thanks, Shannoea, you've always been there for me. I wish there was some way I could have you go with me. I know Lucas will be there, but I can't shake this feeling of being an outsider!" I felt panicked; an online game-room full of people who were seasoned video gamers was more than enough to make me shake all over.

"Don't start worrying now, Gale. You'll scare yourself right out of doing this with him! You and Luke are a beautiful couple, girl! I've watched you work your feathers off, trying to keep him protected and keep him as close as possible without smothering him." She reached over and adjusted the collar of my jacket. "Just don't forget, we're here for you if you ever need us—even ol' sour-butt Brenna." She winked.

I smiled, then hugged her. "I know. Thank you for being patient and for being so generous. It's been discouraging since I left my father, but to hear you say all that is honestly enough to keep me strong." I was so overjoyed. I barely noticed being watched by Sarah and Brenna. Sarah was sympathizing with a smile of her own across her face, while Brenna kept a vigil stance, hands on her hips and her signature half-cocked grin.

"Sour-butt Brenna, huh? You're lucky I treated myself to the most expensive wine they have, or I may have gotten angry the second I heard you say that!" Brenna retorted.

Shannoea broke free of our hug, but held onto both my shoulders, glanced over at Sarah, then looked me in the eyes. "See what I mean? We're all here for you, Gale. We know things are hard right now, which is even more reason to support you and Luke! Now, for the love of God, lady-up so you can get back to him and nerd it up with some serious gaming!" She had a way of ignoring Brenna that only added to the humor of the moment.

Times like these made our friendship priceless. I glanced at all three of them, standing the way they always had, each one of them holding their own personal character, each one as much a treasure as the other. Regardless of how things unfolded in our lives, we would always back one another up—there was no question, even now, that they supported my decision—even had the White-Raven not appeared. I nodded, smiling at each of them, then all four of us leapt off the wooden loft and took on our raven forms, flying toward Cleveland.

CHAPTER 25: GALE

We searched most of the residential area of Cleveland and Brenna spotted a cluster of massacred animal carcasses, as well as a trail of claw marks across the sides of buildings and power-line posts. They were chasing something, or someone.

After nearly four hours of following their trail, Sarah caught sight of something horrifying. *Look! Down there!* she mentally exclaimed to the rest of us.

I swooped in with Shannoea for a closer look, while Sarah and Brenna stood watch on two buildings in the area, making sure we wouldn't walk into a trap. I landed behind a dumpster then took human form out of sight of human eyes, while Shannoea took her human form in an alley. I emerged from behind the dumpster to find splattered blood, more claw marks, and to my shocked surprise, the bodies of human victims! Right there, in broad daylight, behind an apartment complex!

Shannoea caught up to me and gasped suddenly, "What?! That's Tomarr! Oh, God, Gale! They're not just killing humans, they're also killing *Corvidae*!!" She was nearly in tears, caught between fear and anger; she put her hands over her mouth and gasped for air.

I checked the body for any sign of his clan or house; when I pulled open his shirt we saw his clan symbol on his chest—a triangle of swords with the eye of a raven inside it. The triangle was wreathed in quills spiking outward, meaning he was a soldier to the house of Avar Sem, a clan from New Mexico.

"I'm-I'm sorry, Shannoea. Did you know him?"

She nodded, still clutching her mouth with both hands.

I stood up, then pulled her over to me, trying to give her comfort. It was a vain attempt, as she welled with anger and sadness, her energy boiled over slowly and it would be only a matter of time before she erupted. "I really am sorry, my friend. This is worse than we originally thought. We need to find these Rostair bastards before they hurt any more of our kind." I couldn't stand to see her like this, so broken and in such disarray. I held on tightly to her, hoping and praying she would allow me to comfort her.

She sobbed into my jacket, soaking my shoulder with her gentle tears, aching with loss. "He, must've been tracking those freaks from the mountains of his territory," she sniffled. "He'd never come this far, unless he had a damn good reason." She broke off from me, then stomped over to his body, *"What the hell was wrong with you? Why didn't you call for help, you overconfident douche-bag?!"* She started kicking his lifeless arm, screaming in a tantrum.

I grabbed her as quickly as I could, then Sarah and Brenna grabbed her as well.

She fought and flailed wildly, hoping to break free and kick him again, hoping it would somehow wake him up and bring him back to life out of pure guilt. "*I would have come! I could have helped you! You knew I was here and you still didn't try to contact me!*"

Sarah pushed her against the nearest building, hoping to calm her down. "Stop this, Shannoea! He's gone from us! You need to let him go!"

Shannoea grabbed Sarah by the neck, clutching it angrily, as if clutching the murderer himself. She gasped and growled behind her teeth.

Sarah stared back at her, completely unaffected by Shannoea's grasp, "*Don't you dare* waste your fury on me, Shannoea,"

I glanced at Brenna, who looked back at me with absolute shock on her face. We swung our eyes back to Sarah and Shannoea, who grappled on.

"Save every last merciless drop of your hate and fury for the ones responsible! When we find those barbarous little savages, I swear, I'll help you pull every one of their heads clean off! But right now, you need to compose yourself. Take a deep breath and clear your head, right now!"

Seconds passed before she calmed down. "I-I'm sorry." she answered slowly closing her eyes; then she released Sarah's neck from her grip. "He was a young soldier—I trained him about a hundred and ten years back. His mom, Grace, won't be happy about this." She wiped her eyes, then walked over to him and knelt down to whisper, "I'm gonna miss you. I'll never forget all those times you made me laugh...or the first time we kissed."

I froze and felt Sarah and Brenna do the same. We exchanged looks as Shannoea spoke the words 'first kiss', then placed one final kiss on his forehead before drinking the last of Tomarr's energies. She stiffened, then began to glow furiously with dark blue arched bolts of lightning as his Corvine powers lanced with hers. Pillars of solid blue light shot from her eye-sockets as she gritted her teeth, screaming with anger and divinity. As the light faded and the energy she'd absorbed subsided, Shannoea came to rest at last. "Let's get outta here," she insisted in a low tone, and then turned to us with a sinister gleam in her eyes, "We have a few dogs to go kick around."

I could tell she was holding back every ounce of her rage as Sarah had suggested, It scared me to see her so far from her usual self, but it made me feel safer about the four of us confronting any Rostair we thought we'd find, with her in such a high state of alert.

I was still reeling from what she'd said, not once had she mentioned having a relationship to me! I was slightly angry about her neglecting to mention him to me before now, but that feeling was overshadowed by the sympathy I had for her loss. She clearly loved him, but the Rostair had cut him down in the prime of his relationship with her. They would answer for this and we would be the ones dealing the killing blow.

"All of a sudden, I feel rather badass knowing you're here with us, Shannoea!" Brenna chuckled slyly.

Shannoea glanced back with narrowed eyes, slowly letting an evil grin cut across her straight face.

We circled the area, finding more and more bodies of our kind, as well as humans. Some from the same clan as Tomarr, each with a soldier-class emblem on their chest and some from the local area. They were chasing these Rostair for several hundred miles, all the while hoping to take them out before they reached whatever goal had drawn their attention in a northward direction.

I looked at Shannoea and confessed, "You were right, Shannoea. Tomarr had a small unit of soldiers with him, but now the questions are building. We need to know where the Rostair horde are now, how many, and what in the world they're after in the first place!"

"It's hard to say. By the pattern we've been following, my guess is they're going somewhere they think is ripe with more of their kind!" she replied with disgust in her mental voice, giving the impression she had some idea where to start looking.

I glided up to Sarah, who was focusing her powers on sensing their vile essences—she'd always had a knack when it came to finding other creatures and different races in general. "Sarah, can you sense any of them down there?"

"I think I've just locked onto a few of them! Down there, near that corner of the airport!"

"Good. Let's go ask them if they'd like to play twenty questions!" Brenna suggested, banking into a dive.

We followed close behind her as she shot like a bullet directly toward the ground below.

"Those three, right there! They're Rostair, I can sense it!" Sarah called out, causing Brenna to dart directly into their group below.

Before they had a chance to react, Brenna shot through the chest of one, passing through him like a phantom with a direct kill-shot, leaving us only two to deal with. I'd never seen Brenna use a kill-shot like that; it was exciting, but frightening all the same. Deep inside, I was relieved that this part of the airport was unoccupied. We really didn't need humans seeing us mangle what to them, would seem like plain, simple animals.

They tried to scramble, attempting to flee and alert the others of our presence. One turned himself into a rabid-looking dog, while the other changed into a wolf, but Sarah managed to fly into the dog, ramming him into the chain-link fence behind him.

Brenna swooped in, changed to her human form, and tackled the wolf. They scuffled until she managed to snap one of his legs in two, then while he howled in agony, she grabbed his neck and choke-slammed the mangy looking wolf right into the asphalt, cracking it. *"A wolf?!* Are you *kidding me*? How absolutely childish! What's next on your list of brainless creatures to turn into, *a bat*?" She spit in his face just as I grabbed him.

Shannoea rushed in and kicked him in the ribs, making him squeal in pain as he hit the ground.

He looked up at us and snarled, *"Yer gonna bleed for hittin' me, ya bit—*"

Shannoea snatched him by the neck and my nerves spiked as she slammed him hard against a nearby metal beam. I glanced at Sarah and Brenna, who were dragging their Rostair back to us.

"Why are you here? *Why are you killing Corvidae?*" Shannoea snapped.

Even in wolf form, he managed to smile. "Choke on my middle finger, ya stupid bimbo-bird!" His southwestern accent was heavy, giving me the impression that this one was just a nearby commoner, who loved the thrill of the hunt. Whoever turned him, simply gave him the means to hunt more than duck or deer; he'd been transformed into a blood-thirsty savage.

I could smell Tomarr's blood on him, even from behind Shannoea. It was thick and heavy to my senses.

She punched him in his stomach, then slammed him against the beam again. "Wrong answer, Fido. Now, turn to your human form. I wanna see your ugly face! *Do it, now!*" she snapped.

He stared at her with tired eyes. He was dazed and had gashes all over his head from our ambush, but slowly managed to take on his human visage.

As I'd suspected, he was a mongrel-class Rostair, shirtless and dirty, only wearing a tattered pair of black jeans with holes torn in both legs. His arm was broken from Brenna snapping it when he tried to escape. "Now, you'd better answer me, you dirty little hobo! Tell me, why are you here, and why are you killing our kind?"

She waited for him to stop gagging and gasping, his breath was breaking as shock settled in. She was pushing too hard, too soon, but he fought off the pain and panted each word under bated breath, "Jer-Jeremiah, he led us. Told us to lure any Cor-Corvidae we could."

Sarah, Brenna and I stood there, mouths hanging open with fright as Shannoea toyed with her prey, keeping him alive only long enough to pull answers out..

"He's the one you want! Said he was gonna start a *new* war! Said he found out about Xander's girl breakin' off and savin' a stupid human! Said it'd be enough to put his crusty ol' ass outta Ohio territory, for keeps!"

My eyes shot open wider. How did a Rostair find out about my saving Lucas? There wasn't a single one in the area! The scenario raced through my head. Blow for blow, I combed over every detail of that night from the time I'd gotten home to text Lucas to the moment I'd gotten him to my house and locked him in my room. But nothing was coming to me! If they knew, that meant there was a Rostair on my families' land. It was someone who knew my family well enough to have some idea where our house was located! Every nerve in my body spiked and fizzled; all at once, I felt afraid and defensive.

"Who told Jeremiah all this? I wish to speak with those who trespassed on sacred Corvine lands to bring him such information!" I spat out, clenching my fists.

He looked at me with a cold glare in his watery eyes.

"Jeremiah's mate, Nali... She saw it from out in the lake. Said she was following her man's orders, watchin' a kid—some meat-sack named Nate. Jeremiah set up the whole thing!"

Tears rushed down my cheeks, I was shaking the same way Shannoea had, when we'd found Tomarr's body. I steadied myself, letting him seal Jeremiah's fate before Shannoea finished him.

"He told the guy to have his whole damn crew wait for the geek to show. Had Nali make sure he got beat to death, then Xander's girl showed, saved him, and left. Then some rich Barbie-girl showed, beat em up more, and tossed 'em in the lake!" He was flagging in and out of consciousness in a torrent of pain and shock.

But I'd heard enough. It was easy to see that Jeremiah plotted the entire death and rebirth of Lucas' life. Then he ordered Nali to save Nathan and his friends long enough to confess to my inclusion in their fight. Most likely, Jeremiah and Nali had killed the whole group by now.

Shannoea released her grip on his neck, letting him fall to the ground. "I can't believe you follow orders from such a coward!" She was angrier, but somehow, she kept just enough composure to get the last of the information we needed.

"There, I told ya what'cha wanted, now can I go?"

She pointed at him with a sinister glare. "One last question, then I'll let you go."

He nodded while he shook from fear. "I'll tell you anything!"

I heard the other remaining Rostair behind us starting to struggle, hoping to free himself from Brenna and Sarah. "*You freakin' swine! Don't be tellin' these broads nothin, ya hear me?*" The mangy-looking dog had taken his human form, flailing in the arms of his two captors. They choked him and kicked him a few times, then broke his neck.

The one we'd been questioning stiffened, then started to panic, huddling against the beam.

"Come on, now! Don't kill me, too!" He shook insanely.

Shannoea grinned. "Where is Jeremiah now? In fact, where are you meeting him?"

"He's in Port Clinton! He's been there the whole damn time! Didn't cha know that? He's always at that bar called Bell Mell. He uses them old run-down houses across the street for his hangouts!"

I watched Shannoea's eyes light up; she seemed more than ready to meet this threat head-on.

"He's been recruitin' for weeks! Said he's gettin' ready to take Xander out! Said he needed leverage, that's when he found out Xander's girl was hangin' with that human-boy! So, he set him up to get killed! I guess he figured it was even sweeter when she saved the boy, instead! At first, he said killin' the boy would make Xander's girl mad enough to split, then he'd take her hostage or somethin'!"

Right then, I wanted to leave and find Jeremiah, this Rostair filth, and tear him apart! He had an elaborate scheme to take my father's land and territory all planned out, and he used Lucas as the key factor! I would not stand for this, not for a single moment!

"Once Xander and his ol' lady get pushed out, he can take the whole damn state, slicker than snot!"

"Thanks for the tip, you stupid skank!" she hissed, then punched him in the chest as hard as she could.

He cried out, pouting and whining as she hit him eight times, and then let him fall into a heap again.

"Get up!" she snarled, picking him up by his neck. "What's your name, punk?"

"God, please, don't kill me!" He pouted then whined, "My name is Edgar."

"All right, Edgar, I'm curious. Do you know what happens when a Rostair drinks the blood of a Corvidae?" she asked, holding his head against the beam as hard as she could without killing him.

He nodded his head to the best of his ability, "*Yes!* Please, *don't!* Ya done said, you'd let me go!"

Her grip tightened considerably, gagging him until he opened his mouth wide, trying to gather any breath he could. "This is for Tommar, *asshole!*" She bit her palm, opening a deep wound, then wrung out a fountain of blood by balling up her fist until it shook with intensity. The blood trailed into his mouth, flooding down his throat. She let go, then watched with an evil glare as he convulsed and gagged.

The four of us stood there, motionless, watching as Edgar writhed in agony. Black veins climbed and branched from his flesh, his eyes rolled back in his head and he curled into a fetal position until his entire body slowly transformed into a pile of what looked like freshly hardened magma, glowing dark red under its thick, onyx surface.

We knew everything now—who was behind it all, where to find him, everything! All that remained, was to rally our forces to meet this threat. We looked at one another, then I nodded silently to them. We would heed the call of battle once more, the Corvidae would strike at the heart of this cancer, and slay every last one of them

CHAPTER 26: GALE

I glided along the evening winds, trying desperately to recompose myself. The fact that this Jeremiah actually targeted Lucas and used him as bait to trigger a war within the Corvine ranks was simply ludicrous! He'd gone to great and thorough strides to put his plan into effect and it might have worked, had my friends and I not intercepted Edgar and his group. I didn't know how to stop him or how to protect Lucas from the coming forces, considering the Rostair *may* have Corvidae aiding their advance.

Once before, during the Victorian era when Deadric and his brother Roma decided to defect, this had happened. They joined forces with Antoine Vancali, a Rostair from the far spans of France. In this case, however, it was a Rostair who defected. He sought to deploy a secret army right under our noses, and we would soon know exactly how many we were dealing with.

I needed to forget about it, for the time being. I had to focus on my night with Lucas. He graciously allowed me to join him on his online adventures with his friends, the very least I could do was honor the time given.

As I approached his house, I saw that he'd left the glass balcony door open. I swooped in, perching on the railing. I needed to be sure it was safe to assume human form. I hopped down onto the wooden balcony then slowly made my way into Lucas' room. I saw him sleeping on the edge of his bed, his video game controller still in his hand as it hung over the side, junk food wrappers all around him. *Oh, Lucas, you're so adorable,* I thought to myself; it made my heart flutter wildly to see him so comfortable. Here he was, in his nerdiest state of being ever—where some would see him as a slob, I felt myself melting inside at the sight of him.

I made sure to stay in raven form, in case his mother walked in to find him sprawled out. I walked over to his dangling hand and pushed the controller from his limp fingers with my beak, then turned off the console by holding down the power button in the middle of the controller.

I needed to get closer to him. I'd missed him so much, even for such a short amount of time. I felt as though I needed to see his face again, even if he was sleeping. I hopped a few times, then flew over to his dresser. As I turned, something caught my eye. Two gorgeous, fresh roses nestled next to a lovely card addressed to me! I tilted my head, fluttering my wings with excitement, before I investigated the card. It had a picture of a rabbit on the front, with a word bubble that read; *You make me all hoppy inside!* My heart was beating like crazy, beneath my feathers. No guy had ever given me a card before! It felt exactly like Christmas! I pulled myself together and tried to open the card with my beak, but I stopped myself.

This isn't right. Lucas went through a lot of trouble to get

*me these things. Just to surprise me, himself! I think it best if
I were to let him do so. It's not fair to spoil a good surprise,* I
told myself, before turning toward his bed. I hopped from the
dresser, gliding over to him, landing gently on his leg, so as not
to wake him. His khaki pants made it easier for my talons to hold
me steady on him as I made my way up to his waist, across his
stomach, then onto his chest. I could feel his strong heartbeat
through my legs as I stood there, watching him breathe slowly.
I sighed with contentment, staring deep into every detail of his
beautiful face. The more I stared at him as he slumbered, the
more assured I became that I would do anything at all, just for
him. I would give up everything, just to spend mere seconds
with him and I would never leave his side, no matter what.

He must have felt me perched on him somehow, his eyes
opened slowly, followed by a quaint smile.

"I'm sorry, Lucas. I didn't mean to disturb you. I only
wanted to feel the warmth of your heartbeat between my talons.
I-I've come to look forward to it, each time you sleep." He took
in a careful, slow breath, stretching his limbs, and then ran his
fingers over my back sending the most beautiful chills across my
feathers. I couldn't help but shiver with delight as he started to
gently scratch the side of my neck.

"I'm just glad you're back. I've been bored since you left;
this place isn't the same when you're gone."

I closed my eyes and leaned in, letting him get deeper along
my neck and chest, the glorious sensation of his hands on me

was enough to make me want to faint with bliss. I wriggled and shuddered out of control as he finished racing his fingertips over my entire body. I came back to my senses, breathing as though I'd flown non-stop for a week. Even after all this time with him, it was hard to believe how wild he drove me, inside and out. I stretched out my right wing and draped it over his face. Then I slowly, gently dragged it over every curve and feature, until I could see his eyes. I let each feather glide over him, eventually letting his smile emerge from underneath. As I'd finished, I kept my eyes locked with his, peeking from behind my wing, as if from behind a black silken curtain.

"I've always wanted to do that. I'm glad you are the one I got the chance to do it to. Your face is so soft, it makes it difficult to be away from you." The way he treated me was more than enough to wash all my concerns away without a trace, his way with me was uncanny.

"That reminds me, I have a surprise for you! It's all right to change back if you want to, my parents are at work." He walked over to the dresser as I assumed human form, sitting on the edge of his bed. "Now, close your eyes and hold out your hands!"

Even though I knew what I was receiving, I was still worked up with excitement. I'd never gotten flowers, let alone a card, from anyone I'd dated! I shuffled my feet, smiling to myself, waiting for him to lay the surprise into my hand. After what seemed like an eternity, I felt him placing objects in my lap and on my palms.

"Okay, now, *open your eyes!*" he exclaimed.

I opened them and nearly fell over in shock! There was more than simply roses and a card—a lot more!

"Lucas! Good Lord above! I don't know what to say! I'm-I'm speechless!" There, in my hands lay the card I'd seen, the two roses, a box of chocolates, a picture of us that he'd drawn, and a large, soft, plushy polar bear! "These are all for me?!" I felt my heart pounding heavily then felt my cheeks grow hot as I blushed.

Lucas leaned against the dresser, smiling with self-satisfaction. "Well, yeah! I drew the picture while you were out, but then I got the idea to find something special to go along with it. The polar bear was sitting in the window display of a store I passed on my way home. He looked so cool I just had to get him for you!"

I hugged the white, velvety bear, then sat him next to me while I looked at the card with trembling hands.

I glanced up at Lucas, who looked extremely pleased with himself, and then returned my attention to the card, reading it softly, "You make me all Hoppy inside!" I opened it up and read, "That makes you worth more than twenty four carrots!" I felt the blush in my cheeks race over my face; I was smiling so much, it started to ache a little. I looked down below the initial writing the card had come with and noticed Lucas had written something of his own, adding to my excitement.

It read: *To my silk-night-Queen, a warm and loving woman,*

whose heart has chased away all the shadow in my life, for that,
I love you. To a woman who has shown me that life itself, is more
precious when spent with the ones you hold dear, for that, I love
you. To a woman who showed me just how far the rabbit hole
really goes and is willing to follow it all the way to the bottom,
just to find me, for that, I love you. Forever and far beyond.
-Lucas-

My eyes moistened, my tongue pressed against my lower lip, then glided across the front of my teeth in rapturous glee. I carefully placed everything he'd given me onto the bed, then trotted over to him, wrapping my arms around his waist, and stroked his back. "Thank you so much, I love all of it, Lucas!"

He brushed my hair away from my neck and kissed the lobe of my ear gently.

"I just wanted to do something for you, for once." He whispered, "Since we've been together, I've been letting you do all the good stuff. Even though I'm not really good at giving anyone presents, I figured I'd take the chance and show you how I feel about what we have."

"I absolutely adore what you've given me. I'll even let you in on a little secret " I put my hand on the side of his head and pulled his ear closer to my lips. "You're the very first person, aside from my parents, to ever give me anything."

His neck tensed up slightly, then he leaned back just enough to lock his eyes with mine. "Are you serious?" He looked shocked, yet unconvinced. "Wait, no way, that can't be right!"

"It's true, not one person I've ever had any relationship with, has ever done what you've done for me, today!" I held back a giggle. Seeing him so frantic about being a cornerstone in my life was priceless.

"But, how did that happen? I mean, I don't understand!"

"Lucas," I sighed, and fluttered my smiling eyes, "most of the time, the men I knew only wanted one thing—sex."

His face froze. He would mostly likely have fallen backward, had I not been holding him firmly against me. "I suppose I should've seen that coming. I've always been the opposite, myself." His confident grin melted into one of curiosity. "Wait, did you ever, uh, you know?"

He became more adorable with every stumble of words. I leaned in and touched the tip of his nose with mine. "Not a one. I'm still quite the virgin, my dear, sweet, Knight." His expression changed and he looked extremely relieved. I kept my eyes locked onto him, hoping he would be reassured by my words. "None of them were ever as uniquely attractive as you are, Lucas. I gladly kept all my purity and loyalties to share with you."

He shied his face to one side, trying to hide apple-red cheeks. "Uh, oho boy," he started to bite his lip, hoping to fight off the growing blush as I leaned my head to meet his face, "You're embarrassing me so bad, right now!" he confessed in a near whisper. He was so cute like this, fragile at heart, but so quick to attempt bravery against my flirtatious nature toward him.

Suddenly, I felt his excitement pressing against my leg, his lap white-hot, even through my jeans!

He tried to put some distance between us, hoping I hadn't noticed. I let my gaze drop to his legs then slowly climb their way back up, followed by a coy smile.

He gasped and his lap became hotter.

I let him get as much distance as he felt necessary, all the while, keeping my hands around his waist. "You've been the first in many aspects of my life, Lucas, " I whispered with the hottest breath I could muster, letting it roll over his neck. "I want you to be my last, first physical experience just as much." I stared into his helpless eyes with a deep hunger in my gaze, I wanted him to know I wasn't about to tease his weaknesses and that I'd much rather save myself just for him, for as long as it took, if it meant having him one step closer to me.

"I admit you make me want you real bad. I'm seriously just happy you're not pushy. I don't think I have the endurance to stick to my decision to stay loyal to that aspect of myself. You're a hard woman to resist!" His breath was quivering insanely.

I kissed his cheek and ran my fingers through his hair. His reactions to my flirting had always been unique; he fell for it all so easily, but kept enough composure to maintain his sense of self-control, a trait I'd come to adore. It not only made me feel attractive, but also gave me a sense of security. It meant I would always have his attention, that I was everything and more.

"I would never push you, Lucas. As I said, I've made my

decision." I locked my eyes with his. "My purity is reserved for only one person, the one person I've vowed myself to. If he should choose to take me today, tomorrow, or next year then I'll gladly submit to him. As you so elegantly put it that night at Perry's monument, I want to make sure that when the time comes, it will be uniquely special and unforgettable."

He put his trembling hand on my neck then slowly allowed it to flow downward over my collarbone, resting gently at my bust-line. I began to sweat with anticipation; I wanted to feel his hands on me, caressing every inch of me, but I could feel him fighting off his urges deep inside. He took his hand from me, exhaled carefully, and said, "I'm really glad you said that. It's hard to find a woman who's willing to hold out for the perfect moment. Not that I've ever had much luck with women, anyway; I mean, I've never even been to second base, as you know," he confessed. I tilted my head, peering at him with narrowed eyes and a broad smile.

I couldn't tell if he'd just proposed the idea of allowing him to grope me, or if he was simply being coy. Either way, I felt a sense of ardor sweep over me as I felt my face take on a light shade of pink. "Rounding the bases in a relationship with a woman depends on how committed you are to the game." I swung my hair over my shoulder as his mouth dropped open in shock. "And you have to be willing to let her play just as much." I could tell my reply nearly knocked him out of his shoes.

"I-I wasn't..." he stammered for a recovering statement,

almost as if he'd hoped I wasn't somehow offended by what he'd said. "I didn't mean it to sound like that, all I meant was, uh, that it's obvious because..." He took in another breath, then exhaled heavily with a defeated look on his face. "I'll just shut up, now," he finally said, leaning against the dresser with his hand resting on his forehead.

Lucas reminded me of a kitten still trying to master crawling on wobbly legs. He tried so hard to recognize the boundaries in every conversation he and I had, even though, I'd made it clear there were none. I was willing to go anywhere he asked, speak of anything he asked about, and do anything he desired. Still, it was somewhat comforting to know he was so stern with his civility.

After several attempts at trying to relax him, I finally managed to convince him to show me his infamous 'game-room'. He led me downstairs into the living room area and to the base of the staircase.The door there took us to the basement; a place where Lucas escaped to whenever his room wasn't secluded enough. He flipped the light switch on and we headed down into the cold, white brick haven, where he'd planned our night of adventure. The fluttering in my stomach gradually worsened with each step as we approached the bottom.

Here it is—the basement. The game-room is off to the right, past the room where my dad keeps his pinball machine collection." He gestured, swaying his hand across in front of him.

"Your father has a *pinball machine* collection?" I could hardly believe my ears.

He nodded, pointing to the room where they were.

I rushed in and nearly fainted. The man had at least twenty-seven different kinds of pinball machines, each one in mint, or near mint condition. Some I hadn't seen in years. "This is amazing; where did he get all these, Lucas?" I slid my fingers carefully over the metal framework of the Xenon machine, one of my personal favorites from the eighties. I'd already let my mind slip, nearly forgetting I'd asked him anything as my thoughts traversed the days of old when I escaped from my Corvidae life to play at the arcades. I'd spent a score of quarters in countless arcade machines, but none quite as often as Xenon. It had been the mar on my servitude during the eighties, keeping my duties to a minimum at best.

"He buys them from all over the place then restores them. My mom hates when he gets too focused, she says he works like a zombie on them."

I was in awe as even the room itself was fashioned to bring a nostalgic feel to all who entered. His father was clearly a closet-nerd, when it came to resurrecting the era of gallery arcades, and I wasn't one to argue. He was very good at it!

Lucas grabbed my hand then led me further in where numerous posters hung on the walls, from video game themes to old movies. I felt as excited as when I entered the Loftrum of my clan; the times of old lingered everywhere, comforting everyone who sought the warmth of simplicity. Books and statues, paintings and people—all as peaceful and welcoming as Lucas' own basement. We came to a huge room, with gleaming white walls, a light gray carpet, and what looked like an endless wall of video games. Video game consoles from the seventies to the most current were presented next to its respective legion of game titles, shelved with care and respect.

"These, uh..." he cleared his throat softly. "I helped him collect some of these a while back. That's what he collects when he's bored with pinball machines." Suddenly it became obvious that his father was responsible for Lucas' shut-in lifestyle. Perhaps his father had secretly managed to relive his own childhood through Lucas, or maybe he simply wanted company in his committed interests. In either case, it was something they'd shared. In my experience of people in general, I'd come to recognize emptiness among multitudes of people due to a lack of parental bonding. Lucas was fortunate even if he had no idea how precious it was to have a father who tried to connect with him.

"I'm impressed!" My eyes cascaded down the towers and walls of hundreds of titles. "I can't imagine how long it took to collect all these; it must've taken years!"

"It did. My dad finds deals on this stuff, all the time. My mom does gardening and my dad collects game stuff—how awkward is that?"

I shot a glance of disfavor at him. "There's nothing wrong

371

with either one, Lucas. Compared to some people, this is complete bliss! You should be proud to have such active parents." His reaction was proof enough I'd proved my point, he let his eyes avert from mine while grimacing. "All I mean to say is your father is a warm, caring person and your mother is much the same. I would so trade with you, if my father hadn't tried to kill you in the driveway." I inched in a smirk, shrugging my shoulders as I stared at him, which managed to lighten his mood.

He threw his arms up sarcastically, "All right, okay, point made," he sighed. "Now, let's get this game-night rolling, I've waited all day for this."

"So have I, let's go!"

CHAPTER 27: GALE

His game room was absolutely incredible! A sleek, black wooden entertainment center built in the center of the back wall was surrounded by black leather couches, each with their own glass coffee table. The television was sixty inches of LCD, flat-screen splendor, equipped with high-definition and surround sound, coupled by two smaller, forty seven inch flat-screens armed with the same features, on either side of the room. Below each of the two smaller televisions stood an endtable with an XBox 360 on top and a copy of *Left 4 Dead* next to each one.

"Wow!" It took my breath away. "What does your father do, as a career?"

"He works for a big name contractor. You know, drawing blueprints for buildings and landscaping jobs," he replied, leading me over to one of the console setups. "Here, I've set it up so you have your very own guest profile." He handed me the controller and the headset. "Your seat is behind you, they're specially designed to keep you comfortable, while you play."

I looked behind me and saw a legless black leather chair waiting for me.

"I've never seen a chair like this before." It looked odd and I failed to imagine how it could possibly be comfortable.

"Just trust me; it's better than you think."

I scooted the chair closer and slowly lowered to sit on it.

"Good—now lean back. It can even rock, when you want it too."

I leaned back, letting the chair caress my weight. As it did, I started to feel exactly what he was talking about. I'd spent time playing video games, either sitting at the edge of my bed or against the headboard surrounded by my pillows, but this was heavenly! "Oh, my! I do like this, Lucas! It's like nothing I've experienced before!" He looked pleased by my reaction, then turned on my console, as well as my television.

"Let's get started. I bet the others are waiting for us." He turned on his console and television, then plopped into his chair.

I put on my headset and logged into my profile. I ached with excitement as I loaded up the game, and then waited for Lucas to invite me to the online session with his friends.

Before I knew it, I was in the video game world with Lucas, armed and dangerous on the first level. Lucas' friend, Jimmy, opted to be on our team and his other two friends, Dwayne and Melissa, were on the opposing team.

I was already feeling the tingling excitement of adventure as the three of us tried desperately to survive in the game as we fought the onslaught brought on by Melissa and Dwayne. They were accepting me easily as one of their own, just a casual, fun-seeking woman with a taste for video game action! Every step we took into the game was another step I gained in their circle of friendship. Every bullet we fired was a friendly promise to watch out for each other, every zombie slain an obstacle overcome.

Jimmy was having the time of his life. He claimed he'd never come across a woman who was anywhere near as well seasoned in this game as Melissa. I was flattered to say the least, but humbly interjected that Melissa was quite skilled, in her own way. During our trek through the game's streets, the five of us chatted about a number of things unrelated to our gaming session.

Dwayne was insightful, with a large knowledge base on nearly everything, prestigious and proud almost like Sarah. Melissa was deeply committed to Japanese animations, respectively called 'anime'. Jimmy reminded me of Shannoea in every aspect, his witty comments and playful analogies made everything fun and humorous, no matter how bleak.

All at once, I found myself embracing the moment I shared with them, as if Lucas were sharing a priceless treasure with me for the first time. The killing I was doing wasn't real and the amount of playful conversations and joking remarks we'd been sharing dulled the intensity. These people didn't demand sacrifice of any kind, they didn't carry rules and laws, aside from the civility they shared in common society. They didn't have murderous secrets looming over them, or shrouded motives. They were every bit as warming as the morning sun and they made me feel as though I were a part of what they had. I never wanted it to end.

I couldn't help but feel slightly turned on when Lucas saved my life during our game and then defended me from his begrudged teammate. I didn't care if it was just a game, Lucas had shown me a very new side of himself. It stirred me deep inside, giving me a thrilled, anxious sensation that tingled not only my heart, but my skin.

Too soon, the game session ended and the results screen appeared.

"Good game, good game, indeed!" Dwayne said with a relishing tone.

I heard Jimmy scoff, "Yeah, you only say that coz Lucas didn't toast you to save his girlfriend."

"Ease off, Broody Mcbroodster; he did it for the sake of love!" Melissa added, "That was the most fun I've ever had playing this game! Maybe next time, it should be girls versus boys, eh?"

I had to admit, the idea sounded intriguing.

Lucas logged out of the game, then loaded up *Ultimate Mortal Kombat Three*. "Actually, I was thinking about some good old-fashioned *UMK;* we can come back to *Left 4 Dead*, later." He sent the invite to the three of us and we each accepted it.

"It ha-as-s begu-un!" Jimmy exclaimed with a somewhat steady, deep tone.

CHAPTER 28: GALE

The night went on as we fought one another in *Mortal Kombat*, battling to see who was the fastest, the strongest, but most of all we battled to see who remembered what button combinations triggered the finishing moves! I could only recall a few while Lucas seemed to be tied with Dwayne with nearly remembering all of them. The entire time we played, I enjoyed the relaxed feeling of being accepted as a member of the group. The extremeness of Lucas' daring rescue in the earlier game kept my heart singing and fluttering wildly, making it hard to concentrate.

"Gale, are you okay?" Melissa asked. "You're totally letting me own you, right now. What gives?"

I'd hardly noticed she was beating me as I had let my mind drift. I looked up at the screen and saw her character finishing a large combo of attacks on my character. But just then, the power went out through the entire house

Lucas was engaged in an intense fight with Dwayne, but gasped as the screen went black on his TV. "What the heck?" He dropped his controller and opened his cell phone, using the back-light of the screen as a flashlight. "I think we just lost power. That's really strange; there weren't any storms headed this way."

He crawled over to me as I stared down at the message

screen on my phone—a text from Shannoea.

1 missed call - Shannoea

1 new text message - Shannoea: *We got attacked on our way 2 C u! Near the police station! Brenna "accidentally" kicked a Rostair into the power-grid thingy! Be there, soon! Hang tight!*

He sat down as I exited back into the home-screen, "Are you all right? You look kind of nervous about something."

Things were getting out of hand. The Rostair hordes were becoming more aggressive and erratic with every encounter. The fact that they effectively ruined another perfectly wonderful night with Lucas was more than enough reason to make me angry; but now was certainly not the time.

I looked into his eyes as the light from his phone softly illuminated his face, making him look like an angel from heaven itself. "I-I'm fine, Lucas. I guess the power shutting off startled me, that's all," I half-lied through my teeth.

I leaned in and gently nipped his ear; his shoulders stiffened and he jerked to attention. "It's a good thing I can see in the dark, though," I whispered softly, letting my eyes glow just enough to replace his cell phone light.

Lucas didn't move at all he looked fascinated by the faint glister of soft, violet light, cast from my eyes.

I crawled behind him then placed my hands on his shoulders. I slid them both onto his chest and his breathing quickened gradually as I leaned over the top of his chair and raised his head to face mine above him before I kissed him, deeply. I wanted him to know how much I wanted him. Even when his lips were upside down to mine, he was still an elegant kisser.

I let my hands glide further down, resting on his belt-line, then nibbled the side of his neck. I watched as he tried to hide his excitement from me, folding his legs over one another, hoping I wouldn't try to capitalize on the situation.

"Since the power is out, we'll have to find some other game to play," I whispered, kissing his earlobe. The entire side of Lucas' neck and cheek turned apple-red, in the blink of an eye. I could practically feel the heat rolling from his rosy skin. He sat silent and playfully helpless while I loomed over him, my hands roaming hungrily over his entire upper-body.

"I nev..." he tried to whisper, but his eyes closed and his breath was far too broken from my attentions. "I never knew you enjoyed being so bad," he finally managed to speak, but gasped again when I nipped the side of his neck.

"All women have a bad side, mine just happens to crave the perfect moment," I added with a slow, heavy exhale. "I want to take you beyond the reaches of ecstasy, Lucas." I kissed him once, making him shudder in delight. "I want to drown with you, in paradise." I kissed him again and he tensed as the heat from my mouth crawled over the side of his face and neck, pushing him further over the edge.

I ran my lips over his neck then gently dragged my nails over his chest, kissing him more and more wildly. He placed one hand on the side of my face, trying to hold me steady, kissing me back with slower, more controlled passion in return to mine.

That he was trying to pace the moment, hoping to resist me for as long as possible, made the situation more delectable. He focused on keeping his composure, while I explored his tantalizing body, seeing how far he'd allow me to go.

My hands were eager and shaking greedily, one sliding over his chest while the other crawled over the front of his leg, prying it gently from the other, then parting it entirely, all the while my tongue sampled more of his earlobe.

He suddenly broke from me, trying to catch his breath, then looked me in the eyes. "Gale," he said in a bated, quivering tone, "do you really wanna do this, after all we said upstairs?" He looked starved, as if I'd pushed some hungry animal inside of him against the bars of its cage. He shook his head slowly as he cupped my head in both of his caressing hands, staring deep into my watering eyes.

I put my hands on either side of his neck gently and kissed his lips, slowly, "I only wanted to go as far as you'd allow me to." I felt my desires speak for me as the yearning for him grew. I was scared and excited all at once. "Is it so wrong, for me to want my chance to round the bases, Lucas?" The words my desire chose to use were beyond my control, I felt myself submitting to its will, confessing anything it desired. "I-I'm..." I felt myself choking up. "I feel helpless, right now—greedy and hungry. And I'm sorry, but I want you to take me, right now, before I go insane."

My emotions overtook me, as if my desire had done more than simply confess its yearning. It felt as if it were begging him to break his morals, to simply unhinge himself from his virtues, and give in to the moment.

His eyebrow lifted and my heart nearly stopped as I attempted to catch my breath. A solemn, guilty tear chased its way down my cheek. He caught it with his thumb, wiping it away completely. I watched his mouth take on a warming smile as I stood perfectly still. I wanted him to see how loyal I was to him. If what I'd confessed was the truth, about never pushing him, I would have to let him make the first move. I held onto my urges, hoping he would sate the fragile, yet feverish desires of my heart.

"I'm not having sex with you, Gale. I've already——"

I interjected, "I never said a thing about *sex*."

"Then, what?" He sounded stern, something he only did when he was standing his ground.

"I don't know. I guess I was trying to make a good time even better, for my hero."

His expression changed, he looked intrigued, "You're still thinking about how I saved your life, in our *Left 4 Dead* game, aren't you?" he asked with a sly-looking glare.

I nodded, biting my lip. True, his actions in the game had been more than enough to turn me on.

He chuckled softly, "Gale, that was only a game. In fact, I wasn't sure it would work, when I did it!"

"I don't care if it was just a game, you're my nerdy hero and every brave hero, nerdy or not, needs a reward every now and again." I gently tapped the tip of my index finger onto the end of his nose, then winked at him.

"Well, since you put it that way..." He leaned in then pushed me from my knees to the floor behind me. Caught off guard and before I could react, he crawled over the top of me, looming over my face. "What exactly did you have in mind?" He asked, tilting his head to one side.

I grabbed him with both hand by the nape of his neck, pulling him straight to my lips, I kissed him deep and hard, thrilled when he returned the favor. Brushing the tip of his tongue against mine, he knew exactly what I liked.

Having him lay next to me, embracing my lips with his, was beyond heavenly. He drove me further over the falls of bliss and ecstasy, but I craved more this time, much more. I traced my hand along his arm until I came to his wrist; I took hold and guided it along my hip, then across my ribs, resting it on my breast. His breathing stopped as soon as I pressed his hand firmly over it with mine. I wanted to be the first experience he'd ever face on a physical level, just as much as I wanted him to be my first experience.

I moaned softly with approval as I continued to dig deeper into his lips with mine, coaxing him to roam my body with his quivering fingertips. After what felt like an eternity, his passion broke loose inside of him. He pinned my wrists to the carpet.

He hungrily stared into my eyes and I stared back, starvation in mine. I'd never been treated in such a way, that I felt helpless. I quickly admitted to myself that I rather enjoyed the sensation of having him pin me down, like a wild beast does to its prey!

He remained silent, slowly lowering his lips to mine, but teasing me with brief nips and brushes. My arousal heightened, my heartbeat quickened as he lowered his mouth the last few times. I desperately tried to catch at least one more kiss, a quick taste of him. Maddening, yet erotic, I finally managed to lick his lower lip just as he brushed the tip of my tongue on his final pass. The game he played was absolute ambrosia, in every sense of the word.

He eventually let go of my wrists and slid one of his arms under my head, so I could rest on his bicep. I let my head fall back and he began to kiss my neck, first a peck, then longer nibbles, until he could hold back no longer and began to bite down along the side. The sensation of his steamy breath and his teeth digging into me shot torrents of rapture through my entire body, making me gasp for control of my sanity.

Suddenly, just as I thought I was beginning to regain a sense of calm about me, I felt his hand slide underneath my shirt and slowly climb over my bare breasts. My breath hitched as I let him explore every single inch of me, something I'd longed for since the night I'd first stayed with him in his bedroom. His fingers seemed to enjoy all they had found, from the cleavage between, to the aching, stiffened summit of each breast.. Without warning, he gently pinched my already throbbing peak, nearly causing me to lose it.

Every move he made was like a miracle in the works; he made me wriggle and tremble restlessly, victimized by his hunger. I couldn't handle much more—I needed to stop him before he caused me to melt entirely! My hands pawed at him insanely, fighting off pins and needles across every nerve. I grabbed his belt, then let my hand glide over his lap. Just as I'd hoped, his actions slowed, allowing me to gradually regain myself. I let my hand grip his hilt, from top to bottom through his khaki's, slowly repaying him for nearly shattering my resistance. His hand stayed firmly cupped over my breast as the base of my shirt slid up his arm, allowing the cool air of the basement to caress my perspiring skin.

The moment we were sharing was tinged in hot, arduous lust, but warded in deep respect for one another. Silent lines were drawn and we stayed behind those lines, while enjoying the fruits of what lay within those boundaries. We'd come so far in our relationship and, this particular night, we'd reached a milestone. Lucas had shown that he would stay true to his love for me, as well as his intent to stay pure until he felt the moment was perfect for us both. I had shown him that I'd do anything for him, even help him stay on the path he'd chosen. It was as if his golden heart had turned to a shimmering diamond, making him more priceless than before.

"Looks like Gale is having a midnight snack, wouldn't you

agree, ladies?" Brenna's annoying, cynical voice came from out of nowhere.

I broke off from Lucas instantly, hoping it was just my mind playing some sadistic joke on me. It wasn't. The lights were dim, but flickering, struggling to stay on and there, standing in the doorway, arms crossed in front of her, was Brenna.

Shannoea and Sarah were on either side of her, blushing as badly as I was. "So is this what you gave everything up for? A horny geek and a petting party in his mother's basement?"

That was more than I could stand. I got up from the floor, tugged my shirt down over my exposed bosom, and slapped her square in the mouth.

"I've had more than enough of your insults. Brenna!" Lucas put himself between us, hoping to moderate, but I was far too upset. "How dare you come here and disrespect him like that!"

Brenna was shocked and stood still, holding her cheek and jaw, dumbfounded that she'd unwittingly gone too far.

Sarah and Shannoea stepped in, dismissing Lucas from between us. "We don't have time for this, Gale," Sarah insisted. "We finished speaking with your father, then came as soon we finished off the Rostair that attacked us. It's far worse than we'd thought," she added.

I was puzzled, wondering how it could be worse. "What do you mean?"

"Gale, they must've caught his scent, somehow. I don't know, but," Shannoea was stammering just as bad as Sarah, "it's

Luke they're after. I heard 'em talking about him, after I spotted the whole group heading this way! If we hurry, we can still catch 'em, but we have to leave, like, now-ish!"

"What? But how could—" Suddenly, it hit me. The only way they could've traced Lucas' scent was when he went out to the store, to buy me those gifts! "Oh no, Lord help us, if you're right!"

Sarah shook Brenna until she finally had her attention. "You need to get your head back into the game, Brenna. But first you should apologize to Gale and Luke. They didn't deserve that sort of guff from you!"

Brenna had a guilty look on her face for the first time ever. I almost wished I could've found a way to get a snapshot of it, before it disappeared forever. "I'm-I'm sorry, to both of you. Sarah's right, I was, uh...an ass. You two are nice together." She squeezed out what looked like a broken smile to appease the rest of us.

Seeing her attempt to be positive was an occasion to remember, so I, for one, was happy with what she'd said. Lucas seemed much the same, in silent agreement as he nodded his head. Shannoea and Sarah joined in Lucas' approving nod, then returned to the subject at hand.

I looked at the three of them while placing a hand on Lucas' shoulder. "Well, if they're after Lucas, I'm not leaving him here!"

Shannoea jumped in. "I agree, honestly, if even one of those creeps manages to get by us, we won't be safe, chasing after him. I say bring him along. Who knows, he may even come in handy!"

"Gale, if you think it's a wise move, then who am I to judge?" Sarah said with a nod.

I turned to Brenna, who was still babying her face, "What about you, don't you have anything to add?" I half expected her to try to sneak in another snide remark, but instead, she lowered her hands from her face, placing them on her hips.

"I shouldn't have to repeat myself, but since you insist, I recall once saying; *La mort apprivoiser les mechents*." I watched her somber expression take on a mischievous look, almost as though she'd completely forgotten about me slapping her. "Let's be off. I don't want to be late for my manicure."

This was it, our final move against the Rostair. They were coming to wage a war in the streets of Port Clinton against us, and we would finally meet them head-on. I grabbed Lucas and followed Shannoea as she whisked to the area where she last spotted them. The hunt was on and we were playing for keeps.

CHAPTER 29: GALE

The streets were quiet and the night air chilled everything to the bone. Somewhere, hidden among the shadows of the streets and houses, the Rostair marched toward the last known location of their prize, Lucas' head. I would see them all dead before they could kill him, they would never have him, so long as I drew breath. We all gathered on the rooftop of an old hotel building, huddled in the center.

I leaned in and whispered, "Now, let's all stay close to one another, and if you need to contact anyone, use your mental bridge. We can't afford for anyone, aside from the one you're speaking with, to hear us."

"We should head on over to the edge of town; that's where I saw them gathering," Shannoea said eagerly.

Sarah interjected, "How many did you see? I mean, we need some idea as to their numbers."

"Nearly twelve. Jeremiah phoned for some help after we took out his three buddies at the airport." She sounded as if she were still thinking about the events, as though they were still fresh in her mind. "He never had near enough time to get the kind of numbers he needed, he's only been at it for a little over a week or so."

I shook my head. "They'll still be hard to deal with. They've most likely fanned out to cover more ground. Maybe we can use Lucas' scent to lure them to an ambush?"

Brenna raised her eyebrow, cracking a smile, "I dare say, I like that plan." She looked positively impressed. "Let's use your boyfriend as bait then pick them off, one by one!" She rubbed her palms together in anticipation, slyly grinning to herself.

"Hey, wait a minute here," Lucas sounded insulted as he pushed his way into our huddle. "How come I don't have any say about being used, like a dog-treat on a string?"

Shannoea put her hand on his shoulder and laughed. "Relax, Luke, we'll protect you! Besides, all we wanna do is have you run through some streets and alleys to spread your scent. When they smell you, they'll come running, but by then you'll already be safe with us guarding you!" She made it sound so simple, as if anything we'd ever planned had gone without incident.

He looked at her, the worry heavy in his eyes, but he also looked convinced it would work. "So that's it, I get their attention then one of you will teleport me out, before they find me?"

Shannoea nodded, followed by Brenna and Sarah. "We won't let anything happen to you, Luke. But we need your help, if this is going to work," Sarah's voice was soft and reassuring, which seemed to comfort him even more.

He turned to me and asked, "What do you think, Gale? I mean, it is *your* plan! If you think it'll work, then I'll do it. But I don't want any part of it, if you don't agree with them." It took a few moments, the idea that he would be risking his life to lure the enemy out into the open was intense enough, but if we were wrong and Jeremiah anticipated this move, we would be facing dire results. I was beginning to regret opening my mouth at all, but any other choice we may have had seemed miles away, I had no better an idea, than the one I'd suggested.

"I need you to trust me, Lucas—we can make this work," I said, looking him in the eyes. He nodded back and I wrapped my arms around him, then leapt into the air, taking on my raven form.

"The rest of us will set up an aerial perimeter. Sarah will use her sensory ability to locate each of them." Brenna spoke to us mentally as we scattered into the air, fanning out just enough to stay within range of our shared mental bridge. It didn't take long before we located the infested areas. Sarah perched on the rooftop nearest the first Rostair as I silently landed near the house, close by.

"Sarah has found the first one. Lucas is going to lure her into the house where I'm hiding. Then I want Brenna to deliver the kill," I informed them. Lucas and I took human form, then positioned ourselves. *"We need to make sure we dispose of them, the way we did with Edgar, so no one will find the bodies."*

"Sounds good to me. I'll keep an eye out for others while you guys focus on icing that one." Shannoea replied, landing on a lamppost.

Lucas waited until he could see the Rostair woman from

across the street then emerged from the shadows, kicking over a metal trash-can by the front door. She jerked to attention and sniffed the air. His acting was superb! He pretended to be startled, backing up slowly as if he had no idea what to do. I was thoroughly impressed!

She darted after him, shifting into the shape of a cougar. As she entered the shadows, I jumped from around the corner and slammed into her.

Brenna swooped in and gashed her across the chest with her talons, before taking on her human form. She bit her own hand the same way Shannoea had. She squeezed the blood into the open wound, then I kicked the Rostair into the corner of the fenced yard, backing away slowly.

"Let's go, she's finished," Brenna scoffed, diving into the air, then shifting to her raven form again.

I looked at Lucas, who seemed to be enjoying himself, to a degree. I whisked him to the rooftop then took flight again, with his soul lanced as the familiar veil of smoke around me, waiting for Sarah's next detection.

"There, those two, by the pickup truck!" Sarah alerted, landing on a lamppost, across the street.

I looked at Shannoea and Brenna. *Can you two handle them?*

"Not a problem. Brenna, you distract 'em, then I'll slam that truck on top of 'em both!"

"A truck? This I simply must see!" Brenna chuckled eagerly. She landed nearby, shifting to her human form, while Shannoea

swooped in stealthily behind the pickup truck. As Brenna approached the two, I landed next to Sarah, watching their plan unfold.

"Well, hello there. Would either of you two, gorgeous young studs care to help a poor, defenseless woman out?" She used the most provocative voice I'd ever heard from her.

The two Rostair looked puzzled, but eager.

"Whoa, get a load of this broad!" one of them exclaimed, hopping to attention. "What seems to be the problem, Miss?" he asked, licking his lips.

She flicked her hair back, making sure they had a view of her cleavage from the neckline of her silk designer sanguine blouse, "It's my car, I think it's out of gas. Would one of you be kind enough to inject me, with some of yours? Just a squirt or two would be heavenly."

They leered at each other, intense lust in their eyes.

I couldn't believe how flirtatious she acted! I'd never seen her like that, ever! Just as they turned back to her, the truck raised from the asphalt, then Shannoea hurled it onto both of them, barely missing Brenna!

"Sorry, girlfriend—didn't mean to cut it so close!" Shannoea cackled just behind the fallen truck.

Brenna looked unamused.

The two Rostair were unconscious, their heads sticking out from underneath the front bumper. Shannoea and Brenna lacerated their arms and dripped their blood into the fallen duo.

"Okay, lets' ice the next few. We're on a roll, tonight!" Shannoea added, flying off.

Brenna followed, shaking her head.

The night dragged on as we picked off the Rostair, thinning their numbers, dramatically. Lucas was doing a splendid job of luring them, and having fun doing it! We'd slain six of their kind in less than two hours and all seemed to be going according to plan. We were approaching the area where Shannoea claimed to have spotted Jeremiah, as well as his more elite forces. She led the way toward Fulton street, near Bell Mell.

Suddenly, out of nowhere, Sarah was knocked out of the air by a Rostair in the form of a large falcon! She hurtled to the ground below, crashing into the dirt.

"Keep going, I'll help Sarah. You guys go after Jeremiah!" Shannoea ordered, then rushed after her, while Brenna, Lucas, and I closed in on Jeremiah's encampment, an abandoned strip of old houses across the street from both Bell Mell and a convenience store. We landed near their group, took on our human form, and let them get a good look at their fate-makers.

Jeremiah turned and smiled, not showing even a sliver of surprise.

"Well, I'd say it's about time you arrived! I was beginning to get the impression that you'd stay hidden behind your worthless father while I ravaged this mud hole of a town!"

Already, I began to hate the sound of his voice, so smooth, yet brusque. His outfit added to his royal, yet beastly visage; a black pauldron of animal fur over a tan-hide, an open-chested trench-coat, and a necklace of small bones and jewels draped around his neck. His black, torn jeans looked grimy in the moonlight. His dark hair was slick-back, almost as if some part of him actually cared about his appearance.

Lucas gasped, frightened, yet curious. "Is that *Nathan's gang?*" He started shaking wildly, as if the reaper itself had shown its face.

"Well, as you know, to make my plan work, I needed numbers. The kind of numbers it's hard to come by when one is forced to recruit in this dull, meaningless wasteland." He grinned from ear to ear. "It worked out well enough, though, if you've made it this far, that means you and your diseased group of pigeons have already killed most of the ones I recruited."

Brenna scoffed, flicking her hair to one side. "Maybe you should just break your own damn neck. Save yourself the humiliation of having Gale and I do it in front of your dirty little cornball army!"

"Lemme kill 'em all for you, sir! I've been wanting some pay-back!"

I recognized the voice; Travis, the first one I attacked the night I saved Lucas' life.

Jeremiah glanced over at him, then looked back at us, contemplating the thought.

"I say, let him have his fun," a female voice purred. She emerged from behind a nearby tree, in the form of a tiger. "And while we're at it, maybe we should let the others play as well, eh?" She shifted to her human form—a skinny, ragged-looking woman, with tight, black daisy-duke shorts, black ribbons wrapped around her calves, and a smaller version of Jeremiah's animal-hide coat. Her face was smooth, but her hair was unkempt, it looked matted and frazzled.

"That's a fabulous idea, my dear. Travis, you and your friends go entertain our guests, my mate and I would so enjoy a good fight, right about now!"

So, this woman was his mate. I thought to myself, *how predictable of him, to choose one as unclean, as he is.*

Matt and Dillon, the other two from Nathan's group attacked Brenna and I, while Travis rushed at Lucas. We scattered, trying to gain distance enough to fight them off.

"Lucas!" I yelled for him, but as I kicked Matt in the chest, two more Rostair leapt out of the darkness and cornered me against a brick building. I fought as hard as I could, but their onslaught was well choreographed. I tried to whisk past them, but they were determined, the three of them hot on my tail, taking the forms of animals faster than my raven form! I looked over and saw Brenna having the same problem, the Rostair, Dillon, was aided by two others!

Travis still had only himself against Lucas, who was defending himself quite well, despite being a mere human.

In the back of my mind, I prayed for him as I dodged each attack from my foes. I needed to end them before they could overrun us. I flew off, swooping over the strip of houses and as I'd suspected, my foes pursued me. *God, help us,* I said to myself.

CHAPTER 30: LUCAS

"I'm gonna eat your guts fresh out of your corpse after I kill you, punk!"

Travis always was one to talk big, but he sucked at being intimidating. I was already sweating from the fight, but I wasn't tired at all. I felt pretty good! He dove onto me, but I kicked him as hard as I could, between his legs and then pushed him off me. He rolled away, clutching his manhood, groaning and snarling. I didn't waste any time, I ran over and kicked the side of his head, like a soccer-ball, stunning him even more. That's when I felt myself losing composure.

"This time, *you're* the one that's gonna die!" I screamed as loud as I could, my chest on fire with rage. I jumped into the air with everything I had, aiming for his head with both feet. He scrambled off, shifting into what looked like a fossa, just before I stomped into the dirt. I recoiled, looking everywhere for the cat-like beast, but couldn't see a trace of it, anywhere.

I heard Jeremiah and his woman laughing in the background, probably having the time of their lives, while I struggled to stay alive

I backed against the same red brick building Gale had flown over. I didn't want this jerk surprising me from behind. *Maybe I should make a run further down Fulton street,* I thought. I knew

I couldn't trust those two freaks, they might finish me off; if I happened to take down Travis! I looked around, hoping to see Brenna, or even Shannoea and Sarah, but no one was anywhere to be seen. I darted off into the cold dimly lit street near Bell Mell, looking for some way to gain an edge in winning this fight, hoping Gale would come back and give me a desperately needed hand.

After about ten minutes of looking, I managed to find a big, rusty lead pipe and a knife someone had dropped near a storm drain. I hid the knife in my leg pocket and held onto the lead pipe firmly. I kept my back to every wall I came across, inching my way against every empty house. Luckily, there were plenty of empty ones, this time of year.

I was doing a good job of being stealthy, but then, I was ambushed by a large gorilla! He rammed into me then pummeled me on the ground. I swung the pipe while shielding my face, praying it would break his arm, or at least stun him!

"Thought you could hide from me, eh? I'm gonna beat you to death and then beat up your corpse!" Even though he sucked at threatening people, I was still scared to death. I was taking a lot of damage all at once. I started to go numb from the heavy barrage of punches he was landing on me. I had to act fast. If he kept this up, I was a dead man, no doubt about it! I kicked him in the crotch again, only this time it barely made him flinch. But he did stop punching me long enough for me to reach up and head-butt him in the nose.

He clutched his face and I rammed the end of the rusty pipe directly into his throat. He collapsed in a heap beside me, trying to get his breath back as I rolled into the street. I had to get some distance. None of those attacks would last long against a gorilla, let alone a Rostair gorilla! I crawled toward the other side of the street, stumbling all over the place like a wounded squirrel. I could hear Travis groaning behind me, I looked back and saw he'd shifted back to his human form again, still clutching his throat.

"Keep runnin', punk!" he coughed. "I got all night!"

The pain was too much. I collapsed in the middle of the street.

Travis caught up to me and flipped me over.

I quickly stabbed him with the knife in the side of his leg just above the knee. He screamed and hollered as I twisted the blade then broke off the handle so he couldn't pull it out. "I might not win this fight, but I'll be *damned* if I let you walk off without something to remember me by, Travis!" I had no idea what had gotten into me, I was like a mad dog, ready to go down fighting! I grabbed him by the neck and stood up. "Tell you what, I'll let your friends know I sent you to hell!"

His eyes watered and he looked terrified—the same terror I'd felt in the woods the night he'd helped Nathan kill me.

I exhaled slowly, a chilling sensation overtook me. My body was pins and needles in a way I'd never felt before.

"Don't, please, don't kill me, man! I'll totally leave you

alone, I friggin' *swear*, man!"

He pleaded for his life, but I'd had more than enough of him. The urge to punch a hole right through him was too overwhelming. I looked down at my hands; they looked fuzzy, distorted almost, as if my entire body was pulsing and vibrating in one spot. I let go of his neck and reached right through his body like a ghost, then touched his heart with my middle and index fingers. I felt it stop cold, as if the energy I was covered in was the breath of the Grim-Reaper himself. I looked down at him as the cold wind over my skin thinned out. He was dead. I'd actually murdered someone for the first time ever.

My throat clenched, followed by a numbing sensation in my legs. I fell to my knees and threw up all over the asphalt.

"Well now, what have we here, eh?"

Just when I thought I had a genuine moment of recovery, a familiar, soul-chilling voice rumbled not more than three feet away. "Bravo, Luke. I gotta admit you've come a long way since that night when I painted those trees with your blood! I also gotta admit I'm glad you saved me the trouble of killing Travis myself, I hated him the most."

The urge to throw up again grew strong. My nerves were on edge as I looked up and saw a terrifyingly familiar shape standing over me...

CHAPTER 31: LUCAS

"*Nathan?!* What in hell—" I didn't even finish my sentence
before he started laughing.

"Hell?!" He snickered with a beyond sinister grin. "It's funny
you mention that coz hell is exactly where I plan on choke-
slamming you down to!" He was *way* more ferocious looking.
The Rostair had done the unthinkable. He was scarier looking
than any nightmare I'd ever had, angrier and hungrier than
any animal I'd ever seen. To top off the already blood-soaked
situation, he had all their powers—speed, strength, agility, and
their unique animal powers. I felt a tinge of fear spill over me. I
couldn't stay focused. "Let's get this over with quick, kid. I've
been waiting to finish you off for weeks!"

He grabbed my shirt and pulled me up from the ground,
closer to him. I looked him square in the eyes and something
extremely deep inside me just snapped. "Don't you ever, *ever*
touch me again!" My body raged out of control; I punched him
in the face as hard as I could, stunning him, then reversed his
grab on me before picking him up over my head. "I've had it
with you, Nate!" I hurled him as hard as I could and he sailed
headfirst into a nearby parked car, totaling the entire front end.
I looked down at my hands in shock; my body was on fire with
anger. Just looking at him was enough to set me off!

I heard him pulling himself from the wreckage of the vehicle so I charged in hard. The second he stood up on the destroyed hood, I slammed into him from behind, hurling both of us through the rest of the car. Metal and glass raked across both our bodies, blood poured from some of the wounds, but healed as quickly as they appeared. I had my hand pressed on the back of his head, making his face drag through every inch of the car-frame, followed by the asphalt behind where it was parked.

We skidded to an abrupt stop. He somehow rose up on his hands and knees—in a flash he turned into a giant python! I didn't have a second to my name before he completely wrapped around my body, crushing me.

He lowered his snake-face to mine and hissed into my ear, "I bet you wish you coulda' seen her one last time, before I *crushed* the life outta you, eh?"

I was losing fast. I turned my head, facing the side of his maw, and instinctively bit down on his eye. He screamed and uncoiled from me, rolling against the curb as I hit the ground.

Under controlled, shallow breaths, I said, "I *will* see her again!" I clutched my chest. "You're going down, Nate!" I felt my lungs reforming, followed by every rib he'd cracked. I broke off a large, sharp piece of the busted car-frame and dove at him. I thought I'd have enough time before his eye healed up, but I was wrong.

He jerked his head up and saw me in midair. Then he whipped his entire python body into me. It sent me flying into a lamppost, which uprooted on impact. It hit the ground, then I landed on top of it, re-breaking my ribs all over again. I couldn't even scream, the wind was totally knocked from me.

I groaned instead, clutching my body. My eyes crept open and I saw Nathan rushing over to me. He stomped on my chest before morphing his right hand into a tiger claw and his entire left arm, into a horse's front leg. "Now let's see how tough you are!" He knelt down onto me, swiped my arms away from my body with his tiger claw, bloodying both of them, and then stamped down hard with the hoof into my rib cage. The damage of both was way more than I could handle, even with Gale's energies still flowing in me. He was doing too much damage for me to focus on any defense at all.

"How's it going down there, little man? Where's your girlfriend at *now*, eh?" I squirmed and wriggled, trying to pry loose, but he was clawing and stamping way too fast. Just as I'd started to give up, I felt the broken piece of the car-frame I'd dropped, near my hand.

"Eat *this*!" I screamed, stabbing him in the shoulder with everything I had left in me. I twisted it as hard as I could then broke it off in his arm to mangle the wound, hoping it would buy me enough time to heal again.

He growled and started swearing, then kicked me like a football, right in the gut.

I nearly blacked out as the pain seared through me, but snapped back after slamming back-first into a house near where the totaled car was parked. I fell into a heap on the sidewalk and with bated breaths hoped the agony in my chest would stop soon. *Gale, where are you? He's gonna slaughter me if you don't hurry up and find me!* I cried out in the back of my head, hoping to God she could hear me.

"You're so damn dead!"

I looked up and saw Nate pulling the bloodied shard of metal from his arm slowly, grunting to himself in pain. He waited for the wound to close up, then shifted his attention back to me. I knew I only had seconds before he'd maul me again. His head slowly took the shape of a rhino, then he charged at me, full speed and full-bore. It was odd seeing the head of a rhino on the body of a human!

I shambled to stand up, despite staring at his misshapen form while thinking I could dive out of his path, but I was too slow. I closed my eyes and gritted my teeth just as he slammed into me. The force was so great the wall behind me caved in! I couldn't feel most of my body as I was helplessly being rammed through chairs, plaster walls, glass, and wood before he stopped. I was barely able to fight going into what felt like a coma after that. I lay draped over the top of a broken desk, gasping desperately for air. My arms and legs were numb and my chest was on fire. I couldn't even open my eyes from the amount of dust and glass I'd been dragged through.

Seriously desperate, my nerves spiked; I needed a chance to heal, maybe even escape. He grabbed me by the throat and

I instinctively grabbed onto his wrist, trying to pry his fingers from me.

"Now, I think I'm gonna slowly pull your head off," he growled.

I felt his hand slowly morphing again—this time it felt like the talon of an eagle, a very *big* eagle! The nails dug into my neck, curving deep into me. I tried to scream, but nothing came out except a painful gagging sound.

"I can't wait to see your girlfriend's face when she finds you dead."

My grip tightened suddenly. My anger grew and I felt something wake inside me. I had one hand on his wrist while balling up the other, clenching it as hard as I could. I re-lived the fear and intensity of the night he'd killed me. My knuckles felt white-hot just before I punched him as hard as I could. He tried to grab my attacking arm, but it didn't stop me, I kept swinging on him, hitting the side of his face harder and faster each time. He tightened his grip on my neck, I could feel the nails of his eagle claw sinking deeper in, time was running out quick, I was losing way too much blood.

Under all the pain and gasping, I felt my body finish healing, but it didn't matter—he'd drained me of everything I had. My flurry of punches slowed enough that he grabbed my arm and pinned it against the arm he'd been strangling me with. Under what was left of my voice, I choked and gasped, "Go ahead, you jer-*jerk*! Jus-s ki-kill m-me!" The taste of my own blood in my mouth made me gag even more, making him chuckle.

He seemed sadistically pleased at himself, "I wish I'd had these Rostair powers years ago! All I have to do is kill whatever I wanna change into, then drink its blood!"

If I could've opened my eyes, I would've seen his face lighting up with blood-stained glee.

"The minute they changed me, all the drugs in me burned up, my head cleared up, and everything made perfect sense! I'm a *hell* of a lot more now than I ever was before!" I started to feel the cold pains of my body shutting down all over again, even Nate's voice was getting fuzzy to my ears. "I know that girl of yours gave you some of her powers, so now, I'm gonna take 'em from *you*!" He bit down on my forearm.

I felt his teeth tear into my weak flesh. I couldn't scream, or cry out, instead, the stinging of my neck raced alongside the agony of my arm. My grip loosened from his wrist, falling limp on the broken tabletop—I had nothing left.

CHAPTER 32: LUCAS

I woke up, still laying on the tabletop. I jerked to attention as I replayed everything in my head, up to that point. My muscled tensed; I glanced around the room, looking for any sign of Nathan. I heard a gagging sound in the next room, a trail of dark red fluid led into another crumbled wall. I kept my arms tensed in case I was walking into a trap. There in the corner, throwing up, was Nathan. His body was going haywire! His arms and legs were morphing out of control, cycling through every creature he'd slaughtered then reforming into human limbs.

He hacked and choked before turning to see me standing in the hole he'd made in the wall. "*You!! What the hell did you do to me?*" he hissed, his face stretching and forming into countless animal heads.

I panicked at the sight of him slipping in and out of so many deadly creatures. I turned and ran as fast as I could, dodging the rubble, hoping to find somewhere to hide until the others found me.

"*Get back here!*"

I heard him behind me, scrambling to catch me. I hopped through the crumbled wall and fell flat on my face. Just then, I felt him pin me down from behind, his arms still shifting in and out from animal to human. "*You almost killed me, you little freak!*" Even his voice was distorting badly, "How come I can't take your powers? *Why does your blood taste so friggin' gross?*" He scowled.

I was still panicking, my limbs were shaking, and I had no idea how I was going to get out from under him before he started tearing at my spine. I glanced onto the road ahead of me, spotting a manhole cover nearby. It gave me an idea, My entire body started to phase again. Just like during my struggle with Travis, I felt the urge to give in to whatever instinctive sensation I was having. I exhaled and suddenly, I fell straight through the asphalt, into the sewer-line below the street! I landed on all fours and quickly started looking for the ladder leading up to street level.

It didn't take long to find and I climbed up. I shoved the man-hole cover as hard as I could. It jumped from its base and landed with a loud, heavy clang next to the opening. I jumped out, hoping Nathan was nowhere near me. I looked across the street and saw Jeremiah leaning against a lamppost.

"Well my newest disciple, you've got quite a resourceful young prey on your hands!"

I'd almost forgotten how smooth and yet brusque his voice sounded; it fit his demeanor perfectly.

"Enough toying with this gutter-trash, Nathan. If you can't handle the tasks I give you, then *I'll* finish him off," he sneered, before approaching me.

This was it. I was as good as dead. Gale said he was a

soldier-class Rostair. I assumed he'd killed quite a lot of wild and deadly creatures over the years. Panic set in all over again, I knew Nathan's weak point was slow torture and fearsome threats, but this guy was different. I had absolutely no idea how fast I'd need to run, before he'd gut me!

He morphed his arm into a white tiger claw and grabbed my torn shirt with his human hand.

I froze with terror as he drew his clawed arm back and I shut my eyes tight.

"I've got a *better* idea, old man!" Nathan voice yelled from behind Jeremiah.

I heard a violent stabbing noise, followed by Jeremiah gasping and choking. I felt a faint spray of warm blood across my chest before I opened my eyes, seeing Nathan with his arm in the shape of a bear-claw, mauling a large chunk out of Jeremiah's collarbone.

"How about I finish *you* off, instead?" Nathan remarked with a sinister grin.

Jeremiah released his grip on me and fell to the ground at Nathan's feet, favoring his wound with his free hand.

Nali came running out screaming, *"No-o! I'll kill you for hurting him, you monster!"* She changed into a Doberman and dove at Nathan, only to end up getting backhanded into a truck parked across the street. She slowly shifted back into human form, groaning in pain from the dent she'd left in the side of the truck.

Despite the pain he was in, Jeremiah still managed to confront Nathan with furious dignity. "What?? Why you-you traitorous *alley mongrel*!" He scowled.

Nathan licked the blood from his bear-claw. "You said it yourself, you crusty, old geezer. The Rostair family has *no room* for the weak! The way I see it, if you felt the need to recruit more Rostair to take care of one or two birds, then you're as weak as they come!" He was getting lost in his arrogance again, I started to back up slowly, hoping he'd keep rambling on about how strong he was. He saw me, of course, smiling while he shook his head, staring at me with the look of a sadist. "This is where I clean out the fridge, take your woman, and leave you where you fall. Don't worry too much about her, Jeremiah. I'll kill her too, once I'm done with her."

"You'll *die* for this, you *filth*! My family will have your *head*!" Jeremiah warned with a clenched tone.

Nathan shot back a husky laugh, "I'm not scared of your little family, old timer. This is *my* new world order! I'll slaughter every damn one of your little dog-faced friends and take over the entire operation!"

I felt a cold breeze brush over my shoulders, the clouds were growing black, swirling around like charred butterflies. I heard cawing in the distance, but I knew it wasn't Gale. It was deeper, darker, and more furious. Wait a minute! *Those aren't clouds!* I realized as I looked closer.

They were ravens, hundreds of ravens circling and cawing—

they were everywhere!

Jeremiah, Nathan, and Nali all noticed after they caught me staring into the sky.

"What's this, some more of your buddies for me to add to the pile?" Nathan smirked.

Jeremiah spit out a mouthful of blood and said, "Not even close, you imbecile! Those are Corvidae, the creatures you *should* be killing! They've found us and now we're all going to die because of your *arrogance!*"

The ravens flew all around us, swirling like a black tornado, devouring all colors and shapes in every direction, replacing everything with a thick veil of black-silken shadows and feathers. None of us dared to make a move, all four of us were far too petrified, we watched as the torrent of ravens converged into a funnel formation between where I stood and where Jeremiah and Nathan were. The man inside the funnel of ravens raised his head and spread his arms causing the torrent of birds to flow directly into him, giving him the remainder of his form. They slowly merged into one solitary shape—a very tall, proud-looking silhouette of a man with a purple glow in his eyes. I recognized him instantly—Alexander, Gale's father!

I was speechless and white with fear, such a brilliant display of raw energy, proud heritage, and absolute authority!

He stared at the other three with piercing eyes. "This ends now!" Dark violet smoke lightly coiled from his deadly gaze. "The Rostair have no business here, yet you wander about our territory, slaughtering human and beast alike—not to mention, the Corvidae you've murdered! By this, you have forsaken your family name and house! Explain yourself, Jeremiah, for you have ever been the bane of your father's lineage! Always playing your hand against the—" he didn't get a chance to finish.

Jeremiah objected, spitting a mouthful of blood at Xander's feet, then looking him dead in the eye from upon the ground. "Shut your overzealous beak, you demented crow! You're no less guilty than I, harboring a human in your filthy little nest!" Xander clenched his fists while Jeremiah rattled on, "The daughter of a noble, cradling a mortal, that alone is far more than adequate evidence to remove not only you from this disgusting mud-pit of land, it would also be enough to cast your feather-brained wife from her place in the High-Wind-House!"

Alexander looked even more furious, the color of energy rolling from him was dark red with a tinge of gray. Jeremiah was treading too close with his insults and Gale's dad was about to unhinge. "You *dare* speak to me of treachery, swine? My daughter has broken no laws!"

Odd to hear him defend her, after all he'd said the day he attacked me. Still, it was comforting to know he had no intention of trying to kill me again!

"You, however, have broken several! Espionage from the Rostair family in territory already claimed by right is trespassing, punishable by immediate trial, in the Ravenic-courts!"

Nathan, Nali, and I tensed at the same time.

Jeremiah, his wound gaping open, rushed at Alexander, who was prepared for him.

"I won't explain myself to you, you filthy simpleton!" Jeremiah sneered, swiping at him with his good arm, in the shape of a gorilla's forearm. "I don't serve you, or my father! I told Nathan and his mindless friends to kill as they pleased, the only sure way to draw you out into the open, Xander!" He was swinging wildly, but Alexander was quicker, dodging every single attack with deadly precision. Jeremiah was obviously trying to buy enough time to heal.

Xander must have known as each time he evaded, he grinned just slightly. It made me cringe to see him toying with his attacker like a sadistic dog against a wounded cat.

I glanced back at Nathan and Nali.

Nate stood, arms folded in front of his chest, laughing as Nali pleaded for him to jump into the fight and help her mate. When she realized he wouldn't budge, she rushed into the fray herself, morphing into a rabid-looking cheetah, then dove after Xander. I glanced from the fight back to Nate several times, wondering if he would try to break my neck as I kept my distance, or if he'd simply watch the action. Nali was fast, almost blinding, but Alexander was still way faster. Jeremiah was nearly healed, as he fought, blow for blow alongside Nali, growling as he missed every strike he threw.

Suddenly, Alexander grabbed Nali by the face, then slammed

her head into the pavement, stunning her as she let out the muffled growl of a wounded cheetah. He whipped her limp body hard into Jeremiah, knocking him back, then tossed her flailing into Jeremiah's face. Half- conscious, she unwittingly diced and clawed her own mate thinking Alexander still had hold of her. When they both hit the asphalt, she scrambled to all four paws and caught up with what had happened. Jeremiah was in worse shape than before, mangled upper-body, with an eye gouged out. Nali shifted to her human form, trying to gather herself, but Gale's dad had other plans. He walked toward them and Nali let out a blood-curdling war cry as she charged him.

I watched as he caught her in mid-air then lifted her over his head as he got down on one knee. I knew what was about to happen, I'd seen it on a few wrestling shows from my childhood, he slammed her down, back-first, onto his outstretched knee, nearly snapping her in half! She went completely limp this time, her head fell back and her limbs dropped.

He looked angrily pleased with himself. "Impetuous little stray, begone!" he ordered. He tossed her broken body aside with a meaty, stomach-churning thud. "Now, Jeremiah Marcuhm Rostair, fifth son to Matthias Hyrum Rostair, you shall answer for your crimes. Come, surrender and face your sentence in the Ravenic-courts, or let the winds of death blow gently over your corpse as I escort your soul to the afterlife, personally."

I could *not* believe how brutal he was! Nathan looked *more* shocked than *me*! If I didn't know better, I could've sworn he was taking serious notes from Gale's dad

"You'll never lay a hand on my soul, you filthy, old vermin!" Jeremiah was barely moving as his wounds slowly closed up. He'd never have enough time to defend himself with Alexander's barbaric onslaught going so well. He gagged and hacked as he tried to stand and then, as if he realized how bleak a chance he had, Jeremiah stood, fists clenched, his blood-soaked knuckles turning white.

This is it, I thought to myself, gawking lifelessly. *This whole corner of town is about to get leveled, Armageddon style. I think I'd better get the heck outta here, before I end up getting sucked up into it!* I began to back away slowly, hoping to get more than enough distance from the upcoming mayhem.

I saw Nate making his way toward Nali's body, trying to stay completely away from the fight.

Jeremiah ran in and grappled with Alexander, their hands interlocked like two wrestlers about to square off. He looked Jeremiah dead in the eye and asked, "Why, Jeremiah? Why have you forsaken your own house? Your father would be infuriated, should he see what you've done!" Their test of mettle shook the road and buildings around them.

"To *hell* with my father! He is naive and shallow!" he spat back. "There is far more to all of this than your feeble mind can comprehend! You are alone, Xander! Your Pillar is cracked and rotten with deceit at its very core and soon it will topple all about you, crushing everything and all your little birdy-friends, as well!" He started to laugh behind rigid coughs, before Alexander head-butted him once, then slammed him against a nearby building.

"Enough riddles, heretic! Speak plainly!" he commanded with a husky tone.

Jeremiah spit in his face. "I don't answer to you, *vulture*! I'll *die* before I give you abominates any sort of aid!" He kicked Alexander in the chest with both legs, pushing him back only ten feet, then, in a split second, morphed into a large, mangy-looking lion! The wounds on his body reappeared, even while his body reshaped itself.

I wondered how he planned to win with all those deep gashes and a missing collarbone

Alexander's eyes smoldered with the familiar purple glowing smoke, "Fine. If the flavor of death is all that you seek, than death is what you shall taste!" His voice was deep and frightening every single time he spoke and I got goosebumps with every syllable

Xander's human form scattered into the swarm of ravens again and they all darted in a funneling torrent around Jeremiah's lion form, pecking and clawing him from every direction. Jeremiah swiped his massive paws and kicked with his hind legs, biting at them, but it was useless. His paws and teeth passed right through each raven like a branch through smoke. The ravens would dissipate and reform almost instantly, then resume their onslaught. He roared and snarled insanely. He rolled and tumbled on the street as if on fire or covered in hornets, hoping to shake off Alexander's attacks.

Stuck in a state of awe, my heartbeat raced at the sight, my breath felt cold as ice, and I was soaked in adrenaline just from watching all the action! Abruptly, the eyes of each and every raven started to light up! They opened their beaks and started cawing ravenously, I fell to my knees in terror as I watched Alexander slowly draining Jeremiah, bit by bit, of his soul. Trails of light tapered from Jeremiah's body into the mouths of several hundred ravens, while he flailed and tumbled all over the surrounding area.

His cries chilled me to the bone, I started to turn away, but it was too late.

The lion reverted to human form, then fell lifelessly to the ground. The storm-cloud of ravens circled him for a few seconds, then funneled back into the shape of Alexander, standing tall and proud next to his prey.

I felt sick to my stomach, it didn't take long for me to feel the urge to vomit from the sight. I closed my eyes and retched hard, I leaned with my arm against the corner of a nearby house until I'd finished. After the constricting inside me subsided, I opened my eyes to see Alexander approaching me. He didn't look mad, but he *did* look concerned. The cold sweat on my forehead, coupled with the relief I'd gotten after throwing up, kept me from feeling scared of him.

"Are you injured?" he asked, his eyes still smoldering faintly with coils of purple energy. I shook my head, feeling my neck still tightening in areas from the tension I'd been put through. "Excellent. My daughter would never forgive me, should I allow harm to befall you."

His tone caught me off guard, it was calming and sincere, the way a father's voice should always sound. The fact that he felt any sort of concern for my well-being made me feel safe and secure near him. I wiped my mouth with my sleeve, then smiled, looking up at him. His eyes stopped glowing, and he offered a very small grin as he said, "I want to apologize to you, Lucas." I could tell right off this wasn't something he did regularly. "Rhune is my only child, and I would prefer to see her happy in these dark times."

I did everything I could not to choke up; I tried to hide it, but I knew he could tell.

"I can see no fault with you, Lucas Carmicheal, and. if our beloved White-Raven has given you grace, then perhaps I too should take notice and support her decision." I let out a sigh of relief. The biggest hurdle I'd ever faced was her father's wrath, and I'd just been given his approval and blessing! A newfound spark of confidence welled up inside of me, I finally felt completely accepted, and I knew things would only get better from now on.

He seemed pleased at my reaction, allowing a slightly bigger smile to push its way onto his face.

I didn't know what to say and all I could think of was

shaking his hand. I fought off what little bit of insecurity remained and held out my hand, hanging onto my smile.

He looked down at me hand, then back to me. I didn't know if he would go for it, but I didn't care either way, the confidence his approval gave me was empowering. I'd won his trust at last, his faith in me began to show through his rough, unforgiving gaze, lighting a new road of hope for Gale and I. As my confidence peaked, I said, "Sir, I really do love Gale. I would never intentionally hurt her, she's everything to me. I honestly just want to do my best to make her happy." For the first time, I didn't feel meek or worried about speaking my mind; I knew he would hear me out and reach some sort of understanding. This level of confidence was astounding! In uncharted territory, I felt like nothing could ruin it!

He wrapped his hand around mine, almost swallowing it with his massive fingers, "I am pleased to hear that, Lucas, because if you should harm her, in any way, you'll share the same fate as our Rostair friend, the late Jeremiah."

Just as quickly as it came, the confidence dried up completely. The stare he gave me impaled every ounce of pride and security I'd mustered. If he was kidding, there was absolutely *no way* to tell. I hated dry humor, if he was using it, that is. I hoped with all my being that he was just testing my diligence in gaining his friendship. I felt my smile slowly collapse, followed by a worried twitch in my eyes.

"Father?" I heard Gale's voice in the distance, breaking the awkward moment Alexander had caused. He turned just as I peeked over his broad shoulder and saw Gale, Shannoea, and Sarah approaching us. "What happened? Is Lucas all right?" She sounded almost frantic.

I stepped from behind him and grinned, despite her dad's earlier overbearing attitude. I was beyond relieved to see her again. After all I'd been through, it was warming to see those gorgeous, purple eyes of hers in the moonlight.

"*Lucas!*" Her eyes widened and she pounced on me, wrapping me in her arms, then she kissed the side of my neck. After the blood-soaked fighting and the close scrapes with death, it was relieving to feel her around me again. It made everything I'd been through worth it. "What happened to your clothes?" she whispered and slowly slid her arms from me.

I looked down at myself, realizing I had multiple tears and shreds of what used to be a gray shirt and black cargo pants hanging on for dear life to my body. "I-uh..." I tried to come up with an answer that wouldn't make her worry, but nothing came to mind. I forced myself to answer nonchalantly, "Nathan attacked me, so I slammed him through a car."

Everyone stiffened, staring with widened eyes as I pointed to the ruined vehicle across the street.

"Then we fought a little more and he put me through that wall, right there."

They were still gawking at me.

I couldn't tell if they believed me or not. "We pretty much

destroyed most of the rooms on the other *side* of the wall he put me through."

None of them blinked, not once.

"He nearly killed me about three times, but then he tried biting me and when he got a taste of my blood, it made his Rostair powers freak out!"

They looked at one another, shocked surprise on their faces.

I didn't know what I'd said, but their reaction looked familiar, as if they knew why my blood reacted with him.

Sarah tilted her head, "Nathan tried to absorb your energy? As in the same manner a Rostair assimilates any animal they've killed?"

I nodded. "Yeah. I'd show you the scars where he dug his talons in, but every wound healed up about ten minutes ago—the same way yours do. Why? Is something wrong?"

"Well, *that* can't be right!" Shannoea blurted, "Only the blood of a *natural born* Corvidae has that effect on the Rostair! Our blood and energies contend with theirs, if a Rostair manages to taste enough Corvidaen blood, *their* blood turns to dust, their heart crystallizes, and they die!" She made hand gestures for each detail, making my stomach churn all over again.

Sarah's curiosity grew, but then she raised one eyebrow with a strange curve on her lips. "Unless..."

Gale turned to her, eyes narrowed in confusion. "Unless, what?" She asked.

"I'm not entirely certain. It's only theoretical, at this point."

Sarah had everyone's attention after that, even mine. "Gale, did you ever feed on Luke?"

"Of course I did, I had to feed on him the day I saved his life—twice." She almost looked ashamed.

I quickly scooped her hand into mine, showing her a grateful smile as she looked over at me.

Sarah's expression looked more serious. "And did you feed on him at any point during your relationship, afterward?"

Gale nodded slowly. "He asked me to, the first time was because I hadn't actually fed for nearly a month." Her face was flushed with shame despite my gripping her hand. "It took nearly the entire night to soak up enough to keep from reverting "

I glanced at her and asked, "Reverting? What does—" I didn't even finish, before she murmured the answer to me, slipping her hand from mine.

"If we Corvidae don't sate our thirst, our essence preserves itself by forcing us into our most basic form in order to use as little of our energy to exist as possible—the raven form you claim to adore." She tried to smile, but I could tell she felt shameful toward her powers and the tolls they took.

I didn't know how to react, I wanted to comfort her, but I could tell by her body language she didn't feel much like being comforted. She stood, guarded, arms folded in front of her, hands over her elbows, giving herself a cradling hug while staring at the ground. My heart started to twinge and ache, seeing her in such inner pain.

I could practically see the wheels turning in Sarah's head as she combed over every detail of her theory.

"So you've fed on his soul three or four times so far " Her brow furrowed, she ran her fingers through her hair and sighed, "If that's the case and each time you fed on Luke, he was left alive then that also means you've had to pour a portion of his energies back into him—am I right?"

Gale nodded slowly in reply, her eyes averted toward the ground.

"Then that explains everything perfectly! Gale, when you pour any portion of a soul you're drinking from back into that body, that soul still has a lot of *your* energies temporarily melding with *his*. Meaning, if you feed on him enough times, the temporary effects given by a Corvidae obviously become more and more durable, thus lasting far longer than any of us ever realized!"

"Kinda like backwash with benefits, eh?" Shannoea chimed in jokingly.

Everyone looked at her with a frustrated glare, even Alexander had a disturbed frown on his face, more prominent than usual.

"What?" Gale asked, breaking the silence.

Sarah grabbed our attention again with a resigned sigh. " It makes sense that Luke has gained hints of Corvidae abilities, which also explains why Nathan's Rostair energies were vexed and dampened when he tried to absorb Luke's Corvine soaked blood. You were lucky Gale's energy was still lingering in you when he did that. Otherwise, it would have simply killed you, with no effects gained in his favor," she said in a fatalistic tone.

I cringed, remembering every detail of our scuffle.

Alexander stiffened, "Lucas, did you happen to dispatch this Nathan during my attack on Jeremiah? I do not see his body, nor do I see the body of Jeremiah's mate, Nali."

I shook my head. "No, I didn't. He ran over to her when you were fighting, but I never saw where he went after you'd finished Jeremiah off."

They all looked around, hoping to catch any sign of either one of them, but Nathan and Nali's body were gone.

Sarah turned to Gale and said, "He couldn't have gotten far. He may intend to revive Nali, in order to claim her for himself, or—"

I interrupted, hoping to cut right to the chase, "He said he wants to destroy the Rostair and take over their operation. He said it right to Jeremiah's face, before he turned on him."

They turned to me again.

"I've known Nate for years, he's always been pretty blunt when it comes to bullying. Though, just looking at him, you'd never be able to see his true nature. He's cold and calculating, a sadistic fiend who loves to savor every twitch and gasp from the people he's hurting. He has days when he's quick and hard about it, but deep down, he's in love with tearing people down inch by inch! What's worse is that his newfound abilities have sobered him up and even made him think more clearly. Now he's even more cunning than before! Any damage his body had from the years of drug use is healed; he's a completely different person, but with the same goals. "

Shannoea slapped her open hand against her fist. "Then we need to find this creep before he does some real damage! We don't need that caveman out there, breeding an army of thugs like him!"

"Fine, let's find him and put an end to this!" Alexander said, clenching his hands eagerly.

Just as we started to break off to look for Nathan, Sarah gasped and pointed toward the rooftop of a nearby house.

"Soldier-class! Jeremiah had backup coming, everyone on your guard!" She screamed as they dropped from the edge of the rooftop to the sidewalk below.

We readied ourselves. There were four of them, but they looked far more experienced than the others. Gale stood as close to me as possible. I took that as her way of saying *You're not leaving my sight, again.* I stood with my fists up, hoping the others would finish them off before I was anywhere near them.

"There's only three of them, perhaps they'll surrender instead?" Sarah added.

"Surrender? Oh, I don't think so, you traitorous little ginger! You and your Corvidae friends killed Jeremiah. For that, you'll *all* die!" one of them shouted with a cackle. They looked at each other with a reassuring glance, then growled before charging at us.

Without thinking, I shut my eyes as hard as I could. With
Gale standing next to me, I didn't see a real reason to bother
fighting at all. I put my fists over my face and held my breath.
I didn't want to go through another battle. Nathan nearly
slaughtered me numerous times, and I wasn't ready for a night
filled with this much conflict!

I heard them yelling as they got into the street, followed by a
low rasping sound, then silence. I heard Gale gasp and then she
put one arm in front of me, pushing me back slowly. I lowered
my fists and opened my eyes. What I saw nearly gave me a
heart-attack

CHAPTER 33: GALE

What in the world is— I stopped in mid-thought.

The ambush the remaining Rostair had put together came to a halt, due to some unseen force. Violet flames highlighted in deep yellow raced over the asphalt; the Rostair attackers were surrounded by the flames as we stood, shocked.

"He is here," my father mumbled in displeasure. "I never imagined I would see the day. "

I looked to him, hoping to hear good news, for once. "*Who*? Who's here, father?"

"He is a Corvine-Elite, from a legendary house and clan of our kind." His voice almost revealed a hint of awe as he spoke, something I'd not felt from him in ages. "Until this day, I had no idea the legends were true, but now it would seem he is all too real," he added in a fatalistic tone. My nerves spiked, as well as my curiosity.

Shannoea spoke up from behind me, "If he's one of us, then he's here to help, right?"

Xander shot her a narrow glare, followed by a slow shake of his head. "Legend claims he is only sent when dire straits have been met, when the actions of a given family or clan have caused attentions to be gained! His name is Vast, a fitting title, given his ability."

As he finished explaining, the four Rostair hurtled over the fire, landing a few yards away, snarling and laughing as if to ignore the blistering heat of the raging flames around them.

"Let's hurry and kill these clowns, then!" Shannoea hollered, leaping into the air, then landing down on one knee. The look on her face was steeped in confusion. "What? Hey, what's the deal? I-I can't go into *raven form!*"" She stiffened, shooting her arms to her sides, "I can't even bring out my wings! *What the hell?*"

"As I said, his name is fitting considering his ability. According to what I've heard, he can block or dampen the powers of all creatures, including Corvidae!"

I'd never heard of such a legend, nor had I ever heard of a Corvidae with such traits, but if my own father was this concerned, then there was definitely a reason to worry! Each of us tried desperately to activate any power we had, but none responded. It appeared not even the Rostair could shift or cast a single spell, despite their efforts.

We looked at one another, terror overtaking each of us as we huddled together.

The Rostair sniffed the air around them, glancing in all directions, hoping to find the one my father spoke of, this *Vast of Corvine legend.*

Suddenly, the night sky lit up with a flash of energy, the flames surrounding us crawled away, gathering into one spot in the middle of the street. They reached up, swirling and lashing upward, and just behind the flames stood the silhouette of a tall figure, with long flowing features. The display of power was far beyond anything I'd ever experienced. I knew nothing about him, nor did I have a clue as to his intentions. All I knew, was a need to protect Lucas. I hoped Vast had come to decimate the remaining forces of Jeremiah's army, but judging by my father's reaction, we were *all* in trouble.

Vast stepped from the veil of flames, revealing his long, straight, gleaming white hair, which flowed over the back of a thick black coat hanging to the ground. Decorative armor covered his forearms, legs, and boots, donning the familiar shape of a raven with wings spread, wrapping around and spiking outward where the feathers connected, acting as blades. His entire outfit was dark, yet regal looking, midnight blue pants, a belt adorned with strange emblems and medallions I'd never encountered, a thick black vest with a metal fastener down the center and three silver chains draping on either side connecting somewhere on the back, behind his coat. The flames melted into his form, leaving no trace behind. His visage was breathtaking, almost royal in his demeanor: a stern complexion; deep, shining violet eyes outlined in yellow; thin, sharp looking lips; and hair like ice vapors caught in the dance of the wind. I was almost mesmerized at the sight of him, like a dangerous, but princely dream, commanding attention amidst the carnage around us

The snarling from the Rostair broke my train of thought as they laughed in their huddle. "Look what we have here, fellas! Why it's a pretty-boy from team-pigeon! Isn't that just precious?" one of them cackled, followed by the laughter of the others. Their attitude and disrespect for nearly everything almost always caused their ruination. This encounter would be no different, considering the obvious underestimation of this newest threat.

In the back of my mind, I hoped Vast would finish them off in such a way that the rest of us would have time to escape.

Their leader stepped forward, readying himself. "I'll handle this foolish little rook. The three of you kill that blasted human boy they're protecting!" He growled and charged at Vast, full speed.

Vast's eyes illuminated with yellow flames as he extended his hand, spreading his fingers apart, stopping his attacker dead in his tracks by some unseen force.

My eyes shot open wider than ever, he was using an ancient form of Corvine telekinesis!

The Rostair lifted from the ground, hovered in mid-air, then burst into flames while screaming and flailing wildly! The others stared with fright as their leader dematerialized into kindling ash, blowing softly away into the night air!

For the first time, I shared sympathy with the enemy. I was as scared as they were, if not more so. If this interloper had that kind of power and could nullify our powers and gifts, what chance did we have?

The remaining Rostair scrambled, hoping to get away, but it was all for nothing.

Three large ravens, each wreathed in flames emerged from Vast's arms, flying straight at the three remaining Rostair.

They were powerless to withstand his attack, the blazing ravens collided into each of their targets, swirling and crackling deep into them. They had no time to scream before they were reduced to cinders. Vast slowly closed his fingers and the fiery ravens returned to him, each bearing the soul of the Rostair they'd slain.

Vast turned his attention to us.

My blood ran as cold as the pale moon above, a terrible feeling swept over me; it was the same feeling I got the day Lucas died!

I felt my father's hand on my shoulder. "Stay here, Rhune. I will speak with him. Perhaps he was not sent to dispatch Corvidae, this night."

I don't know what it was about him; maybe, simply because he was my father, or perhaps the way he carried himself; but whenever he spoke to me, it was as if he spoke from reassuring experience. Even in this grave and dire circumstance, he made me feel safe and protected!

This Vast, a dark and ominous Corvidae from the deepest shadows of legend, chilled me to my core; but somehow, my father was still able to keep himself well composed and perfectly attuned with clarity. Despite his attitude toward Lucas, I was grateful he was here with us.

"Berhtna Ta, Vast! Reh'er nos eliece't uhnde'ne tuet!"

Hearing my father not only greet, but confess to being pleased that Vast had come made me feel sick to my stomach.

Vast's face remained unchanged and he looked un-amused, as though he were lifeless on the inside.

"Nir dashen uhnde, reh couf'het bettak hyhes Rostair kastuhashen weno."

Hearing father thank him for his aid against the Rostair abominations didn't make me feel any better either. It was hard to get any sort of reading from Vast. He stood towering over my father, motionless, his eyes deadlocked to father's, as if to peer into his very soul.

"You remain un-afflicted by my barriers." Vast's voice sounded soft, but stern, deep and gentle at the same time. "Unexpected," he added with a sinister glare.

We gasped in unison as Vast grabbed my father by the front of his shirt, charged more energy along his arm, then shot him like a bullet into a tree, uprooting it entirely.

I ran toward him, but was knocked back by Vast's telekinetic force.

Sarah, Brenna, and Shannoea rushed toward Vast.

Without so much as a flinch, he tossed them about like playthings, sending Brenna through a brick wall, Shannoea slammed into a parked car, and Sarah hurtled down a nearby alley!

"Why are you doing this?" I demanded, tears streaming down my face. "You're Corvidae, just like us! What do you gain

432

by attacking your own kind?"

Vast didn't even look at me. He simply levitated, gliding like a phantom over to Lucas, who backed against the wall of a house behind him. Suddenly, it all made sense *Someone sent him to destroy Lucas!*

"*Get away from him!*" I shouted as loud as I could, hoping to get his attention long enough for Lucas to escape, "*I won't let you take him from me!*" I got up, then rushed toward him, flames appeared on my sleeves, then my hair began to catch fire, the flames grew hotter with each stride, growing brighter the closer I came to them both. I didn't care in the least, Lucas was in danger, and there was no telling what Vast would do to him once he had him

Lucas tried to escape, but Vast held his prey in place with a tornado of purple and yellowish flames. They spiked and licked all around him, threatening to consume him should he resist.

"*Lucas, run!*" I charged in hard, the flames were burning away my clothes and hair, my skin started to blister from the inferno. I gritted my teeth and clenched my fists, but my body felt heavier from his telekinetic energy weighting my strides. I was a mere five feet away and I could hardly move; the force holding me down also kept the flames from engulfing me entirely!

Lucas was petrified. He didn't speak or move an inch. I couldn't tell if Vast had any sort of hold on him, and it didn't matter, I simply had to save him!

He loomed over Lucas before grabbing him by the forehead. I could hardly move or breathe; I was helpless to help him! The tears in my eyes were hot to the touch as they mixed with the charred blood on my face. On my knees, I tried desperately to gather enough strength to move another inch. He sent a pulse of energy surging through Lucas, knocking him out cold, then levitated his limp body next to his.

"By order of Emeroth, King of the Corvine Dae Anhar and High-Ave of the Pillar-of-Wings, I hereby place this mortal under custody of His Majesty."

I stopped struggling long enough to hear a name I hadn't heard in nearly one hundred years. Emeroth, the king of our people had somehow caught word of my saving Lucas' life! The pain began to overtake me; no matter how hard I tried, I could not move. I watched in horror, as Vast engulfed Lucas into a torrent of flames then vanished with him.

The blistering pain of my flesh was nothing compared to the searing agony in the halls of my heart—I'd lost him. I couldn't keep my promise to protect him—I wasn't as strong as I needed to be.

Agony swept over me, both inside and out. I fell at last, to the pavement, the flames faded, leaving me in plumes of defeated smoke. Empty, I lay motionless. "I'm sorry, Lucas. Please forgive me," I heard myself say in a quivering breath as my senses spun me into unconsciousness.

THE
NIGHT
AND
GALE

Daniel Carrier, author of published short-stories, Evellyn and Amber and the Iron Wolf, finds inspiration for his writing through books, video games and movie trailers. He regularly works on story concepts and character ideas to create a new piece that will potentially exceed his previous publications. Daniel resides in Heath, Ohio, with his wife, Amber, and three cats, Cali, Aj and Mora.

CPSIA information can be obtained at www.ICGtesting.com
Printed in the USA
BVOW012029300712

296578BV00001B/1/P